FIRE AND ICE

"Just think of it, Captain. No scheming woman will be able to entrap you. You can go your own way and I will go mine . . . but with the protection of a convenient marriage. And if you come across a woman who changes your low opinion of wedlock, we can have our marriage annulled. All you need to do is notify me at my estate."

"You have thought this out thoroughly, Catrina!" Brant exclaimed, amusement dancing in his eyes.

"Actually, the idea just came to me," she said proudly.

A pensive frown plowed Brant's brow. "You realize this perfect solution you have dreamed up could cause new problems. There is never a simple answer."

"I will make no demands on you," Catrina insisted.

A slow smile worked its way across his lips. His golden gaze flooded over her delectable curves. "I fear I cannot be so generous. I want you," Brant told her. "And without a fight. If I am to have a wife, I intend to be the first to sample her charms . . ."

SIZZLING ROMANCE
from Zebra Books

WILD ISLAND SANDS   (1135, $3.75)
by Sonya T. Pelton

All beautiful Pandora could think of was Rogan Thorn. His kiss was the first taste of desire she'd ever known. But the captain was a wealthy, womanizing shipping tycoon whose only love was the sea. Once he took Pandora's innocence, he was forever branded by her fierce, fiery love!

PASSION'S PARADISE   (1618, $3.75)
by Sonya T. Pelton

Angel was certain that Captain Ty would treat her only as a slave. She plotted to use her body to trick the handsome devil into freeing her, but before she knew what happened to her resolve, she was planning to keep him by her side forever.

TEXAS TIGRESS   (1714, $3.95)
by Sonya T. Pelton

As the bold ranger swaggered back into town, Tanya couldn't stop the flush of desire that scorched her from head to toe. But all she could think of was how to break his heart like he had shattered hers — and show him only love could tame a wild TEXAS TIGRESS.

WILD EMBRACE   (1713, $3.95)
by Myra Rowe

Marisa was a young innocent, but she had to follow Nicholas into the Louisiana wilderness to spend all of her days by his side and her nights in his bed. . . . He didn't want her as his bride until she surrendered to his WILD EMBRACE.

TENDER TORMENT   (1550, $3.95)
by Joyce Myrus

From their first meeting, Caitlin knew Quinn would be a fearsome enemy, a powerful ally and a magnificent lover. Together they'd risk danger and defy convention by stealing away to his isolated Canadian castle to share the magic of the Northern lights.

DIAMOND FIRE

GINA ROBINS

ZEBRA BOOKS
KENSINGTON PUBLISHING CORP.

ZEBRA BOOKS

are published by

Kensington Publishing Corp.
475 Park Avenue South
New York, NY 10016

First printing: December 1986

Printed in the United States of America

To Kathe Robin And Her Love Of Swashbuckling Pirates

A special thanks to Ed and Janet Preble
for their interest and support

And To My Hero At Home . . .

Note to Readers

The raid on St. Mary's Isle was an actual event in history. John Paul Jones did attempt to take the Earl of Selkirk hostage. Since the earl was not in residence, Jones did permit his pirate crew to steal the family's silver. Impressed with Lady Hamilton's courage in the face of adversity, Jones sent a letter to her when he arrived in Brest, France, and promised to return the silver at his earliest convenience. Jones kept his word. The silver was delivered to Selkirk at the end of the Revolutionary War.

The earl's son, Basil Lord Daer, chanced to meet John Paul Jones in Paris in 1791. Daer and Jones discussed the raid and Daer conveyed the earl's gratitude for returning the sentimental pieces of silver. Despite the previous conflict, Daer found Jones to be a likable character and he came away impressed with the privateer.

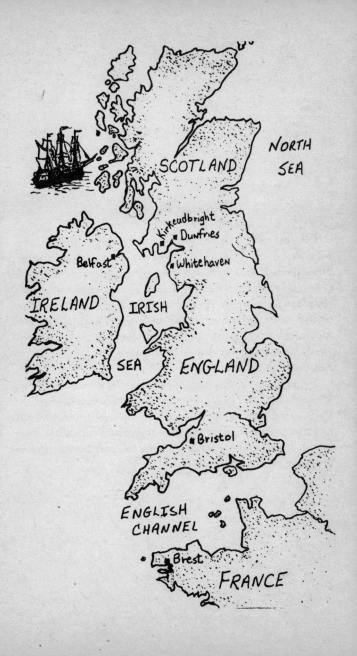

Chapter One

April 23, 1778
Kircudbright Bay, Scotland

Captain Brant Diamond fastened his pensive gaze on the white foam that rimmed the sandy beaches of St. Mary's Isle. The soft lap of waves against the shore mingled with the occasional cry of a sea gull. The peninsula stretched out into the ocean, marking the ragged coastline of the Mother Country. The fields that sprawled across the peninsula were tender green, capped with windblown waves of daffodils, irises, and narcissi. The oak and beech trees were in early bud and the coast of Scotland lay in peaceful silence.

But not for long, Brant reckoned. His discerning eyes swung to Captain John Paul Jones who sat across from him in the cutter that glided toward the Point of Isle. When John Paul had sprung the idea of this dramatic raid on Brant, he had been too numb with ale to give it careful consideration. Brant had applauded the idea of taking the battles of the American Revolution to British shores. He had seen his share of destruction on New England soil and he was anxious to reciprocate the British offense. But when John Paul summoned Brant's privateer to aid the fleet, Brant expected to do

9

battle with His Majesty's sloops of war and seize merchant ships that were heaping with prizes for him and his crew.

Brant attributed his rash decision to his overindulgence of liquor the previous night. He had been in the process of celebrating the capture of a London-bound vessel that was brimming with sugar, rum, wine, and twelve cannons. He must have drowned his good sense in his mug, Brant lectured himself. How else could John Paul have persuaded him to join in this madness?

John Paul had explained his scheme of sneaking ashore to kidnap Dunbar Hamilton, Earl of Selkirk. The infamous captain maintained that the earl was an influential leader and that the British Parliament would pay handsomely for the return of such an important citizen. John Paul surmised that if he took the earl hostage he could negotiate for the release of American prisoners who were being held in the notorious Dartmoor and Mill Prisons in England.

The previous evening, under the influence of liquor, the plot had sounded ingenious and daring. But in full light, when his head had cleared, Brant was having serious misgivings about such a scheme. If the nearby village was alerted to the presence of American privateers, the handful of men in the cutter could be rotting in the dungeons of Mill Prison.

Despite his reservations, Brant found himself surrounded by sailors who would follow John Paul to the edge of the earth if they thought there was profit in it. Grumbling about his involvement in this raid, Brant unfolded himself from the cutter and stepped ashore. Keen amber eyes swept the sprawling brick mansion that sat upon the hill. How could one earl effect the release of several hundred prisoners, Brant asked himself. This scheme wasn't going to work and it was a pity he hadn't voiced an objection to John Paul the previous night.

After Captain Jones ordered two of his men to stand guard on the cutter, the procession of well-armed sailors marched up the path toward the "castle" of Selkirk. The head gardener paused from his chores to survey the motley group who were garbed in an array of uniforms. He would have turned tail and run, but he feared being shot in the back.

"We are the press gang from His Majesty's Navy here to seek recruits," John Paul announced to the wary gardener.

Brant bit back a wry smile. Like hell they were! These were American privateers who carried a letter of marque issued by the Continental Congress. The license gave private American vessels the right to prey on British ships. That wasn't exactly what they were doing at the moment, Brant mused sourly. But at least John Paul's bold-faced lie would offer them meager protection.

The rustle in the underbrush brought Brant's head around. Several young men scampered off, fearing they were about to be impressed into his His Majesty's Navy. Brant breathed a constricted sigh of relief. There would be no battle on the front steps of the Selkirk mansion. Those who might have offered resistance to Captain Jones's hare-brained scheme had just bounded off like frightened rabbits.

The elderly gardener drew himself up and gave the lie without batting an eye. "Sorry, sir. There are few stout young men left here. Most of them have already joined the navy to serve in this frightful war against the colonies."

"I still have orders to speak personally with the Earl of Selkirk about the matter," John Paul insisted.

"I'm afraid that is impossible." The gardener forced an uneasy smile. "The earl is absent. He is taking the waters at Buxton in Derbyshire and is not expected to return for several days."

Muttering over his stroke of rotten luck, John Paul reversed direction and aimed himself toward the cutter. Brant followed in his wake, relieved that this crazed scheme had not materialized.

" 'Tis just as well," he consoled the disgruntled captain. "I had doubts that the seizure of one man could bring about the release of our fellow countrymen. Although I am eager to engage in battle with His Majesty's Navy at sea, I have no . . ."

Brant was rudely interrupted by David Cullam, one of John Paul's outspoken officers. "Surely we are not leaving here empty-handed?" he hooted incredulously. "We received nothing for our efforts in Whitehaven except burning a British man of war. We owe ourselves something for our efforts. The British have burned and raided the houses of our families and friends in New England. We should be allowed to loot the mansion and receive our share of the booty," Cullam insisted.

Brant surveyed the stern faces of the men who had crowded about them. He had dealt with such greedy pirates in the past and had found several such characters among his own crew. Before John Paul could respond, Brant knew what the captain would say. There was naught else to do but allow these independent sailors the chance to reap whatever rewards could be procured from the Selkirk mansion.

Nodding, John Paul reluctantly gave his consent. "You can demand the family silver and jewels, but there will be no molestation of the castle's inhabitants," he stipulated. His solemn gaze swung from his savory crew to the tall, muscular captain of the *Sea Lady*, who had accompanied him on this futile raid. "I ask you to join my men to ensure my commands are followed to the letter. I will wait at the cutter and fire two shots of warning if I anticipate trouble."

Brant would have adamantly declined the request and returned to the skiff, but John Paul was in no mood for further argument. His plans had been foiled and his disposition had soured. Realizing that his only course of action was to accompany the greedy crew and protect the inhabitants of Selkirk from bodily harm, Brant made an about-face. Heaving an exasperated sigh, he followed the men toward the mansion while John Paul returned to the cutter.

Damn, he should never have thrown in with Captain Jones, Brant lectured himself. He was captain of his own ship and he was not accustomed to doing another's bidding. Although Brant respected John Paul and his energetic efforts to aid the

Americans, it was not easy to be second in command. Perhaps it would be best for him to strike out on his own to confront British warships, Brant thought to himself. At least then he wouldn't find himself put ashore to steal the family silver. Confound it, this was war, not a looting party!

Lady Helen Hamilton had just finished taking breakfast when she spied the horrid-looking wretches who were armed with pistols, swords, and muskets. As the group approached the mansion Lady Helen realized they were not dressed in recognizable uniforms. Each man was garbed in a different color of clothing, not in the customary dress of His Majesty's Navy. Fearing the mansion was about to be overrun with pirates, she sent her family and guests to the top story for safekeeping. When the butler summoned her to meet the spokesman of the surly crew, Lady Helen gathered her composure and stepped into the foyer.

Her apprehensive gaze swung past the stubble-faced group to the tall, swarthy rogue who towered above the others. The man was almost handsome in a rugged sort of way. His nose was straight and his mouth was sensual. There was nothing refined about his tanned features, but he made the perfect picture of a reckless, swashbuckling pirate who could turn a lady's head.

The sailor was garbed in a smart green uniform with anchors carved on its buttons. There was a derisive slant to his lips and a daring glitter in his golden eyes. His stern facial expression alerted Lady Helen that here was a man to be reckoned with if he were provoked. And, being without protection, she decided it best to treat the leader and his surly cohorts with caution and respect.

"We are here for the family silver and jewels," Cullam blurted out. "If you give us what we want you will come to no harm."

Lady Helen was taken aback when the demand came from the stout buccaneer in the blue suit instead of the rogue she

13

had assumed to be in command. But then how could one know for certain who was the leader when dealing with a den of pirates, Lady Helen reminded herself. She did not dare insult or anger any of these rough-edged heathens. Her eight-year-old son and her guests, Mrs. Woods and her young daughters were stashed in the attic. The last thing Lady Helen wanted was to lose her family and friends, as well as her valuables.

Nodding in compliance, Lady Helen pivoted on her heels and entered the pantry. There she found the butler hurriedly cramming the silver into one of the maid's aprons. When the pirates filed into the room, the butler smiled bleakly and retrieved the valuables.

"Put them in the sack," Cullam ordered gruffly, thrusting the cloth bag at the servant. "And don't omit even one piece of silver."

Brant begrudgingly watched the procedure until a movement beneath the pantry window caught his attention. While the loot was being confiscated by John Paul's junior officers, Brant strode back to the front entrance to see who had been spying on them. A grim frown clouded his brow when he saw a shabbily dressed urchin scampering along the side of the house. As the scrawny waif made a mad dash for the horse that was tethered in the trees, Brant bounded off the porch in hasty pursuit.

If the daring ragamuffin reached the village to alert the people, innocent lives might be lost. Brant had seen enough useless destruction on American shores and he did not relish the idea of battling elderly men, women, and children over a silver tea pot. His only recourse was to apprehend the stripling and tie him down to something solid until this grizzly business was concluded.

Brant's long, swift strides closed the distance between him and the escaping waif. When the lad sprang into the saddle, Brant grabbed a handful of his baggy shirt and sent the youth tumbling to the ground. The boy's startled squawk caused the birds to flutter from their perches in the trees above them.

14

Fearing the racket would raise the dead, Brant made another grab for the urchin who had vaulted back to his feet to make a second attempt at escape.

"Not so fast, lad. Where do you think you're stealing off to in such a . . . Ouch!" Brant sucked in his breath when the grimy-faced waif bit into his hand. The painful attack only served to infuriate the pirate captain who was already out of sorts. "Damn you, brat," he sneered maliciously as he yanked the waif off the ground. "I ought to . . . Ouch!"

The wretch came uncoiled like a striking snake. The boy clawed Brant's furious face and left severe dents in his shins. Instinctively, Brant released the vicious wildcat and brushed the back of his hand over the bloody claw marks that sliced his cheek. When the waif bounded toward the underbrush, Brant, cursing a blue streak, gave chase. Why he didn't draw his pistol and drop the troublesome wretch in his tracks, Brant wasn't certain. It could only have been his effort not to draw the attention of the servants and nearby villagers, he decided as he plunged into the shrubbery. But he damned well intended to quietly reciprocate the painful blows to his face and shins, he vowed to himself. Brant was not about to be bested by the likes of this skinny ragamuffin!

When Brant caught sight of the fleeing youth, he pounced like a panther devouring his prey. His low growl brought a frightened shriek from his victim's lips. Brant found small consolation in scaring the scraggly urchin half to death, but he hungered to teach the lad a thing or two about striking an officer in the Continental Navy.

But even when Brant had forced the struggling wretch to the ground he felt as if he had a tiger by the tail. The boy was a mass of wormy energy and it was difficult to contain him.

"Pirates!" Milton screamed for all he was worth. "Get help. Pir—"

Brant clamped his callused hand over the urchin's open mouth. Too late he realized that had been another painful

15

mistake. Brant became the victim of another nasty bite. But this time he contained his pained yelp and snatched his dagger from his belt. Brant rolled the struggling urchin to his back and laid the blade to his throat, daring him to shout out another cry of alarm. When Milton felt the prick of the stiletto against his neck, he released the hand that had been clamped between his teeth.

Milton glowered at Captain Brant Diamond's menacing smile. Eyes that glittered like the first rays of sunlight burned down at him. Milton was reasonably assured that the pirate captain would not only slit his throat, but that he would also derive immense pleasure in doing so. There was a daredevil glint in those fathomless pools of amber. The captain's strong jaw and chin were set in grim determination and Milton wondered if he were about to meet his Maker. The pirate's high cheekbones were scratched and bleeding, but the sardonic smile that captured the deep-set lines of his face offered no compromise. Milton was in one hell of a scrape and he was smart enough to know it. But that didn't mean he liked it. Indeed, if Milton could have gotten his hand on the pistol that was draped on the pirate captain's hip, he would have blown a hole through the rebel's black heart.

Brant stared down at the urchin's bruised and battered face, one that had been abused long before Brant got hold of it. The scrawny lad had obviously been beaten, but Brant's critical gaze held no sympathy. After the painful attack on his person, Brant spitefully decided the brat deserved to be whipped . . . or worse.

The boy was a handful. And, skinny and underfed though he was, he could fight like an alley cat. Brant had done battle with better men than this, but he had yet to be scratched, clawed, and bitten as he had been the past few minutes.

Beneath the brimmed cap that set down around Milton's ears were a pair of flaming green eyes that sought to fry Brant to a crisp. A fringe of dark lashes rimmed those frothy emerald pools. The boy's mouth was so tightly compressed it gave the

16

impression that the waif had no lips at all. Milton's body was so rigid and tense that Brant swore he was sitting a bag of bones and brittle nerves.

While Brant was surveying his captive, Milton writhed beneath him. He attempted to knock his assailant off balance. Brant braced a muscled arm against the waif's shoulder, pinning him flat against the ground. "Don't be a bigger fool than you already are." A ruthless smile rippled across his lips, giving Brant a satanic appearance.

The grizzly pirate wore the expression well, Milton thought to himself. The deep resonance of the man's voice vibrated down the boy's spine. The scoundrel looked positively predatory as he loomed over Milton. It was like being pinned down by a starved panther.

"After the pain you inflicted on me, I ought to separate your empty head from your bony shoulders. And I shall if you provoke me further," Brant assured his rigid captive.

"Then be done with it," Milton jeered in his twangy Scottish accent. "If yer such a coward to pick on a wee lad then draw my blood. In so doin' you will become less a man and I will be a martyr. *I* could do worse, but *you* cannot!"

Brant was taken aback by the smudged-faced urchin's temerity. It seemed the wretch knew nothing of fear. The boy had openly invited his assailant to finish the deed. But he had voiced the suggestion in such a way that Brant would feel as tall as a weed if he permanently silenced this troublesome ragamuffin.

"'Tis little wonder you have bruises about your face," Brant smirked, careful not to ease his grip on this wiry bundle of energy. "No doubt your lack of discretion with your razor-sharp tongue has earned you this black eye and swollen cheek. Are you such a blundering imbecile that you do not know when it is wise to keep silent and pray for mercy?"

The waif puffed up like an indignant toad, even while he was being squashed flat by one hundred and eighty pounds of brawn and muscle. "What does a pirate know about gentlemanly behavior or good manners?" he sniped in a venomous tone. "You came to Selkirk to prey on defenseless women and children. *You* are the one lackin' in etiquette. *I* was only tryin' to prevent the injustice *you* were performin'!"

"I am not a pirate," Brant snapped back, his voice carrying a distinctly unpleasant edge.

Brant clenched Milton's shirt so tightly around his neck the lad could barely inhale a breath. "Then what do you want with Lady Helen's silver?" Milton croaked in taunt. "Have you come borrowin' it for an elaborate party you are hostin' for the residents of the village?"

Brant could not believe the brat had such unmitigated gall! The scrawny wretch lay beneath the blade, subdued and conquered, yet he still wagged his barbed tongue. Towing in the remains of his temper, Brant vaulted to his feet and hauled the urchin up beside him. Holding the blade to the boy's throat, Brant marched his hostage around to the front entrance of the mansion.

"Your foolhardy bravado has earned you a year's hitch in the American Navy, brat," he ground out. Brant had decided it best not to release the waif because he would have the entire village up in arms. The crew would never reach the schooner before the isle was swarming with defenders. And this brazen urchin would be leading the attack, Brant surmised. "Perhaps after you have served under my command you will learn to respect your elders and control that vicious tongue of yours."

"I'll not join a gang of bloodthirsty pirates," the waif snorted and then made one last attempt at freedom. Arms as unrelenting as bands of steel clamped around Milton's shoulders, stifling all movement.

"And I'll not leave you to scream our presence to the entire countryside," Brant countered.

When the surly crew filed out the front door to close in around the captive, Brant felt the lad slump in defeat. At least the boy had enough sense to realize he couldn't win against impossible odds, Brant mused.

"What are you doing with that scrawny bag of bones, Cap'n?" Cullam smirked. He raked the thin lad with scornful mockery. "We need able-bodied men to serve our cause, not a babe in arms. He don't look like he could fight his way out of a feed sack . . ." Cullam's attention swung from the boy's battered face to the claw marks that marred Captain Diamond's cheeks. "But maybe I'm wrong. Did you get into a scrap with this guttersnipe?"

"We had a slight disagreement," Brant grumbled as he herded the waif along ahead of him. "The boy had a notion to alert the countryside to our presence and no amount of *friendly* persuasion would deter him. His misplaced courage may be worth more if he exerts his efforts on the *right* side of the war."

Milton opened his mouth to hurl a sarcastic rejoinder and then thought better of provoking a swarm of ruthless pirates. Although the waif had no objection to granting the colonists their independence, he considered these buccaneers to be hypocrites. They were all too eager to howl of injustice and proclaim *their* freedom. But they thought nothing of impressing a defenseless waif into their service. It seemed a rather lopsided freedom and Milton sorely wished he had his! Blast it, this had not been his week. He had gotten himself into one scrape after another. Milton had attempted to play the good Samaritan by aiding the residents of Selkirk. But in so doing, he had bought himself a peck of trouble.

Milton gulped over the lump that had suddenly collected in his throat. He had heard horror stories about these buccaneers. If he made waves among this burly crew of heathens, he faced a fate worse than death. Begrudgingly, the boy allowed Captain Diamond to shuffle him along the path that led to John Paul Jones and the waiting cutter.

A muddled frown plowed John Paul's brow when he spied the hostage Brant held under one arm. He would have expected Cullam or Wallingford to disobey orders, but not Captain Diamond. Brant was a sensible man. Indeed, that was one of the reasons John Paul had befriended Brant when they met

19

several years earlier in the West Indies. When those about Captain Diamond were losing their heads and tearing off in panic, Brant quickly considered his alternatives and proceeded to take the best possible course of action.

Brant Diamond was a superb navigator who could smell his way through fog by night with his eyes closed. And John Paul had witnessed this brilliant captain's nautical maneuvers in the face of adversity. Brant was a calculating man who rarely gave way to sudden impulse. Yet, here he was, uprooting this bruised and battered urchin from his native soil and toting him toward the cutter. For what practical purpose, John Paul could not imagine.

"I requested that no hostages be taken . . . if not Dunbar Hamilton, Earl of Selkirk himself," John Paul reminded Brant. "Would you mind explaining why you are making off with this undernourished waif?"

"Necessity dictated that I employ the boy's services," Brant grumbled, veering around John Paul to deposit his troublesome bundle in the cutter. His stern gaze swung from the boy's mutinous glower to the outstretched peninsula where a crowd of villagers had congregated. "Damn, the boy's cry of alarm must have alerted the town. They plan to attack us."

John Paul's hazel eyes homed in on the throng of men who were running toward the small bulwark of defense. Scowling, he scrambled into the skiff and took up the oars to hasten their flight back to the schooners that were anchored in the bay. When he glanced over his shoulder, he saw the daring waif making a grab for Cullam's dagger. The lad was either a fool or he had been plagued with incredible nerve, John Paul decided as he alerted Brant to the boy's abrupt movement.

Brant subdued his captive and then flinched when the roar of a single cannon echoed about them. The shell fell short of its mark, spraying the passengers of the skiff with nothing more than water. From across the frothy bay, Brant could hear the shouts of the villagers who had come to retaliate against the raid. But their efforts were in vain, Brant thought in relief.

There was not a marksman among them. The exploding shells caused no damage and, unhindered, the cutter glided toward the awaiting schooners.

A quiet chuckle rumbled in John Paul's chest. "Perhaps my mission failed, but the citizens of the British Isles will sit up and take note of their colonial cousins. We will bring this war to their doorstep. It seems only fair that both sides should suffer the harassment of war."

"While I approve of the burning of warships at Whitehaven and the theft of supplies that will aid America's cause, I have no taste for looting homes along the coast." Brant's remark was directed toward Cullam and Wallingford, who had greedily insisted on taking prizes.

"What? A shred of decency in the pirate captain?" Milton smirked, only loud enough for his captor to overhear. "And all this time I mistook you for a maraudin' scavenger, hellbent on rainin' terror on innocent victims."

"I still have not cast aside the possibility of bobbing your tongue, brat," Brant hissed, flinging his captive the evil eye. "Guard your words or you will find yourself afloat in a bay that is being shelled by yonder cannon."

Resentfully, Milton bit his lip and sat brooding on his perch. He was mulling over dozens of sarcastic jibes to hurl at the two pirate captains and their burly crew. But he wisely kept his comments to himself. After all, if not for his daring remarks he would be safely tucked away at Selkirk. Because of his quick tongue Milton found himself being rowed out into the bay to take his place among a surly crew of rebels.

Lord have mercy on his wretched soul! Why hadn't he minded his own business and darted to safety at the first sign of trouble? But nay, he had attempted to portray the martyr, he thought sourly. While the able-bodied servants took to their hiding places in the underbrush, Milton foolishly took it upon himself to call for help.

A thoughtful frown furrowed Brant's brow. His attention swung from the coastline to the sulking waif he held chained in his arms. Why hadn't he shoved the insolent urchin overboard and allowed the boy to sink or swim back to shore, Brant asked himself. When he stared at the lad's bruised face, Brant became hypnotized by the living fire that flickered in the waif's big green eyes. For some unexplainable reason, Brant was magnetically drawn to the lad. Maybe Brant saw something of himself in the boy—a wild, free spirit who had flourished in another lifetime. There was a frown of grim determination stamped on the boy's grimy features. The expression assured Brant the lad might eventually give out but he would never give up. Here was the restless energy of youth, often misdirected but no less fierce. This daring waif could make something of himself with a little instruction and guidance, Brant predicted. Aye, the boy was scrawny and unkempt, but he had spunk. He could be molded into the kind of man that others would respect. Perhaps if Brant showed the waif kindness and took him under his wing, he could earn the lad's undying loyalty. As a member of the crew, the lad would be rewarded with a share of the prizes. What did the urchin have to anticipate in Scotland's rigid society? Brant was offering the boy opportunity and it was worth a king's ransom.

Grappling with that encouraging thought, Brant focused his gaze on the two schooners that awaited them. He would teach this lad all he knew about life and the sea. If fate smiled upon the skinny urchin he would come through this war with flying colors and strike out on his own in a land that brimmed with opportunity. In time, the waif would realize his captivity was a blessing in disguise and come around to his captain's way of thinking. But first the stubborn wretch needed a bath and duties to preoccupy him, Brant reminded himself. Once the boy had settled into the routine aboard the privateer, he would not be so disagreeable.

While Brant was making positive plans for the waif's future, Milton was plotting to undermine the captain's every move. He was not about to make life easy for this renegade captain with hair the color of midnight and eyes the color of the sun. He would spite Captain Diamond at every turn, frustrating him until he put Milton ashore to go about his own business. A wry smile pursed Milton's lips as the cutter pulled alongside the *Sea Lady*. Pirate Captain Diamond only thought he had trouble when he faced His Majesty's man-of-war, Milton thought smugly. The arrogant captain was about to learn the true meaning of the word.

Chapter Two

Once Brant and his captive had climbed aboard the *Sea Lady*, John Paul rowed to the *Ranger* to await the younger captain's return for a conference. Brant propelled his captive through the throng of curious crewmen and aimed him toward the captain's cabin beneath the quarterdeck. When the door had been locked behind him, Brant struck a sophisticated pose and stared pointedly at the disgruntled waif.

"Now that you are a member of my crew, there are several rules I expect you to obey without question." Brant strolled over to his desk to retrieve a cigar and then lit it from the lantern. After blowing a smoke ring about his head, Brant bent his gaze to the grimy-faced urchin who stood in the middle of the cabin like a stone statue. A go-to-hell look was carved in the boy's fragile features but Brant ignored the spiteful glare and continued. "You will refer to me as Captain Diamond, not *pirate captain*. I am the captain of a privateer who has orders to inflict punishing blows on the enemy, capture the prizes for my reward, and ship necessary supplies back to the colonies."

"In other words, yer a leech. You prey on English shores for yer own personal gain with the pretense of bein' a patriot of the colonies." Glittering green eyes raked Brant up and down, mocking him and all he stood for. "A pirate by any other name is still a cussed pirate," Milton sneered.

25

Biting into the end of his cigar, Brant stalked up to the insolent waif and counted to ten—twice. It would be difficult to treat this ragamuffin with tender loving care if he persisted in goading Brant's male pride. But Brant had set his mind to making something of this scrawny bag of bones. And, by damned, he would!

"The name is Captain Brant Diamond," he ground out. "You and I can and will lead a tolerable coexistence. You will be my cabin boy and you will do as I command when I command. I do not wish to threaten you with the loss of life and limb . . . unless you provoke me into taking drastic measures." Drawing himself up, Brant inhaled a deep breath and then slowly expelled it. "Now, young man, what name shall I call you when I request your services?"

The waif sized up the towering mass of brawn and muscle that cast a long shadow over him. How he itched to claw that haughty expression off the pirate captain's craggy features. Resisting the urge, the urchin resigned himself to his fate. "You may call me Milton," the boy begrudgingly replied.

"Very well, Milton it shall be. Your duty aboard this ship will not involve doing battle until you are capable of handling weapons. I expect you to care for my quarters and see that my meals are delivered. When I return from my conference with Captain Jones, I will see about finding you a cot."

"I will room with you?" the lad squeaked in dismay.

It was the first time Brant had witnessed terror on the waif's face. Milton had fought valiantly for his freedom at Selkirk, but the thought of sleeping under the same roof with the captain seemed to horrify him. Did the lad expect to be used in some sort of perverted method of pleasure? Most likely, Brant concluded. Milton seemed to have a distorted opinion of patriots.

A rakish grin spread across Brant's features, sending dimples diving into his cheeks. "Set your mind at ease, Milton. I do not derive sordid satisfaction from toying with boys. I am a man with a man's appetite for *women*." Brant puffed on his cigar and then sent the waif a playful wink. "And if you behave yourself, I will introduce you to the pleasures women can give after we sell our prizes in France."

The crude subject of their conversation caused Milton's face to flame with color. "That won't be necessary," the waif grumbled.

Brant arched a bushy brow. "You have already been introduced to passion?" he questioned, surveying the splotches of red in the boy's cheeks.

"I have no urge to dally with men or women," Milton told him in no uncertain terms. "I will do yer biddin' since I ain't left with no choice, but you needna fret over furtherin' my education about the birds and bees. I want no part of it."

A deep skirl of laughter bubbled from Brant's chest. "I suppose you are a mite young to enjoy the finer things in life," he speculated before he wheeled toward the door. "You can begin by tidying up my cabin while I'm away. I'll send one of my men to fill the tub. See if you can scrub away a few layers of dirt. I prefer not to bunk with a boy who smells like a horse."

"And I would prefer a hitch in hell to a cruise with cutthroat pirates," Milton spouted, glaring holes in Brant's departing back.

Summoning what was left of his patience, Brant turned to face Milton's smoldering glower. "Heed my words, Milton. I can be charming and good-natured or I can be an irascible monster. You have already brought out the beast within me once today. I advise you not to do it again. I could gobble you up in one bite . . ." Brant flexed his sore hand, the one with Milton's teeth marks in it. "You may have chewed on me, my young friend. But 'tis little of nothing compared to what I will do to you if you provoke me to violence." He opened the door and leisurely propped himself against it. "The choice is yours, Milton. I will respond according to your behavior. You decide if you prefer to room with a devil or a saint." The faintest hint of a smile caught the corner of his mouth. "I am most anxious to return from my conference with Captain Jones to learn if I should polish my halo or file the tips of my horns."

When the door drifted shut behind the strutting captain, the waif childishly pulled a face and cursed his predicament. Pacing the confines of the cabin like a caged predator, the urchin impatiently waited for the sailor to fetch water for a bath. In the privacy of the captain's cabin, the ragamuffin pulled off the dingy cap. A waterfall of flaming auburn hair cascaded over Milton's shoulders and tumbled down her back. The lad was no lad at all, but rather a sophisticated young heiress disguised in men's clothes. Her fiery green eyes swung to the waiting bath and then darted back to the bolted door.

"The finer things in life? Indeed!" Catrina Hamilton sniffed distastefully as she peeled off the tattered shirt that disguised her true identity. "Fie on you, pirate captain," she muttered, unwrapping the thick cloth that had been tightly bound about her breasts. "You are making my life miserable and I shall see that you are justly rewarded for it."

Flouncing across the room, Catrina sank into the water to cool her smoldering temper. But it didn't help. She was infuriated to find herself in such an exasperating predicament. After a harrowing week, Catrina had come to the conclusion that the entire male population was a herd of horrible creatures and a woman was much better off without them.

Carefully she inspected her bruised cheek that was still a mite tender to the touch. The menacing face of the man who had viciously struck her rose in her mind's eye. Catrina cursed the vision and the man's devious scheme to make her his prize. But suffering a black eye was the lesser of the two evils, she reckoned. Catrina would gladly take another beating if it would help her escape what would have been a disastrous marriage.

Sighing at the soothing effect of the tepid water, Catrina eased back to relax for the first time in a week. Her thoughts drifted back to the past few months, recalling how drastically her life had changed.

Once she had been happy and carefree, blossoming in the warmth of her parents' love, living in a safe, secure world. Her

28

father had doted over her, allowing her to nurture her free spirit, permitting her to enjoy her zest for life. Catrina's mother had been the epitome of gentleness, subtly coaxing her young daughter toward womanhood.

Aye, she was a mite spoiled, Catrina admitted to herself. When the devil dished out orneriness, Catrina had sneaked through the serving line twice for an extra helping. But she did not consider herself wicked, only a bit mischievous. She could portray the genteel lady when the situation demanded. Her mother had seen to that.

And yet, when Catrina was residing at their sprawling country estate she galloped against the wind on the back of her chestnut stallion. She was wild, free, and uninhibited. That was the real Catrina Hamilton, she reminded herself. Catrina had her faults, but then everyone did. She and her parents had lived in contentment, enjoying each other's redeeming qualities.

But suddenly Catrina awakened to find herself living a horrible nightmare. Catrina had declined her parents' invitation to travel to their town house for a week's sojourn. A few days later she received word that her family had tragically perished in a fire that destroyed their mansion. Catrina had been thoroughly devastated. The life she had known had gone up in flames and she wished she, too, had died in the fire.

For several weeks she had merely existed, walking about in a daze of grief and disbelief. Even the vast country estate near Dumfries was haunted with ghosts and the suffering Catrina endured was almost impossible to bear.

And then along came Derrick Redmund to console her. He had happened along, requesting to purchase a fresh mount when his steed went lame during his journey. Derrick had been concerned about her welfare. When he learned of her recent tragedy, he offered a shoulder to cry on. He had waylaid his journey to become Catrina's constant companion. Like a trusting fool, she allowed herself to be taken in by what she deemed sincerity. For several months Catrina was indifferent to all that transpired about her, making no attempt to take control of her life. When Derrick proposed, Catrina accepted simply because she felt she needed someone.

But gradually her independence and spirit returned. Catrina realized she had only been using Derrick as a crutch to help her survive. What she felt for Derrick was not love. It was then that Catrina began to detect telltale signs of Derrick's pretentiousness. He made careless slips of the tongue and cast her calculating glances. More and more, Catrina doubted Derrick's sincerity and became wary of what she had gotten herself into.

When Catrina tried to explain her true feelings the week before the wedding, Derrick's disposition changed drastically. She confessed that she was grateful for his friendship and compassion, but it was not enough upon which to build a stable marriage. To her utter amazement Derrick exploded in outrage, muttering something about his well-laid plans going awry. He insisted that the wedding would be held as planned. Catrina firmly rejected his demand and a heated argument ensued. Derrick had become a madman, issuing spiteful threats that were meant to frighten Catrina into submission. Because of her own volatile temper she snapped back at him and he fell into a fit of violence. Derrick backhanded her not once but thrice when she canceled the wedding arrangements.

Although several of the servants managed to contain Derrick and hustle him out of the manor, Catrina knew she had not seen the last of him. Deciding it best not to argue with a maniac and fearing for her personal safety she went into hiding. She had later learned that Derrick had lied to her. He was virtually without a means of support and his appearance at the manor had not been left to chance. He had purposely sought out a wealthy heiress to prey upon in her time of grief.

Derrick pretended to be from an upstanding family in England. He was the cousin of an earl, one to whom he constantly referred, as if they were the closest of friends. But all his life Derrick had stood in the shadow of rank, influence,

30

and fortune. Derrick had been close enough to the earl, only to be snubbed as poor relation. He detested his lack of prosperity and had set out to marry money. Since he had twice failed to strike a match with a wealthy heiress he decided to join the Royal Navy. He had hoped to gain prominence and prestige in the Admiralty and then began another search for a wife who could afford his expensive tastes.

Boasting of his association with the Earl of Cottingham and decorated with medals, ones probably stolen from his crew, Derrick appeared on Catrina's doorstep. His compassion for her plight was no more than a ploy. Derrick had been wife-hunting, calculating his every move, drawing Catrina into his web of deceit like a black widow luring a defenseless fly.

After canceling the wedding and sustaining a painful beating at Derrick's hand, Catrina sent a message to her lawyer. She requested that all monies be kept in a trust and that he pay for the upkeep of the estate until she returned from an extended holiday. Garbing herself as a homeless waif she went in search of sanctuary, somewhere Derrick would not think to look for her.

Traveling cross-country, avoiding the crowded roads, Catrina lived off wild berries and fruit. From Dumfries she blazed a path south to Selkirk "Castle." Dunbar Hamilton was a distant cousin of her father and there had always been a compatibility between the two families. Dunbar had invited Catrina to stay at Selkirk after her parents' tragic death and she decided to accept the offer.

It was there on the peaceful peninsula of St. Mary's Isle that Catrina had intended to take refuge until Derrick gave her up for lost. She knew she would be welcome in Lady Helen's home and she would have been safely tucked inside the brick mansion if not for these pesky American privateers.

The past weeks had found her tripping on the borderline of calamity so many times it made her head spin. Catrina grumbled at her misfortune and carefully washed around her swollen eye and bruised cheek. Was it not enough that she had

31

lost her family and then found herself very nearly tied to a man who hungered for her money? Why had fate frowned so severely upon her?

There she was, fleeing from an unwanted marriage, emerging from the underbrush to spy the key to her salvation—Selkirk. A smile of relief had claimed her battered features when she saw the magnificent mansion sitting before her. But her spirits tumbled down around her like an avalanche when she noticed the surly crew of pirates swarming the estate. Fearing for her cousins' safety, Catrina had sneaked to the back of the manor and crouched behind a window to determine the buccaneers' purpose. Realizing Lady Helen was about to be robbed . . . or worse, Catrina attempted to ride to the village for help.

Catrina had been plagued by yet another stroke of rotten luck. The alert Pirate Captain Diamond had sniffed at her heels, thwarting her attempt to summon reinforcements. She found herself wrestled to the ground by a swarthy, swash-buckling pirate who came like an invading army. A menagerie of weapons was draped about his waist and shoulders and he could have withstood the attack of an infantry singlehandedly. But he had directed his assault on an unarmed ragamuffin and emerged the victor, she thought resentfully.

Damn all men everywhere! If it were not one man itching to do her bodily harm, it was another, Catrina thought cynically. Now she was trapped aboard the enemy's pirate ship, disguised as a pauper. Ironic, she mused as she rinsed the soap from her arms. Who would believe a wealthy Scottish heiress who had cleverly eluded the sinister Derrick Redmund would wind up playing lackey to the dashing Captain Diamond?

What a distasteful predicament, Catrina contemplated. The very thought of portraying a cabin boy for that strutting peacock peeved her. Aye, Captain Diamond was a handsome rogue with glistening raven hair and a charismatic smile. But she had also seen the vicious side of this renegade pirate. In the span of a few hours Catrina had learned a great deal about

Brant Diamond. She feared she would learn far more about him while they were caged in the same cabin, things a proper young lady should never know about a man until she had wed one.

It seemed most men had tendencies of gentleness. But they all leaned toward their dark, foreboding sides when they were not allowed to have their way, especially with women. Catrina had instantly decided that she would never tie herself to a man. She had managed twenty years without one and she could certainly exist three scores more. If she survived to the ripe old age of eighty she would do so without a man. They were an abusive, deceitful lot and she would avoid them like the plague.

A worried frown knitted her brow. How could she keep her identity a secret in such close quarters with Captain Diamond? Should she risk confronting the captain with the truth when he returned from his conference? Should she explain her plight and beg to be put ashore anywhere along the English coast? Or should she continue to hide behind her disguise until Derrick relinquished his search for his runaway fiancée?

Catrina absently brushed her index finger over her bruised cheek. What if Captain Diamond took advantage of her once he learned the truth? He was a man, wasn't he? And he had most certainly boasted his eagerness for women, Catrina reminded herself. Nay, a confession would serve no useful purpose. It would be wiser to masquerade as a homeless vagabond for several weeks and then sneak ashore when the *Sea Lady* dropped anchor.

John Paul Jones and his cohort, Brant Diamond, would inevitably return to the coast, just as they had in Whitehaven and St. Mary's Isle. These bold privateers had already stolen merchandise from a British frigate, set the empty vessel afire, and raided Selkirk in search of an influential hostage. When Jones and Diamond next put ashore to go about their grizzly business, Catrina would make her escape and alert the villagers. Let those rascals rot in Mill Prison, she thought spitefully. They deserved no better for piracy under the *pretense* of patriotism.

A wicked smile pursed her heart-shaped lips. She wondered what the haughty pirate captain would say when he discovered his cabin boy was a woman and that she was responsible for seeing that he was locked away in a musty prison cell. Perhaps the skirt-chasing captain who undoubtedly kept a mistress in every port would learn to respect those of the female persuasion. Brant Diamond deserved to learn his lesson the hard way. He could contemplate his unfair treatment of women and innocent civilians while he paced the gloomy dungeon.

Her association with Brant Diamond would be brief, Catrina assured herself. She would tolerate his presence and then flee when opportunity presented itself. And in the meantime she would subtly disrupt the captain's orderly life.

Clinging to that spiteful thought, Catrina climbed back into her grimy clothes and wound her auburn hair inside her oversized cap. First she would set about to sabotage the captain's cabin by reorganizing his belongings and stashing them in the most unlikely of places. An ornery smile rippled across her lips as she plotted her strategy. She would give the pretense of making an honest but bungling attempt to serve her captain. By the time she finished with Brant Diamond he would beg her to return to shore and leave him in peace!

Grinning in wicked anticipation of the captain's return, Catrina Hamilton aimed herself toward the trunk that sat at the foot of Brant's bed. If he intended to wear his breeches he would have to hunt to find them, she mused. And where else would the good captain expect to find his sailing ledgers? Certainly not in his desk. Dancing green eyes circled the cabin searching for a most unlikely place to store Captain Diamond's official papers. The chamber pot perhaps? Giving way to that wicked thought, Catrina scooped up the ledgers and proceeded to stash them in the commode.

*   *   *

John Paul shot forth a glance at his silent companion and then drained his glass of wine. Gathering his feet beneath him, he gestured for Brant to accompany him to the desk. John Paul stretched out the map and drew Brant's attention to the coast of Ireland.

"My next offensive is to sail into Belfast Lough," he announced. "I intend to keep my crew below deck and face the stern of the ship toward the harbor. The gun ports will not be visible, even with a spyglass. The unsuspecting British will not know if we are peaceful traders or warships until it is too late." A wry smile flitted across his ruddy face before he turned his attention back to the map. "Once we have gained the harbor we will turn about to fire upon His Majesty's ships before the officers determine our true purpose."

Brant nodded agreeably to John Paul's ingenious scheme. Although the Scottish-born captain had very little common sense when it came to women, whether they be married or single, he was a brilliant strategist and talented navigator. Brant admired John Paul's uncanny ability of making the British appear the buffoons.

The notorious Captain Jones had taken so many frigates in tow during the first years of the Revolution that he could have equipped an entire fleet to encircle the Mother Country and blockade *her* ports. It was a pity the commander of the Continental Navy Committee had not thought to give John Paul free rein, Brant thought to himself.

"If all goes well, we will slide through the narrow channel between Copeland Island and the headland of Belfast. If the winds veer south as they have a habit of doing during the spring season we will return to the French port of Brest, northabout around Ireland, inflicting damage along the way."

A low chuckle rumbled in Brant's broad chest as he pushed away from the desk and rose to full stature. "And if all goes well, we shall have so many prizes in tow that the British will be whispering your name in awe and fear." The smile gradually faded and his countenance sobered. "I need not remind you

35

that the Royal Navy will have a high price on your head and they will do their best to snare us. These daring raids will only incense them."

John Paul issued a sly grin to his comrade. "They will also hunger to serve your head to the king on a silver platter. I trust you have not grown overly fond of your raven locks and cleft chin."

Brant shrugged carelessly. "The bounty for my capture in Charleston was so temptingly high that I contemplated turning myself in to collect the reward for the patriot cause."

"I doubt that," he said with a chortle. "The challenge of escaping the Royal Navy unscathed makes the entire effort worthwhile, does it not, Captain Diamond? We are alike in many ways, you and I. The thrill of adventure often becomes an obsession. I cannot honestly say which I value most, the riches we receive from victory or the victory itself."

Although Brant had never been one to turn his back on prosperity when it came his way, he was far more dedicated to the American cause than John Paul. Brant had traded with the colonies from Diamond's Den, his private island in the West Indies. He had many friends along the southern seaboard who had suffered beneath the hands of the British. Since he had already acquired a sizable fortune it was the victory of independence that motivated Brant. The prizes he took from enemy ships were no more than a method of keeping score.

"What have you done with that vicious wretch you hauled on board your ship?" John Paul questioned as he sank back into his tuft chair to enjoy his second glass of wine. Earlier, John Paul had noticed the scratches on Brant's cheek and teeth marks that were imprinted on his hand. Begrudgingly, Brant had explained the incident. "Frankly, I was bewildered that you had taken that misfit captive. After he clawed you to shreds I would have expected you to hang him from the tallest tree on the estate."

"Believe me, I considered several medieval methods of torture." Brant snorted. "And yet, young Milton impressed me

36

with his courage. Although he appears to be undernourished he is made of sturdy stuff. I only thought to offer him an escape from a life without a future. There is nothing in the British social system for a wayward youth who is without funds."

One dark brow tilted to a skeptical angle. "Since when have you begun taking vagabonds under your wing and molding them into upstanding citizens?" he snickered. "I thought you usually spent your idle time in the company of some fetching beauty. I cannot imagine your strapping yourself to that frightful bag of bones. It will take some doing to win his loyalty. He would have stabbed all of us this morning if he could have gotten his grimy hands on Cullam's stiletto."

"'Tis that bold daring that intrigues me," Brant confessed before taking a puff on his cheroot. A roguish grin skitted across his lips. "But put your fears to rest, my friend. I have not lost my fascination for the fairer sex, though I cannot boast of conquering as many hearts as have fallen beneath your feet."

John Paul heaved a deep sigh and thoughtfully stared into his glass. "I envy your discretion in affairs of the heart," he confessed. "It seems to be my lot in life to suddenly fall in love. And then just as quickly I feel this unexplainable urge to seek out another's affection. You, on the other hand, have the good sense not to become emotionally involved when a pretty face catches your eye. What is it you seek in a woman that you have yet to find?" John Paul questioned curiously. "God knows you have sampled your fair share of women. Yet you always manage to walk away unaffected while I pine each loss as if the wench were the first and only love of my life."

A merry twinkle glistened in Brant's golden eyes. Slowly, he sipped his wine, peering at John Paul over the rim of his stemmed goblet. "I have an inborn instinct for flight when I find that I am no longer the one in pursuit," he admitted. "In love and in war, 'tis the challenge that lures me, not the ultimate conquest. I relish my freedom and I fear I will always long for distant shores. The wound caused from the enemy's

37

shells is not as painful as the prick of cupid's arrow."

"I have often lamented the loss of a lover and I think you may be right," John Paul breathed forlornly. "My one weakness is women and I will be the first to admit it."

Brant checked his timepiece and hurriedly set his glass of wine aside. "If we are to make Belfast Lough by first light, it would be best that I take command of my ship. I will follow your lead, Captain Jones."

"Your excuse for leaving wouldn't perchance be compounded by your apprehension about your feisty hostage, would it?" John Paul teased. "I would not put it past Milton to organize a mutiny during your absence."

"The thought has crossed my mind," Brant admitted on a short laugh. "The wretch is like a mongrel mutt that has grown accustomed to running wild. Milton is capable of anything at the moment and it may take some time to earn his devotion and respect."

"I admire your interest in taming that ragamuffin and bettering his station in life," John Paul remarked as he followed Brant up the steps that led to the quarterdeck. "Perhaps I should take on such a task to distract me from this obsessive acquisition of beautiful women."

"When I have domesticated the unruly waif, I will send him to you for further training," Brant offered.

"And leave the ladies of Brest in *your* capable hands?" John Paul hooted. "Nay, I think not. I am too set in my ways to change and I do not possess the patience to mold a man from that skinny bag of bones. I wish you luck, my friend. I fear you have undertaken an impossible task."

One bushy brow elevated to a challenging angle. "Would you care to wager against my success?" Brant fished into his pocket to extract a gold coin, one of the many Spanish doubloons he had received in return for confiscated merchandise sold in foreign ports.

John Paul dug into his pocket to match the coin, his eyes dancing with amusement. "If you have not tamed the waif by the time we dock in Brest, the money is mine," he challenged.

"We shall see who is the better judge of my abilities. The bet stands as it is made. When we drop anchor in France the wretch will be eating out of my hand instead of *biting* it," he prophesied.

"We shall see about that." John Paul leaned over the taffrail to watch Brant descend into the skiff. "I'll wager there will be fresh wounds upon your person, ones that are not the result of doing battle with the British. Sometimes 'tis best to let a sleeping dog lie," he reminded Brant. "By the time we reach France, you may wish you had heeded my good advice."

"The little sea dog will be trained to fetch and heel within a few weeks," Brant predicted as he waved to the commander of the *Ranger*.

When Brant sank down on the seat of the cutter, his beaming smile faded into an apprehensive frown. Boasting his ability to conform Milton could well have been an oversight, Brant lectured himself. His gaze swung to the schooner that was riding the waves in the distance. There were no signs of smoke drifting from below decks. Hopefully, Milton had not decided to set the sloop afire during Brant's absence. As bold as the boy had shown himself to be, he would think nothing of transforming the *Sea Lady* into a floating inferno and singlehandedly crushing the opposition of the American forces in British waters.

Brant would prefer to proceed with kindness where Milton was concerned. The boy could be brought around, given time. One day he would become a proficient sailor and he would thank Brant for taking an interest in his welfare. But Rome was not built in a day, Brant reminded himself. And he could not expect to work miracles. The process of reform would be a gradual one with Milton. The lad had a lot to learn and he was as stubborn as a team of mules!

"What have you done to my cabin?" Brant croaked like a sick bullfrog.

The most pitiful expression claimed Milton's bruised features. Attempting to milk Brant's sympathy, she heaved a deflated sigh and set her book aside to survey the room, a disaster though it was.

"I thought it would please you, Cap'n Diamond. I figured a change would be nice. I worked until I had not one ounce of energy left in my body." Sighing wearily, Milton struggled to her feet. "But if my efforts don't please you I'll put everythin' back where it was. I was only tryin' to make myself useful, like you suggested."

Brant had the uneasy feeling he had treaded on the waif's sensitive feelings. Milton had tried to meet his captain halfway. And since Brant had bet John Paul that the ragamuffin would be trailing on his heels like an obedient pup, he felt obliged to praise Milton's efforts rather than condemn them.

"No need to move anything." Brant waved the long-faced waif back to her seat. "I was only startled by the change. I'm sure I will adjust to the new furniture arrangement."

After striding across the room to shed his green jacket and retrieve a casual shirt, Brant pulled up short. Smiling sheepishly, he reversed direction to navigate his way around the misplaced cot to reach the newly positioned wardrobe closet. "I suppose it will take time to adju—" His jaw sagged on its hinges when he flung open the double doors to find his books stacked on the bottom shelf and his liquor lined up on the top shelf. His pistols and belts hung on the hooks and not a stitch of clothing was in its proper place!

"It seemed to me the wardrobe closet would make a better cabinet for yer library and liquors. And them hooks were dandy for hangin' yer pistols," Milton insisted, sounding quite pleased with the ingenious idea. "I thought it best to store all yer clothes in yer trunk right here at the head of yer bed so you didna even have to move to fetch them." She hastened over to lift the lid of the trunk. "You see? All yer garments are neatly

42

folded and tucked away within arm's reach. I took special care to stack them one upon the other." The radiant smile that was plastered on her face faded into a woebegone expression. "But if you object, I s'pose I could undo all my efforts and . . ."

Although Brant was grumbling under his breath, he forced the semblance of a smile. "Nay, your arrangement will be fine." His encouraging tone sounded a mite flat, even to him. "Fetch me a clean shirt. I'm eager to shed this wool uniform and don something comfortable."

Milton's usually agile fingers fumbled over the garment when Brant shrugged off his coat and peeled his shirt from his broad shoulders. It was difficult not to gape at the wide expanse of Brant's chest and the dark furring of hair that trickled down his hard, lean belly. Brant's bronzed skin strained across his finely tuned muscles as he moved with lionlike grace.

Milton was unaccustomed to viewing a man in any state of undress and the arousing sight of him caused Milton's legs to go boneless. Captain Diamond was so vibrant and masculine that any woman could not help but admire his physique. It was with considerable effort that she went about her task of retrieving the fresh shirt and presenting it to Brant.

A muddled frown shaded Brant's brow when he noticed Milton's uneasiness. The boy seemed to find the sight of bare flesh unsettling. My, but this waif was difficult to understand. Milton had fought like an enraged wildcat when he was threatened. And yet, he was actually blushing at the sight of another man's naked skin. Deciding it best not to taunt Milton's apparent modesty, Brant overlooked the odd reaction. It was not wise to tamper with the truce that had fallen between him and the waif. After all, Milton was making an honest effort to be compatible and Brant did not wish to ruffle the boy's feathers.

With her eyes glued to the porthole, Milton thrust the fresh shirt in Brant's general direction. Once he had retrieved it from her outstretched hand she retreated to the corner and stood in it. This living arrangement could have serious repercussions, Milton thought bleakly. She had told herself she could endure Brant's presence and various states of undress without losing her composure, but this might prove most embarrassing! Brant Diamond had no modesty and he thought nothing of exposing himself to what he assumed to be another creature of the male species.

After thrusting his muscled arms through the sleeves of his white linen shirt, Brant absently reached for a cheroot. His hand bumped against the lantern, threatening to topple it from the edge of the desk. With pantherlike grace he lunged forward to catch the falling lantern before it shattered to the planked floor.

Damn, he felt like a bull in a china closet. Actions that had once been as reflexive as the batting of an eye now had him blundering like a clumsy imbecile. How could he earn Milton's undying devotion if he couldn't swagger across the room without upending the furniture or falling on his face?

"I will see about rounding up your cot if you will kindly fetch my black breeches from wherever you have relocated them," Brant mumbled for lack of much else to say.

When Brant began unbuttoning the matching green pants, he heard a startled squawk erupt from Milton's lips. Brant jerked up his head to see the flush-faced waif burying his head in the trunk like a frightened ostrich.

"What the hell is . . ." Brant quickly rephrased his question. "What the devil is the matter?"

"I ain't accustomed to watchin' others undress," Milton chirped, fighting for hard-won composure. "Ain't there a niche in a storeroom where I could stay and grant both of us privacy?"

Soft laughter bubbled from Brant's chest, one still exposed by his gaping shirt. "Nay, I'm afraid not. Every available space is filled to capacity. You will have to adjust to the situation. There is nothing wrong with two men sharing the same quarters. The rest of my crew live under conditions far more cramped than this." An encouraging smile bordered his lips.

44

"You will overcome your unnecessary modesty in time, Milton. There is nothing shameful about this situation. After all, there are very little differences between us."

Nothing shameful? No differences? Brant didn't have the foggiest notion that he was about to bare his anatomy to a cabin boy who was not a boy. Milton could feel the gush of color rising in her bruised cheeks. This wasn't going to work! Captain Diamond was going to drop his breeches and she was going to be forced to stand calmly by, as if nothing extraordinary had happened.

God strike her blind, she prayed frantically. Her overworked heart tore loose and slammed against her ribs when Brant shoved his breeches over his hips. His lower torso was completely bared to Milton's naive gaze. Brant stood there in all his masculine glory—almost as naked as the moment he made his appearance in the world. There was not an ounce of flab on the captain's virile body. His tapered waist and narrow hips were a mass of rippling muscles. Long, hard tendons wrapped around his well-shaped legs and his calves bulged each time he moved.

Milton did not even dare to mentally describe the more private parts of his anatomy. The very fact that she was confronted with the full frontal view of a naked man was enough to cause heart seizure. Milton felt as if she had wrapped her hand around a lightning bolt. The shock that sizzled through her would have had her hair standing on end if the auburn tendrils had not been crammed inside her cap. She was so stricken with self-conscious mortification that she nearly died. And that would have been a blessing, she thought to herself.

"Would you kindly hand me my breeches, Milt?" Brant extended a hand, patiently waiting for Milton to unclamp the pants that were clenched in her fist and raise her gawking gaze.

Brant's husky voice finally filtered into her stunned brain. When she unglued her wide green eyes to focus them on the captain's wry smile, she gulped down the lump that had practically strangled her. Striving to rewind her unraveled composure, Milton willed her trembling arm to move toward the captain's outstretched hand. She half-collapsed before she was able to get a firm grip on herself. But even when Brant covered his private parts, Milton swore the man's naked body would be forever branded on her mind. Aye, she was about to receive an education, but not the type Brant Diamond had in mind for his lackey! She was learning things she didn't want to know, intimate things that kept her blushing profusely.

When Brant had buttoned himself into his clothes he gestured for his flaming-faced cabin boy to follow in his wake. "I'll show you around the schooner while I search out an extra cot," he offered.

Wobbling on legs that had suddenly turned to rubber, Milton followed in Brant's footsteps. She had endured the worst, she reassured herself. After suffering through the past several minutes she could surely survive anything. But her encouraging thoughts did nothing to lift her sinking spirits. Now she was vividly aware of Brant Diamond as a man, intrigued and awed by his masculinity. Beneath the outer layers of linen were hair-roughened flesh and taut muscles. Brant Diamond was all male, every hard, sinewy inch of him. Milton could testify to that and, Lord, how she wished she couldn't!

After Brant had shown his not-so-naive servant to the scullery and galley where the dishes were washed and the food was prepared, he weaved through the various storage rooms that were heaping with prizes. Once he had located the extra cot, he ascended to the quarterdeck.

Since Milton appeared less hostile and more willing to please, Brant decided to give the waif the run of the ship. Brant was surprised that Milton had mellowed, but he was most grateful for the boy's change in attitude. A friendship had begun to take root and Brant did not wish to undermine it by confining the boy to his quarters like a prisoner.

While Brant manned the wheel at the helm to follow John

Paul to Belfast Lough, Milton was assigned to the senior officer, Thomas Haynes. The stout, crusty old sailor hustled Milton around the schooner, acquainting her with a myriad of nautical terms she doubted she could remember since they were thrown at her at such incredible speed.

Thomas pointed out the tackles—the sets of heavy ropes that were used to hoist the sails on each of the three masts. "Have a care, lest you git tangled in these flyin' ropes," he warned. "I've seen many a green sailor peel the hide off his hands tryin' to steady a risin' sail."

Milton's wide-eyed gaze swung to the huge strips of canvas that billowed in the wind. The mere thought of climbing about on the riggings as several of the sailors were doing left her weak-kneed. She had always had an aversion to height, even as a child. If she were requested to perform a task that took her high above the quarterdeck, Milton swore it would take the entire crew to unclamp her fingers from the mast and haul her back to the deck.

Brant had informed her that her duties would involve menial chores, she reminded herself shakily. Surely she would not be called upon to repair the ripped sails while they were flapping in the wind.

Motioning for Milton to follow at his heels, Thomas weaved his way through the sailors who snickered at the new arrival. "Don't mind them," Thomas insisted. "There ain't one among them who didn't come aboard green or turn that particular color durin' rough weather. They got a haughty air about them now, but they didn't when they first enlisted. Once you git yer sea legs under you, you'll do fine. And you could do worse, you know." Thomas paused to bark an order at one of the sailors who was performing acrobatic maneuvers on the mizzen mast. "You can learn a lot from Cap'n Diamond. I've been sailin' with him for nigh on to ten years. I ain't seen him make one foolish maneuver at sea. He knows the workin's of a ship like the back of his hand."

As long as someone didn't rearrange his organized world,

Milton silently tacked on. She had seen Brant Diamond fumbling his way around his room the previous hour. He certainly hadn't appeared the competent commander Thomas was boasting about when he knocked the lantern from the edge of his desk.

When Milton completed her tour of the schooner, Brant called her back to the helm. "You see, Milt, we patriots are not such a ferocious lot," he insisted. A smile pursed his sensuous lips and Milton mentally kicked herself for being affected by his charismatic charm. "Do you still see me as a blackhearted scoundrel who wishes you bodily harm?"

Her pensive gaze stretched across the white caps that danced in front of the schooner's bow. Oddly enough, she no longer felt threatened. But she quickly reminded herself that every member of this crew was a privateer and, worse than that, a man. Men could be civil and accommodating until they were provoked. Brant Diamond could portray the honorable captain and gentle friend until the beast within him reared his vicious head.

"Nay, you are not a blackhearted scoundrel," she replied and then stipulated, "Not at the moment. But I ain't easily swayed by a charmin' smile. I'm tryin' to get along, but I won't soon be forgettin' that you snatched me away from my homeland and forced me to turn traitor."

Milton's bitter tone drew Brant's disgruntled frown. "I had hoped you would view my ship as a means of escape from a grim future. In Scotland you cannot rise above your family's social position." Carefully, Brant raised his hand to trace a lean finger over the waif's discolored cheek. "Who did this to you and for what reason? Have I treated you so abominably since you boarded my schooner? Would you prefer to take a beating than to keep company with me?"

Milton jerked away as if she had been stung. Although Captain Diamond was only investigating the tender bruise on her cheek, she experienced far more than the mere brush of his fingertips against her face. She was far too aware of the man,

48

unwillingly attracted to this powerfully built mass of brawn and muscle. And that changed everything, Milton cautioned herself. She had to guard her emotions and stifle any romantic notions she might be having about the strikingly handsome pirate captain.

"'Tis no matter now who struck me or for what reason," Milton murmured, returning her gaze to the choppy sea and the lead ship that sailed a half league ahead of them.

"'Tis not my want to harm you, but to help you," Brant insisted softly.

"Why?" Wide, questioning eyes swung back to the captain's craggy features, ones that had softened considerably since their scrap on St. Mary's Isle.

"Because I admire your spirit," Brant told the waif honestly. "You have gumption. While all the able-bodied young men of Selkirk were scampering off to prevent what they believed to be a call for enlistments in the Royal Navy, you made an attempt to save the day. You showed your true colors while the other men concerned themselves with saving their precious hides."

"Have you no concern for yers, Cap'n?" Milton questioned point-blank. "What kind of man dares to confront the ominous British fleet in her own waters? You must know you will be outnumbered four to one. It seems to me one would have to be utterly fearless or incredibly foolish to undertake such a darin' mission."

Brant chuckled at the urchin's candor. "I am fighting for what I believe is right. Captain Jones and I are of the opinion that we should take the war to our enemy rather than waiting for them to come to us. Would you say that makes me a daredevil or a fool?"

"The truth?" Milton inquired, curious to know if the captain wanted her to inflate his male pride or voice an honest answer to a direct question.

"Regardless of what you think, I do not thrive on empty praise," Brant solemnly assured Milton. "An honest, straightforward man makes a worthy friend, but a liar will abandon a man when fair weather turns foul. I asked for an honest answer and you will not be condemned for giving it."

Milton's first impression of Captain Brant Diamond was rapidly changing. Despite her attempt to remain cool and aloof where Brant was concerned, Milton was irresistibly drawn to the man. He may have been a mite self-confident, but perhaps with just cause. Captain Diamond was no average man and he obviously held the respect of his crew. Although Milt had her heart set on bringing Brant down a notch or two she had to respect him and his firm convictions, even if they were in contrast with hers.

"In truth, I admire yer darin', but I oppose yer methods," she told him bluntly. "The victims of war ain't always the enemy, but rather his innocent family and friends."

"Perhaps if you had witnessed the desolation of American homes and found your womenfolk raped and abused, you would not cling to your pious stand," Brant countered, his tone harsher than he had intended. "The colonies also had their innocent victims and their numbers are far greater than those who have unintentionally suffered an injustice at our hands."

Milton watched the emotions ripple across Brant's dark features, wondering just how close to home the invading British infantries had struck. Maybe she was being naive to think her fellow countrymen would always conduct themselve like officers and gentlemen. Come to think of it, she *was* deluding herself. Derrick Redmund was an officer in the Royal Navy and she knew exactly how abusive he could be.

"The good citizens of England have only *heard* there is a war going on," Brant continued, his golden eyes fixed on the sprawling seas. "They have not lived it until now. Captain Jones and I do not wish to harm the innocent, only to strike back against those who have performed injustices."

Heaving a sigh, Brant forcefully tucked away his serious thoughts. He was in no mood to debate the issues of war with

50

Milton. His immediate purpose was to befriend this homeless ragamuffin and mold the boy into a respectable man.

"Fetch my meal from the galley, Milton," he ordered in his authoritative tone. "I will return to my cabin after I confer with my senior officers."

Offering a saucy salute, she spun on her heels and strode across the quarterdeck with a bouncy spring in her walk. Should she pursue her scheme of portraying the bungling cabin boy until Brant gave her up for a lost cause and put her ashore? The devilish side of her nature won out. Let Captain Diamond choke down a meal that was unfit for human consumption, the voice of mischief encouraged. She had to make herself appear to be useless baggage, she reminded herself. The good captain would soon realize his newly acquired cabin boy was not cut out to be a sailor and that he would fare better on his native soil. Chewing on that thought, Milton bounded down the steps to the galley to plan a meal that would assault Brant's taste buds.

After Brant informed his officers of the plans for the following day, he returned to his cabin to partake his evening meal. The table had been set, but the eating utensils were improperly arranged. Brant overlooked the lad's obvious lack of sophistication and took fork in hand to sample his meal. When he nibbled on his first morsel fire blazed in his throat.

"I hope my efforts please you, Cap'n Diamond," Milton remarked with a mouthful of food. She stifled a giggle when smoke rolled from the edge of Brant's collar and his eyes popped from their sockets. "I begged the cook to allow me to prepare a special seasoning for the meat. It was my mother's recipe, God rest her soul. She taught me to prepare Hotch-Potch when our meager rations sorely lacked in taste."

Wheezing to catch his breath, Brant grasped what he assumed to be his dinner wine. After one gulp he realized Milton had concocted a new drink as well. The potion served to add fuel to an already smoldering fire!

Noting Brant's discomfort, Milton vaulted from her chair to

whack the red-faced captain between the shoulder blades. Brant groaned in agony when the spicy morsel and its chaser landed in the pit of his stomach like a ball of fire. Lord, the lad would be the death of him, Brant swore to himself. The waif must have had a lead-lined stomach if he could consume the same meal. The food tasted as if it had been seasoned with gun powder and the drink must surely have been spiked with kerosene. Brant cautiously warned himself to avoid an open flame, lest he become a human torch.

"Once you grow accustomed to the taste, you won't be satisfied with bland food," Milton assured the bug-eyed captain and then loudly smacked her lips. "And I canna quench my thirst unless I down a glass of my dear mother's home remedy. She used to say this toddy was good for what ails a man and that it was like preventive medicine. 'A sip a day keeps the grippe away,' she always lectured." Biting back a devilish grin Milton rattled on. "Do you know, Cap'n, I ain't been sick a day in my life since I took to drinkin' this home remedy. Well, except for once. During a nasty cold spell when the roof leaked and I awoke in a pool of water. I couldna seem to get warm enough after that . . . until I fetched a bottle of the healin' spirits to toast my chilled insides. Finally my teeth quit chatterin' before they shook themselves out of my head . . ."

Brant's pallor changed from crimson red to putrid green. It was difficult to concentrate on Milton's rambling conversation. Brant would have given his right arm for a glass of French wine and a plain sea biscuit, but he didn't dare insult the waif when he had just begun to make headway.

Resolutely, Brant stabbed another morsel with his fork and mentally prepared himself to eat fire. His innards wretched in pain as the highly seasoned food lit a torch to his tongue and scalded the passage to his already flaming belly. Upon reflex, Brant gulped the drink and then silently cursed the stupidity of chasing fire with fire. He was about to die. He knew it. His epitaph would read: The courageous captain of the *Sea Lady* did not fall in battle. He went up in a cloud of smoke during his evening meal.

"You don't look too good, Cap'n," Milton observed. "Maybe you should lie down a bit. I'll fetch another plate of food. I guess I was overanxious to try out my mother's recipe on you. I should have left well enough alone. I canna seem to do nothin' right."

"The meal was fine," Brant breathed hoarsely. Instinctively, he moved toward the cot and wound up walking into the wardrobe closet.

Milton grasped the staggering captain's arm and aimed him toward the misplaced bed. "I'm relieved to hear you say it. 'Tis been ages since I had the fixin's for my dear mother's recipes. Just one taste brings back the sweet memories of days when I had a home and family to . . ." When Brant broke loose from her grasp and shot across the room, Milton stared bewilderedly at his departing back. "Cap'n Diamond? Whatever are you doin'?"

Brant told himself he was man enough to endure the raging wildfire that was burning holes in the lining of his stomach, but his overheated insides weren't listening. In desperation he stumbled through the maze of furniture to gulp down the water in the pitcher that set on the commode. But it was not water that sailed past his blistered lips. It was kerosene.

Milton had landed on the ingenious notion that it would be easier to fill the lantern from the pitcher. So naturally she had made the switch to make her menial tasks easier.

"Arghh!" Brant choked on the taste, wheeled around, and charged toward the bathtub. At the moment he had not the slightest qualm about gulping down Milton's leftover bath water. Anything was better than having his digestive system burned to a crisp.

"Cap'n Diamond?" Milton's bruised features wore a mock innocent expression. "Are you certain yer feelin' up to snuff? Yer actin' a mite strange. Would you like me to brew up my dear mother's potion for settlin' a queasy stomach?"

"Nay." Brant's voice was no more than a strained whisper.

"I fear I have no stomach left to settle."

Milton hung her head, playing the role of the ashamed misfit to the hilt. "I know you have been tryin' to be nice to me, Cap'n. I do appreciate it. I truly do. But I can tell I've botched up yer meal." She heaved a melodramatic sigh when Brant's head emerged from the tub. "I never could do nothin' right. Not that I don't try, mind you. My last employer said I was a walkin' disaster. I don't mean to be. I guess I'm jinxed. When I'm underfoot accidents happen."

Brant was beginning to believe it, but he didn't voice such a remark. He couldn't. No words would form on a tongue that had sustained third-degree burns.

"Why don't you lie down a bit. I'll fetch you some wine from the closet. Maybe that will bring you 'round."

Milton retrieved a glass and bottle and sank down on the edge of the cot where Brant was now sprawled. A grin of wicked satisfaction brimmed her lips. "Here, drink this." Milton grasped his shoulder and eased him to his back, watching the color rise and then ebb in his rugged features. "I promise not to tamper with yer meal again. I may have clawed at you in desperation this mornin', but I really don't wish you no harm. I guess I was just too overeager to please you. You've tried to be good to me and all. And don't think I don't know it," she hastily assured Brant as she lifted the glass to his lips a second time. "Yer tryin' to make me a better man. I don't mean to sound ungrateful, but I ain't sure even you can make a man out of me. Some things just ain't possible."

The underlying meaning escaped Brant. But then, he was incapable of all thought. His brain was on the verge of malfunction. The worst hangover could not hold a candle to the side effects of the meal Milton had placed on the table.

"You know, Cap'n, it might be wise to put me ashore. I could bring you bad luck, like I did my last employer. It seems I've been walkin' under a black cloud the past few years. I might jinx yer mission." Rising from the edge of the bed and guarding the slip of an ornery grin, Milton presented her back to the

54

nauseated captain. "I'll be takin' the plates back to the scullery. If you don't mind, I'd like to go above deck for a breath of fresh air."

Brant nodded his consent, wondering if he would ever speak again. When he was left alone, he expelled a tormented groan. If anyone else had served him live coals for supper, Brant would have been furious. But young Milton was different. Dammit, the waif was only trying to be helpful, Brant assured himself. And he *had* made this ridiculous bet with John Paul. That in itself was an incentive to overlook the uneducated waif's bungling attempt to please his captain.

He would give the urchin time to adjust to his surroundings, Brant told himself and then clutched his midsection when another wave of fire rippled through his sensitive stomach. *If* he lived through the period of adjustment, Brant thought sickly. Maybe the boy was right. Maybe he should be put ashore. Milton might best serve the patriot cause if he were on the enemy's side. The faintest hint of a smile spread across Brant's ashen lips when he landed on that thought. If he could devise a way to transplant Milton on one of His Majesty's warships the tub might self-destruct.

After Milton left the captain alone with his misery, she ambled along the deck, watching the moonlight splatter across the sea. Sighing wearily, she paused to lean on the rail. Why was she battling this tug-of-war of emotions where Brant Diamond was concerned? She was doing everything possible to spite him because he was a patriot pirate. And yet, she felt a twinge of guilt for putting him through this last bit of deviltry.

Try as she might, she could not rout the vision of the man. Even when she stared across the ocean she could see dancing gold eyes peering back at her. And even more unsettling was the picture of Brant Diamond standing before her, wearing little more than a smile. She could see the broad expanse of his chest that rippled with finely tuned muscles, the dark matting of hair that clung to his tanned skin. His thighs and calves were well shaped and when he moved he was like a

55

lean, powerful panther.

Banish the thought of him! Milton chided herself. It was only that she had been intrigued by the obvious differences between a man and woman. It was only natural that she would be more curious after the sight she had seen that afternoon.

Crimson red crept into her bruised cheeks, remembering how her eyes had flowed over his virile physique. She had been overwhelmed by the insane urge to touch what her gaze caressed. Now *that* was unnatural, Milton lectured herself. There was nothing between her and the rakish captain. He didn't even know he was rooming with a woman.

Milton expelled an exasperated sigh, praying her stay on the *Sea Lady* would be brief. She was uncomfortable with this ill-founded attraction for Brant Diamond. No other man had affected her the way he had. It was only that she had seen him in the altogether and her feminine curiosity had been piqued, she reassured herself. Besides, men were trouble, one and all. It was because of a violent man that she had been forced to flee from her own home. And because of another man, no one knew what had become of her. Even Helen and Dunbar Hamilton were unaware that she had been on her way to seek refuge at Selkirk. She could drop off the face of the earth and not a soul would think to become concerned until months had elapsed. Now, here she was, serving the captain of the enemy's privateer, wondering if she would perish during a sea battle before anyone realized the not-so-boyish cabin boy was out of her element. And by then it would be too late to remedy the situation, Milton thought sullenly.

Her gaze sank into the murky depths of the sea. Perhaps she should throw herself overboard and pray she could swim ashore. Pensively, Milton measured the distance to the faint lights of the coast. She was an adept swimmer, she thought confidently. Maybe she could ride the waves and let them wash her back onto the beach.

Giving way to impulse, something she had the habit of doing, Milton swung a leg over the taffrail. It was only then that she

56

remembered her fear of heights. The thought of plunging from the bulwark of the ship to the water made her stomach flip-flop. With her mouth set in grim determination, she closed her eyes and leaned out toward the welcoming arms of the sea. She could take the plunge, Milton told herself over and over again. The worst part would be over in a matter of seconds.

Brant had just set foot on the deck when Milton hoisted herself onto the taffrail. He swallowed air when he realized what the waif intended. The poor boy, Brant thought sympathetically. Milton was so overwrought with despair that he had decided to commit suicide to spare his captain the possibility of being jinxed.

Forgetting his own misery, Brant silently crept toward the stern, praying he could snatch Milton into his arms before it was too late. Just as the waif unclamped his hands from the rail and prepared to dive into the sea, Brant pounced. Like a hawk swooping down on his prey Brant whisked Milton from midair and clutched him to his chest.

A startled squeak erupted from Milton's lips when she felt Brant's lean fingers dig into her ribs. But worse than having her plans foiled was the feel of his muscular body pressing into her feminine contours. Odd sensations sizzled through her limbs and ricocheted down her spine. Instinctively, she squirmed for release but Brant held her to him, fearing the waif would make a second attempt to lunge into the sea.

"I won't let you kill yourself," Brant growled, fighting to keep a firm grasp on the wriggling lad.

"You'd be better off without me," Milton insisted. "I ain't done nothin' but botch up yer life and it ain't even been a full day since we met." She was not about to tell Brant she had purposely sabotaged him and was about to make her daring escape to freedom.

Swiftly, Brant carried his wiggling bundle toward the steps that led to his cabin. "I took you as my personal servant and you will be," he told Milton in a tone that antici-pated no argument, but he found himself in the middle of

57

one, nevertheless.

"Dammit, you don't need me. My middle name is trouble," Milton flung at him.

"We'll *change* your middle name and don't use foul language," Brant shot back. "Vulgarity doesn't become a lad your age."

"Put me down!" Milton all but screamed. This closeness was playing havoc with her brittle emotions. Her heart was pounding like rain pattering against a billowed sail.

"Not until you are safely locked in my cabin!"

"Hell's bells," Milton muttered in exasperation. The last thing she wanted was a pirate guardian angel. Why couldn't he leave her alone?

"Mind . . . your . . . tongue!" Brant barked brusquely. His patience had been worn thin and his belly was violently reacting to the overexertion of attempting to contain this feisty wildcat.

After Brant kicked the door shut with his boot heel, he set the irate waif to her feet. "I have a good mind to pound some sense into you, young man," Brant scowled irritably.

Milton tilted a defiant chin, her glittering green eyes focused on Brant's sour frown. "It won't be the first time I've taken a beatin'," she scoffed at him. "That's always the way it is, ain't it? If a man don't get his way he resorts to violence."

Brant's aggravation ebbed when he noticed Milton's bitter tone. "Promise me you won't pull another stunt like that," he coaxed. "I feel responsible for your welfare. I do not want your death on my conscience." Offering a peace treaty smile, Brant tugged the hem of his shirt from his breeches. "Let's put aside our harsh words and call it a night, shall we? 'Tis been a long day."

Milton nodded mutely as Brant discarded his shirt, exposing his upper torso to her admiring gaze. The assault on her senses was to begin again, she thought bleakly. "I'll snuff the lantern," she offered, praying darkness would close in around them before Brant stripped completely naked. One eyeful was enough for one day and Milton wasn't certain she could endure another lesson in anatomy.

"Nay, not until I have undressed for bed," Brant insisted as he sank down on the cot to doff his boots. "I'll never find my way around this new furniture arrangement in the dark."

Milton cursed her spiteful prank. It had come back to haunt her. Helplessly, she stared at the rippling muscles that flexed and relaxed as Brant went about his task.

When Brant stood up to shed his breeches Milton's bruised face wore a sick expression. "Is something amiss?" He was surprised to see that he was the object of Milton's undivided attention.

Amiss? Milton mused. Brant was seeing to it that she *missed* nothing! "Nay," she lied through her teeth.

When the waif turned on his heels and plopped down on his own bed, Brant frowned puzzledly. "Surely you do not intend to sleep in your clothes."

Milton tugged the sheet over her shoulder. "Well, I sure as hell ain't sleepin' in the raw!" she snorted distastefully. "It don't seem natural. If the good Lord didna intend for a body to wear wool clothes He wouldn't have created sheep," she pointed out.

Brant burst out laughing at the urchin's strange logic. "And following that reasoning, I suppose you feel it necessary to sleep in your *leather* boots since God also invented cows."

"Aye, it seems perfectly sensible to me. Why else would there be cows if not for leather and an occasional glass of milk?" Milton parried with smooth sarcasm.

"You have a lot to learn, m'boy," Brant chortled. "I predict when you're a mite older, you will have no aversion to sleeping in the buff, especially when you are abed with a bit of fluff."

His insensitive attitude toward women inflamed her temper. "Is that what you call every woman, a bit of fluff? Is that the only purpose a woman serves for you?" Milton snorted disgustedly. "Now who's the one with distorted logic, Cap'n? Next you'll be tellin' me the Lord put females on earth to warm a man's bed."

A clouded frown shaded Brant's craggy features. "If you knew women as I do, I doubt you would find cause to defend them. They are devious creatures who delight in using a man for their own selfish purposes. 'Tis best for a man to take what women have to offer and then leave before he finds himself entangled in their treacherous webs. I realize you hold your mother in high esteem, but she might be the one exception to the rule."

His cynical remarks set Milton to wondering why Brant held such a low opinion of women. Was his bitter attitude caused by an unfaithful lover? Had he been deeply hurt by a woman's betrayal? Perhaps she and the captain *did* have something in common, Milton thought to herself. Brant considered women to be necessary evils and she deemed men to be worthless creatures.

Stifling a yawn, Brant let the subject die a quiet death and then proceeded to shed his breeches. When he ambled across the cabin to snuff the lantern, Milton buried her head in her pillow, her face flushing seven shades of red. She would never adjust to seeing this virile specimen of a man traipsing about stark naked. Milton swore, then and there, to make it a point never to be in the cabin while Brant was stripping from his clothes. This bold display of hair-covered flesh was her undoing! She could recite from memory the location of every battle scar on his sinewy body.

Unbeknownst to Milton, Brant had turned to voice one last comment and witnessed the waif's reaction. A befuddled frown plowed Brant's brow. The boy refused to shed his own clothes and he cringed each time Brant did. Was the waif ashamed of his masculinity . . . or lack of it? Strange lad, Brant mused as he smothered the light. Not only did Milton refuse to be seen without every stitch of clothing in place, but he had never once removed his grimy cap. No doubt the urchin possessed lily white skin. Brant doubted that even an inch of Milton's flesh had been exposed to sunlight.

After feeling his way through the maze of furniture, Brant plopped down on his cot. He needed a restful night's sleep. The following day would require that he keep his wits about him. There was trouble brewing along the English coast and he and John Paul were the cause of it. Brant was certain news of the raids had reached the Admiralty. British warships would be swarming the sea to dispose of the American privateers who had dared to infiltrate the Mother Country's home waters.

While Brant was mentally preparing himself for another raid on Ireland's shore, Milton was flouncing on her bed like a fish out of water. No matter which way she turned there was a tormenting vision to haunt her. Twinkling golden eyes and a radiant smile were shining like a beacon in the darkness, luring her ever closer.

Brant Diamond was no more than a pirate, Milton tried to convince herself. Just because his masculine physique could put a Greek god to shame was no reason for her to overlook his faults. It was suicide to wonder how it would feel to be held in his powerful arms, to feel his hard, muscular body pressing intimately to hers. But Milton had considered it and she hated herself for dwelling on the thought. She had to find a way to flee the ship and quickly. It would never do to find herself emotionally involved with Brant Diamond. Any affection she might feel for this pirate could only lead to further disaster. She found herself tripping on the borderline of catastrophe often enough without openly inviting trouble.

Determined to ignore the strong physical attraction that was growing out of proportion, Milton forced the vision of the handsome captain from her thoughts. Counting Brant's peccadilloes instead of sheep, Milton begged for sleep. She prayed she could maintain her composure when next assaulted by an overexposure of Brant's bare flesh. Hopefully, there wouldn't be a next time, Milton thought to herself. She was going to take extreme measures to prevent it!

Chapter Four

At the first light of dawn, Brant was at the helm, staring pensively at the enemy schooners that hugged the wharf of Belfast Lough. The harbor was abound with fishing boats and ominous warships, ones Brant was itching to confront. His astute gaze shifted to the *Ranger*, John Paul's sloop of war, and then to the *H.M.S. Drake*. The British frigate had raised her sails to the wind and cruised out of the harbor to investigate the unidentified vessels. Off the leeward bow, Brant studied the approach of the *Drake*'s sister ship.

As John Paul had requested, Brant had kept a skeleton crew on the main deck and ordered the greater force of manpower to prepare the cannons on the lower decks. The crew had been instructed to await the order to fire and to take care not to damage the hull of the enemy ships with cannon fire. The privateers fully intended to emerge from battle with the Royal Navy's vessels as prizes.

Brant anxiously watched the *H.M.S. Drake* sail within cannon range. John Paul quickly turned his ship into the wind, exposing his guns. Brant followed his lead to attack the other brigantine. The British were outraged when the *Ranger* and *Sea Lady* displayed a flag of stars and stripes. Before the enemy could man the guns, the American privateers fired broadside, bombarding the decks and cutting the sails to shreds.

For more than thirty minutes the vessels exchanged fire before the *Drake*'s sister ship wheeled about and pointed its bow toward the inland channel. Scowling at the cowardly enemy captain, Brant gave chase. The frigate slipped into the narrow channel to hide like a frightened rabbit, leaving the *Drake* at the privateer's mercy.

Although the Scottish-born Jones had sailed these waters since childhood, Brant had not. He was wary of navigating unfamiliar waters to pursue the sister ship. Disappointed that he was unable to capture the cowardly captain, Brant tracked a course back to aid John Paul in disabling the *Drake*, offering her no means of escape. When the privateers had shot away the headsails, leaving them dangling from the masts, and cut the riggings to pieces, a boarding party swarmed the ship to seize command.

Since the *Drake* was incapable of sailing, the *Ranger* took her in tow. Brant aimed his schooner southward to pass between Copeland Island and the headland of Belfast Lough, searching for safe waters to refit the *Drake* for sailing.

As the daring privateers cruised away with the British warship in tow, Derrick Redmund lowered his spyglass and snarled bitterly. The Admiralty had sent Derrick to protect the North Channel and its trade ports. But the Americans had made him look the blundering fool. He would not soon forget that he had chosen to retreat instead of becoming a Patriot prize. He had seen that particular schooner before and he detested the sight of it and the bitter memories it evoked. The next time he spied the *Sea Lady* sitting arrogantly on the sea, he would set it ablaze with cannon fire, Derrick swore to himself. Aye, he and the American captain would meet again, Derrick vowed. And when they did, the outcome would not be as disastrous as their past encounters.

Derrick's reputation as a naval officer was at stake and his pride had already been sorely put upon the previous week. Catrina Hamilton's refusal to follow through with the wedding plans had incensed him. The stubborn chit had defied him and

Derrick's temper had exploded. When she had fled from her estate to elude him, Derrick had intended to give chase. Unfortunately, he had been called back to his command.

After the raids on Whitehaven and the surrounding area, all available manpower was ordered to defend the coast and capture the slippery American captains who had wreaked havoc on the Mother Country. Now the privateers had struck again, leaving destruction in their wake. Grumbling, Captain Redmund assessed the damage to his fore- and main-topsails. It would take the remainder of the day to repair the vessel. By then, Jones and Diamond would have plundered another harbor and seized only God knew how many prizes at the Crown's expense.

It seemed he was not to be granted even a smidgeon of luck, Derrick thought resentfully. First he had lost the young heiress and her vast fortune. Now his record had been blemished by the notorious Captain Diamond. But one day his luck would change, Derrick reassured himself. One day he would have a position of power and prestige and no one would stand in his way.

Squelching the feeling of nausea, Milton weaved her way across the splintered deck of the *Sea Lady* to aid the wounded sailors. Although Captain Diamond had ordered her to remain in the cabin, she had not been able to endure the suspense.

While she was tucked inside the stairwell, her eyes had been glued to Brant, fearing he was making himself an easy target at the helm. Just watching him during battle brought an unexpected sense of pride. Milton was completely bewildered by that emotion, especially since she had spent the previous night mentally listing complaints about the man.

Even while cannons were exploding about him, Brant manned the wheel, taking his schooner alongside the enemy to inflict a barrage of gun fire. The American attack was so fast and furious that the British could not match the damaging blows. Limping like a wounded dog, the frigate had headed for cover while she could still sail.

Brant Diamond must have been blessed with the nine lives of a cat, Milton mused. Although he had used up two of them that morning, dodging musket balls that bore his name, it did not discourage him. Brant's reckless daring might have been admirable, but Milton viewed it as nothing more than foolhardy valor. He could have gotten himself killed, she thought furiously and then asked herself why that mattered.

Flinging aside her straying thoughts, Milton knelt to inspect the wound Thomas Haynes had sustained. Luckily, it was only a nick, caused by a splinter of wood. When she had extracted the sliver from Thomas's thigh, she tightly wrapped the wound and then moved on to assist another sailor.

A lump welled up in her throat when she glanced down at one young crewman. Wheeling around, Milton fought back another wave of nausea, painfully aware there was nothing to be done for the fallen sailor. The sight of a ship's deck strewn with maimed bodies was too much. Instinctively, Milton darted toward the steps and shut herself in the cabin. Once she was alone, the dam of tears burst and she mourned the waste of lives. God, how she wanted to go home, back to the peaceful meadows of Dirkshire, away from the roar of cannons and flaming sails.

"You disobeyed me" came the harsh voice from so close beside her that she nearly jumped out of her skin. "I would have spared you this grisly scene of battle, but you defied my orders."

Milton pushed up into an upright position to meet Brant's furious frown. "If you truly wanted to spare me this misery you would have left me on St. Mary's Isle."

"To do what?" Brant queried in scornful mockery. "Sweep out the stables? Just by being a member of my crew you are entitled to a share of the booty to be gained from the cargo and sale of the *Drake*. You have made more in one day than you could have earned in a month working for some snobbish

66

Scottish aristocrat."

"'Tis blood money," Milton insisted. "Bought and paid for by those who fought and died on deck. I want none of it."

Brant let his breath out in a rush. This waif knew nothing of the ways of the world and it was downright exasperating to attempt to explain them to him. "My crew knows the risks they face. They chose to live and die by the code of the sea. Their lost shares become ours and that is the way of things."

Milton bounded to her feet, returning the black look that was plastered on Brant's craggy features. "If that is the way of things why did you order me to remain in this cabin?" she countered, her voice rising testily. "If I am to have a pirate's share I should have fought a pirate's battle."

"Dammit, I was trying to protect you. You, Milton, are a green sailor, as green as they come," he spat sarcastically.

"And yer behavin' like an overprotective father," Milton flung back at him. "If I got a notion to throw myself overboard or man one of them cannons, 'tis *my* business and *my* life. I'll thank you to let me make my own decisions!"

Impulsively, Brant grasped the insolent waif's arms and gave him a sound shake. "Now, you listen to me, brat, I am . . ." His voice changed to a pained grunt when Milton raised her knee and jabbed it into his midsection.

Before Brant could recover she shot around the corner of the desk to place a sturdy obstacle between them. The captain's touch caused a riptide of emotions within her, ones Milton refused to tolerate. "You keep yer hands off me, Cap'n," she growled.

For a long moment, Brant could only stare incredulously at the fiery waif. Didn't that boy know he could have been flogged for striking a superior officer? This ragged urchin had unbelievable nerve! Infuriated, Brant stalked toward the waif. Milton let out a shriek, shot across the room, and sailed out the door before Brant could fight his way through the rearranged furniture to apprehend her.

"I should have that brat shot!" Brant muttered under his

breath and then reconsidered his hasty decision. "Nay, first I will strangle that scrawny bag of bones and *then* I will put him before a firing squad," he amended.

Brant stalked back to the main deck with revenge gnawing at his insides. But when he spied Milton kneeling beside one of the sailors who had been mortally wounded his disposition mellowed. The lad sat on the plank, cradling the sailor's head in his lap. Milton was offering what the crewman needed most— compassion and reassurance.

Brant's irritation evaporated. Besides, he would look the tyrant if he stormed up to the waif and jerked him to his feet. Why did that cussed urchin set off so many conflicting emotions within him, Brant asked himself as he strode across the deck to assess the damages. One minute Brant was laughing at the boy's naïveté and the next moment he was infuriated by Milton's razor-sharp tongue. Damnation, that boy constantly had him walking an emotional tightrope!

The signal flags rising on the *Ranger's* mast disrupted Brant's contemplations. John Paul was requesting that they put ashore in an inconspicuous cove to begin the repairs on the captured frigate. Tossing aside all thoughts of Milton, Brant climbed to the helm to fetch his spyglass.

After another hour Brant noticed another brigantine sailing toward them. A wry smile pursed his lips. He ordered his crew to prepare to seize the *Patience,* a schooner from Whitehaven bound to Norway. When John Paul closed in on the starboard side, Brant hemmed in the unsuspecting vessel from the port side. Like a swarm of hornets, the privateers cast out their grappling irons to snare the ship and quickly boarded. In a matter of minutes the vessel was taken and one of Brant's senior officers was made prizemaster of the acquisition.

By sunset Brant spotted a cove where the crew could lay-to for repairs. Keeping a watchful eye on Milton, Brant supervised the overhaul of the damaged sails. The crew worked through the night to make the *Drake* seaworthy. Finally, the prize frigate was prepared to sail under her own power.

Since the wind now veered south, John Paul decided to sail north around Ireland to escape pursuers and return to France. Brant heartily agreed with the decision. He was anxious to sell the cargo and pay his crew for their efforts in the North Sea.

Before John Paul returned to his command, he pulled Brant aside to question him about his progress with the contrary lad. "How have you fared with that skinny wretch? I am most relieved to see the waif hasn't buried the hatchet in your back."

Brant's gaze shifted to young Milton who had thrown himself into the task of preparing the shredded sails that were stretched out on the deck. "The lad is coming along," he insisted and then begrudgingly added, "slowly but surely."

"Ah well, the loss of one Spanish doubloon will be of no consequence to you," John Paul taunted. "You will be well compensated when we enter Brest to sell our prizes."

"I still have a fortnight to bring young Milton to heel," Brant reminded him. "'Tis time enough. You could well be the one fishing a gold coin from your pocket when we set foot in France."

"Time will out," John Paul chuckled. With a snappy spring in his walk he sauntered across the gangplank. "Roll out your moonraker, Captain Diamond. I am anxious to see the shores of France and keep company with the gentle ladies of court. 'Tis been too long since I have felt something warm and soft beside me."

His hazel eyes danced in the moonlight and Brant chuckled at the grin of rakish anticipation that settled on John Paul's features. "Aye, I share your hunger. I only pray that our roving eyes do not land on the same vision of loveliness. It would be a pity if we were vying for the same damsel's attention. You would be most disgruntled if you were forced to make a second selection."

John Paul sniffed at the jibe and then saluted the taunting captain. "We shall see who claims the loveliest prize on land, Captain Diamond," he challenged before striding away.

Milton frowned after overhearing the conversation between the two captains. No doubt the privateers would pray for a strong wind to take them to Brest while she spitefully wished to be becalmed off the shore of Ireland. The thought of Brant sharing his bed with a willing wench turned her eyes a darker shade of green.

Oh, what did she care if Brant bedded everything in skirts? Because each passing day found her more involved with a man who didn't realize she existed, Milton told herself drearily. It had been easier to hate the dashing captain. But like a fool, her attitude toward him had mellowed. And she should have known better than to feel anything at all for Brant Diamond. She, of all people, knew how it hurt to lose someone she truly cared about. Milton had promised herself never to get that close to anyone again. She didn't want to suffer that stabbing pain of loss, the agonizing grief she had endured when her parents died. To care brought inevitable misery and Milton had had enough of it to last her a lifetime.

Despair closed in around her as she made her way to the cabin . . . after Brant had retired for the night. There was no escape, Milton realized. She was vividly aware of the dashing buccaneer with dancing amber eyes and raven hair. And she was bound for France aboard a pirate ship. Nothing short of a miracle could save her.

A startled gasp gushed from Milton's lips when she opened the cabin door. Damn, she had expected Brant to be tucked in bed by now. But he wasn't, much to her chagrin. Brant was lounging in his bath. His hair-matted chest glistened with water droplets that danced on his skin each time he inhaled a breath. One well-proportioned leg was draped over the rim of the undersized tub. A cigar dangled from the fingers of his left hand and a glass of brandy occupied the other.

The naked rake, Milton thought in exasperation. She was not up for this. Her emotions were already in an uproar and her unraveled composure would come completely unwound if she had to endure another nerve-racking incident.

When Milton pivoted on her heels to exit before she exposed herself to another embarrassing incident, Brant called her back. "Ah, there you are, Milt. And just in time. Come here, boy. I require your services. Scrub my back."

Milton's shoulders slumped in defeat. It seemed she was destined to learn every inch of this man's body by touch as well as by sight. Begrudgingly, she trudged across the room and dropped to her knees, careful to keep her eyes pinned to the far wall.

"It seems to me a grown man ought to be able to give himself a bath," she muttered grouchily. "If you would set yer vices aside, Cap'n, you would have enough hands to see to this task of scrubbin' yerself clean."

Brant was in good humor after successfully battling the British—too good to have his disposition soured by Milton's taunting jibe. "It requires two hands to celebrate our victory and the acquisition of our prizes," he said nonchalantly. His body curled forward, exposing the muscled expanse of his back to Milton's reluctant gaze. "Fetch the sponge and scrub, Milt. And I could use a massage to ease away the lingering tension. 'Tis been a hectic day."

Milton would have preferred to swim through shark-infested waters than to place her hands on his masculine flesh. Heaving a frustrated sigh, she snatched up the soap and sponge to lather Brant's back. Nervous energy spurted through her, causing her ministrations to be rough and jerky.

When Brant tried to take a sip of brandy it slopped on his face and trickled down his chest. "Damn, boy, I wanted you to scrub my back, not scratch the hide off it," he snorted.

Gritting her teeth, Milton slowed her frantic pace of scouring Brant's back. But her attempt at gentleness became her downfall. She could feel his hard muscles beneath her palms. It was impossible not to notice the bronzed flesh that stretched across his wide shoulders and curled around his hips.

The room suddenly overheated. Milton was prepared to swear the *Sea Lady* had caught afire. The white-hot sensations that

71

riveted through her naive body caused beads of perspiration to break out on her forehead. The potential mass of power beneath her hands was difficult to ignore and her feminine curiosity was triggering emotions Milton was unprepared to deal with.

Brant sighed contentedly when Milton's gentle massage erased the tension. Ah, it felt good to relax, he mused. "Lower, Milton," he requested, pushing forward in the tub. "Concentrate on the muscles along my spine. It still feels as if they are tied in knots."

His backbone may have been wrapped in a sailor's knot, but her entire body had become entangled in arousing sensations. When Brant eased forward to expose the muscled curve of his derriere, Milton swallowed air . . . a room full of it. Her throat constricted and she nearly strangled. When she attempted to inhale a steadying breath, Brant's male scent invaded her nostrils, suffocating her.

A curious frown gathered on Brant's brow. Milton was just sitting there like a stick of furniture, her hands dangling over the rim of the tub. Brant glanced back over his shoulder to see a flaming blush climbing from Milton's neck to her smudged cheeks.

"I am only a man, for God's sake," Brant admonished. "And I don't bite. That is *your* favorite prank."

Gulping down her apprehension, Milton placed her trembling hands on the small of his back and began to massage. But ah, at what tremendous cost to her composure. She was splitting apart at the seams, trying to remain cool and calm and failing miserably.

"Mmmmm . . . that feels good," Brant purred in satisfaction.

Milton thought she had endured the worst until Brant eased back in the tub and tapped his chest.

"And now here . . ." Brant instructed.

With a determined frown Milton lathered the sponge once again and laid it to the thick, crisp hair that covered his upper torso. The sight and feel of this powerfully built panther had her overworked heart doing back somersaults. Milton detested the emotions that were leaping through her taut body. She didn't want to enjoy touching him, looking at him, but she was. God forgive her, she was!

Brant lounged against the back of the tub, his eyes closed, his naked body relaxed like a mountain lion in repose. Unwillingly, Milton admired the chiseled lines of his face, the sensuous curve of his lips. She wondered how it would feel to press her mouth to his in a kiss, to touch his muscular flesh in a caress instead of a dedicated scrubbing. Would his body come alive, rousing to tenderness? Or would this dark pirate be a fierce, demanding lover, just as he was a fierce and unrelenting warrior in battle?

The question penetrated her mind with such startling potency that Milton jerked back. Brant cocked his head to the side and pried open one eye to determine why Milton had recoiled on her knees. Oh, how she detested that innocent expression that settled on his bronzed features. How she despised his ignorance and her own attempt to hoodwink this rebel pirate. She was not having the last laugh. She was dying of embarrassment, bit by excruciating bit!

Milton's temper got the best of her. She was not Brant Diamond's personal slave and she did not have to endure these unfamiliar sensations, she told herself. "Here, you do the rest," she grumbled, flinging the wet sponge at his handsome face. "My fingers are shriveled up and they ain't no use to either of us."

Brant snatched the sponge from his cheek, tossed it in the tub, and climbed to his feet. "Now look here, Milton," he ground out, the muscles of his jaw twitching in annoyance. "I asked a simple favor and . . ."

The view caused Milton to gasp in dismay. She could not look up into Brant's angry face without staring at every inch of his flesh between his knees and his neck. Flustered, Milton scrambled to her feet and dived onto her cot. She clutched her pillow and pulled it over her head to muffle her squeal of frustration.

Brant stood there, calf-deep in water, his hands resting on his hips, his jaw sagging on its hinges. "What the sweet loving hell is wrong with you, Milt?" he questioned bewilderedly.

Milton didn't know what to say. She just pounded her fist into the cot and growled under her breath. *Damn, damn, double damn*, she thought to herself. Never in all her life had she been swamped and buffeted by such overwhelming sensations. She was humiliated, bewildered, embarrassed . . .

"Milton, do you have these fits often?" Brant inquired as he snatched up a towel and draped it around his hips. He watched in amusement as the boy beat his legs up and down on his cot and punched his sheet. "Perhaps when we dock in Brest I should have a doctor look you over. You are behaving very strangely."

He wouldn't have thought her actions odd if he knew his lackey was a woman, Milton speculated. But she didn't give the thought to tongue. She just kept on throwing her tantrum until all the pent-up frustrations drained from her body.

Brant made no more attempt to communicate with Milton. It seemed the lad was unable to speak audibly when he was having a seizure. Occasionally, Brant glanced in Milton's direction and chuckled to himself. My, but the boy had difficulty dealing with nudity. He had never seen a young man so horrified of bare flesh. Most men showed no signs of modesty but Milton was a walking bundle of self-consciousness. But why should that surprise him, Brant asked himself. The boy never stripped from his own clothes. He barely knew how his own physique looked, much less any other man's.

Well, Milton would simply have to adjust, Brant mused as he swung his legs onto his own cot. The waif could not wander through life without a smidgen of an education. It was a fact of life that most people didn't wear clothes twenty-four hours a day the way Milton did. The sooner Milton accepted the notion of seeing Brant in the altogether occasionally, the less strained their relationship.

Once Milton could look to his captain, man to man, realizing there were no real differences between them, they could become friends. And Milton sorely needed one, Brant reminded himself. Someone had to care for this peculiar bag of bones. The world was not prepared for a boy like Milton and Milton was unprepared to take his place in society when he climbed into his shell like a frightened turtle each time a little bare flesh passed his line of vision.

As the days blended into a week, Milton resigned herself to the fact that she was doomed to ride out the voyage to France. She had recovered from the late-night incident that caused her such mortification and accepted the fact that she would never cure Brant Diamond of traipsing about in front of her without his clothes. Resorting to ingenuity and excuses, Milton managed to slip from the cabin before Brant rose from bed in the morning and she was conveniently absent when he collapsed on his cot for the night. Since she could not change Brant's ways she merely avoided any situation that might cause her embarrassment. The sleeping arrangements were tolerable and Milton discreetly saw to her toiletries while Captain Diamond was on the main deck.

She had whiled away the hours with the crew members, learning the workings of the ship under Thomas's watchful eyes and Brant's careful instruction. Milton almost found herself enjoying the raillery of the sailors who had accepted her as their comrade.

Considering the circumstances, she lived a peaceful co-existence with the privateers and their handsome captain. Milton kept asking herself if this misadventure weren't better than ambling through her country estate, haunted by the memories of her parents and the bitter incident with

Derrick Redmund.

All in all, Milton found little complaint with the cruise. Begrudgingly, she attributed her contentment to her ever-growing fascination with the raven-haired, golden-eyed captain. Her gaze often drifted to Brant while he stood at the helm, peering across the sea. Her ears pricked each time she heard that deep skirl of laughter bubbling from his chest. And she could not help remembering the sight and feel of his hard, lean flesh, the way his muscles flexed and relaxed as he strode across his cabin in some indecent fashion that kept her blushing even days later.

Milton had come to the conclusion that Pirate Captain Diamond was a complex man. She had seen him at his best, worst, and all phases in between. Brant could be fierce and forceful when the situation demanded. And at other times he could be playfully amusing. He was a man of many moods and Milton chided herself for being so magnetically drawn to a rogue who didn't even know she existed.

One afternoon after Brant finished logging his diary of the cruise, he decided to further Milton's education. With pistol and dagger in hand, Brant explained the correct procedure for hurling a knife and taking aim with a flintlock. He bragged on about Milton's ability and praised the cabin boy for being a quick learner.

Brant encouraged the lad to practice in his spare time and Milton devoted much time and energy to the art of self-defense. Her father had overlooked that facet of her education. After her scuffle with Derrick Redmund, Milton was determined to become her adversary's worthy opponent, should the situation arise. Milton was also aware that part of her purpose for becoming proficient with a pistol and knife was to impress Brant. She could not help herself from grinning back at him when he praised her talents. The painful truth was that she was experiencing her first bout with love, even when the voice of reason warned her of the hazards of such nonsense.

Milton hungered for Brant's attention, his radiant smiles.

Although she kept lecturing herself that this secretive crush was childish and temporary, she craved to be the recipient of Brant's affection, platonic though it was and would always be. Milton had not, however, relinquished her attempt to taunt him at every turn. She still delighted in watching the self-confident captain blunder around the cabin she rearranged each time he became familiar with the layout of furniture. But Milton was certain Brant intended to seek revenge for her madcap pranks when he ordered her to climb the main mast to check the riggings.

Brant couldn't have known she had a fierce, uncontrollable apprehension of falling, she tried to tell herself as she shinnied up the beam. The captain had instructed his young apprentice to check the ropes and sails after a stout gale had played havoc with the canvas the previous night. Forcing herself not to look down, Milton extended a shaky hand toward the lower supporting beam on the fore-sail. But her intention of overcoming her anxiety evaporated when her booted foot failed to make contact with the rough timber. And for a heart-stopping instant Milton was suspended in midair.

A blood curdling scream burst from her lips as she clawed at the horizontal beam that steadied the sail. Her first mistake was not guarding her step and the second was glancing down in the direction she had come. Her stomach fell and splattered on the main deck that was suddenly crowded with anxious sailors. They were simultaneously shouting instructions, but Milton could make no sense of their words. Her heart was drumming in her ears. She resorted to pure instinct—she screamed for all she was worth, clung to the timber, and prayed religiously while her life passed before her eyes.

Brant jerked up his head when he heard the commotion. His breath lodged in his throat when he spied the ragamuffin dangling from the beam like a fallen sail. Brant raced down the ladder and sprinted toward the mast. A fearful gasp broke loose when he saw Milton's colorless fingers slide from the beam. But he was not the only sailor whose heart had catapulted to his throat. The entire crew stood paralyzed, certain the feisty wretch was about to break every bone in his body when he splattered on the deck.

Never had Brant moved so quickly in his life. In less than a heartbeat he scrambled up the mast to perch on the beam. His anxious gaze focused on Milton's whitened knuckles that rewrapped themselves around the timber. The haunted look in Milton's eyes cut through Brant like a knife and he cursed himself for putting the waif through such a horrifying experience.

Milton knew she was staring at Brant for the last time. There was no strength left in her arms, no circulation in her fingers. She screeched again when her hands, as if they possessed a mind of their own, slipped from the beam, giving her up as a lost cause.

Just as Milton's grasp relaxed to send her plunging to certain death Brant uncoiled like a striking snake. He snagged her forearm and hoisted her up beside him.

Instinctively, Milton molded herself to Brant's hard strength. She was like a choking vine wrapped around a lattice. Before she could stop herself she was sobbing against his shirt, her head buried on his sturdy shoulder.

Milton's reaction startled Brant. He felt a mite ridiculous when the urchin squeezed the stuffing out of him with the entire crew as witness.

"'Tis all right now," Brant reassured the trembling waif. "You can let go. You are safe."

But Milton didn't feel safe with nothing but air beneath her. She was petrified and she couldn't unclamp her stranglehold on Brant. "I'm afraid of height," she managed to choke out.

Brant rolled his eyes heavenward. "'Tis one hell of a time to inform me," he muttered, attempting to pry Milton's clenched fists from the collar of his shirt. "Why didn't you mention that minor detail *before* I sent you up here?"

"I wanted to please you, Cap'n," Milton blurted out, and

then muffled her sniff. "I didna want you to poke fun at me because of my fear. But 'tis very real to me and I canna let go!"

Heaving an exasperated sigh that affected Milton as well since she was plastered against his chest, Brant inched his way toward the mast. "Close your eyes, lad, and hang on a few more minutes," he instructed.

As if she could have let go, Milton thought sickly. She knew she must have looked ridiculous clinging to the captain. But she didn't care if the entire lot of sailors were snickering at her. All she wanted was to plant her feet on the solid planks of the deck.

"Milton, could you ease your grasp on my neck," Brant requested in a strangled voice. "You are choking me." The boy's head was butted up against Brant's throat and his fingers were like a vise-grip on Brant's shoulders and neck. With a great deal of effort, Brant leaned out with a free arm to grasp the mast, but still he couldn't breathe, much less see where he was going. "Dammit, Milt, you're smothering me!"

Mustering every ounce of willpower she had left, Milton tried to loosen her grip. But her arms and legs were frozen to Brant's shoulders and hips. For what seemed forever, Milton endured the discomfort of the rough mast scraping her back since Brant was forced to shimmy down the beam with her plastered between him and the timber.

A sign of relief escaped Brant's lips when he felt Thomas reach up to support him and his vining bundle. Finally, Brant set one foot on the deck and attempted to untangle the boy's rigid body from his own. But still Milton wouldn't budge. The waif was a mass of petrified bone and flesh.

"Milton, for God's sake, let go!" Brant thundered. "We are standing on the damned deck!"

Milton pried one eye open to ensure it was no lie Brant gave her and then collapsed in relief. She eased her fierce grip but her legs were like a mass of quivering jelly. With a tiny yelp, she slumped against the captain and dragged in a shuddering breath.

79

"I ain't goin' atop again for all the king's gold," she chirped.

"You won't be asked." Brant rearranged the shirt Milton had twisted about his neck. "What you need is a stiff drink to settle your nerves," he diagnosed as he spun Milton around and propelled her toward the steps.

One of the sailors opened his mouth to interject a teasing remark. But he was immediately discouraged from putting the thought to tongue when he noticed the black look that was chiseled in Brant's features. After the captain whisked the wobbly-legged waif away, Jacob Powers flashed Thomas a wry grin.

"The captain is getting a mite touchy about his apprentice. He already warned us not to make young Milton the brunt of any jokes. I didn't see any harm in razzing that half-pint lad about the way he was squeezing the captain in two."

"The boy will have a difficult enough time facin' us as it is," Thomas reminded the young sailor. "Besides, we all got our secret fears. You wouldn't want nobody exposin' yers, now would you, Jacob? After all, it ain't been so long ago that you was just a novice at sea."

The grin that claimed Jacob's boyish features vanished. "Nay, I suppose not. I'll tell the rest of the men not to ride Milton about being scared of heights."

"Good idea," Thomas murmured absently as he watched Brant herd the skinny urchin toward the lower deck. "The lad's got spunk. I don't want to see it destroyed when he's just beginnin' to emerge from his shell."

Thomas had grown very attached to Milton the previous week. The waif was like a playful puppy, bounding along at Thomas's heels. Thomas had often been rewarded with young Milton's beaming smiles and he felt the need to protect the unfortunate lad, who was so pitifully thin and unsuited for his new life-style. And there was that glittering sparkle in Milton's eyes, Thomas reminded himself. It was the twinkling of youth, something Thomas would never recapture except when he stared into Milton's lively emerald eyes.

But he wasn't the only one who had taken pity on that little bundle of spirit, Thomas reminded himself. Captain Diamond's growing attachment to the lad was obvious. Brant always stood like a sentinel, keeping a watchful eye on the boy, teaching him the ways of the sea.

In all the years Thomas had served with Brant, he could not recall the captain taking such an active interest in one of his young recruits. But there was something different about Milton, something mysteriously intriguing beneath that pile of nervous energy and rambunctious spirit. The boy drew Brant like a magnet. It was as if Brant were claiming the son he never had and probably never would have since he had such an aversion to marriage.

But then, Brant's pessimistic attitude toward women and wedlock was not unwarranted, Thomas reminded himself cynically. Females were a scheming, troublesome lot. That was the reason Thomas had never planted himself on land. He was content to frequent the brothels when he docked. And when he sailed away, there was no anchor of affection to weigh him down.

If Captain Diamond chose to adopt Milton as his son, what could it hurt, Thomas reasoned. At least Brant wouldn't find himself forced to seek out a woman to bear him a child. Milton looked to be thirteen or fourteen. Brant wouldn't have to fuss with diapers and thumb-sucking. Aye, if a man wanted a son, adoption was the only answer, Thomas decided.

Chapter Five

"Here." Brant thrust a glass of French wine at Milton, who drained the liquor in a matter of seconds. When the boy choked on the taste, Brant whacked him on the back. "It isn't your dear mother's remedy, but it will take the edge off your nerves," he encouraged.

Milton chugged a second glass of wine, relieved that the first sips had numbed her throat. But still the unnerving sensations had not subsided. She could feel herself dangling from the towering beam, losing her grasp, knowing she was about to meet her untimely death. Blinking back the dismal thought, Milton snatched the bottle away and poured her third drink. Again the frightening incident flashed before her eyes and she sought to chase it away with hand-to-glass combat.

"Slow down," Brant chuckled. "This liquor can take you every bit as high as your perch on the main mast. You're inviting a dreadful hangover."

"It canna be worse than thinkin' yer about to have yer innards splattered all over the main deck for all to see," Milton countered between gulps.

One dark brow lifted to a mocking angle. "Are you so certain, Milt? Speaking from my own personal experience I can honestly say there were times when I wished I were dead after a bout with liquor."

By the time Milton guzzled her fourth glass of wine, the edge to which Brant referred had been smoothed over. Her nose tingled and her limbs felt as if a thousand tiny fires had been set within them. As the tension eased, Milton slumped negligently in her chair. A silly smile dangled on the corner of her mouth.

"I'm sorry about the way I clung to you," she apologized and then hiccupped. Embarrassed, she covered her mouth. "S'cuse me."

"At least you are still in one piece," Brant snickered, joining Milton in a glass of wine. "For a while, I wondered if we would be forced to glue you back together."

Milton's fuzzy gaze worked its way across her torso. She smiled a mysterious little smile. "You might have been a wee bit surprised when all the pieces didna fit, Cap'n."

Brant chuckled, unaware of her true meaning. "If we would have had a few spare parts left over we would have randomly stitched them back on."

Feeling reckless Milton grabbed one of Brant's cigars and lit it from the lantern. After taking a small puff she eased back in her chair and propped one leg over the edge of the table. "Tell me about yerself, Cap'n," she demanded suddenly. "Where do you call home when you ain't floatin' about in this leaky tub, scarin' the wits from stuffy Englishmen and Scottish clans?"

Brant would have bet his cargo that this was the first cigar Milton had puffed upon. He stifled a chuckle when he detected the slur in the lad's voice. The waif was well into his cups, Brant predicted. At the moment Milton didn't have a care. He was escaping a fright, one he was most eager to forget.

Swallowing his amused grin, Brant patronized the intoxicated waif with an answer. "I own a sugar plantation on a quaint out-of-the-way island in the West Indies," he informed Milton. "Diamond's Den is an ocean paradise, brimming with gurgling waterfalls, colorful parrots, and fruit trees. When this dreadful war is over, I may even drop anchor and allow some other reckless adventurer to sail the high seas in my stead."

Milton skewed her smudged face up in a dubious frown. "You? Give up the sea?" She scoffed at the absurdity. She had come to know the daredevil captain well enough to realize he would be restless and unhappy if he were to run aground indefinitely. "Why, that would be as preposterous as askin' a fish to live out of water."

Brant chortled at the comical expression that twisted Milton's features. "A fish, am I? If you weren't soused, young man, I would take that as an insult." The laughter died in his eyes as he stared across the cabin. A faraway look settled on his craggy features. "There was a time when I wanted no more than a home and family, a time when I was young and in love. But the angel of my dreams turned out to be a witch in a nightmare. Cynthia Marsh was impressed with my self-made fortune, but she had her heart set on old, established money, the kind one procures from British aristocracy. She consented to marry me in case she could catch no worthier prize. But the moment she found a wealthy British officer, stationed in Charleston, she latched on to him."

"Then she was a fool," Milton blurted out, unable to stop herself before her tongue outdistanced her pickled brain.

"Oh? How so?" Brant's gaze swung back to the waif, noting the glaze that covered the boy's sea-green eyes.

"Despite my first impression, you seem a likable sort," she admitted, the wine working like a truth serum. "You ain't built like a pole, for one thing. And you ain't hard to look at for another. If yer lady wasn't smart enough to know old money can sometimes be moldy, she didna deserve a man like you."

A wry smile pursed Brant's lips. He peered at Milton over the rim of his glass. The boy was gradually sliding down in his chair like melted butter dripping over the edge of a hot stove. "Those were my thoughts exactly, Milt," Brant remarked on an arrogant note. "And I was well rid of that scheming witch."

"And because of this Cynthia chit you've set about to wench yer way across the seven seas," she surmised.

"'Tis better than pining a lost love," Brant argued.

85

"Women have their purposes and a wise man will not soon forget that." Heaving a sigh, Brant studied the shaft of light that slanted through the porthole. "Perhaps you consider my opinion of women distasteful, but the scars of love are the hardest to bear. I saw Cynthia shortly after her marriage and I . . ." His voice trailed off when he heard the clank of the glass on the planked floor.

Milton had been treading liquor so long he had finally drowned in his cups. The boy's head dropped on his shoulder and his arms dangled lifelessly over the edge of his chair. It would take the remainder of the day to sleep off this wine-induced stupor, Brant speculated. Milton had barely paused to inhale a breath since he began pouring down the liquor. The lad would be in for one miserable evening *if* he managed to wake before dawn.

Setting the glass aside, Brant scooped the limp waif into his arms. He located the cot that seemed to sprout legs and walk to a new corner of the cabin each time Brant turned his back. When he laid Milton's sleeping form on the bed, Brant stepped back to appraise the drunken waif.

In all the weeks they had been rooming together, Brant had never seen the boy without that dingy, oversized cap pulled down around his ears. Come to think of it, Brant didn't even know if the lad had ears. He had no idea if Milton had one strand of hair on his head, much less what color it might be. And although the discolorations around Milton's eyes and upon his cheeks were fading, there was always a smudge of grime on the boy's nose, cheeks, and chin. Brant had often wondered if Milt was permanently stained or if he simply had an aversion to washing his face.

Several times the past week Brant had suggested that Milt discard the dingy cap, but Milton insisted it was his good-luck piece and that it kept him out of trouble. But then, Milton had also admitted that trouble was his middle name. Brant pointed out that perhaps the soiled hat was a curse rather than a good-luck charm. Milton refused to be swayed from his conviction and he refused to remove that confounded cap, no matter what the occasion.

Curiosity got the best of Brant. What would it hurt to remove Milton's soiled cap and have a look-see? The lad would never know, Brant rationalized. Just as he reached out to remove the hat a rap resounded behind the portal. Brant jerked back as if he were about to be caught stealing. Grumbling at the interruption, Brant pivoted on his heel to answer the knock.

"Cap'n, our sister ship just raised her signal flags," Thomas announced to Brant and then peered around Brant's broad shoulders to appraise Milton. "Is the boy all right?"

A wry smile rippled across Brant's lips. "Aye, he tried to calm his frayed nerves in a bottle of French wine. He reminded me of a thirsty seaman gulping fresh water after being becalmed in the Doldrums. I don't imagine Milton will come around for several hours."

Thomas snickered at the small form that was sprawled on the cot. "I s'pose this will be his first exposure to a hangover." He whistled and rolled his eyes when he spied the empty bottle on the table. "Lordy, did the boy inhale the whole flask?"

"Very nearly," Brant snickered. "He allowed me one small portion before he polished off the rest of the wine."

Thomas shook his head in dismay and then closed the door behind them. "I wouldn't want to have little Milt's head when he wakes up."

"No doubt the boy will accuse us of implanting a bass drum in his skull while he was sleeping."

While Milt lay in a wine-drugged stupor, Brant climbed to the helm to see John Paul's signal flags flapping in the breeze. Off the leeward bow, Brant noticed a merchant ship that appeared to be an interesting prize.

Eager for another capture to satisfy himself and his crew, John Paul decided to give chase. He ordered Brant and Lieutenant Simpson, prizemaster of the captured *Drake*, to follow in his wake. Although Brant complied with John Paul's request and reversed direction to pursue the northbound ship,

87

the *Drake* did not. To Brant's disbelief, Lieutenant Simpson continued on his southbound course to France.

When the sloop identified itself as a neutral Swede, Jones and Diamond came about and turned south again to catch up with the *Drake*. Brant was annoyed with Prizemaster Simpson for disobeying orders. And knowing John Paul as he did, Brant speculated the good captain would be hopping up and down with fury when he got his hands on the bungling lieutenant.

As the *Ranger* eased alongside the *Sea Lady* and her captured prize, the *Patience*, John Paul's face appeared fuming red. "Simpson deliberately disobeyed me!" he spumed when Brant was within shouting distance. "Give chase to the *Drake*. When we catch up with her I intend to suspend that wooden-headed lieutenant and send another man to assume command. I'll not have an idiot at the helm of my prize ship!"

Brant bit back an amused grin. John Paul's usually quiet voice and calm manner had exploded like an erupting volcano. Captain Jones would have the lieutenant under arrest by the time the sun set, Brant prophesied. Either Simpson had misunderstood the command or he had not seen it at all. But whatever his excuse it would not satisfy the irate John Paul. Jones was in a huff and nothing short of a lynching would pacify him.

After ordering the helmsman to plot a course due south, Brant returned to the cabin to see if Milton had roused from sleep. When he stepped into the room, a fond smile bordered his lips. Milton had not moved during the four-hour absence. He still lay sprawled on his back, his arms and legs dangling off the edge of the cot.

Brant ambled across the room to peer down at the grimy-faced lad. Earlier, he had been compelled to remove Milton's oversized hat that continually shadowed the young face. Demons of curiosity were hounding Brant again.

One quick peek at the boy's head wouldn't hurt, Brant argued with himself. Milton would never know and Brant's curiosity would be appeased. Deciding to yield to temptation

Brant carefully tipped back the grimy hat. When Milton stirred in his sleep and wormed to his side, the hidden mane of fiery auburn hair spilled across the pillow.

Brant's eyes very nearly popped out of his head. His jaw gaped wide enough for a sea gull to roost. His bug-eyed gaze swung back to Milton's not so frail but delicate face and Brant sat down before he fell down.

Good God! His cabin boy wasn't a boy at all, Brant's astounded brain shouted at him. Brant had been hoodwinked by a mischievous young woman. When the shock wore off Brant was assaulted by a mixture of indignation and anger. For several minutes he sat there smoldering. When the irritation dwindled, he mellowed into a smile. Shaking his head in disbelief, Brant gathered his feet beneath him and strode over to uncork another bottle of wine and light a cheroot. With drink in hand and a cigar clamped between his teeth, Brant replanted himself in his chair to stare at the sleeping beauty.

The wench could not be much over twenty, if even that, Brant surmised. What Brant had assumed to be a smooth-faced urchin of thirteen was really a clever young chit in disguise . . . and a very convincing one at that. His astute gaze fell to her baggy shirt, wondering what truly lay beneath what appeared to be a flat chest. Curiosity was chewing him up. It took every ounce of self-restraint to remain glued to his seat when he yearned to fully investigate his discovery.

As Brant sat there grappling with his churning emotions, the images of Milton's antics swirled about his head. He could see her biting and clawing at him like a vicious she-cat when he found her eavesdropping at Selkirk. Brant had mocked her bruised and battered face. Now he was curious to know if the donor of those forceful blows knew he was abusing a woman, not a boy.

Brant slumped back in his chair, cursing himself for handling Milton so roughly that morning in Scotland. Although he had not been as merciless as he would have been if he were assaulting a grown man, Brant had clamped several bone-crushing holds on the wriggling youth. The poor chit must have suffered bruises on the tender flesh of her arms after their scuffle.

The split second before Brant gave way to pity for this mysterious sprite he landed on another thought. Milton had rearranged his room and fed him live coals for supper. Brant was willing to bet his fortune this little termagant had purposely tried to trip him up and burn holes in his insides. All the while she was babbling about her dear mother's recipes, Brant was being made to look like a fool.

Brant snorted derisively and puffed on his cheroot until he sat amid a cloud of smoke. Damn, this feisty imp had played the devil's advocate as if she were born to the role. She had scooted furniture around the room to ensure Brant's toes were permanently stubbed and his shins bruised. She had delighted in watching him make a mule of himself. Damnation, he should shake the stuffing out of Milton for those ornery pranks. Milton had punctured Brant's pride so often it was permanently deflated.

Another thought skipped across Brant's mind, making his eyes sparkle like gold nuggets. A low chuckle erupted from his lips. Now he knew why Milton turned several shades of red when he stripped from his clothes. It was feminine modesty that had caused her profuse blush, he reckoned. He had unknowingly given the chit an eyeful. She knew exactly how he looked in the raw and Brant was at the disadvantage. He was itching to remove the baggy garments to expose the woman who hid beneath them. He had never been one to deny himself with women. And why should he waver from that policy now? This chit knew him far better than any lover after he strutted in front of Milton, as naked as the day he was born.

Turn about was fair play, wasn't it? Indecision etched Brant's brow. Should he appease his bruised pride and male curiosity? The chit deserved to be ogled after Brant had exposed himself to her inquisitive gaze, he thought spitefully.

Brant frowned again. He didn't dare announce Milton's true

90

identity to the crew. They would be sniffing at her heels, flirting outrageously with her. These sailors had been more than a month without women. Milton might find herself compromised so many times before they docked in Brest that she would throw herself overboard as she attempted to do at the onset of the voyage.

A pensive frown plowed Brant's brow when he recalled the incident that left Milton perched on the taffrail, prepared to dive into the arms of the sea. Had the girl been so embarrassed that she considered suicide? Surely she realized she could not survive a swim to shore, even at high tide. Or was it that she perceived sailing with privateers to be a fate worse than death?

He well remembered Milton spouting that pirates were the lowest forms of life on earth. She had boldly criticized his mission and hotly defended the innocent. Did she truly despise him, Brant wondered.

His eyes flowed over her refined features. He could have sworn Milton had begun to warm to him and he to him. Her, Brant hastily corrected himself. Brant had grown fond of this playful waif. He had taken Milton under his wing, teaching her the art of self-defense. 'Twas a wonder the lass hadn't turned the pistol on him, blown him to smithereens, and then assumed command of the ship! All this time Brant had been flirting with disaster and never knew it.

Who the devil was this woman? Why was she masquerading as a boy? Who had dared to mar her soft face and why was she sneaking around Selkirk in the first place? The rapid-fire questions came at Brant like a barrage of exploding cannons. But he could attach no answers to his questions. Milton remained a mystery and Brant was stung by the urge to shake her awake and force her to supply an explanation.

But something stopped him. Perhaps it was his thirst for revenge against her ornery pranks or his fear for her safety among his crew. Although the sailors had grown fond of young Milton, Brant wasn't prepared to trust them with the knowledge that Milton was a woman . . . and probably an inexperienced one at that, judging by the way she lost her composure each time Brant innocently dropped his breeches. That thought sent an amused grin spreading across his lips. Aye, he had given Milton an education, one she probably hadn't anticipated.

Deciding that to do nothing at all about his discovery was the best course of action, Brant rose to full stature. While he towered over the sleeping chit, his eyes fell to the long silky strands of auburn that sprayed across the pillow. Impulsively, Brant bent to lift the fiery tendrils and let them trickle through his fingers. A tender smile grazed his lips as he surveyed the thick fringe of lashes that lay against her smudged cheeks. Beneath that grime was probably a very attractive young minx with spellbinding green eyes. No wonder Milton had taken such great care to disguise her features with soot and grease. A clean face would have set a man to wondering . . .

A soft chuckle bubbled from Brant's chest as he tucked the mass of auburn hair beneath the oversized cap and repositioned it on Milton's head. "One day, my ornery little vixen, you will explain yourself to me. 'Tis not the time or place, but very soon you will reveal yourself to me . . . as plainly as I have exposed myself to you."

Wearing a mischievous grin, Brant strode toward the portal and silently exited. He had plans to make, he reminded himself. The next time mysterious Milton found herself in his arms, clinging to him like a choking vine, it might well be for an entirely different purpose. She had climbed all over him because of her fear of height. But next time . . . Brant's grin broadened to encompass every bronzed feature of his face. The anticipation of reciprocating to all Milton's madcap pranks would be a delightful escapade, he assured himself.

Beneath those concealing clothes was a woman with a woman's body. Brant was eager to know just how soft and shapely it truly was. That very thought continued to arouse him as he went through the paces of commanding the ship. But Brant fought to hold himself in check. Milton was no ordinary woman and he could not approach her in the same manner he would the common trollops who satiated his passions. He knew how quickly Milton could become a wildcat. He had been on the receiving end of her bared claws once too often.

Brant had made a wager with John Paul and he intended to tame this tigress . . . but not in the manner in which he proposed the bet. John Paul . . . Brant inwardly groaned. If Jones knew this daring waif was a woman he would immediately set his sights on her. Suddenly Brant felt like a she-lion protecting her cub. If Milton was as lovely as Brant imagined, John Paul would be fawning over her. John Paul had an obsessive craving for beautiful women. The saucier, more spirited they were, the more enamored he became.

Well, Brant wasn't handing his fiery-haired, green-eyed pixie over to John Paul for all the British prizes to be captured in the Atlantic! He would keep Milton as his pet, he told himself. Share and share alike may have been the code of the privateers, but Brant had one amendment to attach to the laws of the sea. Mysterious, mischievous Milton was not part of any crew's booty, Brant promised himself. He had found her first and he was not giving her up!

So much for adopting Milton as the son he never had, Brant thought to himself. Nor could he look upon this young maid as his kid sister, not while these arousing thoughts were dancing in his head. What he wanted from Milton could no longer be shrugged off as platonic affection. He wanted to know everything about her, intimate things that would have her blushing if she could read his mind.

The elusive sprite had suddenly become Brant's secret conquest. He wanted to see those sparkling green eyes laughing with him, not *at* him as they had done the past weeks. He wanted to rain kisses on her bruised cheek and erase the pain she had suffered. There was a living fire blazing in those emerald orbs and Brant wondered how hot that flame could burn. He was like a moth fascinated by a mysterious blaze and he wouldn't be satisfied until Milton . . .

Milton? Wherever had this playful pixie come up with such a ridiculous name? That in itself was enough to throw an unsuspecting man off course. It seemed to fit a scrawny ragamuffin but not a petite young woman.

Patience, man, Brant lectured himself. Soon, very soon, he would see the woman who lurked beneath those concealing clothes and dingy hat. It could prove well worth the wait. Much would come to pass before he and Milton came to terms with the truth. But for now it was best Milton didn't know that Brant knew.

Brant also wondered if both of them would have been better off if they weren't so aware of each other. He might be getting himself in over his head. His fascination with Milton had crossed wider horizons and Brant's perspective had changed. What he didn't need in the middle of a war was more trouble. Milton had warned him she was just that—trouble. She had also claimed that Brant could never make her into a man. She hadn't lied about that either!

Maybe it would be wiser to leave well enough alone, Brant advised himself. Perhaps he should pretend nothing had happened and set Milton free when they docked at Brest. And let her trip off to Scotland without learning her true identity? Allow her to saunter away without knowing why she disguised herself as a waif, the voice of curiosity sniffed distastefully. If Brant let her go without knowing anything about her, he would never be able to forget her. Nay, he couldn't turn his back on the situation, he realized. Milton was going to answer this rash of questions, even if Brant had to squeeze them out of her. A rakish grin caught the corner of his mouth. Now there was an interesting solution to the problem and it was much to Brant's liking.

Chapter Six

Through a hazy cloud, Milton drifted back to reality to the beat of a drum that was pounding in her head. Lord, she felt awful. Her mouth was as dry as cotton. Even her eyebrows ached. Her entire body rebelled when she attempted to push up on one elbow. An involuntary groan flew from her lips when the room began to spin furiously about her. Her stomach lurched like a ship tossed about on a windblown sea.

"A bit under the weather, I see," Brant observed from his lookout post at the desk. Rising, he swaggered toward Milton with a cup of tea in his hand. "'Tis not your dear mother's cure for a queasy stomach, I fear. But 'tis the best I have to offer."

Milton accepted the drink, nodding gratefully as Brant sank down beside her. Her glazed eyes were glued to the bronzed flesh that stretched across his bare chest. The transfer of the cup from steady hand to shaky hand ended in disaster. Milton was too busy staring at Brant's virile physique to make a smooth exchange. A pained shriek burst free when the steaming tea splattered on her shirt.

Brant hurriedly grabbed a rag to dry her clothes. His hand brazenly investigated the swell of her breast that was flattened as close as possible to her chest. When Milton shoved his hand away, Brant bit back a secretive smile. He had felt the tight wrap of cloth beneath her shirt. If Mother Nature had not blessed this sprite with a voluptuous figure she would have no need to strap a tourniquet across her bosom, he speculated.

"I can see to the spill myself," Milton grumbled grouchily and then groaned when the bass drum struck up another agonizing tune in her head.

Now it was Brant's turn to pretend his feelings had been trounced upon. And he did it very well. Milton almost apologized for snapping Brant's head off.

"I was only trying to help, son," Brant murmured, wearing a long face. "You were so good to tend to me while I was ailing that I thought this my chance to return your unselfish compassion." Brant moved the half-empty cup toward Milton's bluish-tinged lips. "Here, take a sip. It will make you feel better."

Milton doubted she would ever feel normal again, but she accepted the drink. When the fluid dripped into her sensitive stomach she groaned in dismay. Too late her numbed taste buds warned her this was not an ordinary cup of tea.

"What did you put in it?" Milton queried hoarsely. "Arsenic?"

Brant drew himself up proudly. "A little of this, a little of that. 'Tis my own remedy for a dreadful hangover," he boasted. "It will bring you back to life."

"Immediately *after* it kills me?" Milton snorted crabbily.

"Most hangovers leave a man with the sensation that he is dying anyway," Brant said with a casual shrug. "What do you have to lose?" When Milton opened her mouth to interject a reply, Brant poured the potion down her raw throat. "Drink up, Milt. I promise you will feel better."

Milton sputtered and coughed on the bitter taste. Her tender head was very nearly jarred loose when Brant pounded her on the back to dislodge the drink that had strangled her. With another groan she collapsed on the cot, wishing her overzealous nursemaid would go away and let her die in peace (or as close to peace as one could come when one was in excruciating misery).

"Is this your first hangover?" Brant questioned with a sympathy-coated smile.

"Aye," she breathed raggedly. "And the last."

"Turn over." Brant eased his green-faced patient to her stomach. "I'll give you a massage to ease your aching muscles."

"I don't want . . ." Milton was not allowed to complete her protest. Brant mashed her face into the pillow to silence her.

"It will relax you," he insisted. Grinning outrageously, Brant speculated on the intriguing indentation of her waist and the curve of her derriere that lay hidden beneath the concealing garb.

His hands closed around her shoulders to massage away the tension. Milton felt her body relax beneath his skillful ministrations . . . until his wandering hands reached the small of her back. She flinched uneasily when his massage flooded over the back of her thigh. Shock waves rippled through her, sensitizing her to a man's touch. Not just any man's touch, but the dashing rogue, Brant Diamond.

When Milton involuntarily winced, Brant chortled devilishly. "A mite touchy, I see. Relax, Milton, I mean no harm. 'Tis for your own good."

But it was truly for Brant's own good, he reminded himself. The taste of revenge was sweet, far sweeter than he anticipated. As a matter of fact, it bordered on painful. It was all Brant could do to prevent his massage from becoming an exploring caress. With deliberate concentration he forced his hands to descend to Milton's rigid calves. He kneaded her legs until they melted beneath his touch.

Milton was being assaulted by various sensations which did more to intensify her awareness of Brant than to ease her overindulgence of wine. She kept imagining what it would be like to truly experience his caresses and she chided herself for even contemplating it.

"That should do it," Brant proclaimed as he came to his feet. "Now for your bath. That should put the finishing touches on

97

my cure for a hangover." Scooping Milton into his arms he carried her to the tub he had filled while she slept. When he had set her to her wobbly legs he inwardly grinned in wicked satisfaction. "I'll fetch you a towel while you undress."

"Nay!" Milton yelped.

She was still suffering from the side effects of being cradled against Brant's bare chest, a condition that hardly went unnoticed, even in her misery. Their close contact had caused a riptide of emotions. Milton was rattled by the experience, knowing the situation was about to get out of hand.

Brant wheeled back around to face her horrified expression. "Would you prefer that I help you disrobe?" he asked, knowing full well what the answer would be. But he was taunting her and loving every minute of it.

"Certainly not!" Milton protested gruffly. "And I ain't takin' a bath while yer here."

A mock innocent expression claimed Brant's tanned features. "Surely you don't think I intended to make something lurid of a bath," he croaked. "Really, Milton, I have given you no reason to be suspicious. I have told you I prefer women to young boys. I do not, I repeat, have a perverted penchant for you. I have grown fond of you, I admit. But I have come to think of you as my own son."

Milton dropped her head, feeling ashamed of herself for deceiving Captain Diamond. He was fond of her, in spite of her mischievous pranks. He had admitted his affection for the lad Milton, but she wondered if their relationship would turn sour if he knew he had been hornswaggled by a woman.

"I've become fond of you, too, Cap'n," she confessed. Her face lifted to meet his waiting gaze, one that was carefully scrutinizing her for reasons she couldn't guess. "But I canna peel off my clothes as easily as you can. I ain't made that way. I'm accustomed to my privacy."

For once Brant understood what she meant. And he was anxious to see exactly how she was made. "Then I shall leave you to your bath, Milton. But you must promise to take it," he

98

insisted, waving a lean finger in her face. "It will make you feel much better. You cannot know how anxious I am for you to return to your old self again."

If she became her old self before his very eyes it would knock the props out from under him, Milton predicted. "I promise," she murmured.

Her appreciative gaze mapped the landscape of Brant's broad chest and tapered waist while he shrugged on his shirt. Before her eyes betrayed her, Milton turned her back, one which Brant began to regard with growing interest. With his curious gaze glued to Milton, Brant blindly navigated his way across the cabin . . . until he rammed into the desk.

When he grunted painfully, Milton's head swiveled around to see Brant clutching his knee. Scowling, Brant limped away, even more determined to have his laugh at Milton's expense. She had most certainly had hers. That ornery chit kept moving the furniture each time he adjusted to an arrangement. Damn, that minx had him walking into walls and colliding with tables and chairs, he reminded himself bitterly. She deserved whatever punishment Brant directed toward her.

Once Milton was alone, she shed her clothes and sank into the tub. She shivered when the cool water wrapped itself around her body. But Brant was right, she soon realized. The bath was invigorating and refreshing. The nausea ebbed and Milton swore, then and there, she would never partake of so much liquor as long as she lived. Why men drank themselves into witless stupors was beyond her. The aftereffects of a bout with wine were enough to discourage her from reliving such misery.

Breathing a tired sigh Milton eased back against the tub and extended a long, shapely leg. Lathering her hands, she soaped her thighs, massaging away the lingering aches and pains. A blush crept to her cheeks, recalling where Brant's capable hands had roamed. It was a mark of heroism that she had remained calm beneath his tender ministrations.

Brant Diamond aroused her, she begrudgingly admitted to

herself. He could make a room shrink when he strolled into it. He could make her eyes betray her when they wandered over his powerful physique. She longed to reach out and touch him, to truly touch him, to run her fingers over the dark furring of hair that splayed across his chest and descended down his lean belly.

More than once she wondered what it would be like to lie in his sinewy arms, her body pressed intimately to his. But Milton knew she shouldn't dwell on such arousing fantasies about Brant. She had come too far, preyed upon his compassion, spited him at every turn. And worst of all, she knew things about him that could complicate matters.

He was a man, Milton reminded herself. He would insist that he be allowed the same privileges that had brought her both embarrassment and wicked pleasure. Whatever might have been between them would become cheap and soiled by this unusual situation, Milton reasoned. Nay, it was best that she leave Brant as she had come—in baggy clothes and a frightfully dingy hat. When she fled the *Sea Lady* and booked passage to Scotland she would forget Brant Diamond and this misadventure.

By now Derrick Redmund should have been called back to duty. Milton had Brant and John Paul to thank for that. No doubt, the Royal Navy had every available vessel searching for the daring privateers. Derrick would be on board his ship, guarding the coastlines, she reasoned. She could return to her estate to enjoy a few months of peace before Derrick returned to pester her.

While Milton was enjoying her bath, Brant was making his way to the bulwark on the main deck. Built into that wooden wall of defense, two cannons sat silent. Beside the mounted nine-pound guns was a small arsenal where ammunition was stored. Inside the niche that was directly above Brant's cabin was a hatch. That was Brant's destination, and he could not reach the arsenal quickly enough to suit himself.

When the *Sea Lady* had been constructed, Brant had

personally installed the opening to the lower cabin. The hatch was covered by a lattice, concealing the true purpose of the opening. In past years, when the schooner served as a merchant vessel, many conferences were held in the great cabin. Brant often presented his proposals and prices to his business associates and then left them in the cabin to make their decisions.

His methods were a bit underhanded, he admitted. And it had been true that, on occasion, an eavesdropper heard nothing good about himself. But the hatch had proven valuable, especially when dealing with less than honorable characters in the transfer of goods from one set of hands to another. From his listening post above the great cabin, Brant had learned interesting facts from traders who played for their own gain between the Mother Country and the colonies. During the war years, Brant had learned the locations and arrivals of British vessels that traded in the West Indies and attacked them before they could sell their goods on the international market.

But tonight it was not his purpose to listen, but to spy. He hadn't meant to stoop as low as a Peeping Tom. Yet, he simply could not help himself. After his last encounter with Milton, massaging her shapely backside, Brant could not endure the suspense. He berated his unscrupulous tactics for about one-half second and then carefully removed the cover on the hatch to peer down at Milton.

First, the soiled cap dropped to the floor, allowing Milton's auburn hair to cascade over her shoulders. Brant held his breath when she stepped out of her breeches, revealing her slender legs. His heart stampeded around his chest like a thoroughbred in full gallop. His blood pressure rose sharply when Milton shed her shirt and unwrapped the cloth that bound her breasts.

Licking his bone-dry lips, Brant squinted through the lattice-covered hatch. He was not disappointed with what he saw. There below, bathed in golden lantern light, was a vision of loveliness that had Brant choking on his breath. Milton's alabaster skin glowed like honey. Her coral-tipped breasts were full and creamy, so temptingly so that Brant ached to touch what his eyes beheld. His all-consuming gaze flooded over her flat stomach to the alluring curve of her hips. Brant gulped over the lump of desire that threatened to strangle him. In all his thirty-three years he had never viewed a vision as enchanting and exquisite as this!

When Milton sank into the tub to wash her face, Brant realized that beneath that grime and soot was a lovely oval face with satiny skin. Her green eyes twinkled in the dim light and her upturned nose shined when she scrubbed it clean. His fascinated gaze dropped to her heart-shaped lips. Brant stared hungrily at them, as if they were the first pair he had ever seen, as if he were contemplating devouring them.

His eyes continued their exploration to note the tiny beads of water that glistened on her skin, lightly caressing the dusky peaks that rose and fell with each breath she took. Brant swore he had died and was staring through the porthole of heaven. This glorious angel left all other females sorely lacking. Brant had seen his fair share of women in his pursuit of passion. But this . . . he breathed appreciatively, this vision would long inflame his dreams.

And then Brant suddenly realized that this bit of mischief could also pave his path to hell. How could he look at Milton in her baggy breeches without seeing her as she was now—shapely, voluptuous, and altogether bewitching? He couldn't, he thought miserably. The vision of this spellbinding enchantress would be branded on his mind and he would remember this night each time he cast the grimy-faced waif a fleeting glance.

At least now they were on equal terms, Brant rationalized. Milton had watched him strip naked. So why should he do the honorable thing by replacing the cover on the hatch? His bird's-eye view of Milton was too delightful to relinquish and he would not stop gawking until she had climbed back into her garb.

When the door creaked and a thin shaft of light splintered through the storeroom, Brant hurriedly replaced the wooden cover and cursed the intruder. He could have happily sat drooling over Milton for the remainder of the night, but he was not to be granted that pleasure.

A muddled frown plowed Thomas Haynes's brow when he eased open the door to see Captain Diamond down on all fours in the corner of the arsenal. "What the sweet lovin' hell are you doin'?"

"I'm checking the ammunition," Brant replied as he rose to his feet to dust dirt from the knees of his breeches.

Thomas frowned again at Brant's odd behavior. "Down on yer knees with yer nose scrapin' the floor?" he snorted sarcastically. "Don't tell me you were countin' specks of gunpowder. I know we ain't that desperate for ammunition."

Brant wondered if he looked as foolish as he felt. To disguise his uneasiness he struck a sophisticated pose and then swaggered out the door. "Do you have something to report or are you merely following me about to ease your boredom?"

"I came to tell you Captain Jones has taken the *Drake* in tow again and relieved Simpson of his duty as prizemaster," Thomas explained, eyeing the nonchalant captain warily. He could not help but wonder if the exploding shells of battle had finally come close enough to rattle Brant's brain. My, but the man was acting peculiar and all too innocent not to be guilty of something. But Thomas could not imagine what! "I thought you might want to haul out the line and take the *Patience* in tow since we are nearin' port."

And then suddenly Brant seemed to regain his senses. He was all business. After snapping to attention he aimed himself toward the helm. "I intend to do just that," he called over his shoulder.

Thomas studied Brant's departing back and then stared bemusedly at the arsenal. Finally he shook his head in puzzlement and closed the door. He prayed the captain's strange fit did not recur. But Thomas vowed to keep a watchful eye on Brant. If the captain were about to crack, Thomas would protect him. He would ensure that the other seamen were unaware Brant's brain was beginning to warp. Thomas was devoted to Brant and he would allow nothing to blemish the captain's reputation.

When Milton came up on deck the following morning she noticed Brant had taken his prize ship in tow, just as Captain Jones had done. But there was an odd look to Jones's vessel. Curious, Milton climbed to the helm to stand beside Brant.

"What's the matter with the *Ranger*? She looks like she's floatin' backwards, but damned if I know why."

Brant flashed Milton a condescending frown. "I thought I told you to mind your tongue. You are not old enough to voice such coarse language."

"My tongue has a mind of its own," she defended with a reckless shrug. "What's amiss with Jones's tub?"

"The *Ranger* is in irons," Brant explained, fighting to keep his mind on the conversation instead of the arousing memory that hounded him.

"In irons?" Milton repeated bemusedly.

Brant gestured a long arm toward the stern of the schooner that was now pointing south. "When a square rigger loses headway and comes about, her sails are caught aback. The *Ranger* is sailing backwards because she can make progress no other way. She is said to be in irons. She suffered more damage during battle than the *Sea Lady*. And towing her prize has taken its toll."

When Brant glanced down at his companion he felt the urge to wipe the smudge from her pert nose and trace her high cheekbones. He knew her skin would feel like satin. But if he gave way to impulse all would be lost. Regrouping his rambling thoughts Brant continued before he was completely steered off course by his arousing thoughts.

"*Ranger* suffered structural damage but it became more severe when John Paul decided to give chase to the ship he spotted yesterday. The maneuver of turning into a strong wind was too much for her. On her return to a southerly direction she passed through the eye of the wind and the sails were taken aback. Captain Jones was already in a fit of temper after the prizemaster of the *Drake* did not heed the signals. Now he is disgruntled because his schooner will be unable to perform necessary maneuvers that are essential in battle. The *Ranger* will be drydocked in Brest and John Paul will be forced to wait another command. I imagine John Paul will be in a snit for several months, fearing he might be missing something at sea."

"And what will become of you when we dock, Cap'n?" Milton questioned, her lashes sweeping up to meet his golden gaze. There was a startling expression mirrored there, something Milton couldn't decode, something different in the way he was staring at her.

Brant tore his eyes away before they betrayed him and fixed his attention on the sea. "Once we have sold our prizes and made repairs, I plan to ship much-needed supplies to the colonies."

Milton did not break the silence. Instead, she turned to amble to the main deck. Brant's eyes followed her, wondering how much longer he could endure this charade. He wanted to confront Milton, to approach her as a man approaches a lovely, desirable woman.

Brant frowned, torn between conflicting emotions. He wanted to know everything about this mischievous pixie and yet the revelation of her identity would change everything. Raking his fingers through his hair, Brant heaved a frustrated sigh. What was he going to do about Milton? Blast it, he had been much happier when he was ignorant.

"Somethin' troublin' you, Cap'n?" Thomas pried. He had been watching Brant like a posted lookout since the previous night. Brant looked distressed and Thomas wanted to know why. "Do you want to talk about it?"

He grumbled about Thomas's uncanny knack of seeing what Brant could discreetly hide from the rest of the crew. "If talking could cure what disturbs me I would eagerly confess it."

"It surely ain't the mission," Thomas mused aloud. "We accomplished our purpose and have taken fair booty to prove it." He stared after the thin urchin who had paused to peer at the *Ranger*. Thomas was quick to note the way Brant's eyes kept drifting to the boy. "Is it Milton? Has he done somethin' to upset you, Cap'n?"

"I'm going below," Brant scowled, refusing to share his knowledge, even with his trusted companion. "Don't disturb me unless an emergency arises."

Thomas muttered at the close-mouthed captain. In the past there had been no secrets between them. But there was one now. Whatever was bothering Brant had him pacing about, preoccupied with some unsettling thought. Surely it would blow over when they docked in France. Brant could see to his male needs, ones that had long been held in check. Aye, that would take the edge off, Thomas diagnosed. It would certainly do Thomas a world of good!

And yet, as the days dragged on, Thomas began to doubt if even passion's pleasure would ease Brant's disposition. Like a private detective on the trail of a suspect, Thomas monitored Brant's every move. For some strange reason Brant kept disappearing into the arsenal after dark and would not emerge for more than a half hour. It was most unusual behavior, Thomas thought to himself. What would he do if the captain lost his sanity? That question continued to hound Thomas while he kept a watchful eye on the mysteriously preoccupied Brant Diamond.

Chapter Seven

The next few days were disturbing ones for Milton. She could feel the unexplainable strain Captain Diamond experienced while she was with him. Yet, she was helpless to explain his distant, remote attitude toward her. Brant had become moody and sulky. He stalked about his cabin and the decks like a captive panther. Although there were less embarrassing moments with which to contend, Milton was oddly discontented. She missed the easy camaraderie between them. But Brant's mood was so sour no one dared to get within ten feet of him without a protective suit of armor.

When land was sighted it came as a great relief. Milton was ready to end this chapter of her life and forget her ill-fated fascination with the pirate captain. As the ships eased into the harbor at Brest, Milton stood on the deck, wondering how and when she should make her break for freedom. Surely when the captain and his crew went ashore, she could sneak away to locate a schooner bound for the British Isles.

As she expected, the eager sailors filed across the gangplank to celebrate their return to land. While she was watching the crew swarm to shore to invade the nearest grog shops and brothels, Brant stalked up to stand rigidly beside her.

"I am going ashore with my men. You stay put," he ordered sternly. "Thomas will be here to guard the ship. When I return

I will take you into Brest, but I'm not turning you loose in France without an escort."

"You don't trust me?" Milton looked pitifully hurt by the insinuation, but her attempt to milk sympathy from Brant failed.

Brant glared irritably at the disguised lass. "Will you give me your word you won't flee from me?"

Milton sorely wished she had kept her mouth shut. "Where would I go? I'm too young for brothels and I've sworn off liquor," she hedged.

"I want your promise," Brant demanded, refusing to be detoured from his original question.

She looked him straight in the eye. "Very well, Cap'n, you have my word, as one man to another."

Two thick brows narrowed over Brant's stormy amber eyes. Milton had just confirmed Brant's suspicions. She would eagerly give her promise as a man since she wasn't one. And since she was not honor-bound to keep it, she would flee when opportunity presented itself, Brant predicted.

"Thank you, Milton. I will be less apprehensive about leaving you to your own devices since I have your word," he said tightly before whirling away.

What devil was gnawing on him, Milton asked herself as Brant stalked across the deck. He should have been bounding off the gangplank with the same enthusiasm that claimed the other sailors. Milton knew the promiscuous rogue would be hopping from one bed to another until he had not the strength to move. That thought soured her mood. As much as she hated to admit it, she was jealous of the women who would find themselves in Brant's arms.

Oh, why couldn't it have been the swarthy Captain Diamond who happened onto her doorstep instead of Derrick Redmund, she thought dismally. Heaving a dreary sigh Milton ambled toward her cabin . . . Brant's cabin, one she would never see again.

Milton had thought through her course of action and she

108

was determined to flee. She had found some suitable garments among the prizes in the hull of the ship. After bathing, she intended to dress in the fashionable clothing. In the cloak of darkness she would sneak into Brest to find accommodations for the night. The following morning she would seek out a northbound vessel. It was as simple as that. Brant would be on his way to the colonies and she would return home where she belonged.

After fetching the water for her bath, Milton laid out her clothes and shed her disguise. Vigorously, she scrubbed her face until it shined. Then she laid her head against the back of the tub and studied the empty cabin. She could see Brant's raven head bent over the ledgers while he labored at his desk. He was there, draped casually in a chair, puffing on his cheroot.

Milton squeezed her eyes shut when another, more arousing vision leaped to mind. She could see Brant standing before her, his muscled body glowing in the lantern light. She could feel his practiced hands gliding over her flesh . . .

Stop this! Milton chided herself. She simply could not carry a picture of a naked man around in her mind for the rest of her life. It was unnatural! Her escapade with the roguish captain was over and done. It had been no romantic interlude, for heaven's sake. Brant thought she was a skinny little urchin and he had treated her well. That was all there was to it. It was ridiculous to fancy herself in love with a man who didn't know she was alive. Aye, it would be best for her to vanish into the night and . . .

Her thoughts came to an abrupt halt when she heard the creak of the door. Panic gripped her. If Thomas came blundering in she would be embarrassed beyond belief! Sweet mercy, what was Thomas doing in the captain's cabin?

"Don't come in yet, Thomas!" Milton ordered, groping for the towel she had dropped somewhere near the tub. Damn, she couldn't reach the towel without exposing herself. "I'm bathin'. I'll be out in a minute."

There was a long silence, much too long. Wide green eyes were glued to the partially open door. "I ain't feelin' myself today, Thomas. I thought a bath might . . ."

Milton's explanation was chopped off by her own startled gasp when the door slammed against the wall. Brant Diamond barged into the cabin, wearing the naughtiest grin she had ever seen plastered on his rugged features.

"I wonder what could keep you from being yourself today or any other day, *Milton*," Brant smirked caustically. When the lady wilted into the tub to protect herself from his hawkish gaze, Brant chuckled devilishly. "It seems you did have a great deal to hide from your captain . . . things that would boggle a man's mind."

Fiery red burst into her cheeks, matching the flaming hair that spilled over her shoulders. "I thought you would be bedded down in a brothel by now," she sputtered, covering herself as best she could. "What are you doing here?"

Brant had aimed himself toward the nearest bawdy house, but the moment he walked inside he knew he would be haunted by the same vision that had hounded him the past week. He had been telling himself that it was wiser to avoid trouble than to walk headlong into it. But all his well-meaning lectures had no effect on the craving that gnawed at him since he took to spying on this enchanting nymph.

Whoever this bewitching lass was, she was running from something or someone. She was no coarse-featured serving maid. The soft lines of her face and her delicate bone structure assured Brant that the lady was of aristocratic breeding.

He had constantly reminded himself there were complications where Milton was concerned, but his body was paying no attention. Brant's battle of self-conquest had taken its toll. His mood had soured and he could not overcome wanting this minx, no matter what the consequences. His need for a woman could not be satisfied in any bed in the brothel. What he wanted was this delightful little witch who was stewing in her kettle in *his* cabin.

"Must I remind you that this is my cabin and I have a right to come and go as I please?" While he spoke his gaze drank in the tantalizing sight of auburn hair and ivory skin. Brant felt the quick rise of desire when his eyes lingered on the creamy swells of her breasts that were barely concealed by her hands. "I also have a right to everything in my cabin, even the mysterious mermaid who is swimming in my tub."

Milton blushed profusely when those probing eyes raked her like golden talons. She had imagined what it might be like to know Brant as a woman knows a man. But her fantasy was a far cry from having him barge in while she was bathing. Damn, she was helplessly trapped in the tub! Milton swallowed hard when her pounding heart vaulted to her throat. Brant was moving toward her like a stalking tiger, his eyes dancing with deviltry, his mouth twitching in a satanic smile.

"At least have the decency to turn your back!" Milton spewed, her temper and humiliation getting the best of her.

He listened to her sharp voice, one that was now void of its twangy Scottish accent. One dark brow lazily drifted to a mocking angle. "Why, Milton, I do believe your voice is changing," he snickered and then stared holes through the hands that were protecting her bare flesh. "Why should I turn my back? You have seen me naked on more occasions than I care to count. You made no attempt to confess your true identity and spare *my* humiliation. I think I have the right to see you as you really are." A rakish grin dangled from the corner of his mouth as his gaze seared across her exposed flesh. "And you are lovely, shapely, and *female*. Or is that that my months at sea have caused me to be visited by hallucinations?"

Milton was swamped and buffeted by the oddest sensations when his eyes caressed her. His gaze blazed a path of fire everywhere it touched, causing her cheeks to flame another shade of red. "I . . . I . . . can explain," she stammered nervously.

Brant dragged a nearby chair up beside him. And, mounting it backward, he plopped down to rest his arms upon its back. "I

111

am counting on that, Milton." His eyes made another deliberate inventory of her titillating assets, ones the scant bubbles couldn't hide. "I'm all ears . . .."

Hardly, Milton thought with a furious sniff. He was all eyes and they were intimately touching her body, just as surely as he had reached out a hand to caress her. "I . . . I was running from catastrophe," she blurted out. "I wanted to keep my identity a secret."

"*That* I could assume on my own," Brant snorted sarcastically. "I want to know who you are and why you were snooping about Selkirk 'Castle.'"

"Could I at least dress before I begin my detailed explanation," she snapped, her voice strongly hinting at a demand, not a request.

Brant gave his raven head a negative shake. His full mouth curved into a roguish smile, one he wore too well to suit Milton. "I prefer to hear the *naked* truth, my dear," he teased, his eyes flitting over her shapely contours.

"I'll shrivel up like a prune," Milton pouted.

"Another disguise?" he taunted, infuriating her and loving every minute of it. "What an ingenious idea. Will you also be changing your name to Ensign Raisin?"

Milton flung him a withering glance. "Your wit is only half what it should be," she sniffed distastefully.

Golden eyes penetrated her flesh, sending a fleet of goose pimples cruising across her skin. "'Tis a wonder I have any wit left after all the pranks you have pulled on me."

A muddled frown knitted her brow. It suddenly occurred to Milton that Brant did not seem surprised to learn his cabin boy was a woman. When he burst into the room he didn't look shocked. But she had been too flustered to make note of that point until now.

Milton eyed Brant suspiciously. "How long have you known I was not a boy?" she demanded to know.

Brant squirmed on his seat, unable to drag his eyes from the delicious sight, even for a split second. Would the newness of

112

this vision ever wear off, he asked himself.

"I've known the truth since the afternoon you drowned in my stock of wine," Brant informed her. "I always wondered what lay beneath your cap." He leaned out to grasp a handful of her hair. "Imagine my surprise when I found this lustrous mane of auburn attached to my cabin boy's head."

Milton grimaced, wondering if Brant intended to pull her hair out by the roots. "Why didn't you call me out when I awoke?" she squeaked uncomfortably.

Damn him. He had teased and taunted her that night, she recalled. No doubt, he had decided to get even.

"I had my reasons," Brant murmured, his voice laced with velvet, his touch becoming an exploration of the silky strands that wound around his wrist. "I was waiting for the perfect moment to confront you, one that would allow me to devote my undivided attention to your explanation. And tonight there will be no interruptions."

Milton swallowed air. She didn't like the sound of that. His eyes and seductive tone were suggesting things she was afraid to consider. Dozens of times she had wondered how it would feel to be loved by this dashing privateer. But wondering and experiencing his caresses were two entirely different matters. She could confront this domineering captain, matching wits with him, while she was dressed as a ragamuffin. But now, facing him man to woman, Milton felt threatened.

Brant made no attempt to disguise his lust and Milton wondered if he would contemplate rape. What else could she expect from a man like Brant Diamond? She doubted he had ever denied himself in his life. And he thrived on challenges. Never in her wildest dreams did she expect to be one of them. If she fought Brant he would probably enjoy it all the more, she speculated.

"I'm waiting, Milton . . . or whoever you are," Brant prompted. "'Tis not that I don't delight in the attractive scenery, but I am a mite curious about you."

Milton took a moment to formulate her thoughts and then

unfolded her tale. "My name is Catrina Ha*milton*." She stressed the partial use of her surname. "I found it necessary to flee when . . ."

"Hamilton!" Brant croaked as he shot straight out of his chair. "Not one of Dunbar Hamilton's children!"

Milton nodded negatively and Brant expelled a sigh of relief before sinking back to his chair. "He is a distant cousin. I was on my way to Selkirk to seek refuge after a near brush with disaster forced me to evacuate my own estate."

Brant stared at her for a long, pensive moment and then slid from the chair to squat on his haunches. When he propped his elbows on the edge of the tub, Catrina shrank away, attempting to cover her nakedness. But his eyes were on her face, his expression solemn.

"The disaster to which you refer? Has it something to do with the bruises you sustained?" His index finger trailed along the delicate arch of her brow and then glided over the ridge of her cheekbone. "Who dared to mar such a bewitching face and why?"

He was so close that his breath whispered across her face like the gentle stirring of wind. Catrina was on fire and the cold bath water did nothing to dampen the flames. His lips were only inches from hers and she was overwhelmed by the insane curiosity to experience his kiss.

"It had everything to do with the bruises," she chirped, her voice failing her when she needed it most.

A knowing smile hovered on his mouth. This nymph was as devastated by this close physical contact as he was. Although he was anxious to hear a full explanation, he longed to press his lips to hers, to caress her . . .

Brant could no longer endure the suspense. His eyes locked with rippling pools of emerald. Like a bee courting nectar his lips whispered over hers, testing her reaction as well as his own. Gently, his mouth slanted over hers, his tongue tracing her lips. When a tiny moan bubbled from Catrina's throat Brant became a creature of instinct. His brain ceased to

114

function when lips like cherry wine melted beneath his.

He had only intended to satisfy his male curiosity, but a wildfire of desire exploded within him. He couldn't have drawn away if his life depended on it. A week of longing had nurtured a craving that one kiss could not appease. Milton had been his ward of war, his constant companion. But it was no longer enough. This auburn-haired temptress was too enchanting to dismiss. What he wanted from her had evolved into something more potent than friendship.

Catrina was terribly inexperienced and she was the first to admit it. But she had been kissed enough to know what she had been missing. Brant Diamond knew how to please and arouse a woman. He had spent years perfecting his techniques, ones that left Catrina trembling like a leaf in a windstorm.

His questing tongue probed the hidden recesses of her mouth and Catrina felt herself melting into a liquid pool of passion. But when Brant's wandering hand flicked the taut peak of her breast, Catrina flinched as if she had been stung. Her wide eyes lifted to Brant's, her expression mirroring a mixture of excitement and fear.

A quiet chuckle tumbled from his lips and his amber eyes danced with amusement. Brant sank back to the floor to watch her cheeks flame crimson red. Flustered, Catrina vaulted from the tub, streaked across the bed, and promptly shut herself in the wardrobe closet. Brant's uproarious laughter nipped at her heels and she cursed her predicament.

Snickering at Catrina's hasty flight, one that granted him an unhindered view of her shapely backside, Brant swaggered over to the closet. "I have had varied effects on women," Brant chuckled. "But 'tis the first time I have sent one into hiding."

When Brant pulled open the double doors the amusement died on his lips. He found himself staring down the barrel of his own flintlock, one Catrina could use with proficiency. He should know, Brant thought to himself. After all, he was the one who taught her to aim and fire without missing her mark. Damn, if his weapons had been stashed in their normal place he would have this feisty minx exactly where he wanted her—cornered and closeted.

Catrina tossed her auburn hair over her shoulder and tilted a proud chin, momentarily forgetting her nakedness. "Unless you want to find yourself useless to *any* woman, you better back off, Captain."

Since this she-cat held the upper hand, the one with a pistol in it, Brant retreated.

"Fetch the gown from my cot," Catrina ordered, using the door as a shield to protect herself from his gawking gaze.

Brant pivoted on his heels to retrieve the dress. Cautiously, he extended his arm to offer the garment to Catrina. "I am still waiting for an explanation."

"You are in no position to demand anything of me," Catrina snapped, clutching the gown to her breasts.

She was leaving . . . now. If she didn't put a safe distance between her and Brant there was no telling what might happen. His kiss and caress had started a fire and Catrina feared it would consume her. She couldn't trust herself with Brant. He was the devil's own temptation.

"So it seems." Brant breathed deflatedly.

But his defeated tone was only a ploy. The moment Catrina dropped her eyes to step into the gown, Brant came uncoiled to spring on his unsuspecting victim. Before Catrina could recover and threaten Brant with the pistol, the door slammed against her arm. Brant snatched the flintlock away and it was Catrina who found herself staring down a silver barrel.

A triumphant smile cut deep lines in Brant's bronzed features. "Now start talking, Cat," he demanded. "You still have not told me who you were running from."

"From a man," she spat at him, fumbling to pull the gown into place. "What other abominable creature would seek to win an argument with his fist?"

Catrina glanced down to survey her daring décolletage that barely covered her heaving breasts. To her dismay, the garment had been made for someone less endowed. One quick

116

move and she would spill from the bodice. Much to the pirate's delight, she thought bitterly.

Brant allowed his eyes to flicker down the tempting display of flesh. What this fiery-haired hellion did to this plain garment should have been labeled a criminal offense. And Brant was contemplating committing one. The pale green satin gown hugged her full breasts and trim waist as he ached to do.

Finally, Brant reined in his tantalizing thoughts and frowned at her curt reply. It seemed Catrina had very little use for men. And with just cause, Brant decided. She had been beaten and forced to flee from her own home . . . A sickening speculation trickled through his mind. Was it her husband who had abused her?

Brant had avoided two kinds of women—married ones and virgins. Although John Paul pursued women for their beauty, giving no regard to their availability, Brant was more discriminating. He respected the boundaries of wedlock, even if his comrade didn't. The thought of Catrina being married caused him to scowl sourly.

"Was this man your husband?" He fired the question, hoping he had jumped to the wrong conclusion.

"Nay, but he intended to be. I am an orphaned heiress. My parents died in a fire six months ago. The man tried to take advantage of my grief. Almost too late I learned what kind of man he truly was and that he was after my fortune."

"I doubt that was all that intrigued him," Brant mused aloud. "Only a blind man would dismiss you as no more than his avenue to wealth." His golden eyes made a slow sweep of her curvaceous figure. "I assure you, 'tis not your fortune that fascinates me."

When Brant advanced, Catrina retreated. "There are scores of women in Brest who would be eager to accommodate you. I cannot," she blurted out. "I know nothing of passion."

Brant stopped short. Damn, toying with virgins was worse than dallying with a married woman, he reminded himself.

Catrina breathed a constricted sigh of relief when Brant

froze in his tracks. Obviously, inexperience did not appeal to him and for that she was most grateful. "I will pay you handsomely if you will let me go," she rushed on. Suddenly, an idea hatched in her mind, one that would solve her dilemma and grant her safety from Derrick. "I will pay you even better if you give me your name to protect myself from my ex-fiancé when he comes to make trouble again." When Brant eyed her warily, Catrina hastened to tempt him with the proposal. Although the scheme had only occurred to her, it seemed a workable solution. "Since you are opposed to lasting entanglements, a marriage between us would put no strains on you, Captain. You and I will be free to come and go as we please. Those who think to get their hands on either of our fortunes will be unable to do so." Catrina beamed at her own ingenuity. What a splendid idea, even if she said so herself.

"Think of it, Captain. No scheming woman will be able to entrap you. You can go your own way and I will go mine . . . but with the protection of a convenient marriage. And if you come across a woman who changes your low opinion of wedlock, we can have our marriage annulled. All you need to do is notify me at my estate."

"You have thought this out thoroughly?" Brant queried, amusement dancing in his eyes.

"Actually, the idea just came to me," she said proudly. "What could be better for two cynical souls such as we? I would be well rid of Derrick Redmund and . . ." Catrina snapped her mouth shut. She had not intended to divulge that viper's name.

A pensive frown plowed Brant's brow. Where had he heard that name? He racked his brain, but he could not attach a face to that name. Brant discarded his wandering thoughts and circled back to her last remark. "You realize this perfect solution you have dreamed up could cause new problems. There is never a simple answer."

"I will make no demands on you," Catrina insisted.

A slow smile worked its way across his lips. His golden gaze flooded over her delectable curves and swells. "I fear I cannot be so generous," he murmured, reaching out to trace the plunging neckline of her gown. "If I consent to this crazed scheme of yours, I expect certain privileges for the use of my name."

The feel of his fingertips skimming over the swells of her bosom set her pulse to racing. She slapped his hand away and thrust out a firm chin. "What is it you are suggesting?" As if she didn't know, Catrina thought acrimoniously.

"I want you," Brant told her simply. "And without a fight. If I am to have a wife, I intend to be the first to sample her charms."

"I'll double the price and purchase my own wedding ring," Catrina bartered, a becoming flush staining her cheeks. The subject of conversation was not one Catrina could discuss as casually as Brant could. He presented the proposal as if he were conducting a business proposition with another merchant.

"Fine," Brant said agreeably. "But you will still share my bed before you depart for Scotland."

"You are being unreasonable!" Catrina stomped her bare foot and glared daggers at his rakish grin.

"It seems a fair exchange to me," Brant argued.

He delighted in watching the sparks fly from those lively green eyes. Cat was devastatingly lovely when she was provoked. She was all fire—like her flaming auburn hair.

"*I* think 'tis a mite lopsided exchange," Catrina sniffed, her chin tilting a notch higher. "What I stand to lose can never be replaced. 'Tis enough that you will be boasting to your herd of pirates that I asked *you* to wed me and that you are being well paid for the use of your name."

A crooked smile dangled from his lips. "But 'tis exactly what you did, nymph," he teased unmercifully. "'Tis your harebrained scheme, not mine. I have merely added stipulations that might tempt me to comply to your proposal."

Catrina stalked over to retrieve the money belt she had kept tucked inside her shirt. "Since we can reach no compromise I shall make my own way without your assistance."

Before Catrina reached the door Brant grasped her arm and pinned her to the wall. "Does the thought of sleeping with me sound so distasteful?" he questioned. His arm slid around her waist, pulling her full length against him, letting her feel his desire for her.

Catrina pressed small but determined hands to the hard wall of his chest, granting her space to breathe. The feel of his body moving suggestively against hers caused her heart to slam against her ribs. Brant's nearness rattled her. She couldn't think when he was so close.

"*Sleeping* with you does not offend me. I have been doing that since I came aboard this ship. 'Tis the other that causes a worrisome thought," she managed to say without her voice failing her.

She could feel Brant's laughter vibrating against her rigid body. She could smell the spicy aroma of his cologne, see the rakish sparkle in those deep-set eyes. Brant was demolishing every barrier of defense she had attempted to construct between them. Damn, how she hated her vulnerability to this pirate. He touched her and her body forgot it had a brain attached to it.

"Do not be so hasty in your judgment, Catrina," he whispered against her flushed cheek. His right hand glided up her back and folded around her neck to tilt her head to his roguish grin. "You may find lovemaking to be a very pleasurable experience. You may even become addicted to it."

His wandering lips found her mouth while his wayward hands made a sensual exploration of her hips. Catrina was caught between his unyielding body and the wall. She struggled to break free, but Brant deepened the kiss and increased the pressure of his arms until she was mashed against him. He stripped the breath from her lungs, breaking her crumbling resistance like a pillar of sand eroding in a brisk wind. Catrina was trapped in a storm of unfamiliar sensations. Senses that Catrina never realized existed came to life, making

120

mincemeat of her fragile emotions.

As her resistance tumbled down her arms went up around his neck. Her fingertips tunneled through the crisp raven hair that capped his head. Wonderingly, she traced the taut tendons of his neck in timid exploration.

Where was the voice of reason when she needed it most? Catrina wondered. This was utter madness! Brant didn't love her. He was only using her to satisfy his lust, just as he had used all other women since the light of his life betrayed him. Catrina would be every kind of fool if she surrendered to his passions, she lectured herself.

Even while she mentally listed all the reasons why she should reject his amorous advances, her body was moving closer to the fire that burned her inside and out. His skillful hands were mapping the curve of her buttocks, tracing the soft flesh that wrapped around her ribs. And she was succumbing to the wild sensations that distorted logic.

Brant was burning alive. He had known what he wanted since the first night he discovered Catrina's identity. It was for this moment he had waited, even when he kept telling himself a wise man would allow this bewitching minx to slip away without becoming involved with her plight. But he had lost the battle of mind over body. He ached to feel this shapely nymph beneath him, to bury himself in her feminine softness.

Catrina had become his obsession, a mystery he wanted solved. Perhaps after he had appeased his craving she would no longer intrigue him, he mused. He would send her on her way and he would be free of the torment. She had haunted him since he learned she was a breathtaking beauty with sharp wit and an endearing touch of deviltry.

When Brant's adventurous hand roamed higher to fold around her breast, Catrina choked on her breath. And when his sensuous lips abandoned hers to tease the throbbing pink crest, she couldn't breathe at all. Helplessly, she arched toward him, hating her weakness, loving the feel of his moist mouth against her quivering flesh.

Having and having not was playing havoc with his sanity. Brant wanted this auburn-haired vixen naked in his arms. Effortlessly, he scooped her from the floor and wheeled toward the bed . . . of where his fogged mind recalled the bed *should* have been. Brant tripped over the chair leg, lost his balance, and, with Catrina in his arms, fell to the floor.

Catrina could not control the gurgle of laughter that bubbled from her lips when they sprawled on the thick fur rug. Her green eyes twinkled with amusement as she peered up at Brant's annoyed scowl. "I always dreamed of having a dashingly handsome rogue fall head over heels for me," she teased, looping her arms about his shoulders.

Brant grinned despite himself. Again Catrina had made him look the clumsy oaf, but when she graced him with that radiant smile he forgot his irritation. "Minx," he chided playfully. "You do have a way of putting a man in a tailspin."

The grin vanished from his lips. Their eyes locked and for a moment it was as if there was no past or future. The banked fire burst into flame. "You captivate me, Cat," he breathed raggedly. His index finger traced the exquisite lines of her face, mesmerized by her youthful beauty. "I want you in ways I've never wanted another woman."

For a moment he was content to merely stare at her, watching the flickering light play on her soft skin. Catrina was a flawless creature made for love. Her long thick hair lay about her shoulders like a fire glowing in the darkness. Her kiss-swollen lips silently parted in a bewitching smile and her cheeks were alive with color.

Gently, Brant eased the gown from her shoulders to expose her upper torso to his appreciative gaze. His caress worshiped the feel of her ripe body beneath his hands and he groaned with a need that was coming dangerously close to burning out of control.

Catrina had always wondered what this moment would be like. But she was too naive to understand the potency of passion, a force so powerful that it swept her up like a raging river overflowing its banks. She could not think of one good reason to reject him and, worst of all, she wasn't even trying.

Curiosity got the best of her. For weeks she had wondered how it would feel to caress him. Trembling fingers hovered over the buttons of his white shirt to lay his expansive chest bare to her caress. Her palm drifted across his hair-roughened skin, feeling his heart thundering beneath her fingertips. Hungry for more, Catrina pushed the gaping shirt from his shoulders and then tracked the long scar that wrapped around his rib cage.

"Did a jealous lover leave her mark?" she teased. "Or was it her irate husband?"

A deep skirl of laughter echoed in his chest. "'Twas one of your fellow countrymen's saber," Brant corrected. "He longed to exact a pound of my flesh, but, fortunately for me, he came up a half pound short."

"And the scar on your hip?" Catrina queried.

Brant broke into a mocking grin. "It seems Milton's keen eyes missed nothing."

His remark caused a blush to invade her face. "I have always been observant," she defended.

Brant slid the dangling gown from her hips and then cast his breeches aside, leaving his hard flesh pressed intimately against hers. When he felt Catrina tense beside him, he offered her a comforting smile.

"I want you, Cat, in ways words cannot convey. I have no intention of hurting you the way your fiancé did. Trust me . . ."

He bent her into his lean contours, making her vividly aware of the differences between a man and a woman. Wild, uncontrollable sensations boiled through her. Catrina could feel herself melting in his arms, surrendering to involuntary sensations that washed away the last of her defenses.

Brant would be a gentle lover, she reassured herself. He was nothing like Derrick. Brant knew how to arouse and excite a woman and his practiced touch was heaven. His roving hands glided across her thighs, across her belly. His lips brushed against the dusky peak of her breast, sending another wave of sensations splashing over her. And then his caress sought out every inch of her skin, following in the wake of his wandering kisses. Over and over again his hands and lips swept over her, flooding and then ebbing like a gentle tide rolling against a sandy shore. Catrina moaned in exquisite pleasure. He was making her want him, weaving his mystical spell about her. She could only respond to the need he created within her, innocently, completely, without restraint.

While Catrina was reveling in desire's sweet pleasure, Brant was fighting for self-control. Never had he been so patient and careful with the woman in his arms. But then, he had never made love to Catrina, an innocent maid who did not have the faintest notion where this rapture would lead. Brant wanted to introduce this sprite to a world reality couldn't touch, to share the ecstasy of wild, sweet love. But it had never been quite like this, he realized. He was giving something of himself to make Catrina's first encounter with love a moment that would inflame her dreams.

As his brazen touch wandered over the sensitive flesh of her thighs, Catrina trembled. Gently, he guided her legs apart. His probing fingers prepared and aroused her, leaving her arching breathessly against him. An incredible coil of longing unfurled within her and she cried out to him to appease the maddening ache. Shamelessly, she clutched him to her, wondering if anything could satisfy the sweet torment that was gnawing at her sanity.

She felt his powerful body surge upon her, felt the hard shaft of his manhood pressing into her tender flesh. And then suddenly the delirious pleasure receded and a stabbing pain replaced it. She couldn't move or draw a breath. Her dreamlike trance shattered and she instinctively writhed for freedom.

Catrina whimpered, certain he was about to tear her in two. But Brant's open mouth swooped down on hers, silencing her, stripping the last breath from her throat.

"Easy, love," he coaxed. "Passion's first pain is the gateway to pleasure. Yield to me . . . Let me make you forget the first unpleasant moment. I need you, Cat, and I have come too far to turn back."

Mustering his willpower, Brant withdrew to brace his arms on either side of her shoulders. When he stared down at her innocent face, her expression stabbed into his heart. Her green eyes were wild with fear. And yet, within those colorful pools was a flicker of trust. She believed in him. She had put her faith in his whispered words and Brant knew he could not disappoint her.

Gently, he moved against her, waiting for her naive body to relax beneath him. His lips skimmed her high, elegant cheekbones and then drifted to her soft, sweet mouth. With all the tenderness he had ever shown in his lifetime, Brant came to her, gently, slowly. He derived a strange sense of pleasure from teaching her the ways of love. And when he took her, it was a new experience for him as well. It was more than physical desire and mindless passion. It was something pure and unique and soul-shattering.

Suddenly, Brant lost control. His body was engulfed by a strange brand of rapture. He was moving without command, lost to the primal needs that he had attempted to hold in check. He thrust deeply within her, aching to free himself of the sweet torture that claimed him, craving to release emotions that boiled through him like a churning volcano.

Catrina gasped when she felt herself lifted onto another indescribable plateau of pleasure. Her nails raked across his back, like a cat digging in her claws to avoid a fall. Brant had promised her a glimpse of paradise and it was there, just beyond her reach.

With each ragged breath he took her higher and higher. Catrina wondered how she would ever find her way back again. Her mind and body were burning with a fever that left her hot and cold and trembly. It was as if she were living and dying in the same moment. And then the darkness parted to reveal shafts of white-hot light. She was dangling in time and space, afraid she was about to fall, swamped by emotions that left her teetering on the brink of insanity.

She clung to Brant as she had that day on the riggings of the schooner, but for an altogether different reason. He had sent her spiraling to towering heights without leaving the circle of his arms. Like an eagle swooping back to earth on a downdraft of wind, Catrina plummeted from passion's pinnacle, her body numb, her mind paralyzed by the exquisite sensations of lovemaking. It was as if she had been dropped into a puffy cloud that cradled her in a strange dimension somewhere between fantasy and reality.

Brant propped himself on an elbow to peer down into Catrina's shadowed face. A quiet smile trickled across his lips as he watched the fire dwindle in her eyes. Passion had never been so sweet, so natural. Catrina's innocent movements had pleased and satisfied him in ways he had not anticipated.

Lovingly, he tunneled his hands through the fiery red cape of hair that sprayed across the rug. "We have struck a bargain, Cat," he murmured hoarsely. "My name is yours, but there is no need for you to pay me for the use of it. The pleasure you gave me far exceeds any wealth to be gained from the proposition."

An impish smile pursed her lips. "But I promised to pay double for the benefit of taking the name of Diamond," she reminded him in a provocative tone. "I could not live with myself if I took unfair advantage of our bargain."

His dark brows shot up, surprised by her insinuation. Cat was such a lively, uninhibited creature that she never ceased to amaze him. Although he was certain once would never satisfy him, he wasn't sure he could move, much less repeat such a physically and emotionally exhausting performance.

"Right now?" he chirped.

"Have I asked the impossible?" she questioned innocently.

Her inquiry caused Brant to burst into a chuckle. Playfully, he flicked her upturned nose. "Naive little imp, do you know

126

nothing of men?"

Catrina's cheeks flamed with heightened color and her lips jutted out in a pout. "You need not tease me because I asked a simple question. How am I to know what a man can and cannot do? I may have disguised myself as one, but I have no way of knowing the capabilities of the male species."

Brant curled his hand beneath her chin, forcing her to meet his piercing golden eyes. "With you, Cat, I am beginning to wonder if nothing is impossible."

His warm mouth captured hers and the flame began to burn. Brant found renewed strength in the rekindling fire that lay amid the smoldering coals of passion. God, what spell had this green-eyed witch cast upon him? He could feel his body rousing, his heart leaping into an accelerated beat. In less than a moment the leaping flames created an inferno of desire. Brant groaned involuntarily when he was swept into another devastating sea of fire.

What madness claimed him, Brant wasn't certain. But he was like a young knight eager to please his lady. If Cat had requested that he fly to the moon, he would have attempted the feat. And why shouldn't he? This spell-casting witch already had him swimming through fire.

But the pleasures were not all hers, Brant realized. He was learning things he had never known about passion, experiencing sensations that words could not begin to touch. She was every bit a woman and she could make Brant feel every bit a man.

Wildly, he drove against her soft, yielding flesh, seeking ultimate depths of intimacy. Catrina had taken him into a wondrous realm of sensual awareness. An uncontrollable shudder claimed him. It was as if he were being tossed about like a windblown wave crashing against a jagged shore. Heart-stopping sensations buffeted him until he collapsed, his breath coming in ragged spurts.

As the embers of passion cooled, Brant fell into an exhausted sleep. The long tense week of waiting had drained his emotions and soured his disposition. But now, he discovered a unique, satisfying tranquillity. He was content where he lay, his arms encircling Catrina's waist, his head nuzzled against the gentle curve of her throat.

For the first time in his life, Brant was in no hurry to flee his lover's arms. Catrina felt so good, so right. She was cuddled against him like a contented kitten resting beside a cozy fire.

It was as if the vagabond pirate had come home at last, home to an inner peace he had never known. And Brant surrendered to the contentment that hovered about him. Even in sleep he could see those mystical green eyes and fiery auburn hair. He could feel Cat's luscious body molded so intimately to his. He was gliding across the horizon with an angel in his arms . . .

Chapter Eight

While Brant was drifting in peaceful dreams, Catrina was peering up at the ceiling, wondering at the odd feelings that were tugging at her heart. She knew she had become enchanted with the pirate captain. Each day her eyes had followed him, captivated by the way his shirt strained sensuously across his chest, noting the way his tight black breeches stretched across his muscled thighs. She had seen him smile in satisfaction and glower in anger. She had witnessed the grim determination that claimed his features when he was doing battle with his enemies. She had come to depend upon his laughter and teasing camaraderie. And each day she awoke she found herself falling deeper in love . . .

The thought caused her heart to lurch. Love? Was that the elusive emotion that had crept into her soul? Was that why she was so helplessly drawn to Brant Diamond, pirate and rogue? Catrina closed her eyes and gulped hard. Sweet mercy, that had not been in her plans. She had been the one spouting about no strings attached to this marriage of convenience.

A pensive frown furrowed her brow as she spared Brant a quick glance. What was it he had said about marriage creating a new set of problems? Aye, they had indeed, Cat mused glumly. Marriage should not be used as a convenient means to solve one's dilemma. It should be founded on mutual love and respect, just as her parents' marriage had been. They had shared something warm and special, something few people found in a lifetime.

Remembering that, Catrina felt ashamed of herself for taking something beautiful and twisting it to fit her purpose. She could almost hear her father denouncing her intentions. If Brant felt something for her, she might not feel so guilty, Cat thought to herself. But she knew Brant was cynical of love and marriage. He had avoided it like the plague and harbored bitter feelings since Cynthia Marsh put his heart in chains.

She could not follow through with this crazed scheme, she realized. Her conscience would not allow it. Cat loved Brant and that changed everything. She would long for more than his name, more than a week of wedded bliss before they went their separate ways. It was best that she find another way to defend herself against Derrick Redmund. Brant had taught her to be proficient with weapons, she reminded herself confidently. The next time Derrick thought to strike her, he would pay for his rough abuse.

If Cat could not have Brant on her terms than she would not have him at all. She loved him enough to let him go, knowing marriage to this cynical pirate would be a mockery. There was naught else to do but vanish into the night and forget she had ever laid eyes on Brant Diamond.

Giving way to impulse, Catrina inched away from the still form beside her. Silently, she shrugged on her clothes and crept toward the door. Taking nothing with her but memories and her money belt, she sailed down the companionway.

'Twas for the best, Cat assured herself. She would not tie Brant to a loveless marriage. It would only remind her of this special night, one that had defied reality and had no place in either of their lives. Once she was on Scottish soil she would forget this adventure ever happened. Her affair with the dashing pirate was over and done and it was time she resumed her proper place in life.

*   *   *

130

Brant roused from his sweet dream. A wry smile trickled across his lips, remembering the splendor he had found in Cat's arms . . . Suddenly, Brant bolted straight off the bed. His head swiveled around the empty room. Where the devil was Cat? When his eyes landed on the cot he saw Milton's baggy breeches and shirt remained behind and the green gown was gone—with Catrina in it, he scowled.

Had it all been a deceitful trick? Had Catrina proposed the idea of marriage to distract him? Had she given herself to him, planning to slip away when opportunity presented itself? Dammit, she had used and discarded him, the fickle woman. If anyone was to leave it should have been him. That was the way of things, Brant thought furiously. Catrina turned the tables on him and his male pride was scorched.

Brant snatched up his breeches and thrust in one leg on his way to the door. When he stumbled against the desk he cursed a blue streak. Cramming his left leg into his breeches, he tore open the door. He was bringing that vixen back, even if he had to turn the town upside down to find her.

When he bounded up the steps, he caught sight of Catrina. Her muted auburn hair glowed in the moonlight as she floated across the deck. "Cat," he growled. "Where the hell do you think you're going?"

Catrina spun around, dismayed to find that Brant had awakened so quickly. My, but he was cranky when he was deprived of a full night's sleep. His golden eyes were flaring like a forest fire and his features were as hard as granite.

Mustering her courage, Catrina put out a defiant chin, even when her shadow was cowardly backing away. Brant did not look the least bit pleased. In fact, Catrina swore he would breathe fire any moment. And for the life of her, she didn't know why. He should have thanked her for walking out of his life.

"I have reconsidered my marriage proposal," she told him. "It was a spur of the moment decision. And, as you pointed out, the solution to one problem could easily create another."

Brant was in no mood to have his words thrown in his face.

131

He was mad as hell and he wasn't even certain why. Perhaps it was because he was in the habit of sending his paramours on their way and it did not set well to have this fickle sprite traipsing off without his permission. Whatever the reason, this entire incident had proceeded backward. He was annoyed with the chit and he had not the time or inclination to sit down and analyze his emotions.

"Well, *I* have not reconsidered." Brant tapped his bare chest to emphasize his point. "*You* asked me to marry you, *I* accepted, and *we* made a bargain," he all but shouted.

"You needn't wake the dead," Catrina snapped. "I thought you would be relieved to learn I had decided to solve my dilemma without involving you. I will find a French merchant ship bound for Britain and book passage on it. My father would roll over in his grave if he knew I had taken the coward's way out. I should have had more sense than to turn to a patriot pirate for salvation."

Brant's chest puffed up indignantly. He most surely would have popped the buttons off his shirt, had he been wearing one. "So I am not good enough to wed a sophisticated Scottish heiress, is that it?" he snorted derisively. "Well, let me tell you something, little miss high and mighty, I am as good as any man!"

He was better than any other man, Catrina thought to herself. But she couldn't tell him that. His male pride would swell and burst. It was enough that she would spend months fretting over his safety during the war. She didn't need to be married to a man who couldn't return her love, not to mention the fact that he happened to be her enemy. For God's sake, their marriage would be a disaster. Brant knew that as well as she did.

"If you don't stop shouting, I'm leaving," Cat told him sharply. "I may be a fool but I am certainly not a deaf one!" Her voice was becoming higher and wilder by the second.

"Now who's shouting?" Brant blared.

"I must if I wish to be heard!" she yelled at him. "We are not getting married. It was an insane idea and I am most thankful I woke from my madness before it was too late."

When Catrina wheeled away, Brant's hand snaked out to snag her arm. "Dammit, you are going nowhere until we have settled this matter to my satisfaction."

"Therein lies the problem," Catrina sniped. "You would never be satisfied, not when you were tied to a woman. And I would be miserable married to a man like you."

Catrina found herself chained in his powerful arms. The feel of his thighs pressing into her soft contours set off a chain reaction, one similar to the prior events that landed them on the floor of his cabin. She would not wind up there again, she promised herself. The intimacy between them had already taken its toll and she dared not risk another interlude. Besides, Brant only wanted a body, any woman's body. Why was he making such ado about nothing? He hadn't really wanted to marry her in the first place. Was it the fact that she was the first to walk away that upset him? The arrogant dolt!

"There is a strange, unexplainable magic between us," he rasped, his face only inches above hers. "Would marriage to me be so distasteful?"

Catrina could endure no more. Brant's persuasive tone and tempting embrace were crumbling her defenses. She had to flee before she surrendered to his compelling magnetism!

"Let me go!" she railed. "A marriage to a man like you would be too painful. Dammit, you mulish man, can't you understand? I cannot marry you because I fear I am falling in love with you!" Catrina could have bit off her tongue when it outdistanced her brain. Damn, she hadn't meant to say that!

Brant froze. His jaw sagged on its hinges. Was that confused logic supposed to make sense? Who could understand the workings of this woman's mind? It seemed to Brant that her reasoning was exactly backward. But why should that surprise him, he asked himself. Everything had been backward since Catrina stepped from her breeches and revealed her true identity.

If Catrina thought she might be in love with him wasn't that the perfect reason to marry? Sweet Jesus, the lady was a lunatic!

Catrina was thoroughly humiliated. She had blurted out her confession and Brant was staring at her as if she had sprouted another head. When Brant's grasp eased, Catrina writhed for freedom. She was prepared to crash through the nearest wall to avoid him. God, she wanted to be anywhere except on the deck when he burst out in triumphant laughter. But when she squirmed, Brant clutched her to him, refusing to release her.

And then it came, that mortifying rumble of laughter. Catrina could not endure the humiliation. She lashed out to unshackle his chaining arms. Her doubled fist slammed against Brant's broad smile, causing it to droop on the side of his mouth. Simultaneously, her foot collided with his already tender shin. The moment he jerked away from the painful blows Catrina shot from his arms like a cannon ball.

Brant darted in front of the gangplank, blocking her flight. "Don't run from me, damn you," he growled.

"I'm not running," Cat corrected. "I am only exercising the noble part of valor. If I stay, I will be sorely tempted to club you over the head for mocking me!"

And then, like an enraged panther attacking his prey, he charged. Catrina glanced frantically about her, seeking another means of escape. While her heart very nearly beat her to death, she darted toward the starboard rail. Clamping her hand over her nose, she bounded onto a nearby barrel and plunged over the side of the schooner. Cat was far more apprehensive of the man who pursued her than she was of leaping into the sea. The moment the cold water swallowed her up, Catrina clawed her way back toward the surface and thrashed through the water to put more distance between her and the infuriating pirate who had stolen her heart.

Scowling, Brant leaned over the railing, amazed that Catrina had dared such a dramatic exit. When she bobbed to the surface, Brant glared at her shadowed form.

134

"You little fool! I hope the hell you can swim!"

"Like a fish," Catrina yelled up at him, and then stretched out to glide through the water with long, flowing strokes.

"Cap'n? What the devil is goin' on?" Thomas questioned as he loped across the deck.

He had heard the commotion and eavesdropped on part of the conversation. Thomas was certain now that Brant's brain had begun to warp. First the captain was railing at this mysterious woman who had supposedly proposed to him after only one night on land. Thomas swore he heard Brant proclaim that he wanted to go through with the marriage. Why? Thomas could not imagine. Brant Diamond was a devoted bachelor. And then suddenly the twosome were wrestling on the deck. And even more quickly the unidentified woman had dived into the harbor.

It was bad enough that Brant had been closeting himself in the ammunition room during his demented seizures. But talking marriage to a woman he could have only just met? My God, Thomas thought to himself, Captain Diamond was not a well man!

Brant wheeled on Thomas, his golden eyes ablaze with frustration. "That woman is crazed!"

Thomas frowned warily. One or the other of them was crazed, Thomas decided. But he wasn't certain which one. Brant was raving like a madman and his paramour had vaulted off the rail. Thomas wasn't sure either reaction was normal.

When Brant muttered under his breath and swung a leg over the rail to pursue the mermaid, Thomas grabbed his arm. "You've already taken one dive off the deep end tonight, Cap'n. That should be enough."

"Confound it, let me go!" Brant growled. "'Tis Milton down there!"

"Milton?" Thomas eyed the rattled captain even more suspiciously. "I thought you said it was a crazy woman, the same one I heard you say you wanted to marry."

Brant grumbled to himself. It was obvious Thomas thought

135

his captain had bats in his belfry. And Brant was wondering the same thing himself. That auburn-haired witch had turned him inside out in the course of one night!

His wandering thoughts scattered when he saw the silhouette of the man who was perched on the docked schooner, adjacent to the *Sea Lady*. Catrina had successfully managed to swim the distance. It seemed the captain of the other vessel had also heard the commotion and had come to investigate. When Catrina neared his ship, the captain tossed a rope ladder over the side to offer her assistance.

When the sailor stepped from the shadows Brant recognized the man. His disposition turned as sour as a lemon. Jean-Martin Turgot, Brant thought disgustedly. He was a rogue if ever there was one. The vision of Catrina in Jean-Martin's capable hands had Brant swearing all over again.

"See there? The girl ain't goin' to drown." Thomas encouraged his exasperated captain. "The Frenchman will take good care of her."

"That's what I'm afraid of," Brant muttered acrimoniously.

Brant was seeing red when Jean-Martin reached down to assist the bedraggled mermaid from the ladder. The Frenchman's arm curled around Catrina's ribs, pressing familiarly against the underside of her breast. While Cat was being hoisted to the deck Brant was turning green. By God, he would chop off Jean-Martin's hands, he swore vindictively.

Jean-Martin waved across to Brant. The smile that stretched across his lips shined like a beacon in the darkness and Brant scowled again. That French Casanova would not lay a hand on Cat!

Furiously, Brant wrestled his way out of Thomas's restraining arms and stormed toward the gangplank. "Are you coming with me or must I rescue Milton alone?" he yelled at Thomas.

"A . . . Cap'n? Don't you think it wise to fetch yer shirt and boots before you go traipsing off to see Jean-Martin?" Thomas said calmly.

Brant broke stride. Mumbling several unrepeatable epithets to Cat's name, and to the French Don Juan as well, Brant reversed direction. When Brant aimed himself toward his cabin, Thomas followed along at a slower pace. Mulling over the strange events of the evening, Thomas stared at Brant's rigid back. It was apparent that Brant's mental affliction had caused hallucinations. The captain's thoughts were jumbled and confused. Brant had himself believing it was Milton who had dived overboard. And yet Brant's twisted mind also had him thinking the mysterious woman was to be his wife.

There was naught else to do but lock the captain in his room until he recovered from his fit and returned to normal, Thomas decided. He hated to deceive the captain, but it was for his own good. Quietly, Thomas eased the door shut and barricaded the portal while Brant was retrieving his clothing.

"Sorry, Cap'n. I know you'll be cursin' a blue streak when you realize you've been locked away. But I don't see no other choice," he said with a heavy-hearted sigh.

Thomas started back up the steps and then paused when he heard the inevitable pounding on the door. His sympathetic gaze swung back to the cabin. "Maybe Milton can talk some sense into you," he murmured.

Since Thomas had seen nothing of the boy that night, he naturally assumed that Milton had returned to the cabin to climb into his cot. Surely he could make Brant realize his fears were ill-founded. And as far as that bit of fluff was concerned, Brant was better off without her.

When Brant roused from his demented trance and realized he had almost wed a stranger, he would thank Thomas for saving him from certain disaster. In the meantime, Thomas had no alternative but to allow Brant's fit to run its course and pray that Milton would not suffer after being locked in with a madman.

Poor Milton. He would be disillusioned when he witnessed Brant's pitiful condition. Heaving a disconcerted sigh, Thomas trudged up the steps. Brant was battle-weary, Thomas diagnosed. The pressure of command had taken its toll. What the captain needed was rest and recuperation. And Thomas would make certain Brant was well rested before they sailed to the colonies.

Jean-Martin surveyed the dripping mermaid with immediate interest. Although she was soaked to the bone and her wet hair was dangling about her in disarray, she was no less bewitching. Indeed, Jean-Martin was mystified by her comely assets. The low-cut gown clung to her shapely swells and curves like a glove.

What a pity Captain Diamond had been forced to relinquish this gorgeous creature. But now that Diamond's jewel was in Jean-Martin's hands, he would not permit her to steal away. He would give this daring beauty no reason to dive overboard.

"*Allez, chérie*, I will fetch you a blanket to warm you," Jean-Martin offered, flashing Cat a persuasive smile. "My name is Jean-Martin Turgot. And what name shall I attach to my lovely guest? Although I am miffed by your unusual arrival upon my ship, I am delighted to share your company."

"My name is Catrina Hamilton."

Catrina studied the swarthy French captain who equalled Brant in size and stature. Although Jean-Martin was dashingly attractive with his dark brown hair and twinkling blue eyes, Catrina was wary of his rakish smile. Men, she thought cynically. A woman couldn't trust anything in breeches. They all wanted something from a woman and this suave, debonair Frenchman was no different, she speculated.

Derrick Redmund wanted her fortune. Brant Diamond wanted her body during the time they would spend together. The Frenchman, she surmised, would find no complaint with whatever she offered him. Catrina cautioned herself to keep a watchful eye on Jean-Martin. His very smile set off warning signals in her head. She had learned a great deal from Brant when it came to the art of seduction and Catrina would make no more compromises. She had barely escaped with her heart when she fled from Brant. She would not become the object of another rake's pleasure.

"I am searching for passage to Scotland," she explained as they descended the steps to the captain's cabin.

A slow smile spread across Jean-Martin's tanned features. "You need not search further, *amie*. My ship is bound for Liverpool and points beyond. We will sail at the end of the week and I will be only too happy to accommodate you."

When the Frenchman laid his arm about her waist, Catrina removed it. "*Merci*, monsieur. I am thankful my swim was a short one. I might have been water-logged if I were forced to paddle from one vessel to another in my desperate search for a northbound ship."

Jean-Martin chuckled lightly as he strolled across his cabin to retrieve a blanket and a glass of wine for his guest. "Your methods seem a bit unconventional, mademoiselle. But I cannot blame you for leaping overboard to avoid the infamous Captain Diamond. He is followed by a notorious reputation, not only as a seaman, but as a philanderer as well."

"You are acquainted with him?" Catrina arched a delicate brow and took a small sip of wine.

"*Mais oui*, we often carouse the streets of Brest when he docks to sell his merchandise." He paused to sip his wine, continuing to peer at Cat from over the rim of his glass. "I cannot say we are close friends. *Vraiment*, it is more accurate to say there is an amicable rivalry between us. I respect him as a man and as a sailor." His blue eyes flickered as they skimmed Catrina's curvaceous figure. "But our conflict is that we share the same taste in women."

Catrina ignored the insinuative glance, her eyes darting uneasily around the room. Part of her was relieved Brant had not come storming after her. And yet, she was a mite disappointed. If Brant cared for her, even a smidgen, he would have tried to retrieve her from this suave Frenchman.

A curious frown knitted her brow, wondering how she could

have so completely misjudged Captain Diamond. She had been dumbfounded when he put up such a fuss on deck. Why had he become angry when she withdrew her proposal? She was the one who had more to gain from taking his name. Aye, it would have granted Brant immunity from scheming women who sought to tie him down, but he had successfully escaped wedlock for the past several years. Obviously Brant was as slippery as an eel or he would have already been snatched up.

An embarrassed blush crept to her cheeks, recalling how she had blurted out the fact that she felt something for that handsome rogue. That had been a foolish blunder. What did Brant care how she felt? If it mattered to him, he would have been hammering on Captain Turgot's door at this very moment.

"You are welcome to sleep in my cabin tonight," Jean-Martin murmured, moving to stand directly in front of her.

"And where will you be sleeping, Captain?" Catrina inquired, flinging him a dubious frown. "I think it fair to warn you that I intend to pay for my passage to Britain . . . in cash. I expect no favors and neither should you."

Jean-Martin bowed elegantly before her. It was obvious it would take cautious wooing to coax this saucy minx into his bed. He would bide his time and win Catrina's affection, he promised himself. Ah, what an enchanting voyage this would be.

"I shall bed down in my first mate's cabin until we sail for the Isles," he said good-naturedly, and then pressed a light kiss to her wrist. "Rest your fears, mademoiselle, I intend to treat you with the courtesy and respect you deserve."

"You are very kind, monsieur." Catrina forced a smile and wormed her hand free to clasp the blanket he had laid over her shoulders.

The Frenchman scooped up the necessary supplies and strode toward the door. Pausing, he cast her a quizzical smile. "If Captain Diamond should come calling, I will be happy to serve as your chaperone . . . or your champion."

"That will not be necessary." Catrina tilted a stubborn chin. "I am making it a point to fight my own battles these days."

"Should the privateer come aboard, I will convey the message to him. He may wish to fetch his sword before he approaches you." He chuckled, watching the sparks fly from her green eyes.

Jean-Martin wheeled away, grinning devilishly. This bewitching vixen was fair game and he would sway her when the American privateer had not. There had been times the past few years when Brant Diamond strutted away with a fetching lady on his arm, the very lady Jean-Martin had set his sights on. Now Brant would know how it felt to be bested. It would goad the American's pride, but Jean-Martin's had been deflated once too often at Diamond's hand. Now the boot was on the other foot and the privateer would feel the pinch, Jean-Martin thought spitefully.

After securing the door, Catrina stripped from her wet gown and climbed into bed. There was much to be done before she sailed to Scotland. The first order of business was to forget the dashing pirate captain. Then she would venture to the boutiques in Brest to purchase suitable clothing for her voyage. Finding clothes would pose no problem, but forgetting the night of splendor she had shared with Brant would be difficult, she thought disheartenedly.

It was only that Brant was the first man to introduce her to passion, Catrina told herself. What she felt for Brant wasn't love. It was physical attraction, pure and simple. She felt guilty for submitting to his amorous assault. Her conscience dictated that she *should* love the man who seduced her.

That was how it should have been. But since it wasn't, she had fancied herself in love to ease her guilt, she reasoned. The situation had gotten out of hand. Her traitorous body had surrendered to Diamond's brand of passion. Her tormented mind had compensated by labeling the emotion as love. But it wasn't love, Catrina convinced herself.

Brant Diamond had several redeeming qualities, she

granted. But he was still a pirate and a rogue. Women were helplessly drawn to outlaws. She had been lured to him because of her strange fascination. She had made a foolish mistake by confusing passion with love. But now that she stood back to analyze the emotion she realized it must not have been love. And besides, she did not want to be in love. She was an independent young woman, she had a mind of her own, and she would never lean on a man again. She had leaned on Derrick and that had proven disastrous. Brant Diamond was no different. If she let herself believe in him he would only disappoint her.

Satisfied with her conviction that once Brant was out of sight he would slip her mind, she settled down to sleep. In time the shame of surrendering would subside. No one would know of her brief, passionate affair with the pirate captain. She would return to her estate and take command of her life. If an ill wind blew Derrick Redmund back to her doorstep, she would deal with him, using the self-defense Brant had taught her.

She would be the strong, willful woman she had been before her parents' death. The tragedy had devastated her, but she had to go on with her life and lock the door on yesterday.

Although she might never truly forget her first taste of passion, the memory would fade. Why, in a few months she would never think of the dashing Captain Diamond at all, she reassured herself. Brant would be no more than a dim shadow of a fading memory.

Clinging to that positive thought, Catrina squirmed to her side and yielded to sleep. But somewhere in the night, she could have sworn soft, sensuous lips were playing softly against hers. Nonsense, Catrina chided herself when she came awake with a start. She was alone in the cabin. It was only the aftereffects of passion that were hounding her. By morning the lingering emotions would have vanished and she would begin the first day of the rest of her life.

*   *   *

Thomas knelt before the keyhole and squinted to see Brant pacing the confines of his cabin. A muddled frown creased Thomas's brow. There was no sign of Milton. Was he lying in an unseen corner, mutilated during Brant's fit of madness?

Cautiously, Thomas removed the blockade and pulled open the door. "Before you have me flogged for mutiny, let me say that I did what I felt I had to do . . . considerin' the circumstances," he blurted out before Brant snatched up his flintlock and dropped his first mate in his tracks.

Brant glared furiously at his well-meaning friend. He had cursed Thomas a thousand times over when he found himself barricaded in his own cabin. "Regardless of what you believe, I am not crazed, nor was I last night."

Thomas shrank away from Brant's booming voice. "Now, Cap'n, don't work yerself into another fit. I . . ."

"Sit down!" Brant's arm shot toward the empty chair. "As soon as I explain the whole of it, you will be dismayed to learn that *you* were the one who made an ass of himself, not I."

Deciding it wise not to argue with a madman, Thomas walked toward the chair and parked himself in it. He would calmly listen to Brant's illogical ravings once again and then contemplate what was to be done.

Brant stalked over to retrieve the baggy garments that lay on the extra cot. "Do you recognize these clothes, Thomas?" he questioned curtly. When Thomas nodded, Brant called his first mate's attention to the cabin. "As you can plainly see, Milton is not in his breeches and cap, nor is he in the room. 'Tis because Milton is no longer aboard the *Sea Lady*. Does that sound logical?" Mocking amber eyes focused on Thomas's ruddy features.

"Aye, Milton must have found himself a clean set of clothes and sneaked off the ship," Thomas patronized his annoyed captain.

"Now that we have agreed on that point, I would like to continue. And you need not stare at me as if I were daft. I am as sane as you are," Brant snorted disdainfully. "You have assumed Milton acquired a new set of clothes, but it has not occurred to you that he might have also taken on a new identity." Brant stalked up in front of the first mate to glower in his face. "The lady who dived overboard last night and my mischievous cabinboy are one and the same."

Thomas's brows shot straight up. "Nay, you only . . ."

"Aye," Brant argued. "The lad I abducted from Selkirk mansion in Scotland was Lady Catrina Hamilton. She was garbed as a ragamuffin to disguise her true identity."

"What!" Thomas's eyes bulged from their sockets.

"Catrina was running from the man who marred her face with bruises. You do remember the bruises, don't you?" he taunted the first mate who wilted in his chair.

"Aye," Thomas said sickly.

"When I discovered the lady's identity, she proposed to me. She planned to marry me and use my name to protect her from her abusive fiancé," Brant went on to say. His tone became more sour by the second. "Then the fickle chit had a change of heart and tried to escape. That is when she jumped from the ship. Running to that French cavalier was like inviting a wolf to guard a lamb. Fearing for Catrina's safety, I planned to immediately retrieve her from Turgot's clutches." Fiery amber eyes burned holes in Thomas's shirt. "But my first mate, thinking me crazed, locked me in my cabin and barricaded the damned door!" Brant's voice grew steadily louder until he was shouting in Thomas's peaked face.

Thomas, realizing he had leaped to the wrong conclusion, smiled bleakly. "Sorry, Cap'n. I thought I was doin' what was best for you. How the hell was I to know Milton was a woman? I thought the girl you had on deck last night was some trollop you dragged off the street. When she took the dive I figured the Frenchman could take his turn with the wench and you would be well rid of her."

That last remark had Brant growling like a disturbed panther. He had spent the better part of the night battling the tormenting vision of Cat in Jean-Martin's capable arms. He could not help but wonder if Cat had sprung the same proposition on the Frenchman. Brant kept hearing Catrina's parting confession, the one she blurted out before she leaped overboard: "I can't marry you because I might be falling in love with you."

Brant rolled his eyes toward the ceiling. The chit made no sense at all and he didn't know why he was stewing over her. Because of her, Thomas thought his captain mad. Because of her, Brant was wrestling with emotions that granted him no peace. If he had any sense he would wash his hands of that high-spirited wench and give her no other thought. But a tiny voice inside him kept whispering to pursue her, to bring her back where she belonged—in his arms.

And, by damned, that was what he was going to do, Brant decided. He was not leaving Cat to Jean-Martin. That French wolf would gobble up that little red-haired hoyden.

"Do you want me to come with you?" Thomas inquired as Brant stalked toward the door.

"I can do without your kind of help," Brant grumbled. "You may suddenly decide to lock me in the Frenchman's brig. If I am to find myself a prisoner, I prefer to be taken by the enemy, not my own first mate!"

A pensive frown plowed Thomas's brow. Brant's apparent fascination with Catrina Hamilton and his instinctive need to protect her from the Frenchman set Thomas to wondering. Only once had Thomas seen Brant in such a tailspin. It had been during his bittersweet affair with Cynthia Marsh. Brant had been twenty-five, the same age as his younger brother was now. The younger Diamond had been enamored with Cynthia and introduced her to Brant, thinking her to be a perfect match for the elder Diamond. When the affair ended on a sour note, Brant's kid brother held himself personally responsible for the disaster. Brant had sworn off women and had flitted about from one bed to another like a bee gathering nectar. There had been no lasting entanglements, only fleeting passion. Brant wanted no more than a smile and a moment from the woman who caught his eye . . . That is, until Catrina had him behaving like a lunatic, Thomas amended.

A wry grin pursed Thomas's lips as he ambled from the cabin. He was anxious to get a look at this misfit who had posed as a boy and roomed with the captain for the past month. Thomas had the oddest notion that beneath that oversized cap and those smudges of soot was a face Brant Diamond was having one helluva time forgetting.

This could be an interesting predicament, Thomas chuckled to himself. The lady had proposed. And for some unknown reason Brant Diamond, the dedicated bachelor, had accepted. When the lady withdrew her proposal it infuriated Brant rather than relieved him. And just what would make a man outraged to have his freedom?

Thomas's grin was as wide as the Atlantic Ocean. There was trouble brewing between the American privateer and this Scottish-born heiress. It had nothing to do with the Revolutionary War, Thomas predicted. Brant didn't even know how close he was to being taken captive by his enemy. But it was not Brant's life that was hanging in the balance of this crucial battle. It was his heart, Thomas thought to himself.

Chapter Nine

Breathing a sigh of relief, Derrick Redmund slumped back in the seat of his carriage. He had completed an extensive cross-examination by the Board of British Admiralty. After his less than courageous encounter with privateers, Diamond and Jones, Derrick had faced court-martial. The Board demanded a detailed explanation of the battle that cost Britain the loss of the *H.M.S. Drake* and its crew.

Derrick had very nearly lost his prestigious position as captain in the Royal Navy. Knowing he would face court-martial for his retreat at Belfast Lough, Derrick had thoroughly prepared himself for the investigation. He also stooped to padding the pockets of those who were called to testify.

Doing some fast footwork, Derrick had contacted several other captains who had the misfortune of encountering Diamond and Jones on the high seas. When he went before the Board of Admiralty he had his story well organized.

Derrick had proclaimed that his ship had suffered extensive damage during the ambush and that the American pirates had stooped to devious ploys to lure the unsuspecting British vessels into battle. After the *Drake* had been heavily bombarded and boarded by the pirates, Derrick deemed he was about to be pelleted by a barrage of cannon fire, not only from the two privateers but by his own sister ship. For those reasons, Derrick surmised that defeat was inevitable and sought cover in the narrow channel off Belfast Lough.

Although the Board of Admiralty had looked upon Derrick with skepticism, he had baited them with a tempting counterattack. Derrick requested permission to set a trap for the slippery privateers when they attempted to transport their prizes and supplies to the colonies.

Calling attention to the fact that the privateers always preyed on the British naval port in the Everlasting Mountains of the Sea, Derrick requested permission to set sail for the Azores. The islands between England and the colonies served as a landing to stock supplies and food for the remainder of the journey across the Atlantic. Because of an ancient treaty, the Portuguese allowed the British to use the Azores as a naval base during war time. Derrick speculated that Diamond and Jones would circle the cluster of islands to steal cargo from the British ships. He had been in touch with several men who had the misfortune of losing merchandise and weapons to these wily pirates while they lay in port in the mid-Atlantic islands. After spouting off the familiar names of other unfortunate captains, the Admiralty sat up and listened to Derrick's scheme.

Intending to use an unseaworthy vessel as a decoy, Derrick planned to lure the privateers within firing range and then blast them out of the water. He suggested camouflaging two men-of-war behind the heavy undergrowth that lined the necks on the bay of Pico Island.

The Board eagerly approved of a plan to lure the pirates into a trap. They wanted Diamond and Jones off the sea and behind bars. Such a feat would break the American's spirit and serve as an example to discourage other rebels who sought to plunder the Mother Country's shores. The Admiralty agreed to allow Derrick to keep his command. They also promised to drop all charges if he successfully captured Jones and Diamond. If he accomplished the feat the Board would even consider offering

Derrick a promotion in the Royal Navy.

Assured that he would not be disgraced, Derrick left the meeting, determined of purpose. His only disappointment the past week had come from his inability to locate Catrina Hamilton. The termagant seemed to have vanished into thin air. No one knew where to find her.

But Derrick was not abandoning his attempt to take control of the vast estate near Dumfries. When he returned from the Azores with Captain Diamond and Jones he would be hailed as a hero. With medals of valor pinned on his chest, he would crawl to Catrina if he must, begging forgiveness. He would explain that he was so upset by the thought of losing her that he had reacted irrationally. He would insist that his fierce love for her had caused him to lose his head when she canceled the wedding. And then he would actively court her again, portraying the perfect gentleman.

A devilish smile pursed Derrick's lips. Time and patience would grant him the power and wealth he craved. At first he had been obsessed with the Hamilton fortune. But when he laid eyes on the auburn-haired heiress, he knew he had to have her as well. She was a breathtaking beauty and Derrick hungered to feel her supple body beneath his. She had come to him in tormenting dreams and he could not forget that bewitching face and those fiery green eyes. During their last, unfortunate confrontation he had seen the evidence of her inbred Scottish temper. There was a living fire in those emerald eyes and Derrick longed to control it.

Catrina Hamilton could provide him with a fortune to sustain him all his days and a passion that no other eligible heiress had instilled in him. Aye, there were wenches to appease his lusts, but none of them could compare to that auburn-haired enchantress. Catrina challenged him, intrigued him. One day he would have her as his own and he would bury himself in her exquisite body, make her a slave to his brand of passion.

That thought alone was the inner driving force that refused

149

to allow Derrick to abandon his scheme to acquire Catrina and her fortune. In the past Derrick had courted money, but not as fiercely as he had laid siege to Catrina Hamilton. She was a rare breed of woman and Derrick wanted her. And, by damned, he would have her . . . just as soon as he delivered Diamond and Jones's heads to the Admiralty on a silver platter! He would prove himself worthy of Catrina's affection and his lifelong dream of prestige and wealth would become reality.

The moment Brant set foot on the French merchant ship, he knew this confrontation would test his strained patience. Gnashing his teeth, Brant fought the urge to plant his fist in Jean-Martin's smug grin.

"Ah, Capitaine Diamond, *quoi de neuf?* I have not seen you in several months," the Frenchman greeted all too cheerfully.

"You can drop the idle prattle, Jean," Brant snorted crabbily. "You know why I'm here. I want to speak with Catrina."

Jean-Martin grinned in wicked satisfaction. "But Mademoiselle Hamilton does not wish to see you."

Brant's golden eyes narrowed. His temper, already sorely put upon the past twenty-four hours, was about to snap. "I want Catrina," he gritted out between clenched teeth.

"I can understand why," the Frenchman cooed, his blue eyes dancing with deviltry. "There are many things about her that attract a man. But I am obliged to grant Mademoiselle amnesty on my schooner. Since France is still at peace with England, I cannot turn my lovely guest over to an American privateer." Jean-Martin sighed heavily. "King Louis is contemplating signing an alliance with the colonies, but as of yet we are a neutral country. You know very well what a touchy situation it is for me. An overt action on my part might enrage the British. We must be careful that this confrontation does not become an international incident. How can I continue to play the role of the apathetic seaman if I sacrifice a citizen of the Crown to an American privateer? Especially one with your notorious reputation?"

The Frenchman was taunting Brant and delighting in every minute of it. Clamping a tight rein on his temper, Brant forced a controlled smile. "If you will not return the lady to my custody then you must at least serve as a mediator during our discussion."

The swarthy Frenchman eyed Brant for a long, pensive moment. "I have always considered myself a fair man, monsieur. If the lady will agree to a meeting, I will serve as your liaison."

When Jean-Martin spun on his heels to relay the message, Brant breathed an exasperated sigh. Damn that minx. If he ever got his hands on her he would shake the stuffing out of her for this last prank. It goaded his pride to use Jean as a go-between. But what peeved him most was having Cat on the Frenchman's ship. Brant could not help but wonder to what extremes the little misfit would go to avoid him. Who could understand that woman! She was a walking contradiction.

"I conveyed the message." Jean-Martin strode back across the deck, pausing in front of his disgruntled guest. "I shall not repeat, verbatim, what the lady replied in answer to your request. It would singe the ears off a priest. I can only say that she wishes you a steamy voyage on the River Styx and that she is not the least bit concerned if you sailed on a one-way cruise to the eternal inferno."

Brant's face clouded with fury. Impulsively, he stalked toward the steps, but Jean blocked his path.

"*S'il vous plaît*, monsieur, do not force me to do something distasteful. You are a friend, but the lady has sought asylum on my ship. I am honor-bound to defend her." Jean-Martin peered soberly at Brant. "Although Benjamin Franklin has been most supportive of you and Jones, he is at this very moment coaxing the French government toward a recognition of American independence and attempting to sway the king into an offensive alliance. Franklin would be most chagrined if you

151

brewed trouble for him in an incident over this Scottish heiress. There is more at stake here than a man obsessed with a high-spirited woman."

Fiery amber eyes clashed with stern blue ones. "No matter what the international repercussions, she is mine, Jean," Brant told him tersely. "We may have called each other *friend* in the past. But if I learn you have taken unfair advantage of Catrina, you will sorely wish you hadn't."

"You presume too much, *mon ami*. If Mademoiselle were yours she would wear your ring and she would not dive overboard to avoid you," Jean mocked. "I have promised to take Mademoiselle to the Isles and I do not feel compelled to answer to you, should any affair occur between us during the voyage."

The thought of leaving Cat with a man who had as many arms as an octopus infuriated Brant. It took every ounce of self-control he could muster to reverse direction and retreat to the gangplank.

"I have news from the Isles," Jean-Martin called after Brant, halting him in his tracks. "During my sojourn in Liverpool I heard of your daring raids and battle in Belfast." A wry smile pursed Jean-Martin's lips. "My sources tell me that you sent the British *capitaine*, Derrick Redmund, into humiliating retreat. I also heard that he faced a court-martial. Your bravery is to be commended, *capitaine*. But I fear you have made yourself a vindictive enemy. My informants predict that Redmund will not forget what you did to him. Beware the man, *ami*. You have soiled his reputation and the price on your head will tempt mercenaries, such as he, to collect it."

Brant's head swiveled around when the name Derrick Redmund popped into the conversation. That was the second time he had heard that name and he cursed himself for being unable to place it. Brant had no doubt that Jean-Martin's information was correct. The Frenchman was an emissary in the secret service alliance that monitored British activities for the rebels. Jean-Martin appeared the nonchalant captain whose only interest was transporting cargo abroad—for the profit in it. He could come and go as he pleased in the Isles and he never returned from a voyage without valuable information.

When Jean-Martin noticed the anger had dwindled in those unnerving golden eyes he broke into a smile. "I thought you might be curious to know who you had done battle with, *capitaine*. I always make it a point to know my enemies. I do not wish us to be on unfriendly terms because of this woman. Perhaps one day soon you and I will be comrades in war, fighting for the cause of colonial freedom." The smile broadened to encompass all his striking features. "I have one more tidbit of information for you, monsieur. Before I left the Isles, I received word that the *H.M.S. Countess* was gathering cargo for a voyage to Canada. She is said to be heavily loaded with supplies for the British Army. There is a good chance that you might run across the *Countess* during your return cruise across the Atlantic. Wouldn't it be a pity if the vessel were to fall into rebel hands?"

Reluctantly, Brant mellowed into a grin. "Aye, Monsieur Turgot. It would be a pity indeed. I shall keep watch for the *Countess. Merci*, monsieur."

Once Brant was pacified and exited from the ship, Jean-Martin chuckled to himself. He had no qualms about passing information to the patriot privateer, but he was reluctant to deliver the enchanting beauty to Brant. Jean-Martin had not bothered to ask Catrina if she would grant Captain Diamond an audience. He had lingered at the bottom of the steps for a reasonable amount of time before returning to the deck.

What Brant and Catrina didn't know wouldn't hurt them, Jean-Martin rationalized. His gaze drifted to the steps and he grinned roguishly. With the handsome privateer out of the way, Jean-Martin could pursue the lovely damsel. He would woo the shapely nymph into his bed and make her forget Brant Diamond existed, he promised himself. Clinging to that

153

arousing thought Jean-Martin strutted toward the cabin to take his lovely guest on a shopping spree.

Inside a tavern on the wharf, Brant sat sipping his ale. But to his dismay, the drink tasted a great deal like sour grapes. Since his morning confrontation with Jean-Martin, Brant had been as ill-tempered as a hornet. Several solutions had skipped through his mind, none of which were satisfactory. He had toyed with the idea of storming the French merchant ship and abducting Catrina. But Thomas had pointed out the dangers of such drastic actions, just as Jean-Martin Turgot had.

Damn, Brant hated to admit that the idea was a mite too bold, considering relations in France. The last thing the American privateers needed was to brew trouble with the French during delicate negotiations. French merchants purchased the goods privateers seized as prizes and quietly applauded any American victory against England.

Brant had considered requesting an audience with Catrina, every hour on the hour, until she relented. But as stubborn as the chit was, Brant would probably wear himself out traipsing back and forth between the two vessels every sixty minutes.

"I thought you would be celebrating," John Paul grumbled as he parked himself in the chair across from Brant. "One of us should be smiling and it should be you. At least you still have a ship."

Brant cast aside his disgruntled thoughts and glanced over to see the frustrated frown that was stamped on John Paul's face. "Haven't you been able to locate a seaworthy schooner?"

John Paul gestured for the waitress to bring him an ale and then slumped in his seat. "I found an East Indiaman schooner that was structurally sound and reasonably swift, but she has already been snatched up."

"Perhaps the *Drake* could be overhauled," Brant suggested.

"I have no wish to have any connection with a ship that does not sail fast," John Paul snorted. "I intend to go into harm's way and I would rather be shot ashore than sent to sea in that floating sieve!" When the waitress set the mug before him, John Paul guzzled his ale and then sighed heavily. "And if that is not enough to spoil my disposition, there are no American senior naval officers in France to hold a court-martial against Lieutenant Simpson. I do not wish to set that bungling imbecile free to botch up someone else's crusade against the British."

"Then there is naught else to do but to keep Simpson in the brig until he can come to trial," Brant reminded him. "As for your new command, surely Dr. Franklin will come to your aid."

John Paul shrugged noncommittally. "Rumors are that money is short and negotiations in Paris are strained. Not only am I forced to table Simpson's court-martial but I have had to make mortgages on our prizes to Comte d'Orvilliers. He was kind enough to aid me in my hour of need. The situation is disgraceful and I seem to be stuck in Brest for God only knows how long before I receive command of another schooner."

A wry smile pursed Brant's lips. "You could travel to Paris to amuse yourself," he suggested. "Franklin declares the best way for a man to polish his French is to find a sleeping dictionary. And he claims the best way to get things done in France is through the wives of influential citizens."

The faintest hint of a smile finally touched the corner of John Paul's mouth. "C'est vrai. Believe me, no man is more anxious to be entertained by a pretty French damsel than I. But if I venture to Paris I might miss something . . . such as the opportunity to equip a vessel for battle. It seems I am stuck in Brest indefinitely." John Paul eased back in his seat to heave another disgusted sigh. "If not for Comte d'Orvilliers my spirits would be scraping bottom. But he has invited us to a grand ball to honor our courage in the fight against the British."

"Have you sent word to Franklin that we have acquired more than a hundred prisoners to exchange with the

Admiralty?" Brant questioned, making a quick change of subject. He was in no mood to consider attending an elaborate party when that auburn-haired hellcat preyed so heavily on his mind. Any other female companion would be a meager substitute for the woman Brant wanted in his arms.

John Paul nodded affirmatively. "The dispatch is on its way. If Franklin can arrange to free the American prisoners that are rotting away in Mill Prison I will feel as if we accomplished a great deal on our mission."

A moment of silence hung between them. And then a fond smile crept to John Paul's lips. "If you were not such a good friend I would be most envious of you," he confessed. "While I am scrambling about in search of a ship, you will be transporting supplies to suffering troops and families in America. I have no wish to part company with you but we shall make Comte d'Orvilliers's gay affair a going away party of sorts." A merry twinkle flickered in his hazel eyes. "Perhaps we will find one or two accommodating maids to make us forget our woes and our forced separation."

"Unfortunately, the lady who is the cause and cure of my torment will not be there," Brant grumbled aloud.

"Has a certain young lady already caught your eye?" he teased.

"Aye, and now Jean-Martin has her in his clutches."

Offering a gesture of consolation, John Paul leaned over to pat Brant on the back. "Then you are destined to meet the light and love of your life again. Turgot will be at the gay affair as well. Surely you have not forgotten that Jean-Martin captains one of Comte d'Orvilliers's merchant ships. It would be an insult not to invite Turgot, *la homme à bonnes fortunes,* the lady's man of Brest."

When a black scowl twisted Brant's lips, John Paul burst into chuckles. "Why is it that you and Jean-Martin have the uncanny knack of being attracted to the same woman? I cannot wait to lay eyes on the mysterious beauty who has again put the two of you at odds."

"I predict you will be fascinated with her as well," Brant smirked. "'Tis bad enough that Turgot has become my rival for her attention, but I imagine you will also be drawn beneath her spell."

John Paul raised his mug in toast. "To the future love of our lives. May she be woman enough for the three of us," he said with a teasing grin.

Brant glared holes in John Paul's flashy uniform. "She will not be shared. I found her first and, by damned, I mean to wed her."

John Paul's mouth dropped open and he stared incredulously at Brant. "Marry a woman you have only met?" he chirped. "That does not sound like you."

"Nay, it doesn't, but the chit has turned my world upside down and damned if I know which way is up," Brant muttered acrimoniously.

"I resolved never to marry unless I could improve my social status and you proclaimed you had sworn off women except to appease your needs," John Paul reminded him. "I do not know what to make of this mysterious chit. Which is it she arouses in you, love or passion?"

The question was point-blank and Brant wasn't even certain *he* knew the answer. All he knew was that he was so frustrated with the turn of events that he was consumed by the urge to throw something, something the size of the Rock of Gibraltar. Dammit, that shapely, high-spirited termagant was giving him fits!

When Brant bolted from his chair, upending it, and stormed toward the door, John Paul frowned bemusedly. It must surely have been a witch who had cast an evil spell on Captain Diamond, he surmised. He had never seen Brant in such a snit over a woman. Indeed, Brant was usually nonchalant about his love affairs.

A curious smile flitted across John Paul's lips. He was most anxious to meet this bewitching nymph who had turned her charms on the infamous Captain Diamond. Brant married?

What an intriguing thought. If it were true that reformed rogues made the best husbands Diamond would be a gem. There was nothing Brant had not attempted. The dashing daredevil had seen and done it all . . . except join the institution of marriage.

John Paul sipped his ale and drowned his laughter. Aye, this sojourn in Brest might not prove to be such a disappointment after all. And who could know for certain? When John Paul met the spellcasting sorceress who had taken up permanent residence in Brant's mind he might also discard his vow of bachelorhood.

In exasperation, Catrina paced the confines of her cabin, grappling with the confused emotions that had hounded her for nearly a week. Although she told herself it was not love that led her thoughts back to that devil Diamond, he was constantly on her mind.

Each time she ventured from the cabin on Jean-Martin's arm, Brant was standing like a posted lookout, spying on her every movement. She could feel Brant's intense gaze upon her. He was like a panther studying his prey, watching, waiting . . . But waiting for what? Catrina didn't know. The man totally baffled her.

Why hadn't Brant come to check on her, she wondered bitterly. Jean-Martin had said nothing about Brant making even one attempt to seek her out. Not that she would have agreed to see him again, Cat reminded herself. But blast it, he could have shown a smidgen of concern for her. So why this sentinel watch over her, she quizzed herself. It made no sense at all.

Heaving a heavy-hearted sigh, Catrina turned to the mirror to complete her coiffure for the ball. Jean-Martin had invited her to accompany him to the party being held at Comte d'Orvilliers's chateau. Catrina accepted, certain it would be easier to keep the amorous Frenchman under control in public than in private. Catrina sought out every opportunity to journey to Brest to avoid situations that might lead to intimacy.

Although the Frenchman seemed eager to please, Catrina did not quite trust his intentions. After her tête-à-tête with Brant, she had learned to detect the look of a man who was hungry for passion. Jean-Martin had that look about him. He was potentially dangerous and Catrina never let her guard down in his presence. Thrice he had attempted to corner her, but she had darted away before he could capture her in his arms.

Catrina was afraid to make comparisons, afraid of what she might learn. The fear that the Frenchman's kisses could not set her aflame the way Brant's did petrified her. If the Frenchman fell short of the mark Catrina would be forced to admit defeat.

Stop this nonsense, Cat chided herself. She was not in love with Brant Diamond. She had been through this same mental debate a dozen times the past week. How many more times must she give herself this lecture before she convinced her foolish heart of the truth?

When Catrina finished pinning the auburn curls on top of her head, she stepped back to view the reflection that stared glumly at her. This was not a happy lady, she realized. Her eyes were dull and lifeless. There was no radiance about her. She felt as enthusiastic and appealing as a damp mop. The only pleasure she had known the past six months had come from playing mischievous pranks on Captain Diamond and surrendering to his brand of passion.

For those few weeks she had been whole and alive, living an adventure she had only dreamed about. But it was over and done and she had to get on with the rest of her life. Brant didn't really want her underfoot. He had only toyed with her, just as he trifled with every other woman. His heart had been torn asunder at a tender age and every female who crossed his path was to pay for his bitter affair. Catrina was only a trinket to him, a plaything. She would never mean anything more to that cynical rogue.

A muddled frown clouded her brow. If that were true, why had Brant put up such a fuss the night she fled his schooner? She still couldn't fathom what motivated his actions. The man was an enigma, Cat assured herself. If there was method to his madness, Cat could not comprehend it.

Was it his male pride that wounded him when she retracted her proposal? And why was he monitoring her actions from the helm of his ship? What could he possibly want from her that he hadn't already taken?

Well, what he had taken was not for sale or lease. Cat was not doling out affection, not ever again. The first time had been a disastrous mistake and she was not about to repeat the blunder. Brant Diamond could wench his way across France and back. She didn't give a whit.

"Mademoiselle? Are you ready?" Jean called from the other side of the locked door.

When Catrina granted him entrance, he swallowed air. Her alabaster skin glowed in the light, making him ache to touch what his eyes beheld. The blue velvet gown made an enticing wrapper for this tempting package. Jean had been patient with Catrina, but his desire for her was smoldering like a log tossed on a blazing flame. He wondered how long he could keep this enchantress underfoot without tossing gentlemanly reserve to the wind.

Each time he maneuvered Catrina into his arms, she managed to elude him. Jean was tired of playing cat and mouse games. He wanted Catrina in the worst way and his patience was wearing thin. Tonight, he promised himself. After they wined, dined, and danced at the ball, he would have Catrina in his bed. And there she would stay until he returned her to Scotland.

Since Captain Diamond had declined to attend the gay affair at Comte d'Orvilliers's chateau, Jean would not have to fret about complications. Things had worked out splendidly. Brant thought Catrina despised him and Catrina surmised that Brant

160

had lost interest in her.

Casting aside his wandering thoughts, Jean raked Catrina's curvaceous figure, not missing the slightest detail. "Mademoiselle, *vous coupez le souffle a . . .*" he murmured appreciatively. Taking her hand, he bowed before her and then pressed a light kiss to her wrist.

"*Merci,* monsieur."

Catrina tried to free her hand, but the Frenchman used it as a tow line, drawing her ever closer. To her dismay, she found herself held hostage in the circle of his arms. Her body was pressed full length against him and his smiling face was dangerously close.

"I have tried to be a patient man, *chérie,* but the mere sight of you arouses me," he breathed raggedly. "I want to make you my pet, to shower you with affection."

"Have you considered taking in an alley cat or mutt?" Catrina questioned, leaning back as far as his encircling arms would allow.

"*Non, ma chérie,* it would not be the same." Jean-Martin frowned when she dodged his intended kiss. "Why do you fight me? Is a harmless kiss too much to ask? It would mean so much to me."

Catrina opened her mouth to retort, but Jean advanced like an invading cavalry. She died a thousand times in that moment. His kiss was not repulsive, but there was no fire, no heat in his touch. When she made the mistake of closing her eyes, a dashingly rugged face flashed through her mind. Fiery amber eyes were laughing down at her. Catrina's heart shriveled in her chest, knowing she would never be free of Brant Diamond's spell. The taproot ran so deep that it would require surgery to remove the raven-haired rogue from her thoughts.

Jean-Martin was like Brant in many ways—suave, charismatic, and handsome. But there was an aura of primitive maleness about Brant, a dark charm that could not be duplicated by the Frenchman. She was not compulsively drawn to Jean-Martin and she never would be.

Catrina twisted away before Jean could deepen the kiss. "Shouldn't we be going?" she questioned, not the slightest bit out of breath.

"I would prefer to remain here . . . with you," he whispered against her neck.

"I am famished, monsieur," Catrina informed him, side-stepping another amorous assault.

"So am I," Jean grumbled as he watched Catrina sail toward the door. "But this hunger cannot be satisfied at the comte's table."

Resigning himself to the fact that Lady Hamilton was not easily swayed by flirtatious smiles and tender kisses, Jean followed in her wake. He would see to it that she was never without a glass of wine during the party. When they returned to the schooner, her defenses would be swamped by liquor and he would take advantage.

Smiling at the thought of having this fiery-haired temptress in his bed, Jean's sour mood sweetened considerably. There was more than one way to skin a feisty cat. His methods might be a bit unscrupulous, but he was a desperate man. Catrina challenged him, stirred him, and he was relentless in his pursuit. Surely she could not hold out for the entire two weeks of the voyage. Even the most obstinate of women had succumbed to his charms . . . eventually, he reminded himself arrogantly. There had to be a way to melt Catrina's ice-encased heart and Jean had two weeks to discover it.

Chapter Ten

While Catrina was staring at her reflection in the mirror Brant was having a long talk with his. Although he had been successful in trading his prizes for much-needed American supplies he had been miserable. It annoyed him that after a week he still could not stare at Catrina from across the distance that separated them without feeling this upheaval of emotion. That unpredictable vixen had gotten under his skin and burrowed into his heart and it would take an exorcist to rout her.

Brant had decided to make one last play to see Catrina before she sailed to Scotland and he opened sail to America. He knew Jean-Martin planned to attend the ball so he waited until the last minute to notify Comte d'Orvilliers that he planned to attend. No doubt, Catrina would not have consented to accompany Jean-Martin if she knew the captain of the *Sea Lady* would be at the chateau. The fickle chit had gone out of her way to avoid him the past week, Brant thought sourly.

Well, by damned, she would not avoid him tonight, Brant assured himself. He wanted to speak to Catrina and nothing short of a worldwide disaster would stop him.

After Brant shrugged on his blue uniform with its white lapels and waistcoat he peered into the mirror. The uniform and white breeches fit his physique like a custom-made suit, but the man within it felt as if he were held together by only one strand of thread. Brant had to admit he had enjoyed better weeks. He had been plagued with a five-foot-two-inch headache, one that refused to go away. That exasperating woman had Brant walking into walls and bumping into furniture. Now she had him meeting himself coming and going. But worst of all . . .

"Are you coming, Captain? Or do you intend to spend the evening staring at your image in the mirror?" John Paul snickered as he strutted through the open door of Brant's cabin. A muddled frown furrowed his brow when he realized the urchin Brant had taken as a cabin boy had made himself scarce the past week. "What became of scrawny Milton? With all my troubles I almost forgot about our wager."

A sly smile rippled across Brant's lips as he snatched up his tricorn and strode toward John Paul. "You will not believe the miraculous transformation in Milton. I hope you brought your gold piece with you since it now belongs in *my* pocket," Brant chortled. "I can honestly say I have made a new person of Milton. I doubt you will recognize the waif when you come face to face."

Scoffing at the boast, John Paul ambled through the companionway beside Brant. "Even you cannot have had such a dramatic effect on that belligerent guttersnipe. And I will not hand over my doubloon until I see Milton for myself."

Bitting back a devilish grin Brant hopped to the gangplank. "You will have the pleasure of Milton's company tonight. The waif will be attending the comte's ball."

John Paul broke stride to gape at his companion. "Surely you did not invite that ill-mannered bumpkin to this social affair," he hooted in disbelief.

Brant burst out laughing at the stricken look that captured John Paul's features. "Believe me, you will find no complaint with Milton," he insisted.

"Really, Brant, this party is strictly for the upper echelon of Brest. I am amazed at your audacity." John Paul plopped down on the carriage seat and cast Brant a condescending frown. "Do you think to pass Milton off as royalty? If he causes a stir I will hold you personally responsible."

"The only *stir* will be of your making," Brant countered.

"I would prefer to meet the goddess who has you contemplating marriage," John Paul snorted. "I will expect her to be causing stirrings, not Milton."

After Brant and John Paul filed through the line of diplomats who waited to greet the guests, John Paul cast his comrade an impatient glance. "Well, where is that ragamuffin? There are dozens of ladies here with whom I prefer to spend my time. Let's settle this wager and be done with it."

The smile that claimed Brant's features faded when he spied Catrina in the Frenchman's arms. His body went rigid when Jean-Martin leaned closer to whisper sweet nothings against the trim column of Catrina's neck. Damn that rogue. If his hands trespassed on Brant's private property they would be chopped off at the elbows, Brant swore vindictively.

Brant gestured a long arm across the sprawling ballroom, calling John Paul's attention to the captivating beauty in Jean-Martin's arms. "Yonder is Milton. Didn't I tell you the transformation was miraculous?"

John Paul did not find the prank the least bit amusing and he intended to say so . . . until he caught a glimpse of those bright green eyes and oddly familiar features. "Good God," he croaked in astonishment.

"The doubloon, John Paul," Brant prompted, holding out an eager hand. When the captain reluctantly fished into his pocket to retrieve the coin, Brant snatched it away from his disgruntled friend. "I will forget the wager since it was won under unusual circumstances . . . if you will grant me a favor."

John Paul's hazel eyes weighed heavily on the curvaceous beauty. There were many attractive ladies at the party, but Milton's delicate face and stunning auburn hair stood out in the crowd. He was eager to reacquaint himself with this daring nymph.

"What is it you wish of me?" he questioned absently, his gaze making another deliberate sweep of her voluptuous figure.

"The lady is the one I intend to wed," Brant told him flatly. "But she won't let me near her and the Frenchman has become her devoted bodyguard. After you renew your acquaintance with Catrina Hamilton, escort her to the terrace so I might have a private word with her."

"Catrina Hamilton?" John Paul's face whitewashed.

"Aye, Dunbar's lovely cousin," Brant hurriedly informed him and then ducked around the corner before Jean and Catrina caught sight of him.

"It seems I owe the lady an apology," John Paul mused aloud. "I will set the matter straight and comply with your request." Remembering their conversation in the tavern, John Paul broke into a knowing smile. "I am beginning to understand why you have been in such a foul temper this week. I would not be at all pleased to have this bewitching beauty in the Frenchman's hands."

"And I am a mite apprehensive about placing her in yours," Brant snorted, flashing the notorious philanderer a pointed stare.

"Ah, my friend, you know me well," he chuckled heartily. "If I do not bring the lady to you within fifteen minutes, it will be a signal that I have reconsidered. I may be calling upon my charms as an officer and a gentleman to gain this nymph's affection.

"*Et tu, Brute?*" Brant grumbled sarcastically. "Can I not count upon even one to return my prize to her rightful owner? There is a code among the privateers, John Paul. You ought to know the pledge by heart. After all, *you* wrote it."

When Brant spun away to exit from the foyer, John Paul frowned sourly. Aye, he had been adamant in proclaiming that a captain's prize was his to keep or dispose of as he saw fit. But that was before he laid eyes on the fetching captive who had been Brant's cabin boy. And during the time Brant had the disguised lass cornered in his cabin, what had transpired? John Paul could well imagine how he would react under such circumstances.

Sporting a rakish smile John Paul weaved his way through the crowded ballroom to confront the lady who had captured his undivided attention. "Jean, be kind enough to introduce me to your lovely companion?" he demanded, never taking his eyes off Catrina.

Grumbling at the interruption, Jean-Martin made the hasty introduction and found himself tactfully replaced by the infamous privateer. When John Paul whisked Catrina across the room, Jean aimed himself toward the study for a tall glass of brandy. But he vowed not to tarry long. John Paul had a way with women and he would *not* have his way with this one! Jean had spent the past week attempting to win Catrina's affection and he would not have it spoiled by another American privateer.

While Jean-Martin was sulking in his brandy, John Paul was assessing the auburn-haired beauty who was trapped in the circle of his arms. "I wish I were the one who had taken you aboard ship," he murmured. "I envy Captain Diamond."

Catrina stiffened, her lashes fluttering up to meet John Paul's sly smile. "You know who I am."

"Your green eyes gave you away, my dear," he chortled softly. "And now that I know your true identity I want to apologize for the mishap at Selkirk mansion. I had not intended to disturb any of the Hamiltons when I learned Dunbar was away. But my men demanded compensation and I felt obliged to give it."

"Yet you would have abducted my cousin and held him hostage." Catrina backed from his arms to cast him a disapproving frown. "You committed a crime of piracy and I cannot dismiss it."

An apologetic smile bordered his lips. "I felt I had just cause for the raids on the Isles," he defended quietly. "The earl is well known throughout Britain. Many of my friends are rotting in prison and I want them released. I thought Britain would make the trade if I took such a distinguished citizen into my custody. If you were in my boots, would you not feel a fierce need to aid your friends, to undo the many injustices of war?"

"I do not condone your methods, but I appreciate your concern for your comrades," Catrina admitted. "Yet the fact remains that you allowed your men to abscond with Lady Helen's jewels and silver like a common pirate."

"I truly lament the incident. Brant told me how gracious and courageous the lady was. I admire the way she conducted herself in the face of adversity. In fact, I sent a letter to Lady Hamilton the day we arrived in Brest. In the message I begged her forgiveness and promised to restore the family silver to her possession when war permits. To this day, the silver remains untouched."

A curious frown knitted Cat's brow. Could it be that this notorious privateer was also a gentleman? His admiration and respect for Lady Helen surprised Cat. Maybe there was a shred of decency among these privateers, she mused.

"I'm sure my cousins will appreciate your consideration," Catrina replied, breaking into a blinding smile.

John Paul, being a man of romantic nature, melted into sentimental mush. Catrina was breathtaking and her smile was as radiant as the summer sun. Gingerly, he wrapped his arm around the shapely sprite to propel her away from the crowd.

"Will you walk with me along the terrace, my dear? I should like to know how you have fared these past weeks aboard the American privateer. I hope you did not find the accommodations too displeasing. If we had known there was a lady in our midst we would have taken great measures to ensure you were comfortable."

"It was a most enlightening experience," Cat assured him, grinning despite herself. "In some ways, the abduction came as a blessing."

"How so?" John Paul frowned bemusedly. He had expected

168

the young lady to be hopping up and down with indignation after her misadventure.

"I found myself in dire straits and fled my . . ." Catrina's voice trailed off when a tall, lithe figure emerged from the shadows that clung to the terrace.

Catrina glared furiously at John Paul. She would have bet her right arm that he knew Brant was on the terrace. These American pirates were as thick as thieves, she thought resentfully. The only reason she had agreed to come to the ball was because Brant was not to be among the guests. Jean-Martin had assured her she would have no run-in with Captain Diamond. And yet, here he was, looking every bit the dashing rake who had turned her world wrong side out.

Catrina felt his golden eyes upon her, caressing her, deteriorating her stubborn defenses. The smile that bordered his lips warned Cat that Brant was fantasizing. He was looking through her velvet gown, seeing her as no other man had. Humiliation and embarrassment flamed her cheeks. She had made such a fool of herself that night on board the *Sea Lady* and John Paul had dragged her back to the very man she was trying to avoid.

"You disappoint me, Captain Jones," she snapped in annoyance. "After what you told me about the Selkirk incident, you restored my faith in your integrity. But now I have lost it again."

Throwing herself away from John Paul, Catrina stormed toward the terrace door and the security of the crowd. But, like a giant panther pouncing on his prey, Brant was upon her in less than a heartbeat.

"John Paul consented to do me a favor," Brant defended. His arm encircled Catrina's waist, holding her tightly to him. "You left me so abruptly last week that we had no time to finish our conversation. We will finish it here and now."

The feel of his hard body mashing into hers was unsettling. The musky fragrance of his cologne was clogging her senses. Catrina was vulnerable to this man, especially at this close

169

range. She was afraid of her weakness, afraid she would blurt out some confession she would later regret.

"Let me go," Cat railed, fighting Brant and the overwhelming sensations his touch evoked. "I said everything I intended to say."

"We have not settled this matter of marriage," Brant insisted. Lord, this close contact was playing havoc with his sanity. He yearned to engage himself in something more stimulating than a heated debate with this firebrand. But this was not the time nor the place. Brant would have sacrificed his fortune if he could snap his fingers and transport them to a secluded niche that was not swarming with unwanted guests.

Feeling a bit uncomfortable, John Paul wedged his way around the struggling couple to take his leave. "If you will excuse me, I will rejoin the festivities. I doubt I am needed here."

"And leave me with this contemptible pirate?" Catrina yelped in dismay.

"Good-bye, John Paul . . ." Brant's firm voice urged his friend toward the door.

Offering Catrina a helpless smile, John Paul made himself scarce as Brant suggested. Although he would have enjoyed lingering to watch the fireworks, he deemed it best to grant Brant privacy. Brant had been like a man stretched out on a torture rack the past week and he needed to resolve his differences with this temptress.

Once they were alone, Brant grabbed Catrina by both arms and held her away from him. The words he had rehearsed escaped him when the moonlight sprayed across her flawless face and tantalizing figure. The trim-fitting gown accented each luscious curve and swell and Brant was having one hell of a time keeping his mind on conversation.

"You look lovely this evening, Cat," he murmured appreciatively.

Catrina did a double take. She had anticipated some mocking comment about their last encounter. But instead he complimented her appearance. Who could understand this pirate? She certainly couldn't. Catrina could have sworn they were in the middle of a fiery argument.

Regathering her composure, Catrina thrust out a defiant chin. "Say what you have come to say and then let me go. My escort is probably concerned about my absence."

That remark soured Brant's disposition. "I'm sure that French werewolf has been licking his chops since you crawled aboard his ship," he snorted acrimoniously. "No doubt he has shown you far more than concern."

"He has shown more concern than you have this past week" came her blistering rejoinder.

"What the hell is that supposed to mean?"

"You didn't care enough to check on me after I jumped overboard."

"I came to fetch you back and you told me to go straight to hell," Brant reminded her, his voice rising testily.

The man was a maniac, Catrina decided. They had not seen each other for more than a week, except at a distance and she had not uttered one word to him. "How could I have said such a thing to you when you have not set foot on the French schooner?"

Brant stared at her for a puzzled moment before the dawn of understanding registered in his eyes. "I came aboard the ship to see you. Jean went below to convey the message and returned to say you had wished me a one-way trip to hell."

The Frenchman had purposely lied to her. Wasn't that just like a man, she thought cynically. Of course, she had no intention of seeing Brant, but that did not give Jean-Martin the right to respond to her messages without consulting her. Men, what a troublesome lot, Catrina muttered under her breath. Derrick had deceived her. Brant had used her. The Frenchman had lied to her. And John Paul had led her into a trap.

"I made no such remark then, but I am making it now!" Catrina spumed, her temper at a slow boil. 'You can go straight to hell, Brant Diamond. I retract my marriage proposal. It was

171

a foolish idea, one made without forethought. I sorely regret ever putting the thought to tongue."

"You said you loved me." A broad grin that displayed even white teeth stretched from ear to ear.

She should have known he would get around to throwing that reckless confession in her face. The only reason he had sought her out was to taunt and torment her. "I said I *might* be falling in love with you," she corrected curtly. "In retrospect I realized I had confused passion and affection. At the time, I was so distressed by what had happened that I tried to ease my guilt by imagining there was something between us besides a reckless moment of physical desire. And why would you need a wife? You have enough mistresses stashed about to appease two normal men. If you were not so clever and elusive you would have been entrapped in marriage long ago." Catrina inhaled a deep breath and plunged on. "I have no intention of solving my problem by hiding behind the name of a man who has not the slightest concern about my welfare."

"Would I be here if I didn't care?" Brant snorted caustically.

"Suppose *you* tell me, Pirate Captain," she sniffed just as sarcastically. "Why *are* you here? It was reported to me that you would not be in attendance. You say one thing and contradict yourself with your actions. I have no idea what motivates a madman!"

Brant's temper was being twisted and stretched out of proportion. This was not the way he had envisioned their meeting. His vision leaned more toward a romantic encounter in the moonlight, one in which he held Catrina's responsive body in his arms and compensated for the frustrating nights he had spent alone. He had not the slightest inclination to become involved in a shouting match, but he was in the middle of one, just the same. The more he learned about Cat, the more he realized she was not, and never would be, the shy, retiring type. She was a stubborn, outspoken, mischievous little termagant who was sent up from the fires of hell to torment him.

172

And just why was he here? Brant asked himself. Catrina didn't appear pleased to see him. Indeed, she never wanted to see him . . . ever. Why else would she have fled to Jean-Martin and booked passage to Scotland on the first northbound ship leaving port?

Before Brant could answer her question, Jean-Martin barged through the terrace doors to interrupt them. "What are you doing here, Diamond?" he grumbled angrily. The sight of Catrina being held hostage by the roguish privateer aggravated Jean. But worse than that was the apprehension that Brant had exposed Jean's lie. If he fell from Catrina's good graces, his chances of wooing her were nonexistent. "Let go of my lady, Diamond!"

"I am *not* your lady," Catrina spouted. "And you are not my champion. You are a scheming man and I want nothing to do with you."

She could guess what his future plans included. Jean-Martin had been catering to her all evening, shoving wineglasses in her hand each time hers went dry. That scoundrel! He was no better than Brant.

Brant grinned devilishly when Jean's face fell down around the collar of his jacket. "It seems the tide has turned. Why don't you run along and find another female companion? Lady Hamilton is no longer in need of your services."

"Nor of yours," Catrina insisted and then elbowed Brant in the midsection.

When Brant doubled over to catch his breath, Catrina dashed toward the terrace rail and sailed over the shrubbery. She had no particular destination in mind. But anywhere had to be better than where she was, she thought as she darted around the side of the chateau and broke into a run.

Before Brant could recover and give chase, Jean rammed him broadside, knocking him from his feet. When the Frenchman swung a leg over the rail to pursue the hot-tempered sprite, Brant charged like a mad bull. Jean yelped in pain when he found himself facedown in the shrubbery with

Brant's heavy body straddling his. While Jean struggled to untangle his limbs from those of the bush, Brant crouched, using the Frenchman as his springboard.

Brant sailed from the shrubbery without a scratch and bounded off in the direction Catrina had taken. By the time Jean wrestled his way free and staggered to his feet Brant had vanished into the darkness.

Grumbling disgustedly, Jean-Martin flicked the leaves from his garments and stalked around to the front of the chateau to find himself a stiff drink. Perhaps Brant Diamond deserved that little hellcat, Jean decided. After all, Jean had no luck coaxing that wary lass into his bed. Brant would receive his just reward *if* he ever caught up with that firebrand. She would probably tear out his heart and feed it to the sharks.

That is one woman I will return to you with my blessing, Jean-Martin silently mused as he chugged his brandy. *Diamond, you may well wish you had never laid eyes on that vixen. By doing so you could very well have outfoxed yourself.*

If Brant could have read the Frenchman's thoughts he would have heartily agreed. But at that moment, Brant had his hands full. When he spied Catrina leaping into a coach, he had raced across the lawn and lofted himself into midair. Clinging to the open window of the fleeing carriage, Brant pulled himself onto the step.

A pained grunt burst from his lips when Catrina discouraged his daring pursuit by pounding his fingers, forcing him to move them or lose them. Tying himself in a human knot, Brant wormed around until he could grasp the door latch. But Catrina held fast, refusing to grant him entrance.

Brant cursed under his breath and then flattened his body against the side of the coach when the driver careened around the corner. "*Arretez!*" Brant bellowed at the coachman.

The groom, realizing a well-dressed gentleman was dangling from the side of his coach, reared back with the reins. The carriage lurched backward, very nearly throwing Brant off balance.

Scowling, Brant grabbed hold of the door. With a forceful jerk, he yanked the handle from Catrina's hands. Before she could scramble out the adjacent door and leap to freedom, Brant sprawled on top of her, forcing her to the floor.

Catrina yelped indignantly when she found herself squashed flat. She couldn't move, much less breathe beneath Brant's solid weight.

"You and I are going to talk this out if I have to hold you down and make you listen," Brant barked at the back of Cat's head. "Blast it, woman, if you run from me one more time I will tie you to the mast of my ship and force you to hear me out."

"What is it you want from me?" Catrina muttered with her last bit of breath.

Finally, Brant eased onto the carriage seat and hauled Catrina up beside him. Keeping a tight grasp on her arm so she couldn't jump from the carriage, Brant leaned out the window to shout directions to the coachman. When his head swiveled around to peer at his furious companion, a dark frown clouded his features.

"You are a ward of war," Brant said in the most civil tone he could muster. "Because of our unusual situation I think 'tis best that we marry. And since I have several years of experience to my advantage I think 'tis best to handle the matter *my* way. You have been roaming willy-nilly about Brest for a week, keeping company with a man who is followed by a questionable reputation."

"As if yours were something to brag about," Catrina sniffed distastefully. Huffily, she resettled her soiled skirt about her legs and glared out the window, refusing to grant Brant the common courtesy of looking at him while they argued. "I am my own woman, Captain. I intend to handle my affairs as *I* see fit. I do not need a pirate telling me what to do. And I did not invite you to rescue me from Jean-Martin. If I ever need your assistance I will ask for it."

This stubborn female would drive him to an early grave, Brant thought sourly. She had his blood boiling like an

175

overheated tea kettle and his nerves were leaping like migrating frogs. He could name several women who would jump at the chance to take his name. But Catrina behaved as if she would rather be whipped than wed him.

"I am making your affairs my business," Brant countered, his voice carrying an unpleasant edge that caused Catrina to bristle like a disturbed cat. "After what happened on board my ship you could well be with child. Have you considered what you will tell your friends when you return home without a husband to await the birth of a baby?"

His sound logic took the wind out of her sails. Catrina had been too preoccupied with keeping Jean-Martin at a safe distance to consider complications. With wide eyes, Catrina peered up at Brant, wondering how she would talk her way out of such a predicament without lying through her teeth.

When Brant finally gained the impetuous imp's attention, he breathed a weary sigh. "As soon as John Paul returns from the ball, he will perform the marriage ceremony."

"Nay," Catrina objected. "I will not be forced . . ."

Brant wrapped his hand over her mouth, stifling her protest. "Dammit, woman, I am trying to do the honorable thing and . . . ouch!"

Catrina bit into his hand and then slapped it from her face. "You should stick to something you are familiar with, Pirate Captain," she smirked, "such as devious, daring, and un-ethical. I doubt you have an honorable bone in your body."

Brant was overwhelmed by the temptation to shake this infuriating minx until her teeth rattled. Damn, but she was making this difficult. "Only a fool would look a gift horse in the mouth," he sniped.

Catrina scoffed disgustedly. "You are not a gift horse, Brant Diamond. You are a horse's a—"

Brant's infuriated growl drowned out the last word and he glared holes in Catrina's gown. "I may not make the perfect husband, but I can provide you with a certain amount of protection."

"I have learned to protect myself," she reminded him flippantly. "And indeed you are correct. Perfect you are not!"

"And you are by far the most obstinate, ornery, mule-headed woman I have ever met!" Brant blared back at her. When the coach rolled to a halt, Brant bounded to the wharf with Catrina in tow. After ordering the groom to stay put Brant went in search of his first mate. "I want you to take the carriage to d'Orvilliers's chateau and tell John Paul to come to my schooner posthaste."

Thomas heard the command, but his appreciative gaze was glued to the flaming-haired enchantress who was chained in Brant's arms. For a long moment he simply stood there, marveling at the shapely beauty he had known as Milton.

"*Now* will be soon enough," Brant snorted. "You can reacquaint yourself with Milton at a later hour. In fact, you will be on hand to give her away in marriage."

"I am not wedding you," Catrina stomped her foot. Her green eyes blazed up like a forest fire. "I do not want you for a husband!" Her angry gaze swung to the first mate who began to snicker at her predicament. "Thomas, will you marry me? I will make no demands on you. I will pay you for the use of your name and . . ."

Brant clamped his hand over her mouth again, careful to avoid having his fingers bit in two. Confound it, this stubborn chit had probably proposed to every man in Brest!

"Be on your way, Thomas. There are several other matters to attend besides my wedding."

Catrina pried Brant's hand away to voice another plea. "Please, Thomas, marry me and save me from inevitable disaster!"

Thomas glanced back and forth between Brant's piercing glower and Catrina's beseeching expression. The glower won out. Nodding in compliance, Thomas made an about-face and strode toward the gangplank.

"Thomas and I have been together too long to have our friendship severed by a woman," Brant boasted, breaking into a triumphant grin. "Unfortunately for you, we are as thick as thieves."

Catrina muttered under her breath. She had found herself thinking that very thought about Brant and John Paul. Thomas was another loyal member of this pirate clan. "How aptly stated," she grumbled resentfully.

Deflated, Catrina allowed Brant to whisk her down the steps to his cabin. No matter what persuasive techniques he employed to convince her to agree to this disastrous wedding, she would counter them, Catrina promised herself. Being married to Brant would be heartbreaking. He would be flitting from port to port, sleeping with every wench who caught his eye while Cat spent the rest of her days trying to recover from her fascination with this cussed pirate.

What kind of future was that? And if she did find herself with child, what would she tell her son about his father? The questions would come and Catrina would be the one to suffer the torment, not Brant. There was no simple solution to their night of reckless passion, but Catrina was determined to make her way alone. It was the only way, she assured herself.

Chapter Eleven

When Brant had locked the door behind him, he stashed the key in his pocket. Catrina stared at him, knowing his waistcoat held the key to her freedom. She wondered how successful she would be if she bodily attacked Brant to retrieve the key. It would be a waste of energy, Catrina decided, sizing up her nemesis. She didn't have a snowball's chance in hell of winning against this potentially dangerous mass of brawn and muscle.

Deciding retreat was the only logical solution, Catrina's gaze swung around the cabin. Tilting a rebellious chin, she stalked over to the farthest corner and stood in it.

Brant's eyes followed her rigid march across the cabin and he grinned at the peevish frown that was plastered on her features. "You once fancied yourself in love with me," he reminded her. Brant moved steadily toward her. When he had Cat backed against the wall he reached out to curl his finger beneath her chin, bringing it down a notch. A charismatic smile bordered his lips. "Whatever the reason for the attraction between us, 'tis enough to make a beginning. I have found something in you that has hounded me this past week while we were apart."

He moved ever closer, his musky fragrance warping her senses, his tender touch burrowing holes in her wall of defense. Catrina cursed herself for being so vulnerable to this swashbuckling pirate, but her body was magnetically drawn to his.

"I missed that mischievous little imp who sabotaged my cabin and played her madcap pranks," he murmured, his breath caressing her cheek, his hard, lean body brushing suggestively against hers. "But more than that, I longed to hold you in my arms, to taste your sweet lips . . ."

His raven head hovered just above hers, his parted lips holding a promise of a brandy-laced kiss. "It was good between us, Cat. Do you remember . . ."

Cat remembered all too well. Her traitorous body arched toward his compelling strength. Maybe she was every kind of fool for caring for this dashing privateer, but telling herself that he meant nothing to her had served no useful purpose. His butterfly kiss and tender touch was stirring a craving that had never gone away. There was a fire smoldering between them, one that all her well-meaning lectures couldn't smother. She was hooked like a helpless schooner snagged by a pirate ship's grappling irons.

"You may kiss me into submission, but I am not changing my mind," Catrina whispered as her body surrendered to his magic spell. "It cannot last. You will go your way and I will . . ."

Brant had grown weary of arguing. His lips longed to engage themselves in something more arousing than debate. The feel of her firm breasts boring into his chest sent a tidal wave of sensations flooding over him. The scent of jasmine fogged his mind. Brant wondered if any price was too great to pay for easing the maddening hunger this fiery-haired hellion created in him.

Maybe he was a little mad to tie himself to the skirts of a hoyden who continually brewed trouble. But at the moment he didn't care if Thomas had him declared insane. He wanted Catrina in his arms, lying beside him, responding to his touch. Beneath her defensive shell lurked a wildly passionate woman. Brant yearned to rediscover every inch of her exquisite body, to bring this vixen to life, to relive the memory of that dreamlike night.

Like a moth flying into a flame, knowing he might be scorched beyond recognition, Brant took her lips and abandoned thought. It felt so right when he touched her. He had introduced her to the world of passion and there was so much more he wanted to teach her.

A groan of pleasure echoed in his chest as his wandering caresses mapped her shapely contours. He ached to rip away the confining gown, to brush his fingertips over her satiny flesh. His kiss, one that had begun as a gentle caress, became an impatient demand. His heart raced in anticipation. His body roused with a hunger that one kiss could never again appease.

His hand dipped beneath the ruffled lace to trace the swells of her breasts. His lips abandoned hers to blaze a path along the slope of her shoulder. Catrina trembled uncontrollably when his tongue flicked at the throbbing peak. Brant knew how to arouse a woman, to make her forget everything that had any resemblance to reality. She wanted to feel his hands and lips upon her skin, to rediscover the rapture she had never been able to forget.

When Brant touched her, she could not pretend indifference. He could crumble the controlled reserve she had constructed about herself. He could make her burn with mindless desire. If this was to be their last night together before she sailed to Scotland, then so be it. She would make it an encounter that would long be branded on Brant's mind. If he took another woman to his bed, he would remember this night, she promised herself. It would be *her* face peering up at him in the darkness. It would be her innocent caresses that sought to stir his passion. Her touch would be embroidered with an emotion that transcended physical desire.

Perhaps it was a spiteful wish to tie him to a memory, but pride demanded it. Catrina would be pining away at her estate, dreaming a dream that would never become reality. The least Brant could do was think of her from time to time, to smile and remember the ardent passion that had blazed between them.

Boldly, she trailed her hand along the band of his breeches and then sketched the ridge of his hip bone with her thumb. When her brazen caresses wandered lower, she felt Brant tense beneath her touch. It gave her a certain sense of power to know that she affected him in the same way he excited her.

Encouraged by his reaction, Catrina unbuttoned his shirt to brush her lips across the broad expanse of his chest. She wanted to return the pleasure he had given her. Like a playful kitten flexing her claws, Catrina raked her nails across the dark furring of hair, following its descent to the band of his breeches.

Brant sucked in his breath and moaned in sweet torment when her sensuous lips drifted over his. The kiss was like the petals of a rose unfolding against his mouth, but the nectar was twice as sweet. Brant closed his eyes and swayed with the hypnotic sensations that weaved a web of indescribable pleasure.

Aye, Cat was a witch, he assured himself. Her mystical powers were too potent to fight. She could make him want her in the wildest way. Catrina's kind of passion was like nothing he had ever experienced. Her innocent, innovative caresses set him ablaze and he knew he would never be satisfied until he had followed her on the most intimate of voyages across the sea of splendor.

"God, do you know how much I want you?" Brant breathed raggedly. "Take this tormenting pain and brew it into pleasure, sweet witch."

Catrina cackled, confirming his belief that she possessed superhuman powers. Playfully, she raked her nails up and down his belly. As her body moved provocatively against his, she murmured unintelligible incantations, casting her spell over him, entrancing him.

"'Tis your soul I seek, my handsome pirate. We witches can be satisfied with nothing less . . ."

Her teasing smile vanished when she saw the fire in his

golden eyes. She knew that look and she well remembered where it led. Memories of ecstasy came rushing back, engulfing her.

"'Tis a vain request, I know. But make love to me as if you truly loved me. Make it special, Brant. Make it a dream that will warm me each night while I am staring out my window at the stars, the same stars that will guide you across the sea."

His sinewy arm curled about her waist and he lifted her from the floor to bring her face to his. "It is you who make dreams collide with reality. I am under your spell, sorceress. Cast out your magical web and bring in the stars. Tonight they shall be ours . . ."

His mouth descended on hers with fierce urgency and Catrina responded in wild abandon. She could feel the rapid beat of his heart matching the frantic rhythm of hers. She could feel his hard, lean body shudder against her quivering flesh. There was no gentleness in his embrace, only a primitive savagery spurred by a week of longing. But it was not tenderness Catrina craved. It would not be enough when her senses had lain dormant for a week. The insatiable yearnings billowed like a thundercloud, feeding on the winds of mindless desire.

The abrupt rap at the door had Brant growling under his breath. Damn, with Cat in his arms he could barely remember his own name, much less recall that Thomas and John Paul were rushing back to the schooner. And blast it, *he* was the one who had sent for them!

Hastily, he buttoned his gaping shirt and rearranged the renegade curls that had tumbled loose from the neat bun that was piled on Catrina's head. Composing himself as best he could, Brant walked over to unlock the door. But nothing short of an ice-cold bath could ease his arousal. When the door swung open Brant positioned himself behind the desk until his disturbed condition became less obvious to his guests.

"You needn't have driven the team of horses into the ground rushing back," Brant grumbled grouchily.

"But you said . . ." Thomas halted his self-defense and then broke into a smile when he glimpsed Catrina's kiss-swollen lips. It was obvious Brant had begun his honeymoon before he spoke the vows. His grin broadened as he turned his attention back to his scowling captain. Brant's shirt had been haphazardly buttoned and the hem dangled from one side of his breeches. "It seems I ain't the only eager swain hereabout."

Brant flashed his first mate a silencing glare and then gestured for John Paul to take his place beside the desk. When Brant could rise without humiliating himself, he did so. "I trust you won't mind officiating at the ceremony, Captain Jones."

"I would be delighted," John Paul assured him with a twinkle in his eyes. He, too, had noticed that Brant did not look as starched and pressed as he had earlier that evening. "But then, I would have no complaint with standing in your stead either." When Brant leveled him a reproachful frown he chuckled good-naturedly. "You need not remind me that you found the lady first. I have many flaws but a bad memory is not among them."

Catrina blushed profusely, knowing there was not one among them who did not know what was going on before the interruption. What was there about Brant Diamond that brought out her ardent passions? She had known they would be receiving guests. And yet she had been unable to control her craving for this lusty pirate. Lord, have mercy on her soul! She had behaved like a harlot. Did she have not one ounce of self-dignity?

The impulse to flee overwhelmed her. Catrina stared at the open door and took flight, determined to disappear into the night before she found herself wed to a man who didn't love her. But Brant, who expected her to break and run, blocked the exit. With a firm grip on Catrina's forearm, Brant spun her around to face John Paul.

"Nay, I will not marry you!" Catrina declared, struggling to escape.

184

Brant's fingers bit into the tender flesh of her arm, cutting off the circulation. "Aye, you will. I have made my decision," he gritted out between clenched teeth.

"Cold feet?" Thomas snickered at the frustrated beauty.

Catrina sent him a pleading glance. "Thomas, try to talk some sense into him. I do not wish to . . ."

When Brant twisted her arm, Catrina yelped and then reacted instinctively. Her foot connected with his shin, forcing a pained grunt from his lips. Brant recovered his composure too quickly for Catrina to make another mad dash toward the door. Holding Cat in a viselike grip, he nodded for John Paul to begin the ceremony, even if the bride objected.

Biting back an amused grin, John Paul began to recite the ritual that would bind the squabbling couple in matrimony. The bride was given away, even though it took two men to contain her. The ring was rammed onto her clenched finger and a toast was made to the less than happy bride and her growling groom.

When the hasty ceremony was completed Brant sent Thomas to the French merchant ship to collect Catrina's belongings. Fearing the fuming bride would attempt another escape, Brant locked her in the cabin and escorted John Paul to the deck.

After inhaling a breath of fresh air, Brant sighed heavily. Although he was relieved to have the matter of marriage settled, he and Catrina were miles away from reaching a working agreement. She had dragged her feet during the wedding and Brant predicted his return to the cabin would be nothing short of a full-scale war.

That stubborn chit would make the prefect rebel, Brant decided. She had been waving the flag of independence in his face since the moment she resumed her identity. But Brant had finally gotten his way and he was not about to ship Catrina off with that French Casanova.

"Troubled thoughts?" John Paul prodded. "I had been under the impression that wedding ceremonies were to be

185

festive occasions. But neither the bride nor the groom seem overjoyed." His pensive gaze probed the depths of Brant's flashing amber eyes. "Why did you marry her, Brant? Granted, she is a most fetching beauty, but 'tis apparent she would have preferred to go her own way."

"Damned if I know." Brant let out the breath he had been holding since the ceremony began. "If I possessed an ounce of sense I would have weighed anchor without looking back. But I couldn't let go and it disturbs me that I have given more thought to that feisty witch than to the war efforts."

"'Tis not like you to become so distracted by a woman," John Paul chuckled. "But then you have yet to become involved with a lass as impetuous and high-spirited as Catrina." A wry grin tripped across his lips. "And 'tis not every day that a captain weds his cabin boy. That in itself should serve to warn a man that he has entangled himself in a most unique predicament."

"Thank you for your words of encouragement," Brant said with smooth sarcasm. "Now if you will kindly hand over your pistol, I should like to kill myself and end this torment."

"And miss seeing how this episode will unfold?" John Paul taunted. "Come now, my friend, you are an adventurer. Consider this one of the most challenging endeavors you have embarked upon."

Brant rolled his eyes heavenward. "I must have been mad."

John Paul chuckled heartily and slapped Brant on the back. "Aren't we all a little mad when it comes to women? They frustrate us, exasperate us, but they are compelling creatures. We cannot live with them, and yet we cannot survive without them." After offering a snappy salute, John Paul strutted away. "Forgive me for saying so, Captain Diamond, but you have met your match. I wish you luck. You, my friend, are going to need it."

He needed more than luck, Brant thought dismally. As he watched John Paul become one of the swaying shadows, Brant expelled a frustrated sigh. He would need an infantry to storm his cabin and bring Cat under control. What a wedding night this would be!

Preoccupied with that troubled thought, Brant stalked down the steps and eased open the door to his cabin. That, he quickly realized, was his first painful mistake. He should have waved a flag of truce. The moment he set foot in the room Catrina flung the pitcher at him. Before he could sidestep the oncoming weapon, it collided with his midsection, slopping water on him.

"Damn you!" Catrina hissed furiously. "I wanted no wedding. And if you think for one moment that I am not taking Jean-Martin's schooner to Scotland than you had better think again."

"You are not sailing with that shark!" Brant protested fiercely.

"'Tis no worse than being wed to one!" she shot back. "I will have this ridiculous marriage annulled the moment I set foot in Scotland."

Brant's temper exploded. When he slammed the door shut, the entire ship shuddered. Looking like black thunder, he stomped toward Catrina. "Over my dead body, woman," he growled.

"Don't tempt me." Catrina's eyes blazed up like torches. "I would do my country a great service if I disposed of you, not to mention the personal gratification I would derive from it. You may defy the king, but do not think to replace him in my eyes. I do not consider you my sovereign and I will never bow to your wishes, Pirate Diamond!"

His hand snaked out to yank her to him. Catrina's head snapped backward, spilling auburn curls about her fuming face. His rough abuse reminded her of another time and another man. Wildly she fought at him, lashing out in self-defense.

Brant froze when he detected that haunted look in her eyes. Dammit, sometimes Cat made him so angry he wanted to strangle her and this was one of those times. When he gave way to that impulse he could have kicked himself. He knew she was comparing him to Derrick Redmund. Not that he didn't deserve to be placed in the same category, he thought disgustedly. Brant had accomplished the feat Derrick attempted—marrying Cat against her will. How could she help but resent him, he asked himself. Brant had given her no choice. He had forced her into a marriage she didn't want.

Reluctantly, Brant let her go before she became hysterical. And thank goodness he did. Catrina was about to split apart at the seams. His brutish handling stirred a turmoil of emotions. The disturbing memories of the past rose like cream on fresh milk, tormenting her. She could almost see Derrick's doubled fist coming at her, feel the sting of the blow on her face. Before Catrina could compose herself, the tears boiled down her cheeks.

"I detest you for that," she sobbed, turning her back on him. "You may have forced me into marriage, but I will not spread myself beneath you to ease your animal lust."

"Cat, I'm sorry," Brant breathed deflatedly.

Tears floated in her green eyes. Catrina spun around to face him, her chin tilting to the belligerent angle Brant had seen once too often. "Saying you are sorry is not enough," she spewed.

"What would you have me do? Throw myself overboard to prove I am sincere?" he grumbled sourly.

"Aye," Cat spitefully agreed. "And I will toss you a rope . . . the one with the anchor attached to it."

Brant cast her a withering glance. "I said I was sorry. Can't you accept my apology without spouting vindictive sarcasm?"

"If you truly repent you will obey my wish to have this marriage dissolved," she told him flatly.

"I cannot do that."

Catrina puffed up indignantly. "Why not? You believe in liberty and justice for all and you are fighting for *your* freedom. Why are you so hellbent on refusing mine?"

How was he to respond to that, Brant asked himself. Catrina's point was well taken, but it changed nothing. They were man and wife and that was the way they would stay.

Cautiously, Brant walked up in front of her. His tanned finger rerouted the stream of tears that trickled down her cheek. "John Paul assured me that I had met my match in you, vixen. I believe he is right. I may be many things, none of which you approve, but I swear I will never treat you the way Derrick did." The faintest hint of a smile surfaced on his lips. "I have no wish to hurt you. I want you, Cat. I want to touch you, to make love to you. I cannot get you off my mind or out of my blood. There has been no other woman. I could not be satisfied with another when 'twas you I wanted."

His tender smile and softly spoken words shattered her defenses when nothing else could. She wanted to believe him. She wanted Brant to chase away the tormenting memories.

When those beguiling amber eyes rippled with gentleness Cat knew all was lost. Her defenses fell around her ankles and she melted when his mouth rolled over hers in the lightest breath of a touch.

Nimble fingers worked the stays of her gown, leaving it in a crumped heap at her feet. His hands worshiped her satiny flesh, spreading pleasure wherever they touched. And suddenly she was burning with a fever a blizzard couldn't cool. She wanted to feel his hair-roughened body pressing intimately to hers, to lose herself in a world of fiery splendor.

Brant was a wizard who could transform anger into blazing passion. Even when her mind warned her against surrendering, her heart cast caution to the wind. Catrina arched against him, loving the feel of his hands and lips upon her flesh. A sigh of pleasure escaped her when his roving caresses sought out each sensitive point and spun her nerves into tangled twine.

For this time in space they would be man and wife, rapt in a dream that only lovers shared. She would be a part of this that time could not erase. No matter how bleak her future, there would be one glorious memory to cherish. Brant would be hers and hers alone for one brief, shining moment.

Streams of sweet agony channeled through Brant's veins

when she returned his caresses. Her touch was achingly tender and the pleasure mounted until Brant feared he would die before he could satisfy this maddening craving. Not once, but over and over again, she traced the taut tendons of his back, melting them to mush. He was like a puppet dancing on a string, moving upon command, mindless to everything except the feel of her hands flooding over him.

"You make me want you in ways that frighten me," Brant breathed raggedly. His right hand slid about her waist and his left hand glided about her neck to tilt her exquisite face to his. She was like a goddess. Her skin was so soft, her features creamy and delicate. He could stare into those emerald eyes and view another horizon, one that stretched out forever. "I hunger and thirst for you. The first time we made love only fed this insane craving. It left me wanting more than before. It was like offering a starving man a morsel when he craved a feast. It seems there is no end to this need you instill in me. Do you understand, temptress? Are you too young and naive to comprehend what I'm trying to say?"

Catrina stared straight into those deep-set eyes and gave her head a negative shake, sending the fiery curls cascading about her in disarray. She was no longer an innocent maid. She understood what he was feeling because she felt it, too. Even after that first night of lovemaking, when passion ebbed, the sweet stirrings lingered. Their need for each other was like an oncoming tide rushing to shore and then receding into the sea. But it would come again and again, just as surely as night followed day. One kiss caused desire's waves to crest. One touch caused a flood of unrestrained passion.

Aye, it was a mad obsession, she realized. She knew the ecstasy that awaited her. She had seen the fires of passion burning in Brant's eyes and she had felt the flames when his hard, muscular body became a part of her. Catrina had become a slave to Diamond's desires, hypnotized by Diamond's fire.

The torment of this obsession came in knowing that what they shared would not last forever. They would go their separate ways, but the coil of longing would never go away, even when they were an ocean apart.

That depressing thought made Catrina clutch at him, eager to lose herself in another soul-shattering kiss. Vaguely, she remembered Brant setting her upon his bed, but his mouth never left hers for even an instant. His hands were upon her, caressing, massaging, arousing. He made her blood run like a cresting river spilling over its banks.

A tiny moan tripped from her lips when his kisses flitted across her collarbone to hover over each dusky peak. As his caresses mapped the shapely terrain of her body, Catrina closed her eyes and mind to all except the budding pleasure that blossomed somewhere deep inside her. It was as if he had suddenly sprouted another pair of hands. They were weaving across her flesh to sensitize her entire body. She could feel his softly spoken words of want and need vibrating against her skin.

Another unrestrained cry of pleasure bubbled forth when his skillful caresses roamed across her inner thighs. His mouth returned to hers, the firm outline of his lips fitting themselves to hers. Their breath mingled as one and Catrina lost her separate identity. When his chest rose and fell she felt the shuddering sensations as if they were her own. She inched closer, her feminine contours molding exactly to his.

Her innocent movement brought Brant's passions to a fervent pitch. He wanted her, wildly, desperately. No other thought infiltrated his mind. Breathlessly, he crouched above her, his arms bulging, his male body rigid with fierce passionate needs. As he guided her thighs apart, he glanced down at the shadowed face below his, seeing an expression of tormented pleasure, a reflection of his own churning emotions.

She wanted him. It was in her eyes. And he came to her to make her his possession. But Brant swore *he* was the one possessed. Powerful crosscurrents of emotions tore at him and he was caught up in a force so overwhelming that his body shuddered in response. He surged toward her, driven by uncontrollable passions, ones that refused to release him until the primal desires had run their windswept course.

Catrina reveled in the rapture that consumed her. She met his driving thrusts as the world careened about her. She was certain she had been drawn into the eye of passion's storm. Sensations piled one upon the other. The sweet, violent whirlwind made her cry out in indescribable pleasure.

For a moment time stood still. They were one living, breathing essence, drifting somewhere in a dimension of space that had no boundaries. It was a vast, dark world, comprehensible only for that brief but endless instant when they were of one body and soul. And then suddenly she was numb to all except the ineffable ecstasy that coursed through every nerve and muscle in her body. Lazily, Catrina drifted back to reality like a weightless feather gliding on a summer breeze.

When the spell of passion lifted, Brant pushed upon one elbow to peer down at the bewitching beauty. Absently, he combed his fingers through the lustrous tendrils that sprayed across his pillow. What was it about this incorrigible nymph that made it impossible for him to retreat when he knew it was the wisest course?

Catrina stretched like a kitten rousing from her nap and Brant chortled huskily. She reminded him of a playful cat in so many ways. She could purr in contentment or she could spring at him with her claws bared. Cat was so unpredictable that Brant never knew if he were to be slashed or caressed until the moment was upon him.

What an enigma this lovely creature was, he thought to himself. She could stoke the fires of his temper, inflame his passions, and amuse him with her mischievousness. His life had not been the same since Cat rearranged the furniture *and* his emotions.

Catrina stared up into Brant's chiseled face, wondering at his pensive silence. Was he beginning to regret this rash marriage? Was he asking himself what possessed him to wed a woman he didn't love? Or had their savage passions stirred a deeper emotion in his heart, one he was not prepared to deal with? Catrina prayed this night would prey heavily on his mind and she intended to ensure that it did!

A provocative smile traced her lips as she twisted to sit upon his belly. She shook out the tangled strands of auburn and giggled seductively. And then her quicksilver mood changed. Her nails raked across his ribs and she yielded to the temptation of tweaking the dark hair on his chest.

Brant flinched and caught her hand in his. "Spiteful witch, you set my soul afire and tied knots in the strings of my heart. Isn't it enough? Must you . . ." His voice trailed off as his all-consuming gaze swam over her shapely body.

The lantern light caressed her flawless features and outlined her feminine curves. Her hair shined with a brilliance that reminded Brant of a distant fire burning in the night. Thinking about their lovemaking aroused him, looking at her excited him. Sweet mercy, would he ever be able to rout this enchantress from his thoughts? Would he ever be free of her spell as long as he could remember the taste and feel of her?

Catrina sketched the sensuous curve of his mouth with a dainty finger. "You have taken your prizes, Pirate Captain, and so shall I have mine," she insisted in a soft, throaty voice that sent an infantry of goose pimples parading over his skin. Her investigating caress tracked the firm line of his jaw and trickled over his shoulder. "It seems a fair exchange. No deed shall be left unanswered. And in one surrender, so shall come another . . ."

Her lips came to his in such a tender kiss that Brant felt as if he would melt onto the cot and eventually drip to the floor in a puddle of liquid fire. Her seductive movements devastated him and he became a willing pawn. She touched him in playful, inventive ways that made him burn like a dry twig of kindling.

From a strength that had been completely drained, energy was created. Desire reared its head like a sleeping lion. She breathed fire into him and Brant came to life. Making love to this spellcasting witch was never the same. Each time they touched he was transported into a new, exciting world. It was as if it were the first time they had loved. And yet the memories of their passion served as stepping-stones that led them down erotic paths that were oddly familiar and sensuously unique.

Was he making any sense, Brant quizzed himself bewilderedly. Passion was passion, wasn't it? And if it were, why was he struck by the feeling that what *should* be the same was ever-changing? Before he could delve into that mind-boggling question, his brain broke down. Cat's imaginative seduction severed the last thread of logic. His body had but one purpose—to satisfy the tingling sensations that engulfed him.

He was flying into a fire that blazed hotter than a thousand suns. The heat was so intense that it was frying him alive. But Brant didn't care. He was prepared to sacrifice his last breath if he could enjoy the rapturous pleasures that awaited him.

Like a shooting star searing its way across the sky, consumed in its own fire, Brant found sweet release. His body spent, his mind numb, he surrendered to the contentment that hovered about him. With Catrina nestled in his arms he drifted into dreams. And the green-eyed angel was there beside him, spreading her wings in motionless flight . . .

Chapter Twelve

A contemplative frown plowed Brant's brow. He stood on the quarterdeck, grappling with emotions that were tearing him in two. He had roused the moment dawn crept into his cabin. For several minutes he had stared at the sleeping beauty beside him.

Catrina's wild mane sprayed about her, glistening with sunbeams. Her heart-shaped lips parted, as if awaiting his kiss. Long, slender arms protruded from the sheet that made such an enticing wrapper for a breathtaking package.

Mustering his willpower, Brant had eased from bed to don his breeches. Quietly, he tiptoed up the steps where he could think without being hampered by that incredibly lovely distraction.

Before the night that had become a dreamlike trance Brant had made plans for Cat's future. But the thought of stashing that alluring temptress in France, under John Paul's tender loving care, sounded less appealing by the second. Brant wasn't certain Cat would be the same when he returned to France . . . *if* he returned to France within the year. John Paul was prone to become helplessly enamored with young beauties. Although Brant would have entrusted John Paul with his life, he could not turn the notorious rake loose on his wife!

And Brant was not about to ship Cat back to Scotland with

Derrick Redmund running loose. After his defeat near Belfast and the threat of court-martial, Derrick might use Cat as his scapegoat . . . among other things. Even if Brant considered Cat safe in Scotland or France (which he most certainly didn't), how could he face the sea without visualizing her green eyes sparkling in those fathomless depths? How could he view a colorful sunset without seeing Cat's exquisite face framed with streams of fire? And worse, how the devil was he to navigate by the same stars they had touched when they blazed a path across the midnight sky?

It was utter madness to even contemplate taking Cat with him on another dangerous cruise. And yet he was pondering the notion. It was insane to become so distracted by a woman, especially when he was in the middle of a war, Brant lectured himself. But distracted he was, so much so that he could not even explain to himself why he was saying and doing the things he found himself doing. He was moonstruck! If he weren't careful that witch would turn him into a mindless toad. And then what use would he be to the patriot cause?

Brant inhaled a deep breath and then raked his fingers through his hair. Crazed or not, he could not live with any other decision than the one that kept Cat by his side. He could stash her in Charleston with Old Matthew while he ran the blockades along the eastern seaboard, delivering supplies to the army. Old Matthew would keep a watchful eye on Cat, he reassured himself. Matthew's apathetic attitude toward the war kept him safely from harm's way. He was a friend of Tory and Whig alike, the watchman who manned the beacon in the lighthouse and caused no one any trouble. Aye, what better place to stash that impetuous young beauty he had taken for his wife, he mused.

Determined in his purpose, Brant reversed direction and aimed himself toward his cabin. When he sprang his plans on Cat he knew he would confront an argument. Indeed that contrary creature thrived on them. But she was going to the colonies with him, even if he had to chain her to the mast for the duration of the cruise.

A lazy smile crept to Catrina's lips when she roused from sleep. She was still drifting in a tantalizing dream, reliving the pleasures of the previous night. As the foggy thoughts parted, her lashes fluttered up to meet the bright morning sun that splattered across the cabin. The spell was broken by the realization that Brant had left her side. Had it all been an erotic fantasy, she asked herself.

Before Cat could further ponder the matter, Brant burst into the room to tower over her. "I'm taking you to the colonies with me," Brant declared, deciding to cast diplomacy to the wind.

When the initial shock subsided, Cat was assaulted by two conflicting emotions. As much as she longed to remain by Brant's side, no matter where destiny led him, she was afraid to go. She had no fear of battle. But what disturbed her most was watching his physical fascination for her dwindle and die. If she returned to Scotland she could live on the memories and pray Brant would never forget the sweet ecstasy they shared. It would break her heart to watch him turn to another woman, knowing he had tired of his own wife and was eager to sleep in a variety of beds.

Cat wrapped the sheet about her and sat up on the edge of the bed. "Nay, I am not going with you," she protested. "I want to go home where I belong."

"Home to what, a possible beating at your ex-fiancé's hands? To an empty mansion that is haunted with painful memories?" he snorted gruffly.

Cat presented her back, refusing to meet his annoyed gaze. After scooping up Brant's discarded shirt, she hurriedly shrugged it on. "We made a bargain and I kept my part of it. We agreed to wed and then go our own ways. I have the protection I need in my new name and you have your freedom. I should think you would be pleased with the arrangement."

197

"Well, I'm not." Brant scowled.

Confound it, this minx was determined to have her way and he was constantly battling for superiority. Damnation, why had he gotten himself entangled with this obstinate wench who was as independent as hell? And why had she bothered to wrap herself in his shirt? She would look more appropriate in the rebel flag—considering how greatly she valued *her* independence.

"I told you I would not permit you to cruise off with that French cavalier. Jean-Martin has designs on you and I will not have my wife dallying with another man. 'Tis enough that you lived with that roué for a week!"

Two delicately arched brows shot straight up. Did Brant think she had allowed the Frenchman to have his way with her? Could Brant actually be jealous? Lord, wonders never ceased.

An impish grin tricked across her lips as she turned to survey the sour frown that puckered Brant's handsome features. "Double standards, is it, Captain?" she scoffed caustically. "You have frolicked with every willing wench from here to the colonies and you dare to complain that I might have fallen into another man's bed?"

"Did you?" Brant questioned point-blank. The thought had tormented him for the past week. Now that he had blundered onto the subject he wanted a blow-by-blow account of their tryst.

"And if I did? Would you deport me to Scotland?" Cat quizzed him.

Brant raked the shapely beauty who had him envying his own shirt. Lord, she looked a tempting sight. Her hair was in tangled disarray. The sunlight streamed through the thin fabric to outline every delicious curve and swell she possessed. He could not help but wonder if she had traipsed about Jean-Martin's cabin dressed in the same improper manner and he became aggravated all over again.

"If you did, I'll wring your lovely neck," Brant threatened.

"Dammit, Cat, why did you?"

"What difference does it make if I did or didn't?" she countered with a reckless shrug. "You and I were not man and wife at the time. I haven't asked you for the sordid details of every affair you have waltzed in and out of."

"That's different. I am a man," Brant defended, his voice rising steadily.

"'Tis not!" she shot back, lifting a rebellious chin.

Brant resisted the urge to shake the stuffing out of this feisty termagant. It still amazed him that he constantly tripped back and forth between anger and desire where Cat was concerned. Regathering his unraveled composure, Brant expelled an exasperated breath. She still had not told him what he wanted to know and they were edging closer to a heated debate. He did not come to argue, but to inform her of his plans.

"Very well, 'tis no different," he begrudgingly concurred for the sake of peace. "What happened between you and that French roué is in the past. But you are my wife now and I will not be shipping you off to Scotland with that lusty shark."

"But you would leave me in the hands of a notorious pirate?" Catrina sashayed toward him, raking his well-sculptured torso with blatant interest. There had been a time when she was embarrassed to stare so boldly. But no more. Brant's virile physique intrigued her and she had no qualms about feasting on the sight of him. "Do you know how difficult it will be for me to resist that provocative pirate?" Cat slid her arms over his bare shoulders and graced him with a blinding smile. "Last night should be proof that 'tis next to impossible." The warm draft of her breath feathered across his neck, causing a flock of goose flesh to flutter over his skin. "Aye, the Frenchman was handsome enough to turn a lady's head, but you . . ." Her lips melted like summer rain against his. "You stir me, Pirate Captain."

"Enough to go with me, even when you would prefer to return to Scotland?" he questioned huskily.

"Will you lead me into another dangerous adventure?" she

whispered against his full lips.

"Does the thought frighten you?" Brant inquired as he nibbled at the corner of her mouth.

"Nay," she chortled, her eyes sparkling with spirit. "I live for thrills."

A low rumble echoed in his chest. Brant didn't doubt that for a moment. This wild, free sprite was every bit as daring as he was. "I admire your spunk, madam." He leaned back, his hawkish gaze wandering over her voluptuous figure. "But 'tis not your spirit that interests me most."

And with that Brant settled down to the serious business of kissing her senseless. Catrina responded, longing for those few stolen moments of ecstasy that engulfed her the previous night.

My God, but he had become possessive, Brant chided himself. He was plagued with a nagging jealousy that gnawed at the pit of his belly. He wanted no other man to touch what belonged to him. He yearned to kiss away any lingering memory of the suave Frenchman.

"I couldn't," Cat confessed as Brant's exploring hands weaved titillating caresses over her body. She had not intended to admit that the Frenchman did not hold the lure of Diamond's fire. But the words slipped out before she could bite them back.

Brant frowned bemusedly. Had he been so preoccupied with kissing and caressing this enchanting nymph that he had missed part of the conversation? "You couldn't what?" he prompted.

Her fingers tunneled through the crisp wavy hair that capped his head and her eyes probed those fascinating depths of gold. "There has been no one else. I slept alone in Jean-Martin's bed." A hint of pain flashed across her flawless features. "I wish you could say the same. It hurts to know other women have shared your embrace . . . that I was not the first. What was special for me was only old habit with you—passion's tryst and nothing more."

Catrina backed from his arms and, with downcast eyes, she pivoted away. Hurriedly, she stepped into her gown and shook off Brant's shirt. Brant just stood there, not knowing exactly what to say in response. The silence between them was so thick he could have stirred it with a stick and he shifted uncomfortably from one foot to the other.

He was not about to blurt out some impulsive confession about how unique their lovemaking had been, that no other woman had affected him as devastatingly as Catrina had. To utter such words would be suicide. Had she baited him, he wondered cynically. Just what was it that this spitfire wanted from him? What did she expect him to say?

Mulling over those questions, Brant strode toward the door. He was well aware that Cat felt a physical attraction for him. She readily admitted to that. But he had dealt with too many scheming women to trust her underlying motives. Only a fool would discard his previous experiences with women and stumble blindly ahead.

Brant had not become cynical of women without just cause. Cat was a British subject, he reminded himself. That alone was enough to cause worry. Although he was irrationally attracted to this fiery-haired hoyden, he had to keep his wits about him if he were to survive. There was no telling what Cat might do. She was a woman of many complex moods and she was as fickle as the wind. If he didn't tread carefully she could undermine his cause and bring about his downfall.

"Well, Cap'n, are we gonna load the rest of the cargo or are you gonna stand there starin' at the sea as if it was the first time you laid eyes on it?" Thomas taunted as he ambled up behind Brant. "I can't imagine what is on yer mind that could distract you so."

Brant bent his gaze to the snickering first mate. "You might be surprised what thoughts are running through my head," he said absently.

A wry smile spread across Thomas's lips. "I doubt it. I should've taken Catrina up on her offer to marry her. *I* would have been the one daydreamin' and *you* would be envy green . . ."

Thomas's voice trailed off when Catrina emerged from the steps in a soft, flowing gown that accented her curvaceous figure. When she glanced at Thomas his knees threatened to buckle beneath him. She was like a breath of fresh air, so vibrant and lovely that Thomas could do nothing but gawk.

Brant frowned disconcertedly. An awestruck expression settled on the crusty sailor's face. Then Brant turned to assess the rest of his crew. All activity had come to a halt the moment this auburn-haired nymph floated onto the deck. Brant scowled under his breath. Was this how it was to be each time Cat prowled the deck? Brant knew what his men were thinking while they ogled her. Lust was printed on their faces in bold letters. Damn, he was destined to spend every waking hour hovering over Cat, wondering if these bold privateers were waiting the opportunity to seize her as their prize.

Those sour thoughts spoiled Brant's disposition. He barked the order for the men to resume their chores and then turned on Cat. She frowned at the granite-hard expression on Brant's face. He looked very put out with her and she could not fathom why. All she had done was emerge from their cabin. But somewhere in that route from cabin to deck she must have done something dreadfully wrong.

Clutching Cat by the arm, Brant propelled her back in the direction she had come. "Have you nothing less provocative to wear on board ship?" he muttered grouchily.

Cat bristled at his harsh tone. Was this the same gentle lover she had known in the darkness? What the devil was the matter with him? He looked as if he had run headlong into a rock wall and the stony features had been imprinted on his face. Her gaze flickered down her torso, seeing nothing revealing about the garment in question. Aye, the bodice was cut low, but not indecently so.

"Would you prefer I dragged out a feed sack and poured myself into it?" she queried, her lips dripping with sarcasm.

"As a matter of fact, I would," Brant grumbled. "I will not have my men gawking at you day and night. Dammit, sometimes I wish you *were* Milton. It would make my life a thousand times easier!"

Catrina drew herself up after being slapped with the insult. Brant seemed so distant and cruel that she wondered if she really knew him at all. It was as if the previous night never existed. Brant was no longer playful and attentive. He behaved as if he resented uttering the vows and regretted their night of splendor.

Her troubled musings evaporated when she noticed the open sails on the French merchant ship. Her gaze stretched to the schooner that was preparing to cruise from the bay. When her eyes locked with Jean-Martin's, Cat began to wonder if the Frenchman hadn't done her a favor by lying to her. At least it had kept her from the torment of squabbling with this ill-tempered American pirate. She could have been on her way to Dumfries, she reminded herself drearily.

A rueful smile rippled across her lips when Jean-Martin struck a sophisticated pose and tipped his hat to her. Aye, the Frenchman could not compare to Brant Diamond, but he was definitely easier on the heart, Cat realized.

Brant muttered in agitation when he noticed the exchange of glances between his newly wedded wife and his charismatic rival. He stormed back to Catrina, whisking her down the steps and out of sight. "Change your clothes and remain in the cabin," he ordered brusquely.

Catrina set her feet, refusing to budge from the spot. "I am not your slave and I will not remain below deck like a prisoner," she assured him hotly. "I see no reason why I should be punished just because of your black mood."

"You are the cause of my foul temper," Brant scowled. "I will not have you flaunting yourself in front of my men. They have work to do and you are distracting them."

"Flaunting?" Cat gasped incredulously. "I merely walked on deck!"

"You *strutted!*" Brant accused, giving her the evil eye.

Cat's hand cracked against his cheek, leaving a fiery red welt. "You are the only one hereabout who struts like a peacock," she spumed, her eyes snapping.

"A peacock, am I?" Brant crowed indignantly.

"Aye, Captain Peacock," Cat mocked scornfully and then spun on her heels to seek refuge in the cabin.

Before she could make her dramatic exit and slam the door in his face, Brant grabbed her by the arm and whirled her around to face his furious snarl. "Don't you dare come on deck unless you garb yourself in Milton's clothes. The only time I wish to see you in a dress is when we are alone in our cabin," he had the unmitigated gall to say.

Catrina could feel the heat of anger burning her cheeks. The nerve of that man! He was treating her like his private whore and ordering her about as if she were his personal servant. Was this the man she thought she loved? Why was he behaving like such a cantankerous scoundrel? At the moment he looked every bit the imposing renegade with his windblown hair lying in disarray, his chiseled features set in a menacing frown, his broad chest heaving with every irate breath he took.

Well, if this cussed pirate wished to fight with razor-sharp words or even pistols and daggers, Cat would accommodate him. Just because she was his wife didn't give him the right to order her about. She would dress in Milton's clothes, but the results would not be what this irascible varmint anticipated, she thought spitefully. If he could play the part of the growling, foul-tempered pirate, then, by damned, she would portray the pirate's wife!

"Very well, Captain, I will don Milton's clothes . . . provided you voice no further complaints. Indeed, if you cannot keep a civil tongue in your head, I would prefer you didn't speak to me at all."

"I will have no complaint if you follow my orders," he bit off.

When Brant wheeled and stomped toward the door, Cat

smiled devilishly. "I will hold you to your word, Captain Diamond. But I wonder if one can depend on a pirate's promise."

"I give you my word, madame," Brant declared, his tone cold and clipped. "As long as you do what I tell you, when I tell you, I will be satisfied."

Catrina raised a mocking brow and assessed the huffy captain from head to toe. "You wouldn't, perchance, be related to Attila the Hun, would you, Captain?" she sassed him. "I have heard it told that the vengeful conqueror tolerated no compromise."

Brant gnashed his teeth until he very nearly ground them smooth. A dozen sarcastic rejoinders flashed across his mind, each one meant to slice this firebrand in half. When he landed on one that suited him he flung it at her.

"Do keep provoking me, Joan of Arc, and I will light a fire under you that you will not soon forget . . ." Brant's voice trailed off when he saw the vulnerability in Catrina's eyes. Damn, he should have kept his mouth shut.

The hurt was suddenly replaced with spewing venom. Catrina did not need to be reminded that her parents had perished in a blaze. Nor did she appreciate the threat of having a torch set to her. "And do keep provoking *me*, Devil Diamond. You might learn that hell hath no fury like a vindictive wife!"

"I have no doubt of that," Brant grumbled as he stormed out the door. "It has been said that some marriages are made in heaven, but *hell* wouldn't claim this one!"

Pausing at the head of the steps, Brant attempted to compose himself. Damn, but he was in a snit. What was gnawing at him? Why was he behaving as if he were jealous of every sailor in the crew? And why was he being so confounded possessive? That was not like him at all. His philosophy had been share and share alike . . . until Cat drew him beneath her evil spell and transformed him into an irrational monster. Not only was he snarling at his crew but he had managed to destroy the

205

companionable serenity between Catrina and himself.

The honeymoon had ended as abruptly as it had begun. But what the hell was a man to do, he asked himself. Let his crew ogle his wife? Allow her to saunter across the deck and disrupt the workings of this ship? If he did not exert some control over Cat and his men the schooner would be mass chaos!

Brant expelled a frustrated sigh. It was foolish to cart Catrina off with him. But dammit, he couldn't leave her in France. There were too many hot-blooded swains in the country, not the least of which was John Paul. And there were too many love-starved sailors on the *Sea Lady* to give Cat the run of the ship when she was decked out in her finery. Brant was damned if he took Cat with him and he was damned if he left her behind.

Catrina was correct when she declared her middle name was trouble, Brant thought dismally. He had never been the same since he laid eyes on that green-eyed witch. Dammit, why couldn't he have taken their marriage in stride and sailed off without looking back? And why hadn't he bowed out when she begged Thomas to marry her?

Now he was plagued with a five-foot-two-inch headache with fiery auburn hair and emerald eyes. And she wasn't going to go away because Brant couldn't let her go. *Couldn't!* The word shot through his mind like a sharp arrow, deflating his spirits.

He was a doomed man. He couldn't bear to leave France without Cat and he couldn't trust his own crew. At least her beauty would be disguised beneath Milton's unflattering garb, he reassured himself. Perhaps when Cat appeared as a scrawny ragamuffin, his men would forget there was a shapely goddess lurking beneath those baggy clothes.

Encouraged by that thought, Brant climbed the steps to issue orders to load the remainder of the supplies bound for the colonies. When the men scampered off to do his bidding, Brant strode across the deck to keep his appointment with John Paul.

*　　　*　　　*

206

The welcoming smile slid off John Paul's face when he noticed that Brant was alone. A stern expression was chiseled in Brant's bronzed features and he approached like a brooding panther. The new groom did not appear to be enjoying wedded bliss, John Paul surmised.

"Trouble in paradise so soon?" John Paul teased.

Brant flounced into his chair and scooped up the mug of ale John Paul had ordered for him. "Aye, plenty of it," he muttered. "The first time Catrina sashayed across deck, my men began hallucinating."

"What did you expect," John Paul chuckled. "Your lady is a stunning beauty. You cannot hang your men for fantasizing about her. But they will recover and turn their minds to the business at hand when Catrina comes ashore and you sail for Charleston."

"I've decided to take Cat with me," Brant informed him flatly.

John Paul's face fell. "But I thought you were leaving her with me. I have made arrangements for her to stay with Comte d'Orvilliers until you return from Charleston. I assured you I would keep a close eye on her."

"That's what I'm afraid of," Brant snorted. "You might take better care of Cat than I intended."

John Paul was a dear friend, but the man was indiscriminate in his taste for women. The fact that Cat was married would not deter John Paul if he found himself irresistibly drawn to the high-spirited beauty.

John Paul broke into a rakish grin. "I must admit I have wondered how I would handle my lovely ward."

"Forgive me for being so frank," Brant began, discarding tact. "But I fear it would be like sending the fox to guard the goose. I think it would put less strain on our friendship if I took Catrina to Charleston and deposited her on Old Matthew's doorstep."

John Paul swirled his ale around in his mug, his hazel eyes twinkling with amusement. "Do you suppose Old Matthew has long forgotten his craving for beautiful women? I fear you will also be testing him greatly if you thrust such a bewitching imp in his lap . . ."

His gaze strayed to the buxom waitress who was eyeing Brant from across the tavern. Brant glanced up to survey the wench who had accommodated him several times while he was in Brest. Her wide smile assured him that he had a standing invitation. When she sauntered closer Brant was stung by a riptide of emotions. He longed to prove to himself that Cat had no special hold on his heart. And yet, he remembered the haunted look on her face when she murmured that it hurt to know she had not been the only woman in his arms.

"I have missed you, monsieur," the maid cooed as she traced the sensuous curve of Brant's mouth. "Perhaps you could come upstairs and we could . . ."

Brant removed her lingering hand, cursing himself for making comparisons. The chit was attractive but she did not arouse him the way Cat did. "I don't think my new wife would approve," he heard himself say to his own amazement.

Shock and disappointment seeped into the girl's features. When she dejectedly turned away, John Paul very nearly fell through his chair. He had been ashore with Brant Diamond dozens of times, but never once had Brant rejected the opportunity to appease his lusts.

"By God, it *must* be love," John Paul choked over his ale.

Brant scowled at the remark. "I would be a fool to fall in love with Cat. She fought like the devil to keep from marrying me and she is a dyed-in-the-wool Loyalist."

"But she must care for you," John Paul insisted. "She seemed eager enough last night . . . before Thomas and I interrupted you."

"*Seemed.*" Brant pounced on John Paul's choice of words. "You forget, my friend, that she is the same minx who charaded as my cabin boy. She can also *seem* docile and agreeable when it meets her mood. But Cat is a free spirit. She had every intention of sailing off to Scotland after the wedding."

John Paul eased back in his seat to pensively sip his drink. Aye, the lady was feisty and independent. She was not the usual maid, but then Diamond was no ordinary man. He had tested his abilities to the very limits and he was relentless in the face of adversity. The match between these two headstrong individuals would be a constant struggle for dominance. Judging by what John Paul had seen of Catrina, Brant would have no easy time controlling her. Aye, she was breathtaking with those wide, intelligent eyes and lustrous auburn hair. But she was also a spitfire. She had kept Brant running in circles the previous week. If the past was any indication of what Brant could anticipate in the future, he would be a weary man.

"Aye, she is a willful woman," John Paul concurred, melting into a wry smile. "But ah, what an intriguing challenge for a man."

"You speak as if I don't face enough challenges by attempting to slip my cargo through the British blockade," Brant snorted. "That should be challenge enough. But to make matters worse I have opened my sails to a windstorm named Cat Diamond."

"I will be most anxious to hear how you fare in both your endeavors," John Paul chuckled. When Brant unfolded himself from the chair, John Paul smiled affectionately. "God speed, Captain. I pray your mission will aid the suffering colonies. And if you decide your lovely wife is more than a handful, bring her to me before you sail. I will attempt to keep my intentions honorable."

Brant clasped John Paul's hand, giving it a fond squeeze. "And I hope you will be back at sea posthaste. The patriots will greatly suffer while you are stranded in France."

"With Benjamin Franklin and Comte d'Orvilliers's assistance I pray I will not be long on land." John Paul heaved a frustrated sigh. "It goes against my grain to be sitting out the war."

Brant knew John Paul was itching for a command. It would not be easy for this overzealous adventurer to sit back while his comrades were sailing the high seas, engaging in battle. "Until we meet again . . .'' Brant scooped up his mug to toast John Paul and then guzzled the remainder of his drink. "God willing, it will be soon, my friend."

Wondering how he would fare if he were in John Paul's position, Brant strode out the door. He had never been satisfied to remain in one port for extended periods of time. Would the day come when he yearned to settle down? The image of a saucy auburn-haired enchantress skipped across his mind. Would he and Cat ever enjoy a true marriage? Would the time come when he would consider giving up the sea and remaining ashore with his wife and family? Would Cat spurn the idea of living somewhere besides Scotland . . . with a man she considered a renegade pirate?

Tossing aside those pensive contemplations, Brant aimed himself toward the wharf. There was no time for idle whims. The war had disrupted everyone's life. He had a mission to complete and daydreaming would only distract him. For the next few weeks he would devote himself to his duties. He had allowed Catrina to preoccupy him far too long as it was. If he continued on this same reckless course he might find himself tossed into the hull of a British prison ship. There were too many people depending on him, he reminded himself. The rebel army needed the supplies and weapons he had confiscated from British ships.

Aye, he had taken an oath to the cause, Brant told himself. And he was going to keep it, even if he had married a Tory in a moment of madness!

All Brant's well-meaning lectures on dedication to the war effort escaped him the moment he hopped onto the gangplank. The scene before him caused him to come unglued. Catrina had garbed herself in men's clothes, as he had demanded. But the ornery wench had altered the garments to fit her curvaceous

210

body like an extra set of skin! There was nothing beneath the thin gauze shirt to disguise the full swell of her breasts. The top two buttons lay open in a most provocative manner. Her black breeches hugged her shapely thighs and hips and polished black boots extended to just beneath her knees. A bright yellow sash hugged her trim waist and the dingy cap had been replaced by a black beret. Across her shoulder lay an auburn braid, intermingling with colorful ribbons. If the sight of this voluptuous vixen were not enough to send a man's blood pressure skyrocketing, the devilish sparkle in her green eyes was. Her face was beaming with so much undaunted spirit that the effect was staggering. Sailors were hovering about her like devoted servants bowing to their queen. *Queen*, hell! Brant thought, giving the matter second consideration. It was more like a she-devil coming to count the number of captured souls she had collected in Hades.

What infuriated Brant most was that his men were actually smiling while they went about their menial chores. They carried double loads from the dock and scurried to catch up with Cat, who was also transporting cargo from the wharf to the deck.

This was not at all what Brant anticipated when he returned to the *Sea Lady*. There was not a glum face in the crowd. Men who rarely smiled were beaming in pleasure when Cat graced them with a glance. And Brant knew damned well what sordid thoughts were dancing in each man's head while he watched the graceful sway of Catrina's hips.

Catrina had purposely defied him. She had made herself so blasted desirable in what *should* have been baggy rags that she had captivated the crew. She was a witch, Brant scowled to himself. She had subtly taken command of the schooner, using her feminine wiles. Not a soul on the *Sea Lady* noticed the captain had returned, nor did anyone care. They were so busy drooling over that curvaceous temptress that they didn't see Brant standing there smoldering, threatening to reduce himself to a pile of ashes.

Although Brant was outraged, he could not utter a word. He had made a vow that if Catrina were to dress in Milton's clothes he would have no complaint. She had done that, he reminded himself furiously. And he knew better than to rant and rave about the alterations she had made to the garments, especially in front of this independent crew of privateers. Brant would wind up looking the irrational culprit and Cat would become the martyr.

Besides, what was there to complain about, he asked himself resentfully. The sailors were doing their chores. But confound it, they didn't have to enjoy it! Catrina had miraculously transformed mundane tasks into pleasure.

Keeping a tight rein on his boiling temper, Brant hopped to the deck and cut his way through the merry laughter on board the enchanted schooner. Without a word to anyone, he marched toward his cabin, wearing a frown that was sour enough to curdle fresh milk.

"What's bothering the captain?" Jacob Powers questioned Thomas.

Grinning wryly, Thomas set his crate beside the hatch. "How do you suppose you would feel if this surly crew was fawnin' over yer wife, Jacob?"

The young man's gaze swung back to Catrina, who had overextended herself to grasp another armload of supplies. His keen eyes sketched her shapely backside and then he broke into a broad grin. "She is a beauty, isn't she? I get a warm, giddy feeling just looking at her. Work doesn't seem so tedious when a man's got such pretty scenery to stare at."

"I don't think the cap'n takes kindly to us starin' at his wife," Thomas speculated. He paused to watch Brant buzz down the steps, looking madder than a disturbed hornet. "But he can't say nothin' about it when the crew is performin' their duties as he ordered. He just ain't none too happy that we're enjoyin' our work."

Jacob wiped the perspiration from his brow and massaged his aching neck. "I have no complaints about working with

Catrina, but I feel as if I've carted a ton of cargo to the deck."

Thomas surveyed the young man's pale features. Jacob did look a bit hollow about the eyes. Lovesick, Thomas diagnosed. Young Jacob had only been sailing with the privateers for a few months and he had probably never found himself in the company of such a fetching beauty. The strain of both was beginning to show on his face.

"The captain is a lucky man," Jacob sighed appreciatively, captivated by Cat's sylphlike movements. "I would gladly exchange places with him."

Thomas burst into snickers. "I'm sure *that* is what haunts Cap'n Diamond the most. And this is one time he don't want to share. He's tied himself to a lady with an overabundance of spirit and *she's* tyin' him in knots."

The captain's biggest problem was himself, Thomas decided. He was magnetically attracted to this feisty sprite, even when he didn't want to be. Brant had never been this protective of his women in the past. But he wanted no other man near Catrina. He hadn't trusted her with Jean-Martin or John Paul and he didn't trust his crew when Cat was underfoot.

Brant was like a man stretched on a torture rack. No matter which way he turned he was tormented by emotions he refused to deal with. Brant tried to remain cool and aloof, but it was damned near impossible.

Aye, the captain had it bad, Thomas assured himself. But Brant was fighting like hell to deny his feelings for this emerald-eyed tigress . . .

"Thomas? Could you lend me a hand?" Catrina questioned breathlessly. The armload of cargo had weighted her down and she feared she was about to drop the heavy crate on her toes.

Like a puppy eager to please his mistress, Thomas bounded off to assist the lady. He pulled up short when it suddenly occurred to him that he was suffering from the same affliction that Brant had contracted. The only difference was Thomas was a tender-hearted softy. He was not as stubborn as Brant Diamond. Thomas would be the first to admit he was plagued

213

by that certain kind of heart trouble that left an unfulfilled ache in a man's chest. But Brant had yet to come to terms with his affliction and his obsession with this Scottish pixie who had turned his well-organized world upside down.

"You ain't got so much as a prayer, Cap'n," Thomas mused half aloud.

Catrina frowned at Thomas's inaudible utterances. "What did you say?"

A sheepish grin pursed Thomas's lips. "Nothin', lass. I was just talkin' to myself," he dismissed with a shrug.

Catrina glanced back over her shoulder to stare at the dark stairwell where Brant had disappeared. When he returned to the ship a few minutes earlier, he looked like a volcano searching out an appropriate place to explode. But to Cat's dismay Brant had said not one word about her attire. It had disturbed him. She could tell by the stormy expression that flashed through those golden eyes. And if looks could kill she would have been pushing up daisies, Cat speculated.

Let him steam and fume, she thought spitefully. He deserved to work himself into a frustrated frenzy after the way he had spoken to her. But she wasn't backing down to that sourpuss, she vowed determinedly. She would fight fire with fire. Before she was through with that dragon pirate he would be smoldering in his scales!

Chapter Thirteen

Brant peered through the spyglass, surveying the heavily loaded vessel that cruised two leagues ahead of them. The ship fit the description of the British schooner Jean-Martin had mentioned to him. A smile spread across Brant's lips for the first time in four days.

"Are you thinkin' of takin' her?" Thomas inquired, staring thoughtfully at the *H.M.S. Countess.*

"When have I turned my back on opportunity?" Brant queried. "Turgot informed me there would be a letter-of-marque ship bound for Quebec, loaded with a cargo of clothing and supplies for the British Army in Canada. Unless I miss my guess we have caught up with her."

"Sounds temptin'," Thomas agreed. "It would be good to see you turnin' some of yer bottled-up frustrations on the enemy for a change."

Brant leveled Thomas a silencing frown, well aware of what the first mate insinuated. Turning away, he shouted orders to the crew to raise the moonraker, increasing their speed. His gaze swung to the main deck, ensuring Catrina was still in the cabin. And that was where she would stay until he had seized his prize, he told himself. They had gone one round when she poked her head on deck at Belfast. She knew better than to try that stunt again.

As the *Sea Lady* surged forward, taking advantage of the stout wind, Brant smiled in satisfaction. This worthy prize would ease his dark mood—the one that had plagued him for the past few days. He yearned to engage in battle, to put that lovely sea witch out of his mind, if only for a few hours.

The beat of a drum reverberated across the deck and through the hatchways, alerting the crew to the presence of a British ship. "All hands to quarters!" Brant barked through the speaking trumpet.

The deck suddenly appeared to be a bustling anthill. Sailors scampered to the twelve-pound cannons on the main deck and to the eighteen-pounders that waited on the lower deck. In the galley, the cook doused the fire and manned his station. Sand was cast across the deck to give a strong grip for the crew's feet.

When the *Sea Lady* turned about, dipping into the trough of an oncoming wave, Brant grasped the wheel. His face was set in grim determination. They were but one hundred feet away from the *Countess* and Brant hungered to take the prize. With practiced ease, he veered around the enemy's stern and then spun about, scraping her broadside. As he sailed away from the damaged ship, the cannons roared from the *Countess*, in attempt to discourage the swifter ship, but Captain Diamond was relentless in his pursuit.

Brant shouted the order to load the guns and then maneuvered the *Sea Lady* into position to rain cannon fire on the enemy. His purpose was not to sink the schooner but to cripple her for boarding.

The commotion brought Catrina to the deck. Her eyes swung across the sandy planks to see the crew hustling to their stations. Most of the seamen had stripped to the waist. Narrow bands of cloth were tied around their heads to muffle the deafening roar of the cannons and to keep the perspiration from dripping in their eyes.

Catrina had witnessed this scene once before, but it was the first time she had seen the seamen doff their shirts to prepare for the heat of battle. The conflict in Belfast had occurred in

216

the spring and the men had no need to shed a few layers of clothes. Catrina's gaze lifted to the helm to see the bare-chested pirate captain manning the wheel. His bronzed skin gleamed in the bright light. His corded muscles rippled as he tensed to steer the *Sea Lady* into position for attack. A cutlass dangled on his hip and a dagger was tucked in his belt.

Brant again reminded her of the swashbuckling pirate she had met at Selkirk. He looked every bit the part of a vengeful devil with his raven hair glistening with a blue-black tinge in the light. He presented an imposing picture at the helm—the strong, invincible pirate who thrived on life-threatening challenges.

Although Brant expected Catrina to remain below in the event of battle, she scurried across the deck to assist Thomas. The first mate directed Jacob Powers to unplug the barrel of the gun and then frowned when he noticed Catrina.

"You shouldn't be here, girl," he said gruffly.

"Aye, I should be in Scotland," she sniffed caustically as she handed Jacob the sponger.

"The cap'n ain't gonna like this one bit," Thomas grumbled.

"Nothing has been to his liking for almost a week," she argued. "It seems impossible to anger an already furious man."

Deciding it a waste of time to debate the issue with the stubborn chit, Thomas turned his attention to his chore. He watched on as Jacob stuffed the loader and sponger into the cannon muzzle and then Thomas swiftly retrieved the plug.

"Load!" Thomas ordered. "The cap'n is almost in position."

The sailors handed the bulky cartridges to the assistant loaders at each cannon. The ammunition was passed through the line as if it were a hot potato. When the cartridge was in place, Thomas snatched the sponger from Catrina's hand and pushed the ammunition home.

"Run out!" Brant shouted through the speaking trumpet.

Upon command the crew grabbed the cannons and shoved them forward until the front edge of the guns were steadied against the side of the ship.

"Prime!" Brant yelled to his competent crew.

Once the crew had poured the gunpowder into the pan to set a fuse, Brant waited until the *Sea Lady* was in her most advantageous position. A swell of water lifted the schooner and then took her down. When the *Countess* was caught in the oncoming wave, Brant gave the order to fire. The *Countess* could not counter the cannons while she was rolling with the swell. The eighteen-pounders scored two direct hits on the stern and one on the bow, scattering debris across the enemy's deck. Before the British could steady their cannons, reload, and fire, the rebel guns rang in the breeze. The *Countess*'s mainsails buckled from the punishing blows, crippling her maneuvering ability.

Brant wheeled hard, putting the helm a-weather. The two ships scraped broadside, setting bow to stern and stern to bow. Brant snatched up his blunderbuss and cutlass and directed his men to toss out the grappling irons. Within minutes the *Countess* was snared by sturdy lines and several planks joined the warring ships. Like a hive of bees swooping down to claim nectar, the pirates swarmed the *Countess* to engage in hand-to-hand combat.

Catrina aimed herself toward the stairwell when a British sailor bounded off the plank, his pistol pointed at her chest. When the man realized he had very nearly made this shapely nymph a victim of battle he dropped the barrel of the flintlock and stared incredulously at her.

For the life of her, Catrina didn't know why she was running from the British. My God, she was one of them, she reminded herself. If she explained her captivity, the sailor would have no choice but to protect her, she reasoned. She could slip aboard the *Countess* and Brant would never know she had fled until he had sailed off with his stolen cargo.

"I'm Scottish," Catrina hastily informed the British officer. "I am Captain Diamond's captive, transported on the high seas against my will."

The officer glanced about him, seeing his fellow countrymen

struggling in hand-to-hand combat. His gaze circled back to Catrina and then he clutched her arm, lifting her to the plank. "Seek cover below deck," he ordered hurriedly. "Your only chance is to hide during the battle."

Tossing the officer a grateful smile, Cat dashed across the gangplank and scampered below deck on the *Countess*. She was free of Brant Diamond at last, she reassured herself. Now she could return to the Isles with the crippled schooner and make her way to Scotland.

A part of her applauded the scheme for freedom. But yet, there was an odd gnawing sensation in the pit of her stomach. It was for the best, Catrina lectured herself. Brant didn't want her with him. He would have preferred her to be the fumbling Milton. Hadn't he said that the day they set sail for Brest? And hadn't he ignored her for four days? Aye, the pirate captain would be relieved to have his unwanted wife off his ship and out of his life forever.

Brant lunged at the enemy captain, taking the man to the deck. But the officer was no match for Brant's superior strength. He was subdued before he could even begin to fight. Brant snatched the captain's pistol away and bolted to his feet. Displaying a menacing smile, Brant nudged the commander with his own flintlock.

"Call off your sea dogs, my friend, or you and your ship will be blown to bits. Surrender is your only hope of survival."

The British captain ground his teeth. He had not anticipated attack, much less defeat. But now he faced certain death if he did not comply with Pirate Diamond's wishes. Begrudgingly, he staggered to his feet and raised the speaking trumpet to his bleeding lips.

After the signal was given for the British soldiers to throw down their weapons, Brant motioned for the captives to retreat to the deck of the *Countess*. When the weapons were confiscated the British were further mortified by bearing the cargo onto the deck of the victory ship.

Thomas wiped the perspiration from his brow and sighed wearily. He trudged up to Brant who was overseeing the transfer of supplies to the *Sea Lady*. "This should keep the patriots in food and clothin' for a long time to come," he chuckled in satisfaction. "Won't the British Army be surprised when the *Countess* doesn't show up in the Canadian port?"

Brant nodded affirmatively. "Aye, it will be a crushing blow for the British to attack rebels who are garbed in the boots and uniforms that were meant for Loyalists."

A thoughtful frown creased Thomas's brow. Where the devil was Catrina? She had been standing beside him until they boarded the *Countess*. His concerned gaze scanned the deck of the privateer, praying the daring nymph had not been brought low by her own countrymen.

Brant had watched the first mate crane his neck to search the decks of the *Sea Lady* as if he had misplaced some valuable possession. Curiosity got the best of Brant. He could not imagine what Thomas sought. "Thomas? What is the matter with you?"

Indecision tore at Thomas's thoughts. If Brant knew Cat had been prowling the deck during the siege, he would be furious. And if the feisty beauty had attempted another escape, Brant would be . . . Thomas frowned. Just how would Brant feel about it, Thomas asked himself.

A sly smile flitted across Thomas's stubbled features. Twice Brant had been granted the chance to put the green-eyed vixen from his life. And twice he had failed to let her go. The captain had been behaving as if he resented his decision to release his new wife. How would he react if he faced the third opportunity to send Cat home with the crippled *Countess*?

"Well?" Brant queried impatiently. "What are you looking for, man?"

Thomas eased against the rail and met Brant's inquisitive stare. "I ain't sure about this, but I think yer lady may be tucked somewhere on the *Countess*, waitin' for us to sail off . . . without her.''

"What!" Brant hooted. "That is impossible. I ordered her to remain below deck when we were engaged in battle. She wouldn't . . ." His voice trailed off, knowing Catrina had defied him once in this situation. That rebellious chit would not bat an eye at doing it again.

"She was standin' beside me and Jacob when I loaded the cannon," Thomas said nonchalantly. "And now she ain't here." His bushy brow lifted to a mocking angle as he regarded the huffy captain. "Yer a bettin' man, Diamond. Where would you wager the lady is at this moment?"

Brant exploded like a misfiring cannon. Cursing a blue streak he glared at the enemy ship. "I'll bet the entire cargo that minx sneaked on board," he ground out. "Damn that she-cat. I wish the hell she would stay put!"

When Brant drew himself up to storm away, Thomas grasped his arm to detain him. "This is yer last chance, Cap'n," he reminded Brant. "If you don't love her, let her go. The girl will reach the Isles with her countrymen. If yer ready to set her free and put her out of yer life, the timin' is perfect . . ."

Brant froze in his tracks, debating his choices . . . for all of five seconds. Roughly, he jerked his arm free and stalked across the deck of the *Countess*, the muscles of his jaw twitching in annoyance. He pushed bodies out of his way in his haste to find his runaway wife and give her a good piece of his mind.

Amusement bubbled in Thomas's throat as he watched Brant take the steps two at a time to retrieve Catrina. "The third time is the charm," he snickered to himself. "If you can't let her go now, Cap'n, you'll never be free of that witch-angel's spell."

Blazing amber eyes seared every nook and cranny on the *Countess*. Damn that troublesome wench, Brant growled under

221

his breath. When he got his hands on that woman he was going to nail her boots to the planks of the *Sea Lady*. Muttering, Brant shoved open the door to one of the cabins. His keen gaze searched the shadows. Seeing no sign of Catrina, his shoulders slumped and he expelled an exasperated sigh. Where could she be? He had torn the damned ship upside down.

His golden eyes recircled the room in final inspection and he frowned when he spied the faintest movement under the cot. The quilt that dangled over the foot of the bed rustled slightly. It was either Cat or a pesky mouse huddling in the corner, Brant decided.

Clamping his hands on either side of the bed, Brant lifted the object and heaved it against the opposite wall. With pantherlike grace he swooped down to jerk Catrina to her feet.

"Damn you," he roared, his voice booming down the companionway. "I spend half my life chasing after you."

Catrina drew herself up in front of him and raised a defiant chin. "Damn you, Brant Diamond," she hurled at him. "Why did you come after me? Just go away and let me alone. Go blow up another ship and feast on your prizes. You don't want me with you. For God's sake, let me go."

Confound that woman. How dare she offer him an out. If he wanted out *he* would make his own exit without her permission. Just who the hell did she think she was anyway? he thought huffily. Women had chased after him for years. They had practically run him down in carriages in an effort to snare him because he was an elusive vagabond. And now this wildcat was showing him the door!

Angrily, Brant slammed her up against the wall, making Catrina wince in pain. There was menace in his eyes, a harsh frown stamped on his features. It was Derrick Redmund all over again and Catrina swore at any moment Brant was going to double his fist and strike her.

The hunted look in her eyes caught him off guard. Although his rigid body pinned her to the wall, his grasp lessened, allowing the blood to recirculate through her arms. "I have

222

decided to take you to Charleston and that is exactly what I am going to do.''

''Why? So you can keep me as your personal harlot? So you can use me when the hunger for battle is replaced with animal lust?'' Cat laughed bitterly. ''If that is your excuse, it holds no logic. You have avoided me for almost a week. What is it you want from me?'' She heaved a tired sigh, relinquishing her attempt to escape from Brant's chaining arms. ''If 'tis responsibility you feel because I might carry your child, you are worrying for naught. We have not created a child.''

''How can you be certain?'' Brant asked frankly.

Catrina flung him a withering glance. Brant Diamond had probably forgotten more about women than she had even learned about womanhood. ''You should know the answer to that,'' she insisted tartly. ''You are a connoisseur of females. And since I am assured that I will not bear your child, I want to go home. At least there I would have my dignity. With you I have nothing at all.''

''You have this . . .''

His mouth came down on hers, ravishing her lips, attempting to exert his superior power over her. It was a rough, forceful kiss, unlike anything Cat had ever experienced in Brant's embrace. It frightened her to know he was capable of hurting, intent on punishing her in what once had been their only display of tenderness.

But suddenly the flame of passion replaced the blazing fire of his temper. He was again fighting the battle of self-conquest and losing miserably. Brant jerked back as if he had been burned and scowled at his lack of willpower. She always emerged the victor in these amorous battles. He touched her and he lost a part of himself. His heart began to rule and his mind did but obey. Dammit, he had promised himself that he would keep his distance from this cunning minx, that he would deny his craving until it no longer tormented him. He fully intended to keep Cat as his wife, but he had no intention of falling prey to the tender emotions she aroused in him. With

223

Cat he was vulnerable and he could not subject himself to weakness.

Gripping her forearm, Brant propelled Catrina through the companionway like a naughty child being dragged home for a spanking. Catrina was fuming, but none of her struggles slowed Brant's long, swift strides. She found herself hauled across the deck, on display for the captives and crew. How she detested that humiliation! Damn that devil!

Without another word, Brant shoved her across the gangplank and hustled her to his cabin. When he slammed and locked the door, Catrina stomped her foot and muttered a long list of disrespectful epithets to Brant's name. She was certain she had married Satan himself. The man was a devil from the top of his raven-black head to the tip of his polished black boots. Aye, he was handsome, she thought bitterly. But that was only a disguise. Beneath that attractive face and muscular physique was the soul of a devil, hellbent on revenge. For what, Catrina didn't know. What had she done to invite the devil's wrath?

"Damn that pirate!" Catrina hissed venomously. He didn't truly care about her, but he considered her his prize, his possession. Now that he had her, he treated her with nothing short of contempt. "He hates me but he won't let me go," she cried to the walls. "The man is crazed! He is punishing both of us for our reckless mistake."

Catrina flounced onto her cot, wondering if she would ever understand that infuriating man. Time and time again he contradicted himself with his deeds and words. His bruising kiss had not spoken of affection, only brute force. His touch was hard and his golden eyes were like stones when he glowered at her.

Aye, he was the devil who wanted her heart to wear as a trinket around his neck, Catrina decided. Well, she was not to become a sacrifice for a one-sided love. Brant Diamond had had his fiendish way, but she would never succumb to that pirate. He could take her body when it met his whim but he could

224

never touch her soul.

They were fighting a private war and she would *not* admit
defeat. Never! She could be as sour and unpleasant as Devil
Diamond, she told herself confidently. Each time he looked at
her he would see the reflection of his own irascible mood.
What he needed was a taste of his own temperament. Let him
stuff that in his cheroot and smoke it, Cat thought vindictively.
And she hoped he choked!

"Don't utter a word," Brant snarled, hurling his first mate a
threatening glare.

Thomas watched Brant stomp up the steps to take command
of his ship. His perceptive eyes ran the full length of the
smoldering captain. "I don't think I need to say a word,"
Thomas replied glibly. "Yer actions said it all."

Brant grunted in response and clutched the wheel, anxious
to put more distance between the *Sea Lady* and the disabled
Countess. What was he going to do with that woman? Brant
interrogated himself. He felt as if he were being pulled in ten
different directions at once.

In attempt to gather his composure, Brant inhaled a deep
breath and let it out slowly. He would have to find some sort of
substitute for his fascination with that fiery-haired minx.
There had to be a way to rout Cat from his mind. He had to
learn to watch his men fawn over her without reducing himself
to a cloud of steam. He had to look at Cat without losing himself in a tormenting fantasy. And he could, Brant told himself
proudly. All he had to do was set his mind to it. Within a few
more days, he would forget his attraction, forget the feel of her
supple body beneath his caresses. Only then could he devote
himself to his duties as he had done before Cat came into his
life.

Determined in that thought, Brant ordered his crew to roll
out full sails and repair the damages they had sustained during
battle. They had taken valuable prizes, Brant reminded

himself. He should be celebrating his victory. And by damned he would! He was an adventurer who thrived on conquest. It was enough to bolster his spirits. It had to be. If it weren't he would have to face the depressing truth that Cat mattered more to him than the life he had known. But she would not always be with him, Brant told himself. And when she was gone, what would he have if not the sea and its dangerous challenges?

His astute gaze sketched the choppy waters that rolled on forever. Aye, he was a part of this vast ocean, just as he was a part of the rebel cause. Women always had a place in his life, but they held no permanent position and he gave them little consideration . . . until . . .

Don't think about that woman, Brant preached to himself. Catrina was no different from any other female. And if he lost sight of that fact he was in a hell of a lot of trouble! Cat Diamond wore his ring, but Brant had the gnawing fear that it would wind up in his nose if he didn't resist that witch's charms. The last thing he wanted was to be led around by that impetuous bundle of spirits. Theirs was a battle of wills and the loser would sacrifice his or her pride to the victor. Damn, Brant never could tolerate defeat. It went against his grain.

He would just have to forget Cat. Once he could view her in the proper perspective he could set her ashore with Old Matthew and go about his business.

The faintest hint of a smile touched Brant's lips as he stared at the horizon. Aye, he was man enough to withstand the temptation. He had to. Cat didn't truly want him as her husband. If she had, she wouldn't have scurried to the *Countess*. She would always abandon him when opportunity presented itself and he was a fool if he ever allowed himself to forget that.

Chapter Fourteen

A condescending frown plowed Thomas's brow while he watched Brant guzzle his third glass of brandy in less than ten minutes. Thomas was sure Brant would drink himself insane if he didn't slow his pace.

"Don't you think you've had enough?" Thomas snorted, snatching the bottle from Brant's grasp.

Brant's glacial glare froze on his features. "Not nearly enough to forget what I am trying not to remember," he blurted out. "Give me the damned bottle."

"You've been drinkin' like a lush for nearly a week," Thomas preached, holding the whiskey just out of Brant's reach. "Don't you think yer overreactin' to marriage? Yer supposed to be celebratin' blissful wedlock. Hell's bells, man, you act like yer grievin' at yer own funeral."

"Spare me your attempt at wit," Brant muttered. "I came to join you in a drink, not sit through a lecture on temperance and a sermon on whether or not there is life after marriage."

"Yer the one who forced Cat to marry you," Thomas reminded the scowling captain. "And you dragged her back when you could have sent her home on the *Countess*."

"And I will probably long live to regret those mistakes," he shot back, eyeing the brandy bottle like an insecure child coveting his cuddly stuffed doll from afar.

"Not at the rate you've been pourin' down the liquor lately," Thomas scoffed. "I've heard of a man drownin' his troubles, but you've gone overboard." Exhaling an agitated breath, Thomas stared straight into Brant's bloodshot eyes. "I used to consider you a good-natured sort, but you've been behavin' as if you've had a steady diet of sour grapes."

"Damn, I could have sworn I requested no sermon," Brant growled sarcastically.

"Just who the hell are you tryin' to punish? Cat or yourself?" Thomas questioned point-blank. "If I was Cat I would load my pistol and put you out of yer misery and hers as well."

"Curb your tongue, old man," Brant blared. "I will hear no more!"

"You will hear an earful if you think to park yerself in my cabin and deplete my stock of liquor," Thomas snapped back, and then tucked the bottle behind his chair.

Brant vaulted to his feet, momentarily weaving to sustain his balance. "Be stingy with your liquor, if you wish," he slurred out as he navigated his way across the cabin. "I'll fetch a bottle from the storeroom. Had I known I was to endure your preaching I would have made the hull my first and final destination."

"You could have retired to yer own cabin," Thomas hurled at his captain. "There's enough liquor stored in yer quarters to sink this ship."

"Ah, but I can't, you see." Brant paused to lean negligently on the door handle. "My cabin is haunted by a green-eyed witch. And wherever she goest, I goest in the opposite direction."

Thomas rolled his eyes toward the ceiling. "Aye, that is a fact," he sniffed, his tone crackling with sarcasm. "The bonds of matrimony joined you and yer lady together so you could pull in opposite directions. You would be a happy man again if you would accept yer fate and admit that woman has gotten beneath yer skin."

228

"Aye, like a festering splinter," Brant snorted derisively. "Were there a doctor on board, I would beg to have her removed."

"You are the one who wanted her with you, the one who twisted her arm to force her to repeat the vows. And yer lucky you got her," Thomas shot back, his bushy brows narrowing in meaningful frown. "Cat ain't no splinter, she's a gem."

"Your poetic nonsense is nauseating."

"It ain't me, it's the liquor," Thomas parried caustically.

"The next thing I know you'll be saying that precious gem should dispose of her *Diamond* in the rough!" he grumbled as he yanked open the door.

"*Rough,* sour, cantankerous, moody . . ."

The door banged shut in the middle of Thomas's lengthy description of Brant's unpleasant disposition of late. Thomas muttered at the dramatic change in the captain's personality. Brant's laughter no longer rang across the decks. The man frowned constantly and he behaved as if he carried a personal vendetta against the world and everyone in it.

Each time Brant spied Catrina engaged in harmless conversation with one of the crew, he scowled. Poor Jacob Powers was one of the worst offenders. The young man had a terminal case of love and it was printed on his face. When Cat walked within ten feet of Jacob he lit up like a lantern burning on a long wick. And when Jacob beamed with the pleasure of Cat's company, Brant Diamond turned pitch black.

Since Brant had purposely ignored his fetching wife, Jacob had devoted his spare time to entertaining Catrina. He had taught her the card games the crew played after their chores were completed. He ambled beside Catrina each time she appeared on deck. And if Jacob dared to brush an unruly strand of auburn hair away from Catrina's face, Brant growled with barely contained fury.

Brant was like a lion trying to defend his cub from within a confining cage, Thomas thought to himself. Although Brant could not tolerate any man staring overly long at his enchanting wife, he remained possessive from a distance. Brant contained his frustrated emotions throughout the day, but he relieved his irritation in a bottle of brandy each night.

Thomas wasn't certain how much longer Brant could endure the punishment he was inflicting upon himself. The captain's affection for his wife had driven him to drink—to excess. And Brant was becoming more irascible with each passing day. The mulish man refused to admit he was vulnerable to Catrina's charms. He tried to treat her as if she were just another member of the crew, but she wasn't and she never would be.

Any man in his right mind should know that when he played with a cat he was bound to get scratched. And Brant Diamond had been raked raw, inside and out. He was paving his private road to hell with broken liquor bottles in attempt to compensate for his anguish. But the captain wasn't going to forget he was attracted to that feisty she-cat, no matter how much whiskey he consumed. Brant would wake in the morning, his head throbbing, and ask himself why he subjected his body to such abuse. The answer would ring in his head like a pounding drum calling sailors to their battle stations. And that inner voice would echo in Brant's ears, Cat Diamond has taken hold of your heart. She sank in her claws and you will never be free.

When Brant confronted the frustrating truth, the vicious cycle would begin again. He would watch his men hover about the auburn-haired beauty by day and then he would try to forget it mattered to him by numbing his tormented mind and body with brandy by night. Aye, the captain was vulnerable all right, Thomas concluded. Brant had an unconquerable weakness for . . .

An explosive crash from below his cabin floor caused Thomas to fly out of his chair. Hurriedly, he scampered down the companionway to seek out the source of the sound, certain he knew who and what had caused it. Another loud racket drifted up the stairs and Thomas charged into the hull. When he reached the last step he heard Brant growling in inaudible curses, saw him flinging crates about as if he were searching for some special object. Most likely his *sanity,* Thomas decided. Brant had misplaced it occasionally these past few months and Cat was the cause and cure of this periodic lunacy. It was indeed true that love caused a person to behave like a madman and often a fool.

"Cap'n, the hour is late. I think you should go to bed," Thomas suggested. His tone was overly calm, as if he were attempting to talk a misbehaving child out of a tantrum.

Brant wheeled around, staggering to maintain an upright position. His golden eyes, tinted with red, flared in response to being patronized by his first mate. His mouth twisted in a disdainful scowl. Impulsively, he clutched a pair of boots, ones that were meant for a rebel soldier's feet *if* they reached the colonies with their soles intact.

Ducking away from the flying boots, Thomas glared at Brant. The captain had surged from the sulking phase of drunkenness into his violent stage, Thomas diagnosed. His conclusion was founded on the fact that he came dangerously close to being slapped in the face with a boot heel.

"Mind your own business, Thomas," Brant snarled. "I'll go to bed when it pleases me and not a moment before." He slumped down onto a nearby crate and clutched the bottle he had found while rummaging through the cargo. "Now get out! I have come here to ponder my problems and you are disturbing me. Why don't you go nest on your whiskey bottles, miser." Brant chuckled at his own cleverness. "Perhaps you can hatch out a *brood* of brandy."

Gritting his teeth, Thomas stalked forward. But he was immediately dissuaded when Brant scooped another leather boot and threateningly cocked his arm.

"Take one more step toward me, my friend, and I swear I will give you the boot. But you won't be wearing it. And if you think to spout off another lecture you may find the footwear stuck in your craw." Brant warned Thomas away as he broke into a devilish grin. "Begone, old man, before you provoke me further . . . or have you acquired a taste for leather?"

When Thomas retreated, Brant sank back on the corner of the crate. He winced uncomfortably when the sharp edge jabbed him in the back. Grumbling, he shoved the crate aside, sending it crashing to the floor, atop the disheveled heap of cargo.

Thomas swore Brant would ransack the storeroom in his fit of temper, given another hour. Muttering over the fact that Brant had developed the personality of a captive rhinoceros, Thomas pivoted around and stomped up the steps. There was no reasoning with Brant when he was in one of these moods. And this was not the first, Thomas reminded himself dismally. Thrice the past week Brant had taken his frustration out on some niche in the bowels of the ship. And thrice Thomas had attempted to steer his captain to his quarters, but without success.

When Thomas heard another crate bang against the floor he broke stride. It was time to fetch Catrina and insist that she put her pet rhinoceros to bed before he completely demolished the ship. Where Thomas failed to cow the brooding beast, Cat could soothe the savage beast.

She wouldn't be pleased that she was called upon to perform the duty, Thomas reckoned. But blast it, without her assistance it would require the services of a dozen sailors and none of them would volunteer for a task above and beyond the call of duty. The entire crew steered clear of Brant Diamond these days. And for good reason. The captain's bite was as bad as his bark!

Staring at her reflection in the mirror, Catrina combed out her hair, letting it form a fiery waterfall over her shoulders. The only sound to reach her ears was her own heavy-hearted sigh. Each night when she retired to her room she was met with deafening silence. Brant had dragged her back to the ship, but he had nothing to do with her. He never entered his cabin until she had crawled onto her cot. And more than once she had been summoned from a sound sleep to corral the cantankerous captain and tuck him into his bed. She had thought he had kept her with him as something to play with in between battles, but he never came near her. The tension between them was like a lightning bolt sizzling from one black cloud to another. How much longer could they . . .

The impatient rap shook the hinges on the door and jolted Catrina from her silent reverie. She laid the brush aside and padded barefoot across the room. The grim expression on Thomas's face made her frown warily.

"Now what is wrong?" she questioned.

"Plenty," Thomas muttered. "The cap'n is havin' one of his drunken fits again. He's down in one of the storage rooms, drinkin' himself into a witless stupor. Would you fetch him to bed before he tears the place to pieces?"

"Why, of course," Cat sniffed caustically. "Why not stuff my hand in a starving tiger's mouth? Why not take a swim in shark-infested waters? It would prove no less dangerous."

"Please, Cat," Thomas implored. "I know you don't like to wrestle with the big brute. But no one else will dare go near him when he's on a binge. But he won't hurt you."

Cat wasn't so certain. The last time she hauled Brant to bed he very nearly squashed her flat when he tripped over his clumsy feet.

Brant spent every day sulking about the ship, avoiding her as if she had contracted leprosy, glaring at everyone who crossed his path. And when he drank he threw things. How could Thomas presume she would be safe from the ferocious dragon when he had been breathing fire for a week? If she angered the red-eyed monster she would be standing directly in harm's way.

"I think you overestimate my powers," Catrina insisted. "I could get myself killed carting him to bed and I am not at all sure he is worth it." When Thomas addressed her with that pitifully helpless expression of his and pleaded again, Cat begrudgingly relented. "Oh, very well. I will try to chain Dragon Diamond to his bed . . . if he will allow me near him. But if I do not return in half an hour with the beast in tow, please read some kind words over me before plunging my battered body into Davy Jones's locker."

Thomas chuckled quietly. "Lass, if I thought yer life was in danger, I wouldn't make the request. The cap'n may snarl and growl at you, but he thinks too much of you to strike you. I, on the other hand, could be knocked out cold by his doubled fist."

"He doesn't think of me at all," Catrina mumbled deflatedly.

"Ah, but he does," Thomas assured her. "I don't think you understand a man like Brant Diamond. He's been footloose for years and he don't know how to handle what he feels. The more he cares about you, the harder he struggles to be free. When a man like Brant Diamond begins to feel constricted he thrashes in earnest. The tighter he's tied, the harder he fights. And you, Cat, have him tied in a Gordian knot."

Although Catrina was certain Thomas had misread the reasons for Brant's idiotic behavior, she agreed to attempt to lead the runaway tiger to his cage. "I will do what I can."

"Thank you." Thomas breathed in relief. He stepped back to allow Catrina to pass. "I'll be hidin' in the companionway. If you meet with difficulty, call out to me."

"If I meet with trouble I will be tempted to club the growling monster over the head and leave him where he lies," Cat grumbled spitefully. "I have grown weary of his drunken shenanigans."

As Catrina made her way into the bowels of the ship, she heard the crash of one crate after another. She paused to gulp down her apprehension and then continued, even though her shadow was cowardly backing up the steps. Brant had been on a terror once or twice, but never had she heard so much commotion while he was roaring drunk.

When she reached the storeroom and peered around the corner of the door she broke into an amused grin. Brant looked a sight. His raven hair was in disarray, as if he had been twisting it in circles while standing on his head. His shirt had come undone during his exhausting battle with the crates and beads of perspiration were dancing on his skin. Even in the dim lantern light Cat could see the streaks of red slashing through the whites of his eyes. There was a harsh scowl hanging on the downturned corners of his mouth.

Aye, this was one of his worst tantrums, she thought as she surveyed the shambles. His hatred for her had driven him to destruction. The neatly stacked crates were now upended and scattered about as if a cyclone had breezed through the storeroom.

Mustering her courage, Cat pushed open the portal and strode inside to appraise the fire-breathing dragon at closer range. "You have certainly made a mess of things tonight," she declared, her eyes making a second inventory of the wrecked niche. "I hope you aren't thinking of making a habit of this. I doubt the *Sea Lady* can endure too many of your destructive outbursts. You have already gutted her innards."

Brant's glazed gaze flickered across Cat's bare knees and ascended to survey his shirt, one that looked considerably more seductive on her than it did on him. She had made it a habit of traipsing about in his shirts, no doubt to annoy him. But the effect of her appearance did more to arouse than to agitate him.

A silly smile tugged at his lips as he propped himself against his crate throne. "Ah, 'tis my lovely wife." His eyes burned through the thin fabric, seeking to unveil what lay so temptingly beneath it. "Have you no clothes of your own, madame? Must you invade my wardrobe?" he slurred out.

Cat was trying very hard not to laugh at the ridiculous smirk that was dripping off his lips. "I saw no reason not to employ your shirt as my robe," she countered. "After you drink yourself to death, all your worldly possessions will belong to me. Why wait until the last moment to make use of this apparel?"

"Aye, why wait?" Brant snorted, but not as effectively as he would have liked. He was too inebriated to sound foreboding when he matched wits with this crafty feline. Sluggishly, he clambered to his feet, steadying himself against the wall. "Would you like my breeches as well? It seems we have been battling over them since we first met." Fumbling fingers hovered about the band of his breeches, threatening to disrobe, then and there.

There was a time when Brant stripped from his clothes and Cat fell to pieces. But no more. She had seen this powerfully built rogue in every state of undress. Although the sight of his rippling muscles and sinewed columns of bronzed flesh aroused her, she had learned to maintain some semblance of composure.

"That won't be necessary," Cat calmly insisted, flinging up a hand to forestall him. "I couldn't keep them up."

"A pity, that," Brant growled suggestively, his roving eyes mapping her well-sculptured contours.

Catrina did a double take. The man had made no attempt to seduce her since their wedding night and now he was leering at her. It must be the liquor, she decided.

Casting aside her wandering thoughts, Cat slowly reached out to retrieve the half-empty bottle that dangled between Brant's thumb and fingers. "Why don't you let me hold the whiskey for you, Captain. If you aren't careful, you might spill it. I know you would hate to waste even a drop." There was the slightest hint of taunt in her voice, but Brant was too far into his cups to detect it. Before he could react, Cat snatched the bottle from his hand. "Come along, my dear husband. 'Tis time to put you to bed."

Brant allowed himself to be led through the demolished storeroom. "Will you be in it?" he questioned, his glassy gaze focused on the back hem of her shirt.

Her lashes swept up as she turned back. Her eyes locked with liquid pools of amber and her heart fluttered in her chest like a caged bird seeking its way to freedom. Was that desire she saw glistening there? Surely not, Cat told herself. Brant was only

236

mocking her. If he truly hungered for her, he would have come to her long before now.

"Nay, Captain, I make it a point never to sleep with dragons. I have a fear of being scorched beyond recognition," she informed him breezily.

"A man's wife should always join him in bed," Brant muttered.

"You could have invited me," she parried.

"You need no invitation. You are my wife!" His slurred voice rose until he was very nearly yelling in her face.

"Aye, your wife, not your whore," she burst out. "But even a wife has more sense than to disturb a sleeping lion. You are constantly looking for something to chew on, but it will not be me!"

Brant remained silent until they trudged up the steps and veered around the corner toward his cabin. Without giving notice, he changed direction and started up the flight of steps to the main deck, much to Cat's chagrin. Lord, she would never get Brant into bed! And as drunk as he was, he would most likely trip and fall overboard. And yet, that might sober him up, she thought spitefully.

As he weaved on his merry way Cat threw up her arms in a gesture of futility and muttered in exasperation. When she turned to give chase, a movement in the companionway caught her attention. She glanced sideways to see Thomas tucked in the shadows.

"You almost had him cornered," Thomas encouraged as he watched Brant disappear from the stairwell.

"*Almost* is never good enough when a dragon is on the loose," she grumbled. "Do you, perchance, have a shield and a whip with you?" Cat thrust the whiskey bottle at the first mate. "It may be the only way to get the beast back into his cage."

Thomas snickered at her down-in-the-mouth expression. "Nay, I'm afraid not. But I suggest another method. You wrestle the brute to the deck while I fetch the honey. After we smear it on him, it should sweeten his disposition."

237

Cat smirked at the suggestion. "I doubt there is enough honey in the galley to coat that man's temperament and make him tolerable, much less pleasant."

"Well, then we have no other choice, lass." Thomas directed her attention to the top of the steps and stifled a grin. "I'll go turn down the bed while you coax the cap'n to his cabin."

Perhaps Thomas found the situation amusing, but Catrina did not. Muttering several unladylike curses, she stalked up the steps in pursuit of the besotted captain. A bemused frown knitted her brow when she glanced around the abandoned deck. Her eyes darted to the helm, but it was not Brant who manned the wheel.

When a hoarse chuckle drifted down to her, Cat raised her eyes and gasped in disbelief. There was Brant, strolling on the supporting beam of the main sail, tripping along like a tightrope walker. Cat rolled her eyes heavenward, requesting more patience to deal with this mindless daredevil.

How the hell was she to coax him from the riggings when he was flirting with danger? She couldn't very well climb up the mast and haul him down when she was terrified of heights. Grinding her teeth, Cat scampered across the deck to stand beneath the oversized bird who was wobbling on his perch. Tensely, she waited for him to grasp a rope before she called to him.

"Brant, come down from there this instant," Cat ordered sharply. "You will break your damned neck."

His glazed eyes fell to the lovely goddess who was bathed in the silver moonlight. "Would you care, madame?" he questioned on a bitter laugh.

"I will not answer that question until you climb down," she stipulated.

"And I refuse to come down until I hear your reply," Brant slurred stubbornly.

If Catrina could have gotten her hands on that confounded pirate she would have slapped him sober. The spiteful thought evaporated when Brant's foot slid sideways and he flapped his arms to regain his balance. Catrina's heart slammed against her ribs and then ceased beating until Brant clutched the rope to save himself from a nasty fall.

Catrina was desperate enough at that point to contemplate shinnying up the beam, but she doubted it would serve a useful purpose. She would freeze up and there would be two fools in the crow's nest. Damn, what was she to do? She couldn't just stand there, waiting for Brant to splatter on the deck.

Her wild eyes flew to the helmsman who was quietly chuckling. The drunken canary who was perched on his branch had suddenly burst into song.

"Please fetch him down before he falls," Cat beseeched.

The officer gave his head a negative shake. "Sorry, Miss Catrina. I would do most anything you asked . . . except that. The captain has the strength of ten men when he's fallen into his cups. He'd push me to my death. I'm too fond of my neck to have it broken . . ."

When the helmsman's voice faded into silence, Catrina's gaze lifted to the sails. She saw Brant grasp the dangling rope and fly through the air with inebriated ease and she choked on her breath. Brant was performing death-defying aerial maneuvers without a net! The man was a lunatic!

"My God, he thinks he is part ape!" To her astonishment, Brant hopped onto the beam of the foresail, beat his chest like an arrogant monkey, pirouetted, and then swung back in the direction he had come—singing at the top of his lungs.

Frustrated by the helmsman's refusal to retrieve Brant before he managed to kill himself, Cat rushed toward the steps to elicit Thomas's assistance. At her frantic call, Thomas appeared. When he laid eyes on the swinging gorilla, he groaned in dismay. The captain had eased from the violent phase of drunkenness and progressed into delusions of grandeur. Obviously, the captain envisioned himself as part monkey, part bird.

"Hell's bells, the man's brain is saturated with so much

whiskey that it quit functionin'."

Three pair of eyes lifted to watch Brant leap to the main mast. With all the self-confidence of an experienced acrobat, Brant extended himself to grab another dangling rope. As Brant glided through midair, his destination the aftsail beam, Cat clutched Thomas's arm and squeezed her eyes shut. Brant was on a collision course with disaster and she didn't want to watch.

But one eye popped open and Cat very nearly pinched Thomas's arm in two. "Oh my God . . ." she chirped, horrified.

Unfortunately, Catrina's premonition proved correct. Brant missed the lower beam and crashed into the back of the sail, knocking the wind out of him. The sagging sail did, however, hold the drunken captain captive, preventing him from plummeting to his death. His unconscious body rolled down the canvas and wedged between the bottom of the sail and the timber. If the sail had been taut with a stout wind, Brant would have bounced off and perished during his acrobatic maneuvers. But his guardian angel was working overtime, seeing to it that Brant survived his drunken escapade in the lofty heights.

Thomas let out the breath he had been holding and scrambled up the mast. "Lordy, if the cap'n would have been sober, it would have killed him," he choked out.

While the helmsman followed Thomas, Catrina manned the wheel. Frantically, she waited for the men to haul Brant's limp body to the deck. Once they had carried him to bed, Catrina hurried to the cabin to survey the damage. She dipped a rag in cool water and dabbed it on the scrapes and bruises that marred his features.

"Silly fool," she chided gruffly. "Why I am catering to you I don't know."

The thought reignited her ire and she sat there smoldering. She was not about to dote over this drunken imbecile. Giving way to that thought, Cat scooped up the basin of cold water and spitefully dumped it on Brant's head, causing Thomas to burst into giggles.

"That should bring him 'round," Thomas chuckled.

"I hope so," she spumed, glaring at Brant. "And when he comes back to life I plan to kill him for scaring the wits out of me!"

Brant sputtered to catch his breath and struggled from the haze of darkness. His thick lashes fluttered up to see two angry Cats glowering down at him. He wasn't certain which image was the real Cat Diamond but she looked mad as hell.

"What happened?" Brant croaked.

"What happened?" she echoed incredulously. "Don't you remember what you have been doing for the past half hour?"

Carefully, Brant gave his tender head a shake and then cautiously inspected his smashed face with shaky fingertips. "My nose feels as if it has come out of joint."

"'Twas out of joint long before you crawled up the mast and began swinging around on the ropes," Cat bit off, her voice acrid with anger. "You were behaving like a gorilla, for God's sake! You went sailing through the air like a damned chimpanzee tripping through the jungle on his grapevine. 'Tis bad enough that you have been acting like the very devil for almost a week, but now you have reduced yourself to a creature who has the intelligence of an ape!"

"Not so loud," Brant groaned miserably, searching for a way to hold his head that didn't hurt. "I am not a well man."

Catrina shook a dainty finger in his bruised face. "You could have been a *dead* man," she scolded him.

Completely exasperated, Catrina stomped toward the door. "I am going to undo the disastrous mess in the storeroom. He is your patient, Thomas. I don't have the compassion or patience to coddle an acrobatic gorilla who sings while he swings through a jungle of sails. Patch up the captain as best you can and we shall see if we can sell him as a sideshow in a circus."

When the door crashed against the casing, Brant collapsed on his cot and rubbed his aching head. Unsympathetically,

Thomas plopped down on the edge of the bed to inspect Brant's swollen nose and scraped cheeks.

"She seems a mite upset," Brant breathed.

"Yer damned right she's upset and so am I," Thomas assured him curtly. "I've seen you pull some madcap stunts while you was feelin' yer liquor, but this has got to be the worst!"

Brant flinched when Thomas's stubby fingers hit a sensitive spot. Impatiently, he brushed the first mate's hand away. "If you came to spout another lecture, leave me alone. I have listened to Cat's tirade and I will not tolerate another."

Shrugging carelessly, Thomas climbed to his feet. "Very well, Cap'n. I'll leave you to yer misery."

"Thank you, I appreciate your consideration." His mocking tone negated his reply. Groaning, Brant pulled the pillow over his rumpled head and heaved an exhausted sigh.

Thomas lingered by the door, sadly shaking his head. "A man's most difficult battle comes when he wars with himself. Ain't you got enough trouble battlin' with the Royal Navy without pickin' fights with yer own wife?"

"Good night, Thomas." Brant's voice was brittle with irritation.

"It wasn't all that good," Thomas mumbled before disappearing into the companionway. "Believe me, Cap'n, I've enjoyed better nights."

Brant gnashed his teeth, cursing himself for behaving like a witless wonder. This constant tug-of-war of emotions was wreaking havoc with his sanity. He was trying hard to keep his distance from Cat, to prove his willpower, to salvage his pride. But the compelling attraction was tugging on him and liquor brought the only relief, temporary though it was. The brandy numbed him to the primitive male needs that fed on Cat's unexcelled passions. He was purposely denying himself as he vowed he would do, substituting brandy for the taste of her intoxicating kisses.

Aye, he had overcome his longings for the time being, but he dreaded the morrow. Brant knew what he would do. The dawn would come and Cat would appear to enchant the crew. Silently, he would watch her charm the sailors with her radiant smiles and carefree laughter. He would adore her and despise her all in the same moment. He would tolerate his men showering her with affection. And then he would lean heavily on his brandy crutch. Futilely, he would try to forget he cared for her. He would pretend the silken bond between them was not as sturdy and unbreakable as an anchor's rope.

He would continue punishing his traitorous body for aching for Catrina. But he would *not* submit to that green-eyed witch. If she wanted him she could come to his bed to ease the yearning of having her so close and yet a hundred leagues away. Chomping on that thought Brant closed his eyes and sank into the lulling aftereffects of his bout with liquor. Quietly, he nursed the bruises he had acquired while he was prancing high above the deck, behaving like an idiot. But just behind the dark silence was a flawless face with heart-shaped lips. Jade green eyes, shaded with desire, peered at him, beckoning him to abandon his vows and follow her. And in that hazy dimension between fantasy and reality, Brant dropped his armor of pride and went in quest of the fiery-haired pixie who had tormented his thoughts.

While Brant was drifting in dreams, Cat was flouncing about the storeroom, replacing the upended crates. She was so irritated with the besotted captain that she felt she had to work off her frustrawtion before she could settle down to sleep.

"I love him," she muttered as she set one crate upright. "I love him not." Roughly, she slammed the second box atop the first. Catrina continued to play her foolish game of I-love-him, I-love-him-not, until she had rearranged the entire room. "I love him . . ." The last crate was stacked in its normal resting place and Catrina expelled a weary breath. She glared at the wooden box, her feet askance, her hands resting on her hips. "Why do I care for him when he acts as if he detests me?" she questioned the empty room.

"Dammit, the man has me talking to myself again," Catrina muttered resentfully.

Catrina grasped the lantern and carried it up the steps. When she tiptoed into the cabin she glanced over at the bulky form of a man who lay sprawled on his cot. Her irritation melted away when the scant light caressed his sleep-softened features. She knew why she cared about this confounded pirate. He stirred each and every emotion, touching her in ways no other man had. Aye, they had weathered a stormy relationship, but the attraction was still there, flickering like an eternal flame.

Impulsively, Catrina set the lantern aside and eased onto the cot. Lovingly, her fingers threaded through the wavy raven locks that capped his head. "Sleep well, my handsome dragon." A rueful smile surfaced as she traced her index finger over the sensuous curve of his lips. "I wish . . ." Catrina sighed wistfully. "I wish you would breathe your fire into me with a kiss instead of searing me with your blazing temper."

Her head moved deliberately toward his, her lips playing softly against his unresponsive mouth. "I wish I could touch your heart and make you understand that all women are not like Cynthia Marsh. I would caress away every cynical thought and come to you with love shining in my eyes."

Cat sat there for a silent moment, wondering what escapade Brant would encounter when next he reached for a whiskey bottle. If only Brant would reach out to her to ease this unbearable longing. Catrina sighed heavily. She would be more successful in capturing Brant's fascination if she stuffed herself in a brandy bottle. It seemed she was determined to survive on the memories of splendor they had made a lifetime ago when Brant made wild sweet love to her. But Brant didn't really want her, Cat reminded herself. He had given her his name because he felt a responsibility. He had consummated their marriage and left her to shrivel up and wither away in unrequited love. Ah, if only they could go back to the way they were, back to those rapturous nights . . .

A startled squawk erupted from her lips when Brant roused in his sleep to sling his heavy arm around her neck. Catrina found herself shoved facedown in the pillow, her body pinned beneath his bent leg. When she tried to squirm free, Brant mumbled inarticulate phrases and pressed closer, molding his hard flesh to hers.

The fires began to burn within her, stirring the sweet memories. She knew Brant would never remember what had transpired this night. And yet, she could not withdraw. She wanted him, wanted to touch him, to kiss him. Perhaps he would not recall their embrace, but it was just as well, she reasoned. He could not see the love she felt for him, nor could he hear the soft whisperings of longing that tumbled from her lips.

Brazenly, her hands slid beneath his gaping shirt, feeling the thick matting of hair on his chest. Her exploring caresses mapped the flat plane of his belly and moved lower to glide along the curve of his hip.

Her brazen touch dragged a moan from his lips as he strained against her. Catrina answered his response, her breasts pressing wantonly against his chest. Her leg slid between his as she moved above him. Adoring eyes looked down into his craggy features, memorizing them, one by one. And then, like the slightest breath of wind, her lips feathered over his.

Unknowingly, Brant responded, his mouth opening to accept her questing tongue. Her kiss deepened, stealing his breath and then graciously sharing it. Her hands folded around his jaw, tilting his face so she could rain kisses along his cheeks and eyelids. Ever so slowly, Catrina withdrew when she felt Brant sink back into his brandy-drugged dreams.

She snuffed out the light and walked to her own cot. A quiet smile tripped across her lips. She had abandoned her pride to join Brant in bed. But he would never know that. She had found a glimpse of the pleasure they had once shared without sacrificing her dignity. And then a soft bubble of laughter erupted when the vision of Brant standing on the beam, pounding on his puffed-up chest, drifted across her mind. If Brant could have known how ridiculous he looked he would have kicked himself.

Mulling over that thought, Catrina slid between the sheets and closed her eyes. She could not imagine what tomfoolery Brant would land upon when he fell into his bottle again. She could only pray that he would prance about on the deck instead of resorting to scraping the clouds on his swinging vine. The drunken daredevil! He had very nearly killed himself!

Chapter Fifteen

By the end of the week, Catrina was reasonably certain the whiskey and salty sea brine had pickled Brant's brain. His temper had become legendary among the crew. He rarely spoke, except to bark an order. Although he and Catrina shared the same space, Brant chose to ignore her. Catrina had come to the conclusion that marriage did not agree with Brant. He had not been the same since the night they took the vows.

Catrina had rearranged the furniture twice, but Brant never mentioned it. He didn't smile or scowl at her. He methodically navigated his way around the misplaced objects until he located his stock of brandy. Without a word he would drop into a chair and sit there, contemplating his drink. Then he would empty the brandy in one swallow and stare out the porthole, as if something there had drawn his undivided attention.

She was at her wit's end. Nothing she did fazed Brant Diamond these days. Although Thomas had diagnosed Brant's ailment as a severe case of heart trouble, Catrina was too naive to comprehend what devil possessed Brant. She attributed his cool, detached manner to disinterest and boredom.

Heaving a frustrated sigh, Catrina plopped down on the cot where she had slept alone for endless nights. It had been lunacy to agree to this cruise, she chastised herself. Brant didn't really want her with him. His attraction for her had quickly faded to dispassion. She had done her fair share of the work on the schooner, hoping for praise. She had taunted Brant to get a rise out of him, but to no avail. The man barely acknowledged that she was present in his cabin or on his ship.

Catrina had been living with the whimsical hope that Brant would come to love her as time went by. But she was beginning to think Brant Diamond was a lost cause. The situation was dissolving her self-confidence and she wondered if anything about her stirred Brant.

Her dismal gaze swung to Brant who looked as approachable as a coiled cobra. She had done everything to make Brant notice her, if only to agitate him. Anything but this strained silence, she thought to herself. She longed to feel Brant's strong arms about her, to taste his fiery kisses . . . especially now when she was feeling so tired and listless. It seemed she had no energy left and the tension between them had spoiled her appetite. Cat needed his affection, needed to feel loved and protected. She lived for his laughter and she could not stir so much as a smile.

Confound it, if she couldn't have his love she would settle for his lust. Silly fool! Cat chided herself. She had finally reached that degrading level where she was willing to take Brant any way she could get him. Her pride was stinging, but it could not overcome this self-maiming emotion called love.

And, weary though she was, Cat set about to lure Brant into her bed, appealing to the lusting beast within him. Humming a soft Scottish ballad, Cat shed her breeches. She bent over to test the temperature of her bath water, knowing full well the hem of her shirt was riding provocatively over her hips.

Brant bit into the end of his cigar when the gauze fabric slid upward to expose Cat's shapely derriere. He inwardly groaned at the enticing sight and gulped another drink to cool the fire of desire she kindled within him. But it didn't help. Nothing did. The woman had tampered too long with his mind and had taken command of his body. She aroused him and there was no getting around it.

After his shenanigans the previous week, Brant had been mortified by his behavior. He had vowed to curb his drunken fits, certain they were deteriorating his brain. An overindulgence of whiskey had not lessened his craving for this green-eyed witch. Indeed, the liquor seemed to intensify his need. He had awakened with a dreadful hangover, struck by the oddest sensation that he had felt Catrina's soft lips playing against his. And he could have sworn her luscious body had been pressed intimately to his. But it had only been a lifelike dream, Brant told himself.

Since that day Brant had taken special pains to erase those lingering sensations. He had made certain he was on deck while Cat was dressing or bathing. But tonight he just sat there. He knew he should gather his feet beneath him and march out the door, but his male body refused to unfold itself from the chair.

For a week he had paced the deck from bow to stern, wearing himself to a frazzle. He had walked thirty miles, fighting this mental tug-of-war, without making progress. Nothing had helped, not the liquor, the lectures, nor the constant pacing. And now he was glued to his chair, his mind mocking him because he had lost his battle of self-conquest. He was enduring Catrina's sensuous assault, but he wondered if he possessed enough willpower not to surrender to the needs he had long left unappeased.

The moment Cat peeled off her shirt and eased into the tub, Brant swiveled his head around to glare at the blank wall. By damn, he would not sit there gawking at her like the rest of his moonstruck crew, he promised himself. He had wed the woman his crew craved, but he was purposely denying himself to prove that he was still a man, not a simpering milksop who was so head over heels in love with a woman that he could no longer function rationally.

Brant cursed under his breath when his traitorous eyes strayed to the delectable witch who was stewing in her bubble bath. The taut peaks of her breasts glistened with water droplets and Brant ached to trail his hand over those moist-tipped buds. One shapely leg rose from the tub and slim fingers lathered the satiny skin of her thigh. Brant groaned in unholy torment. It had finally happened, he thought bitterly. He had lost what little sense he had left. What man in his right mind would long to exchange places with a bar of soap? He yearned to glide cross her alabaster skin, to trace the titillating curves and swells in a never-ending caress.

Brant braced himself when a chain reaction of sensations toppled over him. He would *not* yield to temptation. He would *not* grovel at Cat's feet, begging for whatever morsels of affection she would toss at him. He was the captain of his own ship, the master of his own soul. He would not allow this mere wisp of a woman to assume complete control of his mind and body! My God, she had already steered him off course, detouring him from the sea lanes of life. She had muddled his purpose. For weeks he could not remember where he intended to go—or why!

He had already stooped to humiliating depths, ones that had depleted his self-esteem. Like a shameless Peeping Tom, he had spied on the shapely nymph. He had monitored Cat's every movement while she was under Jean-Martin's protection. He had bribed John Paul to steal her from the French cavalier's arms and deliver her to the terrace. When Cat tried to escape, Brant had chased after her and forced her into a marriage she didn't want.

Now was he a man or a two-legged mouse, Brant asked himself proudly. A man would hold his ground while a mouse would scamper to the lady, mindless of its self-respect and its firm resolve. To Brant's way of thinking he had compromised his manhood far too often. If Cat felt anything for him she would not have dressed in that outlandish garb and roamed the deck, tempting his crew. If she cared she wouldn't taunt him with that delicious body of hers. She would have come to him with her heart in her eyes, asking that they make amends and attempt to share a true marriage.

But not this fiery-haired wildcat, Brant grumbled to himself.

Angrily, he threw down the rest of his brandy and, out of reflex, promptly refilled his glass. That minx was so damned independent that, not only would she never break, but she wouldn't even bend toward a compromise. She was so cynical of men that she would never trust her own husband, never accept him as anything but a money-hungry pirate.

And if he didn't watch his step he would be so henpecked he would moult twice a year. By God, he still had his pride, Brant reminded himself. And since that was all he had left, he would cling fiercely to it! If Cat wouldn't bend, neither would he.

Brant chugged his brandy and puffed his cigar, substituting liquor and tobacco for what he craved most—Cat's kisses and caresses. Determined to resist the lure of the curvaceous mermaid who was frolicking in his tub, Brant smoked and drank until he very nearly made himself sick.

Catrina frowned disappointedly as she wiped the beads of perspiration from her brow. What else could a woman do to make a man notice her? There was nothing more drastic or suggestive than stripping naked before him, was there? It was obvious the man was carved from stone, that he had lost all desire for her.

Oh, what was the use, she thought tiredly. Nothing she had done affected Brant these days. Dejectedly, she sank into the tub, shivering from a sudden chill. What was the matter with her? She felt hot and cold all in the same moment.

When Brant summoned every ounce of willpower and rose from his chair, Catrina's heart fell to the bottom of the tub. She watched in dismay as Brant, with bottle in hand, strode out the door.

He just doesn't give a damn about you anymore, her anguished soul screamed at her. She could never win Brant's love, not in seven days or seven years. Cynthia Marsh had locked his heart in granite and no other woman could chisel her way through solid rock to retrieve it.

Catrina expelled an exhausted sigh. She was too tired and achy to devise another method of luring Brant into her arms.

Obviously, this emotional upheaval had sapped her strength, she diagnosed. Absently, she sponged her face, relieved that the tepid water had cooled her feverish brow. Could one become physically ill because of a bleeding heart, she asked herself. At the moment it seemed entirely possible to Cat. She was feeling miserable and she could think of no other reason why her arms and legs felt as if they had anchors strapped to them.

Another chill shot down her spine. Cat frowned puzzledly as the room turned a hazy shade of gray and a hollow ringing echoed in her ears. She was more than lovesick, she realized when a wave of nausea set her stomach to churning.

Something was very wrong! With grim determination, Catrina hoisted herself from the tub and stumbled blindly toward her cot. As the schooner pitched and rolled on the choppy sea, her stomach flip-flopped against her ribs. Perhaps she was only exhausted from doing a man's work on the ship, she thought sickly. Maybe it was weariness and depression that was tormenting her. Once she had a decent night's sleep she would be her old self again.

Clinging to that encouraging thought, Catrina rolled herself into a tight ball and shivered beneath the quilts. Rest was what she needed. The fever and nausea would go away after she had treated herself to a full night's sleep. Tomorrow she would be bounding about the ship in her usual, energetic manner . . .

Brant guzzled the last of his brandy and hurled the bottle into the ocean. Damn, how much more of Catrina's seductive taunting could he endure before he buckled beneath the desires that were raging through him like wildfire? If he hadn't pried himself from the chair and taken his leave, he would have been crawling to Cat like a shameless mouse!

Bitter laughter bubbled from Brant's chest when he realized why he was so distressed. For the past few years he had waltzed from one woman to another without emotional ties. And now he had stumbled upon a female who was so unlike his other lovers. Catrina never catered to him or chased after him. She didn't murmur words of love in moments of passion or whimper when he walked away. All she had ever wanted was to return to her estate in Scotland. Since Brant refused, Cat was spiting him at every turn. Her ploy that evening had been no more than a taunt, an attempt to prove her magic powers over him, to humiliate him.

Brant had not been this frustrated after his sour affair with Cynthia Marsh. Those same painful sensations were recoiling inside him, but they were fiercer than they had once been. The affection he had once felt for Cynthia shriveled and died when he realized what a selfish, scheming woman she really was. But Cat was different in most ways and Brant was drawn to her, even when he didn't want to be. That mischievous misfit had crept into his heart and monopolized his thoughts.

What a foolish mistake it had been to learn her many moods, to find pleasure in her exquisite body. Caring for a woman always brought pain, Brant reminded himself. Catrina was ornery, fickle, and he should have allowed her to remain on the *Countess*. . . .

"Cap'n?" Thomas strode up behind Brant. "I think you better take a look at Jacob Powers. The lad is ailin'."

Brant tore himself from his troubled reverie to focus his attention on the grim-faced first mate. Lord, he had been so preoccupied with Catrina that he had no regard for his crew. Especially Jacob, Brant thought to himself. The young man hovered about Cat, and Brant spent most of his time trying to ignore that fact.

"What is the matter with him? He should be the healthiest man on board the *Sea Lady* since he has been exercising his male desires by running circles around my wife," he snorted unsympathetically.

"He's been feelin' a bit under the weather the past week. I didn't think much about it at first. But he collapsed this mornin'. When I went to check on him tonight he was burnin'

253

with fever.''

Brant grumbled sourly at the news. He and his crew had been fortunate the past year, but Brant was beginning to think their luck had run out. The last thing he needed was an epidemic while he was en route to the Azores to capture another British prize.

''When I noticed Jacob lookin' peaked, I quarantined him,'' Thomas informed the captain as they descended the steps. ''He's kept to himself the last day or two . . . 'cept when yer lady was about. He always perked up and followed her around. At first I thought it was a simple case of puppy love for Cat.'' Thomas broke stride, his weather-beaten features paling. ''Lord, I hope she don't come down with the fever, too. If anyone has been exposed, 'tis her.''

The thought stabbed Brant like a knife. He had watched able-bodied men die from fevers at sea. The vision of Cat thrashing in bed from the fever frightened him. She was so energetic and alive, so full of spirit. Nay, she was well enough, Brant consoled himself. After all, she had attempted to seduce him in a quiet, subtle way only a half hour earlier.

A worried frown creased Brant's brow when he pushed open the door to see Jacob Powers tossing and turning on his cot. It was obvious the lad was out of his mind with putrid fever. Brant had seen the symptoms several times during voyages and had suffered from them once or twice himself.

''He don't look good, Cap'n,'' Thomas whispered.

Jacob's ashen face was dripping with perspiration. Brant reached down to brush his palm across the young man's forehead and then jerked away as if he had been scorched.

''Damn, he's frying alive!'' he gasped in genuine concern.

His dark brows drew thoughtfully together as he watched Jacob flounder on his cot. A conversation he had once had with John Paul suddenly popped to mind. He knew John Paul had suffered a severe case of the intermittent fever. Jones had informed Brant that he had tried the cold bath treatments once while he was in the colonies. Since John Paul had survived a devastating form of the fever he had attributed his recovery to the revolutionary new treatments developed by a doctor in New England.

Brant decided to test the theory. Jacob looked so pitifully ill that Brant was certain it would require drastic measures to bring down the fever before it affected Jacob's brain and cost him his life.

"I'll fetch the tub from my cabin." Brant wheeled around and started toward the door. "Have some of the men haul cold water down here. We haven't much time if we hope to save the boy."

As Brant hurried toward his cabin he could hear the lad whimpering in fevered dreams. When he stepped into the room he found Catrina sound asleep in her bed. Although he tried not to cause a stir it was inevitable that he clanked the buckets when he emptied the tub. But to his surprise Catrina didn't rouse during the commotion.

When Brant completed his time-consuming chore, he lifted the awkward tub and negotiated his way around the misplaced furniture to reach the door. Once outside, Brant braced himself and his armload against the wall to catch his breath. At the sound of approaching footsteps Brant glanced up to see the somber expression that claimed Thomas's face.

"There ain't no need for the tub," Thomas mumbled. "A bath won't do Jacob no good now. By the time I got back with the last bucket of water, he was gone . . ."

The dismal news hit Brant like a hard slap in the face. He eased the tub to the floor and cursed under his breath. Damn, it wasn't fair. The lad was young. Jacob's life had only begun and now it had come to an abrupt end. The sailor was not accustomed to the confinement of the ship and his body had not adjusted to the sea rations. Why was it usually the young and inexperienced seamen who buckled to the fever?

Leaving the tub where it sat, Brant returned to Jacob's quarters to have it thoroughly scoured and disinfected. The regrettable task of preparing for burial at sea took the remainder of the evening. It was well after midnight before Brant crawled into bed, exhausted and in low spirits.

Shortly before dawn, Brant was dragged from his dreams by odd, muffled noises. Groggily, he sat up in bed to locate the source of the sounds. When his senses cleared he realized Catrina was thrashing in her sheets, her head rolling from side to side as if she were possessed by demon spirits.

Brant was wide awake in less than a heart beat. His bare feet had only hit the floor before he was by Catrina's side. "Cat, can you hear me?"

When her heavily lidded eyes opened in a blank stare, Brant sucked in his breath. Cat was peering straight at him, but she couldn't see him. Brant recalled Catrina had seemed a mite pale the previous evening but he had been too busy trying to ignore her to give it much thought. Now her face was crimson red, as if she were burning from inside out.

Brant's deep voice came to Catrina through a long, echoing tunnel. Instinctively, she shrank away from the fuzzy shadow that loomed over her. It wasn't the handsome Captain Diamond who hovered over her. It was Derrick Redmund. He was snarling at her, cursing her, threatening to strike her. And behind that dark, foreboding face were two other shapeless images, ones that rose from the leaping flames of a fire.

Catrina became hysterical. She could hear Derrick's booming voice intermingling with the tormented cries of her parents. The torturous vision receded momentarily and Catrina collapsed in relief. But then the images lunged at her again, growing until they were blown out of proportion, terrifying her.

A bloodcurdling scream burst from Catrina's lips and tears boiled down her cheeks as she attempted to shove the nightmare away. She was drifting somewhere beyond reality, trapped in a world of horror. She was assaulted by the hazy images that had long haunted her thoughts. For months she had successfully held the tormenting visions at bay. But now those carefully guarded memories rose like banshees in the night, wailing and jeering, overwhelming her tortured mind.

"Nay, please, don't strike me again," she cried out and then cowered against the wall. "Mama . . . Papa . . . please come home. I miss you so . . . help me . . ."

When Catrina broke into breathless sobs, Brant grimaced at the hunted look on her face. "Cat, 'tis me, Brant. Wake up!"

Brant scooped her tense body from the cot to enfold her in his comforting embrace. The moment he touched her he knew she was not sleeping in the arms of an ordinary nightmare.

The fever! a frantic voice shouted at him. It only took an instant to recall what Thomas had said about the possibility of Catrina being exposed to Jacob's affliction. The young sailor had infected Catrina!

Panic gripped him. The morbid picture that flashed through his mind was that of Jacob lying lifeless on his cot after his fevered thrashings had drained the last of his strength. Like a frightened little boy fiercely clinging to his one and only possession, Brant crushed Catrina's smoldering body to his. For a dazed moment he sat there, hugging her to him, afraid to let go.

In the face of adversity Brant had always been quick to react. But Catrina's serious affliction stunned him. He couldn't think. He just held her to him, haunted by the terrifying premonition that if he let her go he would lose her.

Jacob had been plagued with the fever. Now the young sailor had gone to Fiddler's Green, the ever-open locker that waited at the bottom of the sea. God, Brant didn't want to think of Catrina following Jacob into those cold, murky depths.

"Brant, where are you?" Catrina sobbed, scratching her way from the confining arms of her delirious dream.

Suddenly she found herself dodging the exploding shells of battle. She wanted to be free of the iron chains that bound her, wanted to reassure herself that Brant had not fallen during the siege. But as she fought for freedom another vision shot across her mind, confusing her boggled thoughts. She was hanging on the supporting beam of the sails, knowing she would take the

257

inevitable fall. From out of nowhere Brant appeared to save her from certain disaster. She held on to him, afraid to unclench her fingers and pry open her eyes.

"Don't let me go!" she whimpered brokenly. "Why do you hate me so . . . ?" Her raspy voice trailed off and she slumped against Brant, exhausted from her fevered ravings.

Brant's emotions were being torn to shreds. First Cat had clawed at him for release. In the next second she was squeezing the stuffing out of him. And just as abruptly she collapsed into a restless sleep. Her head rolled against his shoulder, sending a waterfall of tarnished fire spilling over his arm. Although Brant was uncertain what distorted images were darting through her mind, her words distressed him.

"I don't hate you, my fiery jewel," he murmured. Fondly, he combed trembling fingers through her damp curls. "Never that . . ."

Sometimes he was cynical of Catrina's purpose. And other times, like now, when he stared into her exquisite face, he could not imagine why he was wary of his intense feelings for her. But she *was* impetuous and ever-changing, he reminded himself. He and Cat had been at cross purposes since he learned there was a woman hiding inside Milton's baggy clothes. Cat had driven him mad with her seductive body and ornery pranks and Brant was trying to maintain what little sanity he had left.

But seeing her like this tormented him. When he peered down at the limp bundle in his arms the wall of ice around his heart melted like snow on a blazing campfire. Cat was no longer the feisty, high-spirited temptress. She was frail and vulnerable. The flames that once danced in her eyes were now boiling through her blood in the form of a deadly fever. And the once-lively expression was a confused stare. What was left was the shell of a woman who could not trust her own mind because it was frying with fever.

The abrupt rap at the door jolted Brant from his pensive contemplations. "Who is it?" he questioned, never taking his eyes off Cat.

"Me, Cap'n," Thomas grumbled. "I hate to be the bearer of more bad news, but Witham and Phelps have taken ill. And Witham ain't fully recovered from his battle wounds." Slowly, Thomas eased open the door. His breath caught in his throat when he saw Brant tucking Catrina's lifeless body beneath the sheet. "Sweet mercy, don't tell me yer lady has come down with the fever, too!"

"Fetch some fresh water, Thomas," Brant ordered as he rose to full stature to retrieve the tub that still sat in the companionway.

Thomas nodded mutely before scampering back in the direction he had come. "It don't seem right to see her layin' there like that. I've never seen her so still. Nay, it just don't seem natural . . ." he mumbled.

Brant's concerned gaze swung to the cot. "Nay, it doesn't," he mused aloud.

Tossing aside his depressing thoughts Brant dragged the wooden tub beside the cot. Nervously, he paced the confines of his cabin, glancing at Catrina every other second to ensure that she was still breathing. Fear rushed through him again when Catrina began thrashing on her bed. Her crimson red face whitewashed, as if the fever had surged on to take possession of another part of her body.

Mumbled bits of sentences trickled from her lips and her arms flailed wildly in the air. Catrina struggled to climb from the depths of another fearful dream. The distorted images leaped at her, making her shriek involuntarily.

Brant stared helplessly at Catrina, wishing he could perform miracles. Dammit, seeing her so seriously ill was cutting him to pieces, bit by excruciating bit. The thought of exposing himself to the intermittent fever didn't disturb him, but watching her waste her strength did. Brant sank down beside her, clasping her arms to restrain movement. He prayed she would not wither away before his eyes. God, he couldn't endure that, he told himself shakily. Ignoring her was one thing, but losing her forever was an altogether different matter and it terrified him to even consider life without her.

After what seemed forever, Thomas and several sailors filed into the room to fill the tub. When they completed their task, Brant ordered his men to search out another tub to begin the cold bath treatments on Phelps and Witham.

Carefully, he lifted Catrina from the cot to the tub. With sponge in hand, he trickled cold water through her hair and across her perspiring brow. With meticulous care Brant washed her fevered body like a compassionate nurse tending his patient.

Compassionate? Brant smiled ruefully to himself while he continued his tender ministrations. Strange, he had come the full circle these past few months. Brant had felt sympathy for young Milton and he had taken the waif under his wing. He had been amused by Milton's orneriness, seeing a reflection of his own youth. But his feelings for Milton had transformed into passion when he learned this staunchly independent, persnickety misfit was a woman. His hunger for Catrina had very nearly swallowed him alive and his jealousy had overshadowed logic. Now he was back to pitying Cat, wishing she were not forced to endure this fevered torment, an affliction from which she might never recover.

This fiery sprite had turned him wrong side out. She was playing havoc with his carefully controlled emotions. Just when he thought he had mastered self-control and recovered from his obsession, Catrina was stricken with the fever. Now the thought of losing her, not just to another man, was driving him out of his mind. He wanted to brush his fingertips over her satiny flesh, giving her pleasure where there was pain. He wanted to kiss her sweet lips, offering her the breath of life that slowly ebbed with each moment that ticked by.

Lord, his friends only thought he was embittered when Cynthia Marsh used him as a rung on the ladder of social prominence. But it would be little of nothing compared to the soul-wretching emotions that would haunt him if he lost Catrina . . .

Brant felt himself go mushy inside when Catrina's tangled lashes swept up. She was staring up at him with that special smile of hers, one that was tritely innocent and a mite mischievous. For a moment she was coherent and she knew who held her close.

"I hoped you would return, Pirate Captain. Even if you despise the sight of me, I adore watching you." A throaty giggle bubbled from her lips and she cuddled against his supporting arm. "Did you know I find you very handsome?"

Brant smiled, despite his deflated spirits. He was lost to that impish grin that cut becoming dimples in her cheeks. "Do you now, my little kitten?"

Cat gave her head a faint nod. The gesture seemed to drain what strength the cold bath revived. "Aye," she admitted groggily. "There is a mystical sparkle in the ruby and sapphire, but it cannot hold a candle to Diamond's fire. It lures me ever closer, even when I know I should back cautiously away . . ." She sighed heavily as reality faded from her grasp and darkness circled like a waiting vulture.

Brant chuckled at her nonsense, but his smile vanished when he felt Catrina go limp in his arms. Deciding Cat had soaked long enough, Brant scooped her onto his lap to dry her. Ever so gently, he toweled her naked body, trying not to dwell on her shapely curves. But it was no use. He was hypnotized by the glorious sight of her, overwhelmed by the sea of memories that swamped him.

When troubled dreams converged on her again, Catrina came uncoiled, clawing at the tormented visions. Keeping a tight grasp on his squirming bundle, Brant eased Catrina back to her cot and tucked the sheet securely about her. Exhaling a depressed sigh, Brant eased into the chair to keep a constant vigil on his patient.

And there he sat, from dawn until midnight, waiting to give Cat a cold bath each time her temperature soared. Her constant rambling amused and frightened. Sometimes she made perfect sense, but usually her utterances were scrambled thoughts recklessly put to tongue. Yet, Brant was there to comfort her when she wept and to smile when she giggled like a child reliving a forgotten memory.

The distance he had put between them the past few weeks became inches instead of miles. Brant could see part of himself withering away each time Catrina heaved a shuddering breath and cried out in her dreams. His large hand enfolded hers, wishing his nervous energy could flow from his taut body to hers, replenishing her will to live.

"Don't leave me, Cat," Brant whispered as his lips skimmed her fevered forehead. "Not like this . . . I would sooner give you up to another man than to lose you forever . . ." Lovingly, he squeezed her limp hand. "Hang on, love. You are fighting for your life and it means everything to both of us . . ."

Chapter Sixteen

Thomas's tired body slumped as he trudged into the captain's cabin with the supper tray. His remorseful gaze swung to the cot where Brant had remained a posted lookout for five days and nights. "Is she doin' better?" he questioned quietly.

Brant rose from his chair to work the kinks from his back. "There has been little change," he muttered grimly.

"Well, at least she ain't gone from bad to worse." Thomas set the tray on the desk and strode over to brush his hand over Catrina's forehead. A concerned frown settled on his weather-beaten features when he noticed the dark circles under her eyes and the hollowness of her cheeks. "Lordy, I hope she rouses soon to eat. She's wastin' away."

That dismal comment did nothing to uplift Brant's sinking spirits. He was beginning to think John Paul's boasting accolades of cold bath treatments were empty praise. Although Cat had survived the past five days she was only a shadow of herself. Her severe fever and wild thrashing had depleted her strength. She lay as still as stone and Brant had to press his head to her breast to ensure she was breathing.

Ignoring Thomas's remark, Brant grasped the glass of brandy and quickly downed it. "Have Witham and Phelps shown any improvement?"

Thomas glanced back at the stubble-faced captain. "We lost Witham this afternoon. Phelps fares no better than Catrina. He's passed the phase of tossin' and turnin' with delirious dreams. He just lays there as if he were . . ." His voice trailed off, refusing to dwell on the dreary thought. "Do you want me to sit with Catrina while you go up on the deck for some air?"

Brant gave his head a negative shake. "Nay, I'm not leaving her," he insisted, his voice showing evidence of strain and lack of sleep.

Thomas frowned disapprovingly. "You ain't left the girl's side since she fell ill. If you don't breathe some fresh air and get some rest, we'll be nursin' *you* through the fever. I don't relish the idea of takin' command . . . permanently."

Brant took another sip of brandy and then reluctantly nodded in compliance. "Very well, Thomas, I'll climb to the quarterdeck to see to the ship, but you must promise to keep your eyes on Cat. If her condition worsens, notify me immediately."

"Do you think I want anythin' to happen to yer lady?" Thomas snorted indignantly. "I can care for her as well as you can!"

A wry smile pursed Brant's lips. "Aye, I suppose you can," he murmured.

"Yer damned right I can," Thomas sniffed, drawing himself up to a proud stature. "You ain't the only one in love with this fetchin' mermaid."

Two black brows formed a hard line over Brant's eyes. "I never said I was in love with Cat," he growled.

Thomas plopped down in the chair beside Catrina's cot. "Yer a stubborn one, Cap'n. I know yer in love with her, even if you won't admit it to yerself. If I was you I'd be shoutin' it to the sails. But bein' the mule-headed man you are, you pretend yer immune to her charms."

"If I want your opinion I will ask for it," Brant snapped brusquely.

"Forgive me for sayin' so, Cap'n, but you ain't foolin'

264

nobody but yerself," Thomas rattled on, undaunted by Brant's terse tone. "Don't you think I've noticed the way you've been actin' since you crossed paths with this girl? Yer worse than you ever was with Cynthia Marsh. That wench tied you in knots, but this one . . ." Thomas snickered as he gestured toward the oval face that was surrounded with tangled auburn curls. "This cat and mouse game you've been playin' is downright amusin'."

"That is quite enough!" Brant gritted out through clenched teeth, determined not to disturb his patient. "I am in no mood to sit through one of your lectures on how I should or shouldn't behave."

"'Tis a pity," Thomas said with a nonchalant shrug. "You've had the disposition of a disturbed shark the past month. I should think you might want to remedy yer sour mood."

Brant had heard enough. His temper was running on a short fuse and he feared it would explode if he didn't put some distance between him and the source of his irritation. Without a word in his defense, Brant stormed out the door, resisting the urge to slam it shut on his outspoken first mate.

Chuckling, Thomas leaned over to pat Catrina's hand. "He'll come 'round, lass. You just hold on till the fever runs its course. One day that stubborn husband of yers will wake up and realize how much he cares about you."

For a moment, Thomas swore Catrina heard and understood him. Her eyes fluttered open and a smile touched her waxen lips. But before Thomas could speak again, Catrina fell back into the possessive arms of fevered darkness.

Fondly, Thomas squeezed her hand and stared into her face. He was not a religious man, but he had been doing some serious praying since Catrina collapsed with the fever. It grieved him to see such a spirited young beauty crippled by illness. How he longed to view that youthful flicker in her eyes again, to hear her carefree laughter echoing through the companionway.

Heaving a discouraged sigh, Thomas wilted into his chair,

wondering if he would ever witness another of Catrina's radiant smiles. Dammit, it wasn't fair to see such a lively lass cut low by the fever. It was so unlike her to be still for even a moment. But there she lay, hovering between life and death, trapped in a world of shadowy dreams.

With tremendous effort Catrina opened her eyes to greet another shade of darkness. It seemed it had been dark forever, she thought to herself. When she tried to pull into an upright position on the cot, her entire body rebelled. Breathing was a costly effort and movement was next to impossible.

Deciding it best to remain where she lay, Catrina turned her head to the side to see Brant slumped in the chair. His drawn features and dark beard were even more formidable in the waning light. My, but he looked the part of the foreboding pirate, she mused.

A puzzled frown claimed her features, wondering how Brant could have grown such a thick beard in the course of a day. And what had come over her? Why did she feel so weary?

Catrina tossed aside her perplexed deliberations when she spied the glass of water sitting on the nightstand. God, she was thirsty. She was certain she could swallow all the water in the Atlantic without being satisfied. With painstaking effort she extended a shaky hand to clasp the glass. Her reflexes were so sluggish that she sent the cup crashing to the planked floor.

Brant came awake with a start. His head swiveled from its resting place on the back of the chair to see Cat's half-nude body stretched toward the nightstand.

"Cat, you've alive!" he breathed in relief.

"You are only humoring me by saying that," she grumbled hoarsely, dismayed that she could barely find her voice and that she had spoiled her chance of quenching her thirst. "Please, I beg a drink."

Brant vaulted from his chair to retrieve another glass of water and hurriedly returned to steady it against her lips.

Catrina gulped it so quickly that Brant snatched it away from her. "Slow down," he ordered. "You have had little nourishment for a week. Your stomach may object to such a thorough soaking."

"A week!" Catrina croaked, her hollowed eyes as wide as saucers.

"One week and one day to be exact," Brant informed her, granting her a dainty sip.

For some strange reason Brant felt the urge to shout down the rafters. Cat had survived the fever! It would be a long road to recovery but she had endured the worst. Witham had not been so fortunate. His battle wounds, complicated with intermittent fever, had taken their toll. Phelps still lay in a deathlike trance, but Catrina's recovery gave Brant hope that the young sailor would also survive his ordeal.

Catrina sank back onto her pillow to peer at the ceiling. "What happened to me? I remember nothing except feeling hot, then cold and weary."

"You came down with the fever," Brant explained. "Perhaps you felt cold, but you were burning alive." A tender smile touched his lips, but he quickly masked the sentimental expression behind a carefully blank stare. "'Tis been a long trying week for all of us. Although you have returned to consciousness you are sorely in need of rest. While I take command of the ship I expect you to do just that."

Her heart nearly broke in two when Brant turned and walked away. For a split second he had almost seemed relieved she was alive, but it was obvious her mind was playing tricks on her. Now Brant behaved as if she had contracted leprosy and he could not wait to escape her.

While she lay abed, her spirits scraping rock bottom, Thomas bounded into the room to display the type of greeting she had hoped to receive from Brant. "Lordy, ain't you a sight for sore eyes, girl," Thomas hooted enthusiastically. "I thought the angels was comin' for you."

"I thought they had." Catrina forced a faint smile. "At least there is one friendly face in heaven."

Thomas frowned at her deflated tone. "Don't tell me Devil Diamond has been breathin' fire on you already." He could tell by the look on her face that Brant had done little to cheer her since she roused from the dead. "Well, don't take it to heart, lass. The God's truth is the cap'n never left yer side unless I insisted. He's kept watch over you day and night."

Catrina eyed Thomas suspiciously. Brant nursed her back to health? It was too inconceivable to even consider. Thomas was only trying to boost her spirits, she decided. But that was Thomas's way. Why, he even rattled off Brant's redeeming qualities each time she made reference to one of the pirate captain's aggravating faults.

"You can put away your bow, Cupid. Your arrow cannot penetrate Diamond. He rivals granite for hardness," she grumbled acrimoniously. "The captain didn't care if I lived or died and you needn't try to make me feel better by saying so. He considers my illness an inconvenience."

Thomas sadly shook his head. "'Twas no lie I gave. The cap'n was worried sick about you."

"Just as surely as this ship sprouted wings to soar across the sky." Catrina smirked sarcastically. "Really, Thomas, if you came to cheer me, don't ply me with obvious lies."

"Confound it, woman, yer as stubborn as he is," Thomas breathed in exasperation. "Yer bound and determined to make each other's lives miserable. Will *you* at least admit you love him?"

Downcast eyes focused on the crumpled sheet that covered her thin body. "Aye, I will admit it to you, but if you breathe a word of it to him, I will bob your tongue. Brant would laugh in my face if he knew. He has little use for women and even less need for his wife. Cynthia Marsh has seen to that. If I ever chance to meet that foolish woman I have a good mind to give her the verbal lynching she deserves. She has made a cynical man of Brant Diamond."

Thomas rolled his eyes in disgust. These two stubbornly

independent individuals would never settle their differences without a matchmaker, he predicted. And if he weren't so fond of both of them he wouldn't risk being caught in the middle.

After informing Catrina that he would fetch her something to eat, Thomas stepped into the companionway. A thoughtful frown gathered on his brow. By damned, he was going to devise a way to crumble the barrier Catrina and Brant had built between them. They were not going to struggle through life, crossways of each other. Not if he had anything to do with it, Thomas thought to himself.

Grappling with several possibilities, Thomas ambled toward the galley. If Brant didn't know what was good for him, Thomas would take matters in hand. Catrina was just the woman who could make Brant believe in love again. It had been a long time in coming, but the time was ripe. This particular lady possessed what Brant needed to captivate him—a fiery temperament, an overabundance of spirit, and unmatched beauty. A wry smile pursed Thomas's lips. He would channel his efforts into a scheme to bring Brant and Catrina together. The course of love could never be smooth sailing for these two, he admitted. But Thomas fully intended to see that Brant and Catrina were at least rowing in the same direction!

A sour frown darkened Brant's features when Catrina poked her head from the stairwell and wobbled upon the deck. It had been four days since she had roused to consciousness and Brant confined her to bed rest. Obviously, his orders meant nothing to the defiant chit. There she stood, her chin held high, her eyes flickering with that determined sparkle Brant had come to expect in them.

The fact that every crewman on board flocked to Catrina did nothing to sweeten Brant's disposition. Catrina had cast her spell on the *Sea Lady* and the ship was under her command. The sailors raced to greet her as if the reigning queen had returned to court.

Although Catrina was swarmed by well-wishers her eyes were on Brant. But even at a distance, his gaze cut into her, slashing her composure. Since the night she regained consciousness, Brant had moved in with Thomas. He had come to check on her occasionally, but the task was generally left to the first mate. Thomas was a godsend. Without his companionship Catrina would have been climbing the walls without a ladder.

To fill the idle hours Thomas told her stories about Brant's first years at sea. When he spoke of their narrow escapes during the war, Catrina could envision Brant at the helm, making split-second decisions. Her admiration for the daring pirate captain had grown by leaps and bounds, just as Thomas had hoped.

Thomas had done her a disfavor, Catrina suddenly realized. She was trying very hard to bury the bittersweet memories, but Thomas would not allow them to die. He continued to offer nothing but praise for Brant. *That* Catrina didn't need to hear.

Tossing aside her wandering thoughts Catrina focused her attention on the sailors. At least they were happy she had survived, she reassured herself. What did she care if the grumpy captain had no time for her? He would only cut a gash in her spirits and send them plummeting again.

"What is she doing on deck?" Brant growled when Thomas ambled up beside him.

"She wanted some fresh air," Thomas explained.

"And if she wanted a slice of the moon, would you have flown off to fetch it?" Brant questioned with sticky sarcasm.

Thomas sent Brant a withering glance. "She ain't that unreasonable. But you know Catrina. She is too restless to stay cooped up. She begged me to let her come to the deck."

"If she suffers a setback it will be on *your* conscience," Brant lectured, wagging his finger in Thomas's face. "She requires plenty of rest. She has no business gallivanting about the ship. Her crowd of admirers will smother her."

A sharp cry from the crow's nest brought everyone to attention. In the distance rose the Azores, the Everlasting Mountains of the Sea. It had been more than three weeks since the crew had seen land. Shouts of cheer echoed across the deck when the sailors laid eyes on something besides the cresting wave that rolled toward the far horizon.

Catrina caught her breath when she spied the mystical domes that glistened like silver. The volcanic peaks rose above the circling halos of clouds, painting a mid-ocean picture of beauty that held Catrina spellbound. The lowlands of the closest island were bright green with foliage, reminding Catrina of an exotic paradise. For several minutes she could do nothing but feast her eyes on the quaint haven that broke the horizon with its jagged precipices.

When Thomas noticed Catrina's awestruck expression, he smiled slyly. He was about to set his plan in motion. "Bed rest ain't what yer lady needs," Thomas diagnosed. "She's had enough of that. What she needs is sunshine, fresh air, and the succulent fruit to be found on these islands." Thomas snapped his fingers as if an ingenious idea had suddenly hatched in his mind when actually he had spent the past few days perfecting his plot. "I got a splendid idea, Cap'n. Why don't you take the lady ashore for a few days of rest and recuperation while me and the men scout out the islands for British prizes."

A wary frown etched Brant's brow. Thomas had a sneaky look about him, a most unnatural one. The man was too honest to wear that mock innocent expression without causing suspicion. "What are you up to, Thomas?" he demanded to know.

"Me?" Thomas squeaked. "I ain't up to nothin'. I just want to see Cat back on her feet. A few days in the Azores will help get her there. Besides, the two of you ain't had a proper honeymoon." A rakish grin stretched across his lips. "If you don't take to the idea, send me in yer stead. I'll see that Cat recuperates from the fever and enjoys her stay on the island."

"I'm sure you would," Brant snorted. Thomas was a long-time friend and good-hearted man. But his affection for Catrina was so obvious that it seeped from the pores of his skin. "No husband in his right mind would turn another man loose with his wife in such a place as this. Lord, he may as well pray for trouble!"

"Well, which of us is it goin' to be?" Thomas prodded the contemplating captain. "You or me? Just take a long look at Catrina. She's spellbound by the islands. Hell, she ain't no sailor and 'tis been almost a month since she set foot on solid ground. If you ain't goin' to take her ashore I will. And I will be only too happy to do it."

"She is *my* wife," Brant snapped irritably. "If she goes anywhere, I'll do the taking."

The words were out before Brant could bite them back and Thomas was not about to let the captain retract the offer. "If that is yer wish, then so be it . . . just as long as the lady wades ashore." Thomas gestured toward the chain of islands that was growing larger on the horizon. "You can take Catrina to Graciosa and me and the men will scout out the warships around Pico Island. When we return with a report, you can decide if you want to do battle with the British before we take the cargo to Charleston."

"On one condition," Brant stipulated, eyeing his first mate with piercing scrutiny. "Do not attempt a seizure without my permission."

"I wouldn't have considered it," Thomas assured him.

"Perhaps you wouldn't, but there are those among the crew who get that greedy look about them when temptation crosses their line of vision. They are reckless without leadership. Misdirection during wartime can be disastrous."

"I ain't lookin' to be a hero," Thomas sniffed. "And I will do my best to keep these rowdy privateers under thumb. But I would rather accompany the lady ashore and have her all to myself. Any man who would prefer a scoutin' cruise in enemy waters to a romantic interlude on an island paradise ain't normal."

"Are you insinuating that I'm a lunatic?" Brant puffed up until he very nearly popped the buttons off his shirt.

"I didn't say nothin' of the sort, Cap'n," Thomas snickered. "However, I'm still a mite puzzled why you spent a week in the ammunition storeroom . . . in the dark . . . down on yer hands and knees." Stroking his chin, he appraised Brant for a long, thoughtful moment. "Mighty strange behavior for a sane man, wouldn't you say, Cap'n?"

When Thomas sauntered off, Brant gnashed his teeth. He was not about to explain his actions to anyone, especially his antics in the arsenal. Cat would think he was a lecherous pervert and Thomas would ridicule him. Brant inwardly groaned at his unscrupulous tactics. He would take that secret to his grave. It would be utterly humiliating to admit to spying on Cat.

Damn that woman. She had him doing things he never expected of himself and he was fighting like hell to deny the attraction. He couldn't trust her, Brant cynically reminded himself. She was Scottish, a loyal subject of the Crown. And worst of all, she was a woman. A man would be a fool to let himself be dragged into a love affair with his own enemy.

Blast it, why had he married that fiery-haired hoyden in the first place? And why hadn't he deposited her in John Paul's hands? Cat would have never come down with the fever and Brant would not be hounded by the myriad of tender sensations that assaulted him while Catrina thrashed in bed, out of her mind with the fever. Brant had made a vow to himself while Cat was deathly ill. He promised himself he would no longer stand in the way of what Cat wanted if she were allowed to live. If she decided to sail back to Scotland he would let her go. If another man caught her eye he would step aside. Those were vows he intended to keep. Catrina had survived the fever. Since Brant's prayer had been answered, he was obliged to stand by his vows.

Heaving a troubled sigh, Brant stared across the waves to the shining mountains. How was he going to control himself for

273

three days while he was alone with that tempting minx? Blast it, he should never have allowed Thomas to talk him into this crazed notion. If he weren't careful he would not escape the Azores with his heart intact. And if she took his heart and demanded to return to her homeland, what would he do? What *could* he do?

But no matter what the consequences of their sojourn in the Azores, Thomas was right. A few days on the shores of Graciosa would bring the color back to Cat's cheeks. But at what cost to *his* emotions, Brant wondered dismally. Sweet mercy, he would be paving his private road to hell by agreeing to Thomas's suggestion!

Although weary from remaining on deck throughout the day, Catrina was thankful for the change of scenery. And it was a relief to be in an upright position once again. During her slow recovery from the fever, Catrina had been forced to conserve her energy. She had counted the cracks in the ceiling so many times she swore she would go stark raving mad before she was allowed to ambulate across the cabin.

Finally Cat could stand no more solitary confinement. Despite Brant's orders, she pleaded with Thomas to help her climb the steps to the deck. She had not been surprised to see the condescending frown stamped on Brant's face. Nor was she shocked when he stalked into the cabin that evening, grumbling about her defiance and total lack of respect for his authority as her husband and captain of his ship. But what knocked the props out from under her was his gruff announcement that they were rowing ashore.

Cat could scarcely believe Brant would consent to go anywhere with her. The moody pirate had avoided her like the plague for weeks on end.

"What errand are we running when we dock on Graciosa?" Catrina questioned curiously.

Brant kept his eyes carefully fixed on the wall directly above Catrina's head to prevent his gaze from mirroring his emotions. He could not look at this nymph without remembering what lay beneath those altered garments. Although Cat was thinner and hollow-eyed, her natural beauty had not faded during her illness. In fact, the vulnerability in her exquisite features evoked feelings Brant had one hell of a time ignoring.

"Thomas and I have decided your health would be greatly improved by a few days' rest on the island. You have been seriously ill and you are not accustomed to spending such long periods of time on board a ship."

His bland explanation was a bitter disappointment. Catrina would have been overjoyed with the idea if Brant had given the slightest indication that he anticipated a rendezvous on secluded shores. But he didn't and she wasn't. Indeed, she could have sworn Brant would prefer to take a beating than to be alone with her.

Her chin tilted to a proud angle. "I appreciate your concern, but waylaying on Graciosa is unnecessary. I am recovering nicely and I do not expect special treatment. If Ensign Phelps is not allowed the privilege after his bout with the fever I do not wish the schooner to detour on my account."

Brant ground his teeth to chew up the sarcastic rejoinder that waited on the tip of his tongue. Why did he even think Cat might be pleased to be alone with him? Arrogant fool, he scolded himself. No doubt, she would rather risk a flogging than to share his company.

Why was he attempting civilized warfare with this rebellious chit, he asked himself. What they needed was a shouting match to air their griefs about this so-called marriage. Once they knew where they stood with each other, they could readjust and strive for a workable peace. Heavens above, Brant was already involved in a world war! What he didn't need was a private battle with Catrina! But he was in the middle of one, just the same. And with Cat, there was no such thing as unconditional victory. Victory? Brant scoffed disdainfully at the thought. Since the situation leaned heavily toward defeat, Brant's only hope was to call a truce. And that mortifying thought turned his disposition as sour as a bushel of green apples.

"I am not asking you if you wish to go," Brant growled, his golden eyes flaring up like torches. "I am *telling* you. Gather a few necessary belongings. I am going to give my final instructions to the crew before they weigh anchor."

With that, Brant reversed direction and stomped toward the door. Oh, how she itched to swab the deck with that infuriating pirate. Childishly, Catrina pulled a face at his departing back, but the spiteful expression evaporated when Brant glanced back.

"I saw that," he informed her curtly.

Since she had been caught red-handed, she couldn't very well deny the childish prank. "I may be dragged ashore with you, but you didn't say I had to *like* the idea."

Brant grinned in spite of himself. Catrina looked comical with her face skewed up and her green eyes crossed. "Nay, I didn't," he conceded. Impulsively, he ambled back to her. His index finger smoothed away the lingering frown that claimed her flawless features. "You mustn't make such dreadful faces, my dear. If you do it often enough the expression will freeze into the muscles and you will spend the rest of your days looking like a cross-eyed ape. I should hate for my friends to think I have married out of my species."

Catrina contemplated slapping the smirk off his face, but she decided to parry his jibe with one of her own. "I wouldn't fret over it, dear husband," she purred through a sugar-coated smile. "I have most certainly married out of my species. My friends on board this ship, pirates though they are, have been considerate enough not to make mention that I have been mismatched with a snake."

Brant's countering smile was so tight Catrina feared it would split his lips. "We do make quite a spectacular pair, don't we, my precious? I wonder if our friends realize how difficult it is for us to pretend wedded bliss. 'Tis comforting to know you are as miserable as I am. At least we have one thing in common.

And since misery loves company we will row ashore to tolerate each other until the *Sea Lady* returns to retrieve us."

Doing a quick about-face, Brant closed the distance to the door in deliberate strides. This time Catrina waited until the door slammed shut behind him before she put out her tongue and pulled a face.

"Now I know how the name *Diamond*back rattlesnake was derived," she sniffed distastefully. "I intend to enjoy my sojourn on Graciosa in spite of you!"

With that positive thought humming through her mind, Cat scooped up a few necessities and crammed them into a satchel. She would frolic in this mid-ocean paradise and Brant Diamond could hide in the underbrush with the rest of the slimy reptiles and *mold* for all she cared!

Chapter Seventeen

Catrina offered Thomas a grateful smile when he met her at the foot of the steps and extended a supporting arm. A curious frown settled on her features when she noted the wide grin that stretched across Thomas's leathery face. What the devil was he so happy about, she wondered. Before she could fire the question, Brant snatched her arm from Thomas's grasp and herded her toward the skiff.

Although Cat resented Brant's cold, remote attitude, she voiced no complaint. Her eyes were on the beauty of her surroundings. The sun had begun its final descent and the evening haze splashed muted shadows of color across the face of the mountains. There was a certain mystique about the island that fascinated Catrina. She found herself wishing she could wait out the war with the natives of the Azores. Here, she would be free from Brant Diamond and Derrick Redmund. Here, she could wander at will and delight in nature's abundant beauty.

As the yawl cut its way toward the white beaches, Cat leaned out to test the water. The Gulf Stream warmed these waters and Catrina was struck by the reckless urge to dive into their enticing depths. When they were fifty yards from shore, Catrina stood up to plunge into the ocean, drifting ashore with the onrushing surf. The water closed in about her, but not before she heard Brant's startled squawk. When she resurfaced to ride the cresting wave, she met Brant's furious scowl.

"Dammit, woman, you nearly capsized the boat," he muttered sourly.

His disapproving frown slid off Catrina like water trickling down a duck's back. She giggled at the sight of Brant's dripping hair and splattered shirt. "Forgive me, Captain. I had no intention of upending you. I thought you would be relieved not to be forced to share the same boat with me."

"You haven't the strength to swim ashore," Brant insisted, straining to row the skiff alongside the impetuous mermaid. "You will damned well drown yourself with this tomfoolery!"

The playful laughter died on her lips. Her eyes met Brant's, holding him hostage for a long moment. "I would imagine that would also come as a relief. Then you would have me out from underfoot forever."

Brant opened his mouth to argue the point, but Catrina dived beneath the surface and disappeared within the depths. In frustration Brant slumped on his perch, letting the skiff drift where it would.

Things would never be right between them. Not even tolerable, Brant told himself. He was a walking contradiction who struck out to hurt Catrina to protect his male pride. He never said what he meant and he never did what he truly wanted to do where Cat was concerned. He ached to hold her, but he pushed her farther away with hateful words. He wanted to tell her how relieved he was when she recovered from the fever, but he growled at her instead.

How could he hope for a compatible coexistence when she thought he wished her an untimely end? And how the devil was he to confide his feelings when he was afraid she would toy with him the way Cynthia had? Cat hadn't wanted marriage. She only wanted the protection his name could offer her, Brant reminded himself for the umpteenth time. If he hadn't twisted her arm behind her back she would never have spoken the vows. And if he had not insisted, she would have sailed away with Jean-Martin. And then there was her escape attempt during the capture of the *Countess*—another evidence that Cat was prepared to do most anything to avoid her unwanted husband.

Brant raked his fingers through his damp hair and sighed in exasperation. This mental tug-of-war was worse than any medieval torture. For years he had swaggered from one shallow affair to another without feeling any attachment or regrets. He had taken passion where he found it . . . until Cat pranced into his life to blow holes in his theory that he was immune to the wiles of any and all females of the species.

Dammit, he *did* care what happened to her. It was this fierce possession that gnawed at his very core, refusing to grant him relief. He wanted her—madly, passionately. Yet, it frustrated him to admit it. Cat had him fighting daily battles of self-conquest. She had become a vision that followed him like his own shadow, a part of him that time and determination had not been able to erase.

The faintest hint of a smile grazed his lips when Catrina burst to the surface and then submerged. Among this chit's other unusual talents, she could swim like a confounded fish! Ah, but she made an entrancing picture, he thought to himself. Her auburn hair flowed about her like a waterfall of fire while she stretched out to glide through the water, putting even the most graceful swan to shame. In the distance, silhouetting this lovely creature, lay the sprawling oyster-white beaches. Above her, like a fairyland castle in the clouds, stood the majestic mountains of the sea. No artist could re-create such a spellbinding setting on canvas, Brant mused with an appreciative sigh.

Pushing side his meandering thoughts, Brant took the oars in hand and rowed toward shore to set up their camp for the night. Despite his attempt to pay little attention to Catrina, his gaze kept circling to the shapely naiad who refused to emerge from the ocean.

She would not have one smidgen of strength left, Brant

convinced himself. And before the day was out, he would be forced to dive into the ocean to retrieve that stubborn Cat. Damnation, cats were supposed to have an aversion to water, weren't they? Well, there was an exception to every rule, Brant reminded himself. But then, the name Cat Diamond was synonymous with contradiction. A man could not set his watch by the pacings of this she-cat because she was unpredictable. A man could not organize routine in his life because this prowling kitten would take daily ritual and claw it to pieces. In short, every day was a new world when Cat was parading about and a man was forced to struggle to keep his life and his wife in hand.

Determined to exercise the small amount of control he had over his reckless wife, Brant marched back to the beach. "You have had enough swimming for one day," Brant called out to her. "Come ashore or I am coming in after you!"

Catrina had mellowed after her relaxing swim. The ocean had washed away her frustrations and drained her energy. Without protest she waded to the beach. Forgetting she intended to remain cool and aloof in Brant's presence, a happy smile rippled across her lips, bringing color to her cheeks.

Brant's knees went boneless when Catrina emerged from the water. Her form-fitting clothes clung to every swell and curve, making Brant vividly aware of the sharp contrast between her feminine body and his. Cat looked so damned tempting, even when she was dripping wet, that Brant felt spontaneous desire channeling through every part of his being. A hunger, the likes he had never known, gnawed at him. All his well-meaning lectures abandoned him when he stared into those dancing emerald eyes. His gaze dropped to caress the pink peaks of her breasts that were outlined with the clinging shirt and then descended to survey the arousing curve of her hips.

To hell with celibacy, the passionate side of his nature growled at him. Catrina was his wife. He had legal right to pleasure himself with her exquisite body. Why should he deny himself? Submitting to his desires for this delicious witch was not an admission of love or devotion, for heaven's sake! He could salvage his pride when he satiated his lusts. He had once been able to take from a woman without giving of himself and he could do it again.

His rationalizations won out. Brant was weary of battling this attraction. They were in a deserted cove. There was no one to mock him for succumbing to the temptation. There were only the two of them and Brant ached to ease the cravings that staring at this enchanting sea witch evoked.

Catrina caught her breath when she deciphered the expression in his golden eyes. Her footsteps slowed to a halt. For a moment it was as if she were paralyzed, unable to move or even look away. She knew Brant had only to touch her and she would dissolve like tracks washing away with the oncoming waves.

A riptide of emotions swirled about her as she peered up at the black-bearded pirate. The sea breeze had tousled his raven hair, carelessly flinging it across his forehead. The deep tan of his face sharply opposed the gaping white shirt that strained across his chest. His tight blue breeches hugged his narrow hips and muscled thighs, taking her thoughts on a most sensuous detour. He was so devastatingly handsome that her overworked heart rattled in her chest.

There was only the warbling of birds in the dense forest beyond the beach, the quiet murmur of waves sifting across the sand. In that moment, as the waning light melted into night, a companionable silence hovered between them. Gone were the stinging jibes and insults. The protective armor of pride fell away like a discarded shield. They were a man and a woman, totally aware of each other, buffeted by needs that had long gone appeased.

It didn't matter why they were here alone. It didn't matter that a mountain of obstacles stood between them. The attraction between them had become more potent with time and self-denial had served to intensify the need.

"God knows I've tried to keep my distance from you," Brant

283

murmured huskily. He took a bold step forward to trace a finger over the gauze shirt that revealed the dusky peaks beneath it. "But you are too damned tempting, Cat." His golden eyes burned over her, drying her from inside out. "I want you in my arms and I don't care if I have hell to pay for admitting it. You are the fire within me. And despite all else, this blaze has never cooled or burned itself out."

There was a reluctance in the way his dark head moved toward her, as if he resented this compulsive attraction he felt for her. His eyes focused on her face, captivated by her heart-shaped mouth. His hand cupped her chin, tilting her head to his, his thumb leisurely caressing the delicate line of her jaw.

Catrina could have sworn lightning struck her. Her body sizzled beneath his touch. She wanted his kiss. Indeed, she would have killed for it. Sensations that had been dead and buried for three endless weeks were resurrected in less than a heartbeat. When his lips slanted across hers, Catrina savored the taste of him. Her arms wound around his neck to press herself full length against him. She reveled in the pleasure of molding her body to his hard, lean contours, feeling his solid frame tremble in response to her touch.

Their bodies were like logs smoldering on an already blazing fire. His caresses seared her flesh, leaving her to burn. The winds of passion fed the eternal flame, fueling it into a raging crown fire. A muffled groan caught in her throat as she edged closer, aching to give herself to the only man who could stir her to mindless passion.

Adrenaline shot through her veins, replenishing the strength she had expended during her swim. The need for Brant was so great that nothing could smother the longings that engulfed her. Passion alone sustained her, carrying her away with the path of fire.

Brant could not break the fiery kiss, even when he scooped Catrina up in his arms. His destination was the pallet beneath the shelter of the trees, but he knew he would not have the patience to wait the extra moment it would take to reach the bed roll of quilts.

Deciding to waste not even a second, Brant came down on bended knee to lay Catrina on the blanket of sand. She voiced no objection when he stretched out beside her to map the graceful curves of her body. She welcomed his expert touch and the maddening sensations he aroused. Later, they would share the bed of quilts, but for now they would make wild, sweet love in the sand, beneath the twilight's sparse smattering of stars.

His exploring hand glided beneath her shirt to make intimate contact with her flesh. Catrina moaned in pleasure as streams of sweet agony trickled over her. Every fiber of her being tingled as his caress feathered over each taut bud and then wandered across her belly. Her breath lodged in her throat when his bold hand dived beneath the band of her breeches to investigate the silky flesh of her inner thigh. As his mouth descended upon hers, his fingertips delved into the soft moistness, creating a need that threatened to consume her.

"What is this incredible need between us, Brant?" she whispered when he allowed her a breath of air. "Does it have a name, a cure? You touch me and there is no rhyme or reason. I cannot think past this insane desire I have for you to ask what the morrow will bring."

His warm kisses tracked across her cheek to seek out the sensitive point beneath her ear as his adventurous hands continued to explore the satiny curve of her hips. "'Tis incurable madness," Brant breathed against her skin. "I can no more control this yearning than I can cast out a seine and drag in the stars. I need you in ways I am helpless to understand. Love me, sweet angel. Hold nothing back. Make this island my paradise for as long as we have together."

His hushed words were like a magician's hypnotic spell. Catrina heard and obeyed. Without feminine reserve she arched toward his seeking hands and drew his lips back to hers. Her teeth nipped at his mouth. Her tongue tugged his lips apart to taste him, to share the ragged breath that sustained her. Another volatile spark bridged the narrow gap between them and the flame burned hotter, consuming them.

His body half covered hers, crushing her into the sand. His hands flowed over her yielding flesh, rediscovering her luscious contours. Catrina accepted the full weight of his lean, powerful body and the pressure built until it became a maddening pain. Tingles ricocheted through her, multiplying until she was shuddering with uncontrollable tremors. His hands and lips were everywhere, roaming unhindered across her skin as he shifted above her and then lowered himself to her. His hips guided her thighs apart as his sleek body covered hers at last . . . totally, completely.

They came together with a wild, reckless urgency that nothing could contain. His hard, quivering body became hers, appeasing the sweet ache that coiled in the very core of her being. Catrina clutched at him as he drove into her, satisfying the craving that had gnawed at her for weeks on end. He sent her spiraling into the haze of clouds that encircled the towering mountains. And for that one glorious moment they were of one heart and soul, their bodies blending in rapturous union. One splendorous sensation after another cascaded over her. Catrina felt as if she were reaching an outstretched hand to touch some intangible emotion that lay just beyond her grasp.

And then she was there, somewhere beyond the moon. Her mind went blank and her body was a mass of quivering sensations. She surrendered to them, one and all. Tiny shards of light poured through the darkness like a pitcher of stars spilling onto the black velvet sky. She was swept into the sparkling stream, flowing with the current of unrivaled passion. For what seemed eternity, she drifted, enjoying the contentment that words could not describe.

Brant gazed down at the goddess who had shown him a new dimension in heaven. He was bewildered by his need to take her again, even when his body had yet to recover from the overwhelming sensations of their ardent lovemaking. What madness was this, he asked himself as he traced the sensuous curve of her lips. He thought himself satiated, that once would be enough. But it wasn't. He still wanted her, still craved the feelings that enveloped him when his body was united with hers in ecstasy. He had denied himself far too long, Brant reasoned. Now he could not get enough of her. His body had been cruelly deprived of pleasure and the craving he had harbored these long weeks refused to go away.

Like a giant panther rolling to his feet, Brant rose to full stature. His gaze circled from the tempting nymph to the silver-capped waves that lapped against the shore. A rakish grin enhanced his shadowed features as he pulled Catrina up beside him.

"'Tis time to return you to the sea from which you came, my lovely mermaid," he chortled softly.

Brant lifted her into his arms and strode across the sand. But he wasn't sure if he had walked into the water or upon it. His body was assaulted by feelings that defied logic. He longed to return to that place in time where eternity was not measured in seconds, where there was nothing but sweet, uninterrupted ecstasy.

Catrina curled her legs about his waist, her breasts brushing provocatively against his hair-matted chest. Her lips came to his like a butterfly flittering about his mouth. He sighed in the pleasure of it all. Her kiss was like a foretaste of paradise, her touch could crumble mountains.

Brant's breath lodged in his throat. Impulsively he crushed her to him, groaning with a need that rose from nowhere to consume him. Her tongue played against his and then probed deeper, stealing the last of his breath, suffocating him in a cocoon of ineffable rapture. A white-hot fire shot through every nerve and muscle. Even though he was standing chest-deep in water, Brant swore the entire Atlantic Ocean couldn't cool the flames that were scorching his body.

Allowing the sea to cradle Catrina, Brant began to weave his sweet magic over her flesh. His hands and lips were upon her, rediscovering and sensitizing every inch of her body. His worshiping caresses triggered mystical sensations that rose and curled until they smothered her.

Catrina could endure no more of the sweet torment. She ached to feel Brant's hair-roughened flesh beneath her hands, to stir his passions to the same breathless pitch. Her caresses sketched the taut muscles of his thighs and followed the hard tendons that ascended his back. She marveled at the potential strength beneath her fingertips, loving the feel of his sinewy body.

When Brant tried to pull her to him to end the maddening agony of having her so close and yet painfully far away, Catrina pressed her hands to his chest. "In due time, Pirate Captain, we will become lovers again. But the night is still young. There are things I wish to know about you, things a wife should know about her husband."

One dark brow raised sharply and then slid back to its normal arch. "What is it you wish to know about me that you do not already know, vixen? Ask and I will tell you."

Catrina purred huskily, her green eyes sparkling with deviltry. "I wish to know you by touch. I want to know if it arouses you when I touch you here . . ."

Her fingers splayed across the broad expanse of his chest to encircle each male nipple and Brant broke into a grin. "It does give me a faint tingle of pleasure," he assured her. "What else has piqued your feline curiosity, Cat?"

"Does this excite you, my handsome pirate?" Catrina whispered as she drew nearer to feather her lips across the dark furring of hair that descended down his belly.

Her long lashes fluttered against his skin and her lips were like soft velvet brushing against him. The fresh feminine scent of her wrapped itself around his senses, setting off a series of shock waves. Her body moved suggestively against his, causing his nerves to dance beneath his flesh.

"Mmmm . . . your curiosity is killing me, Cat," he breathed raggedly.

"And this?" Catrina's roving hand swam across the lean muscles that hugged his ribs and then her fingertips dived beneath the water's surface to further investigate the rugged terrain of his lower torso."

"I'm not certain I can endure this line of questioning," Brant gasped in shaky spurts. "A man has just so much resistance. I lost most of mine when you walked from sea to land.''

''Does this disturb you?'' Her touch explored the tapering of his waist and the masculine hardness of his thighs.

''Very much so.'' His voice was so heavy with unfulfilled passion that his words were no more than a ragged whisper.

When her wandering caresses roamed lower Brant flinched. It was as he feared. All the water in the ocean couldn't cool the fires that blazed within him. He pulled Cat to him, aching to make them one living, breathing essence.

''No more games, minx,'' he murmured as he stared into her eyes, seeing a sparkle that outshined the stars. ''Your touch is not enough. I feel like loving you again . . .''

His mouth swooped down on hers, savoring and devouring her in a kiss that carried enough heat to set the sea in a rolling boil. Their bodies moved in flowing rhythm, seeking ultimate depths of intimacy, straining to ease needs that were as ancient as time itself.

Torrents of pleasure streamed through him as their bodies came together like two pieces of a puzzle that made no sense at all until they were one. Brant groaned uncontrollably, clutching her ever closer. Passion raged along its windswept course, uplifting him, flinging him into a sea storm that was more devastating than any he had ever endured. It was as if his soul had taken flight to escape the tempest. His mind was swirling with chaotic emotions. His flesh was assaulted with tumultuous sensations. And when he swore he had sacrificed life for another glimpse of paradise, Catrina's moist lips returned to his. She offered him that critical breath of life that grew and blossomed until he was a whole man again . . . the man he had been before he surrendered to the one woman who was fiery enough to match his passions and gentle enough to take his restless heart.

They lingered in the waves until the embers cooled and sanity returned. Their lips hovered together in soft, wispy kisses, their hands gently stroking in the aftermath of passion. When Brant carried Catrina to their lean-to beneath the trees, she glanced down to see the separate bed rolls. Her eyes lifted to lock with the shimmering pools of amber.

"Must you sleep so far away tonight?" Trembling fingers traced the thick beard that lined his jaw. "Don't leave me, Brant. It would be too much to bear just now . . ."

A soft chuckle rumbled in his chest. Lovingly, he glided his hand through the damp tendrils that cascaded down her arm. "Where would I go when all roads lead back to you?" he murmured, pressing a light kiss to her brow. "You have me running in circles, temptress. Don't you know that? We fight like two warring countries battling for supremacy, but when we make love, the walls come tumbling down. I cannot forget those precious moments. And they lure me back to you."

As Brant dragged the quilts together Catrina's quiet laughter drifted off with the breeze that rushed ashore. "What is there about us, my dark pirate? We are like two planets revolving around the same sun, hopelessly attracted by a fire nothing can extinguish. And yet we rival each other's purpose, throwing shadows as we go. Where will it end?"

Her question was the same one that continued to haunt Brant's thoughts. He had no answer, at least not one he could accept. "I know not, my fiery gem, I know not . . ."

As the blanket of contentment settled over them Catrina drifted into splendorous dreams, securely cradled in Brant's arms. Catrina could not name another time when she felt so whole and alive. Each time Brant had smiled at her she found her heart swelling with such pleasure that she swore it would burst. And when he murmured his need for her during the night, she surrendered to the love she could no longer deny existed.

Aye, it was an emotion so deep that nothing could rout it, she mused as she resettled in the circle of his arms. Just touching his sleek, muscular body set her soul to singing. It might not be forever, Catrina warned herself. But for a time, she would tarry in paradise.

Chapter Eighteen

Brant's lashes fluttered up to greet the morning sun. When his senses cleared he realized a stout, bronzed-faced native and his wiry-haired dog were staring curiously at him. Discreetly, Brant reached beneath the pallet to retrieve his flintlock, but the intruder raised his hand to forestall him.

"My name is Manuel Alvarez. I have not come to harm you, *amigo*," he said in broken English.

The sound of voices brought Catrina slowly awake. When she noticed the dark-skinned stranger she gasped, startled. Catrina clutched the quilt under her chin and glanced expectantly at Brant, waiting an explanation. "Who is this man?"

Brant shrugged a bare shoulder. "He says his name is Manuel. When I woke up he was standing there, grinning at me as if we were long lost friends."

Although Brant had offered a quiet explanation, Manuel was quick to note his accent. "You are American," he guessed, his smile broadening. "I once visited the colonies when I was a young man and I found much difficulty in making myself understood. Then I met a man who took me under his care and taught me the language. I vowed to my good saint that I would always treat strangers with kindness when they ventured to my homeland."

"You are very kind, Manuel," Catrina murmured.

Manuel pricked his ears. "Ah, *senora adoravel*, you must be Scottish," he speculated. "I pride myself in determining the nationality of the strangers who happen onto our shores." His gaze made a fast sweep of the lean-to, noting the scant rations Brant had brought with him from the *Sea Lady*. "You have not taken advantage of the fresh fruits and vegetables that grow in abundance on our island. We have much to offer castaways, *amigo*."

While Manuel was praising the produce to be found in the Azores, Brant was squirming uneasily beneath the quilt, wishing he had not been caught without his breeches. Damn, their deserted cove suddenly had one too many inhabitants.

When Manuel realized what disturbed the bearded American he grinned wryly. "I have come to invite you to the feast of the great saint." He gestured toward the path that wound up the side of the cliff. "When you are prepared to join me, come to my wagon."

Without waiting for Catrina and Brant to accept or reject his invitation, Manuel turned and walked away, his devoted canine trotting along at his heels. Brant grumbled under his breath. He had no desire to partake of fresh fruits when he could feast on his delicious wife.

Cat snatched up her discarded clothes and wiggled into them. Her eyes sparkled with humor when she glanced at the sour frown that was plastered on Brant's rugged features. "For a man who has been invited to gorge himself on fine food, you look none too happy about it."

"My hunger pangs are the least of my concern," Brant pouted, clutching his breeches. "I could live for a week without rations . . . other than you as dessert . . ."

Cat was delighted with the compliment, but she could not resist taunting him. "Why, Captain, you said the purpose of this sojourn was to stuff me with fresh fruits so I might regain my strength."

It was obvious that his adventurous wife was anxious to

acquaint herself with the islanders and enjoy the feast of the great saint. Begrudgingly, Brant pulled his breeches into place and ambled up beside Catrina. "Aye, I suppose that was what I said," he mumbled.

While Catrina bounded up the path to join Manuel Alvarez, Brant followed at a slower pace. Why the hell would he wish to munch on plums, pineapples, and bananas when he could be devouring Catrina, he asked himself bitterly. He had expected to have Cat all to himself, but it was not to be. Along came Manuel to interrupt what could have been a long morning of splendorous lovemaking.

"Quicken your step," Catrina called to the lagging captain. "Manuel and I are eager to join the festivities."

Brant growled under his breath. He wasn't going to enjoy the day. He just knew it! And his prediction proved correct. He found himself loaded in a wagon brimming with fruit and carted off to a village swarming with vivacious natives. The islanders crowded around Catrina, chattering in their foreign tongue, uncaring that their lovely guest could not interpret their words. Brant was separated from his wife time and time again and Cat was too preoccupied to notice that Brant was sulking.

Catrina was bubbling with enthusiasm, delighting in watching the islanders perform their folk dances. When Manuel grabbed Catrina's arm and led her into the circle to teach her the dance steps, Brant plopped down on the ground, feeling sorely out of place amid the cheerful group. His ill-humored disposition mellowed when his eyes followed Catrina through the crowd. He was mesmerized by her sylphlike grace, her ability to pick up the dance steps and perform them as if she had attended these rituals all her life. She floated in perfect rhythm to the musical accompaniment of the acoustical guitars and reed flutes. Her carefree laughter mingled with the lively folk tunes of the *chulas* and *viras*.

When Catrina finally caught a glimpse of Brant he was propped on an elbow. Leaving the circle of Manuel's arms she strode across the grass to peer at the wallflower who had yet to join in the festivities.

"A mite stuffy today, aren't we?" Cat teased. "You have been offered a gracious invitation, but you will have Manuel thinking you are ungrateful. Do you intend to spend the entire day pouting, or only the better part of the afternoon?"

"There are other physical activities that tickle my fancy far more than dancing," Brant snapped more harshly than he intended. Before Brant could expound upon the specific form of recreation that appealed to him, Manuel whisked Catrina back into the circle to teach her another folk dance.

"I think my husband needs coaxing. He has yet to adapt the festive spirit," Catrina commented.

Manuel glanced at the long-faced American and then nodded in agreement. "*Não se aflija*, I will see to it that your *marido* enjoys himself."

Manuel rattled off a request in his native tongue and a crowd of females swooped down on Brant. Before he could object, Brant was plucked off the ground and herded into the circle to be passed from one partner to another like a hot potato. His mutinous glare pelleted over Catrina, but she shrugged carelessly and continued to follow Manuel's lead.

Despite his attempt to have a miserable time during the gay affair, Brant found himself enjoying the enthusiasm of the islanders. Later, he promised himself. Later he would make Catrina compensate for dragging him into the throng of humanity.

When the feast began Brant and Catrina were handed plates heaping with fresh bread, vegetables, fruits, and white cheese. Catrina devoured the succulent food. After her bout with the fever her appetite had returned and she could not seem to get enough to eat. Never had she dined on such a delicious feast.

A curious frown knitted her brow when she chewed on the meat that had found its way to her plate. "What delicacy is this?" she questioned Manuel.

"Dog," he said matter-of-factly.

Catrina choked on the morsel of meat in her mouth and turned a pale shade of green. Grinning, Brant leaned over to whack her between the shoulder blades.

"Did you help yourself to too large a bite, my dear wife?" he taunted. Mischievously, he gestured for Manuel to fetch more of the meat that was roasting over the coals. "When Manuel returns I will take personal pains to cut your meat into bite-sized pieces. I should hate for you to strangle on it."

Catrina felt nauseated, but the feeling grew worse when she glanced up to see the Portuguese Water Dog that was bounding at Manuel's heels. "Why didn't you tell me what I was about to eat before I ate it?" she croaked, glaring disdainfully at Brant.

"You were the one who insisted on joining the islanders and learning their customs," he reminded her. "If you are going to dance their dances, then you will also partake of their food without complaint." Brant pointed a tanned finger toward the black, curly-haired canine. "To these islanders, the Portuguese Water Dog is bred to serve a useful purpose. The breed is noted for its swimming abilities. It can swim as far as five miles without tiring and dives to depths of ten or twelve feet. The islanders use these prized dogs to pull fish and nets from the ocean. The dogs also serve as messengers between ships. But to these natives, a mutt serves another purpose. These people enjoy the taste of dog, as well as fish. After all, one cannot make a steady diet of clams."

When Manuel eagerly offered Catrina another portion of smoked meat, she forced a smile and halfheartedly took a dainty helping. "I will never be able to look another dog in the eye," she muttered at Brant.

His quiet laughter echoed about her. "Eat your meal, kitten, and do not squabble over your cut of meat. After all, our purpose for cruising to the island was to put some *meat* on your bones." A devilish twinkle sparkled in his eyes as he summoned Manuel's pet and tossed the dog a scrap of bread, leaving Cat to glance back and forth between her plate and the canine. "You still look a mite green," Brant observed, stifling a chuckle. "Shall I fetch you some wine? To my knowledge, the drink is only made from grapes, sour though they may be."

Catrina eagerly clutched the mug to wash down the taste that clung to her palate. Damn that Brant, he was enjoying her misery. Determined not to offend Manuel and the kindly islanders, Catrina choked down the remainder of her meal, certain she would never forget that taste as long as she lived.

When a sudden gust of wind whipped through the village, every object that was not tied down went flying into the air. Catrina lifted her eyes to see heavy black clouds scraping the precipices of the mountains. A rumble of thunder sent the islanders scurrying to unload the food from their makeshift tables. The celebration site suddenly looked like a disturbed anthill. The natives were buzzing about, anxious to seek shelter in their huts.

Brant scowled in irritation as he surveyed the threatening sky. The forceful gale was a forewarning of the devastating tempests that were known to wreak havoc in the Azores. There was no time to return to the beach before the storm engulfed the island. He and Cat were stranded.

When Manuel motioned for them to follow, Brant grasped Cat's hand and dragged her along behind him. Before they could enter the thatched hut, the heavens opened and buckets of rain spilled from the sky. Gasping for breath and drenched to the bone, Brant shoved Catrina ahead of him and then ducked inside the shack to find himself surrounded by Manuel's large family and, God forbid, the family's livestock. The hut provided protection from the storm, but the inhabitants, both friend and fowl, were squeezed into the tiny niche like sardines trapped in a net.

The walls quivered as the howling gale swept through the village. The pounding rain tapped against the roof like the drumming of impatient fingers. Manuel and his guests were huddled in their cramped shelter, anxiously waiting for the destructive storm to run its course.

An amused giggle bubbled from Cat's lips when one of

Manuel's chickens took roost in Brant's lap. It was difficult to keep a straight face when the hen began cackling to rival the thunder that boomed about them. Catrina could tell Brant had neared the end of his patience. He sat there, his jaw taut, his big body wadded into a tight ball in the corner. After several minutes, the hen fluttered away, leaving an egg on Brant's thigh.

His smoldering amber eyes riveted over Cat. "Don't you dare say one word," he gritted out as he leaned over to set the hen's offering on the table.

Catrina made a valiant attempt to remain somber. But the thought of the cackling hen using the black-bearded corsair as a nest was too much. Cat burst into irrepressible giggles.

Her laughter stoked the fires of Brant's temper. "The next time you think to accept an invitation from Manuel, you will go alone," Brant scowled as he pulled his knees to his chin and wedged himself deeper into the corner. He glared at her as if she were personally responsible for every unpleasant event he had ever encountered.

"'Tis hardly my fault a storm interrupted the festivities," Cat smirked. "It seems a stroke of luck we accepted Manuel's invitation. We could be huddled in that flimsy lean-to you constructed."

"Flimsy!" Brant snorted. He would have puffed up with indignation, but there was no room in the crowded corner. "That shelter withstood the storm that raged within it last night."

Catrina glowered at the bearded pirate, refusing to dignify his off-color comment with a reply. Silently fuming, Catrina crouched in the corner. Oh, how she would delight in wiping that smug expression all over his craggy features. That scoundrel! Leave it to Brant Diamond to take something wild and sweet and turn it sour with his crude innuendoes.

After what seemed eternity, the storm passed and Catrina was most thankful. She had tired of pretending to be civil to that raven-haired galloot. Extending her appreciation to

Manuel's family, Catrina walked back outside to climb into the wagon. She turned a cold shoulder to Brant, one complete with icicles, and chatted with Manuel during their short journey to the beach.

When she had bid Manuel good-bye, Catrina stalked off, determined to put a greater distance between herself and the annoying corsair. After she was out of earshot Brant clasped Manuel's hand.

"We appreciate your generosity and kindness," Brant said, and then slid his departing wife a quick glance. "But this is our honeymoon of sorts." A rakish grin highlighted his bronzed features. "I was hoping to have the *senhora* all to myself."

Manuel smiled a knowing smile. "*Compreendi.* I will see to it that you and the *senhora* are not disturbed." He handed Brant a basket heaping with fresh fruits, bread, and cheese. "*Adeus, amigo.*"

When Brant appeared behind Catrina, toting a basket of food, she quickened her step. But that proved to be folly on the slippery path. A surprised yelp burst free when her feet flew out from under her. Catrina landed with a thud, grimacing when the mud oozed through her clothes. Brant's amused chuckle did nothing to ease her temper. Impulsively, she scooped up a handful of mud and hurled it at Brant's chest.

Brant's laughter evaporated. He glanced down at the glob on his shirt and glared at his furious wife. "So you wish to fight dirty, do you, woman?" A wide smile, displaying gleaming white teeth, stretched across his lips. With one lithe movement, Brant set the basket aside and dipped up a handful of gooey retaliation. Taking aim, he slung the mud, leaving a blob on the side of her fuming face.

After being slapped on the cheek with mud, Catrina came uncoiled. Using both hands, she hurled mud at Brant until he was covered with muck from head to toe. But she did not escape unscathed. Brant answered each assault with one of his own. Her anger vanished when she wiped her eyes to peer at her muddy opponent.

How foolish they were to become irritated over little or nothing when there were mountains of major problems between them. They were squabbling over molehills. Well, at least this mudslinging was a harmless release of frustration, Cat rationalized. Perhaps she could not make the rebel pirates fall in love with his British enemy, but she could enjoy his reckless laughter once again. And Brant was laughing. He had not seemed so carefree and impetuous in weeks. Mud fights were far better than the strained silence that had once stood like an invisible partition between them.

"I have had enough," Catrina surrendered. Without further ado, she peeled off the stained shirt and breeches and sauntered down the path, leaving Brant to repair his unhinged jaw and close his gaping mouth.

When Brant recovered, his eyes soared skyward. Lord, would he ever learn to adjust to this witch's quicksilver moods? One moment they were engaged in mudslinging and the next moment, Cat was shaking off her clothes, arousing him, even when she wasn't trying. He was compelled to follow and follow her he did. By the time she reached the sand Brant was one step behind her. His fingers clamped around her elbow, slowing her pace.

"I delight in teasing you," he confessed as he combed his hand through her muddy hair. "I adore the fire in your eyes, minx. You are spectacular when you are angry. Even our battles provide a certain amount of pleasure." His lips brushed across hers. Gently, he pulled her into his arms, feeling her soft flesh forge against his. "But if I were allowed my way, we would spend all our time doing this . . ."

Catrina sighed contentedly as his kiss deepened. She had never been able to resist this pirate's dark charm. He had but to touch her and she melted all over him, forgetting the obstacles between them.

"I have no complaint," Catrina murmured against his sensuous lips. Her hands glided over the hard muscles of his chest to toy with the shiny black hair that curled against the nape of his neck. "After a quick bath, shall we retire to the lean-to to see if it can withstand another passionate storm?"

Brant withdrew, his expression sober. "I'm sorry," he apologized. "Earlier, I spoke in anger. I was none too happy about sharing you with the islanders. I did not intend to imply that I found fault with your lovemaking. Indeed, you are very proficient . . ."

"As proficient as Cynthia Marsh . . ." Catrina could have cut out her runaway tongue. Silently, she cursed herself for asking Brant to make such a comparison.

With her face flaming she twisted away to rush along the shore. She longed to know the answer to that haunting question and yet she didn't want to know either. It would have destroyed her to learn she was merely a substitute for the woman who had once possessed Brant's heart. Did Brant look into her eyes and see another woman? Was he pretending he possessed the one woman he could never have?

Eluding those tormenting thoughts, Catrina scampered up the boulders above the beach to sink into one of the many warm pools that were fed by hot springs that bubbled from the volcanic mountains. When Brant appeared on the rock ledge, stripped naked, Catrina glided away, refusing to look in his direction.

Stifling an amused smile Brant eased into the steamy water and swam toward his retreating wife. When he had pinned her against the rocks, he turned her in his arms, forcing her to meet his level gaze.

"You didn't let me answer your question, vixen," he murmured, his eyes roaming over her soft, delicate features, ones that seemed more vulnerable since her illness.

"I don't think I want to know. After giving the inquiry a moment of consideration I realize I should not have asked," she grumbled.

Shrugging, Brant released her to drift on his back. "Very well then, if you don't want an answer . . ."

Cat glared at his ornery smile, once her eyes ran past his

300

masculine form floating upon the water. "I sorely wish I had been promiscuous these past years," she muttered spitefully. "Then I could compare your techniques to my scores of lovers. Perhaps I should take a survey when I return to civilization. Then I can determine how you match up to other men who might be persuaded to join me in bed."

Brant tucked his legs beneath him and stood up. His fists were clenched on his hips and his eyes were as hard as gold nuggets. "I do not find those remarks the least bit amusing."

"Nor do I find any humor in the fact that you have probably slept with more women than I have known in my lifetime!" Catrina spewed.

"Had I cavorted with as many women as your wild imagination leads you to believe, I would have spent more time in bed than on my feet this past decade," Brant snorted sarcastically. "I can assure you that is not at all the case, madame."

"How many, Brant?" Catrina blurted out, her irritation causing her tongue to outrun her brain. "Can you count them on one hand . . . or even two?" Dammit, she knew no matter what he said she was going to be mad as hell.

One heavy brow lifted in taunt. "Aren't you the same young lady who once proclaimed you are not going to quiz me about the sordid details of my affairs or demand to examine the chronicles of my wayward youth?" he flung at her, grinning all the while.

Aye, she had said that, but curiosity was killing Cat. Blast it, why had she dared to dredge up his past? It was only going to upset her. Willfully, Catrina held her tongue, speculating on the number of women Brant had seduced to earn him the reputation of a masterful lover.

Aware of her sulking silence, Brant held out his arms, urging her closer. "Come here, minx. We were supposedly finished with our quarreling and mudslinging."

Reluctantly, Catrina swam toward him. She was too tired to go another round. Her vigorous activities during the celebration had sapped her strength. She just wanted to be held in Brant's arms and forget everything that had any resemblance to reality.

Brant nuzzled his chin against her head and sighed. "Let's go back to the lean-to. 'Tis been a long day and you have already overexerted yourself. I did not come here to watch you suffer a relapse."

Nodding mutely, Catrina allowed Brant to hoist her from the bubbling pool and lead her down the path to the beach. When they reached the lean-to, Brant swore under his breath. The blustery gale had caused the lean-to to sway until it collapsed in a heap in the sand.

"I stand corrected," Brant muttered. "It appears my flimsy accommodations have buckled beneath the storm."

He hurriedly dug into the rubble to drag out the quilts and directed Catrina to plant herself on the pallet. "You rest while I rebuild our humble abode," he instructed.

Brant untied the twisted ropes and restrung the tarp. With that accomplished he gathered the stray limbs and situated them in a row to form a wall. He worked quickly, anticipating the possibility of making love to Cat all through the night.

When he completed his task and turned back to Catrina, his shoulders slumped in disappointment. Catrina was asleep, her arms flung across the pallet, her chest rising and falling in methodical breaths. Brant settled down beside her, staring at her for a long, silent moment. The little nymph had depleted her energy during the celebration and there was nothing left. Reluctantly, he reminded himself that she needed to recuperate after her illness. The last thing she needed after a full day was to be deprived of her rest.

And where did that leave Brant? Frustrated. Gnashing his teeth to combat his unfulfilled passions, Brant scooped up the sleeping bundle and deposited her inside the lean-to. Catrina roused for only a moment. But the instant Brant laid her down she curled into a ball and moaned drowsily.

Brant peered down at the naked beauty and then dragged a

302

quilt over her. "Tomorrow, my sleeping beauty, when you are well rested, I will expect full compensation for my noble restraint," he mused, half aloud.

Contemplating that thought, Brant settled down to sleep . . . although it had been the furthest thing from his mind when he drew this shapely minx from her bubbling bath and led her back to the lean-to.

Chapter Nineteen

A contented smile rippled across Brant's lips as he lay basking in the sun. His gaze drifted to the bewitching naiad who dipped and dived in the water. When Cat tossed her wet hair over her shoulders and walked ashore, Brant's smile faded into a wary frown. Cat had that mischievous look about her and he could not imagine what wicked thoughts were dancing in her head.

"Why are you looking at me like that?" he demanded to know.

Her green eyes glittered with deviltry. Boldly, she raked his masculine form, not missing even the smallest detail. When Cat reached down to retrieve the stiletto and tested the blade, the dubious expression settled deeper into Brant's tanned features.

"Do you plan to do some carving, madam?" he interrogated.

Cat glanced up, beaming with impish delight. "Aye, as a matter of fact, I do."

"Carving on what . . . or dare I ask," Brant prodded, propping himself up on both elbows to regard the ornery nymph.

"On you, Pirate Captain," she informed him glibly.

Brant met her wicked grin and then focused on the sharp blade. "I thought we were on friendly terms. Surely you aren't

305

thinking of cutting out a pound or two of my flesh."

A devilish chuckle bubbled from her lips as she crept closer, the dagger blade gleaming in the bright sunlight. "Nay, Captain."

Brant slumped in relief. For a moment there he thought she was going to slice him to bits and feed him to the fish. But she wasn't angry with him, he reassured himself. They had not argued since the previous evening.

"'Tis not what I intend to cut *out* that should concern you," she chuckled fiendishly. "'Tis what I plan to cut *off!*"

Her visual communication was downright sinful and Brant flinched in response. She assessed him from head to toe, and all parts in between. Before Brant could gather his feet beneath him and make a dash to safety, Cat grasped the front of his shirt and carved off the buttons, leaving the garment dangling at his sides. Wide, disbelieving eyes lifted to her wicked grin and Brant stared at her as if she had gone mad.

"What the sweet loving hell did you do that for?" he squawked, surveying his mutilated shirt.

"Because you are such a stuffy pirate," she chided playfully. "Yesterday you pouted your way through the feast of the great saint and today you have garbed yourself in far too many clothes to suit this warm climate."

After shoving the shirt from his broad shoulders, Cat clutched the leg of his breeches high above the knees. With two quick slashes of the stiletto she transformed his long pants into provocative shorts.

Brant opened his mouth to protest the destruction of his clothes, but the words died on his lips when Cat plopped down on his belly, forcing the wind out of him. Threateningly, she waved the blade in front of his nose and then lightly laid it against his neck.

"You were about to voice a comment, Captain?" she taunted, a deliciously mischievous smile twitching her lips.

Brant addressed his playful assailant with a subdued grin. "I was about to say I make it a *point* never to argue with a witch

306

who holds a knife to my throat, especially when I know how adept she is with the weapon."

" 'Tis a wise rule to follow," she concurred. Bounding to her feet, Cat stepped back to appraise her handiwork. The effect of his bare chest and exposed legs was devastating. Brant's powerful physique did wonders with the most elegant of clothes. But he was even more stimulating to the eye in these scant garments. "I heartily approve of the transformation." Her compliment was substantiated by a slow, deliberate survey of his bared anatomy.

With a quick flick of her wrist, Cat flung the dagger into the sand, leaving it quivering not four inches from Brant's left forearm. His narrowed gaze swung from the nearby weapon to Cat's unconcerned countenance.

"You could have laid me open," Brant admonished.

Catrina lifted a nonchalant shoulder. "I could have," she agreed. "*If* that had been my purpose. But the blade stands upon its target. You had no need to fear that I might have drawn blood if 'twas not my intention. I was taught to handle a knife by the most notorious of pirates. I have learned many things from the daring renegade. Hurling stilettos was the least of them," she added with a teasing smile. Cat strolled around Brant, surveying him from all angles. "Aye, your new wardrobe is very appealing." She gestured toward his bare legs and chest. "Now you look the part of a castaway on a mid-Atlantic island."

Brant retrieved the knife and rolled to his feet to tower over Cat. "But you, madam, are the one who is shamefully overdressed. 'Tis my turn to remedy that."

Ah, how she adored watching the smile lines spray from his golden eyes and the dimples dive into his heavy beard. He looked so ruggedly handsome that Catrina fell in love with him all over again.

When Brant stalked toward her, Cat retreated. "Beast," she shrieked in mock horror. "You wouldn't dare lay a hand on me!"

"A hand?" One dark brow climbed to a roguish angle. He came at her like a prowling panther waiting the right moment to pounce. "I intend to lay more than a hand on you . . . after I have chopped off a few unnecessary yards of fabric."

The buttons of her shirt went flying and the garment parted to reveal the cleavage of her bosom, much to Brant's delight. Deftly, he inserted the blade into the leg of her breeches and proceeded to design a garment that allowed his gaze free access to her shapely thighs. A mite indecent though it was, the short breeches were most enticing to the rakish eye. The mere sight of her creamy flesh glowing in the sunlight aroused him. Tiring of their game, Brant recklessly tossed the stiletto aside.

"Come here, woman," he growled, his voice raspy with unappeased desire. "Your skimpy clothes tantalize me. But I still prefer to see you without a stitch."

When Brant reached out to remove the dangling shirt, Cat agilely sidestepped and dashed toward the ocean. Her merry giggle rang in his ears, luring him to give chase. His long, swift strides closed the distance between them. When he clutched at the collar of her shirt, Cat sarificed the garment for her freedom and dived into the oncoming surf. Inhaling a frustrated breath, Brant glared at the empty shirt that was clenched in his fist. But a roguish grin replaced his disappointed frown when the rolling wave brought her discarded breeches to his feet.

Catrina rose from the water and tossed him a silent invitation to join her. Brant swore he would evaporate into a steamy fog when the water receded to reveal Catrina's exquisite body to his leering gaze. He mapped the luscious landscape of her body, entranced by the way the tiny droplets glistened on her bare shoulders and full breasts. Lord, he ached to touch what his eyes hungrily devoured. He could almost feel her moist skin beneath his inquiring hand, taste the hint of salt water on her heart-shaped lips. Brant tore off his clothes and waded into the water, anxious to put actions to the sensuous thoughts that were skipping through his mind.

"I wondered if you would come to join me in a swim," Cat murmured, her attention focused on his sleek, well-sculptured torso.

"I have not the slightest inclination to tread water with you," he told her, his voice low and provocative. "'Tis something else that entices me into the ocean . . ."

Before Brant could capture her in his arms, Catrina dived beneath the surface. With Brant in pursuit she made her way to the cave formed by the constant force of the ocean lashing against the rocks. During her explorations of the coast she had discovered an underwater entrance to a most intriguing cavern.

When Brant burst to the surface he found a dome of glazed rock above him. A small opening near the peak of the cave offered light to guide them to the smooth boulder that sat like a tiny island amid the whirlpool.

"Is this the haven where mermaids dwell?" Brant questioned bewilderedly. It was as if he had surfaced in shadowed dream. He was surrounded by the echo of his own voice and the strange, mystical formations of rock.

Cat eased onto the boulder and leaned back on her arms to study the darkly attractive face that protruded from the pool. "There is an old Scottish legend stating that mermaids lure sailors into the depths. These sirens of the sea yearn for a human soul and they can only acquire one by marrying a mortal."

Brant pulled himself from the swirling whirlpool to curl his arm around Cat's waist. The feel of her soft body molded to his sent his passions rising like the high tides. "Tell me more, sweet siren. I'm fascinated," he murmured against the swanlike column of her neck.

Her wandering hand drifted over his collarbone to trace the bulging muscles of his upper arm. "These mermaids often entice men to live with them in the sea." Her voice was like a soft, enchanting melody, luring him deeper into her spell. "Her song can put a man into a hypnotic trance or drive him mad . . . depending on how fond she is of the mortal she has lured into her lair . . ."

Her hushed words whispered through the cavern. Her caress flowed over his hip like a wave unfolding on the sandy shore. Her sweet mouth brushed against his, tempting and teasing him until he moaned involuntarily. The taste of her lingered on his lips, leaving him craving a dozen more kisses, just like the one she had bestowed on him.

"And which is it you intend for me?" Brant breathed raggedly.

Her caresses became more intimate, more arousing. "I plan to drive you mad . . ." Cat murmured against his hair-matted flesh. "Mad with passion . . ."

Brant struggled for about half a second. But in that short span of time he knew it was futile to fight against the wiles of this enchanting sea witch. Her touch spun a silky web of rapture around him and it was impossible to ignore the entangling sensations. He had every intention of seducing *her*. But it seemed Cat intended for it to be the other way around.

He could feel the taut peaks of her breasts searing his heaving chest. The clean scent of her absorbed into his skin. Desire, like a dense fog, enveloped him. His body stirred, longing to satisfy a need that this siren alone created.

In the past, his fervent passion had raged like the savage storm that had wrought destruction on the island the previous afternoon. But this was altogether different, he realized, grasping to pursue the contemplative thought. Aye, the craving was there, bordering on insanity. But it built slowly, creeping up on him inch by inch as Catrina's kisses and caresses investigated his muscular body. She had set the cadence for their lovemaking with those long, stroking caresses and feathery kisses that offered gentle pleasure and promised unleashed passion.

Her embrace was like the subtle erosion of the sea upon the rocks, flooding and then ebbing, constantly moving over his flesh until he melted into a pool of liquid desire. What had

310

once been the muscled contours of a man were now smooth, pliant planes. What had once lain rough and ragged beneath the surface was now polished to sweet perfection.

This was passion in its pure form. It was the unique blend of desire embroidered with love. Brant could feel the sensations spilling through him, devastating him in a quiet, penetrating way.

His thick lashes fluttered up to see Cat's flawless face hovering only a few breathless inches from his. As her lips mated with his, her body took possession of what had once been a mass of masculine strength. But no longer, Brant mused as she moved sensuously upon him. The potency of her lovemaking lay in overpowering tenderness. She had taken command of his mind and body without the slightest force.

The crescendo built ever so slowly, like a siren's song playing softly on his soul, enticing him deeper into her spell. She left him reveling in each arousing sensation until they piled one upon the other, gradually intensifying the need until it became a sweet tormenting ache. The maddening craving had sneaked up on him so silently, so completely, there was no time to take control of his mounting passions. It was as if he had unknowingly drifted to the edge of a waterfall and then plummeted into the churning pool of rapture before he realized what had transpired.

Incredible sensations splashed over him and he gasped to catch his breath before he drowned in the soul-shuddering emotions. Instinctively, Brant clutched Catrina to him, clinging to the only stable force in a world of dark, erotic ecstasy.

In that wild, delicious moment that pursued and captured time, Brant dangled in an echoing chamber of rapture. He couldn't breathe. His heart ceased beating. His body was numb from the assault of so many tantalizing sensations. The feeling that spread through him was like nothing he had ever experienced. He could not begin to describe the moment, even to himself. It was far more than an enchanted dream. There were no words to express the quintessence of Catrina's lovemaking.

Catrina bent to press a light kiss to his parted lips and then slid into the cool whirlpool. Her body tingled from their passionate encounter and she did not trust herself to remain by Brant's side until the haze of emotions had cleared. What she felt for this rogue threatened to translate itself into words—words the cynical pirate could not understand.

Aye, she loved him with all her heart, Catrina admitted to herself. But it was a secret love, one that could only be expressed in moments of passion. She could touch him with love and kiss him with all the pent-up emotion that coiled inside her. She could only speak to him in the language of one soul reaching out to another. But words of love would only fall on deaf ears. Cat would not risk breaking this enchanting spell by putting her deep feelings to tongue.

Perhaps she could not confess what she felt, but the unselfish affection was there, just the same. It was in the way she caressed him, the way her lips worshiped the feel of his beneath her kiss, the way she offered herself to him, giving and sharing the splendorous pleasures of love.

Heaving a weary sigh, Brant eased onto his stomach and propped his chin on his hands. Silently, he watched the graceful siren swim circles in the underground pool. He felt oddly serene on his rock island, viewing this breathtaking creature who had done impossible things to his self-control. She had made him her pawn and he had moved upon command, responding to the delightful sensations she had created with her touch.

When Cat glided toward him he outstretched a hand to tilt her face to his. "Tell me another Scottish legend of the sea," he beseeched her, his tone still husky with the side effects of passion. "And if the enchanting tale ends as dramatically as the first, you can have my soul, lovely mermaid. Do with it what you will . . ."

With his eyes lost in the depths of emerald green, Brant slid his arm around her waist to lift her from the pool. His mouth swooped down on hers, devouring her as if he were starved for the dewy sweetness of her lips. Catrina surrendered to his ravenous kiss and the exciting feel of his masculine body straining intimately against hers. This was Diamond's brand of passion, she mused with a sigh. It was more forceful, more impatient, but every bit as satisfying as the tender love she had offered him.

The wild savagery of his lovemaking was like being dragged into a turbulent current. She was tossed from one waveswept emotion into another. His kiss sizzled like a boiling river and his caress was a devastating flood rushing over her trembling flesh. Brant Diamond could be a gentle lover when it met his mood. But it was this reckless, untamed renegade who yielded to his primal instincts who captivated her. She eagerly responded to his embrace, caught up in the chaotic sensations that swirled about her.

And it was almost an hour later before passion's rolling river became a quiet pool and Catrina could collect her wits to relate the Scottish legend. When she did, Brant was most receptive to the tale of the mystical creature that raced across the sand to entice innocent mortals to live within the boundless depths of the sea. At least he was receptive to the story of magical kelpies *until* he became distracted by a need that ran as swift and deep as an eternal spring. . . .

While Brant and Catrina were delighting in their carefree existence of love and laughter, Thomas was making his way toward the port on Pico Island. His scouting mission had proved successful, almost too successful. A British frigate, its flag undulating in the breeze, sat alone in the harbor. The temptation to advance and capture was more than the independent crew of privateers could bear.

Thomas, although he was popular among the crew, did not carry the prestige nor the dominating influence of Captain

Diamond. When several sailors approached the first mate, insisting they take the prize, Thomas met with difficulty.

"The rest of us have decided to seize the sloop," Clifton Perkins, the spokesman for the crew, declared. "If we wait until we retrieve the captain, the bay may be crawling with British."

"That may be so, but Cap'n Diamond gave us strict orders not to engage in battle on this cruise," Thomas reminded him sharply. His wary gaze swung to the congregation of sailors who frowned at the first mate's objection. "I gave my word to Diamond and I'm obliged to keep it."

"Hell, the frigate is ripe for plucking," Clifton argued. "And we didn't make no solemn pact with the captain. We're entitled to the prize . . . with or without your consent."

The greedy scoundrel, Thomas thought sourly. A man's disposition changed drastically when he was confronted with the temptation of more wealth. Thomas tilted a determined chin and stared Clifton straight in the eye. "I say we return to Graciosa to report the position of the brigantine to the cap'n."

"Look yonder, fool," Clifton snorted, indicating the seemingly unsuspecting warship. "She sits heavy in the water. No doubt her hull is heaping with valuable cargo, goods that could aid our patriot army."

"It ain't the supplies you covet, Perkins," Thomas sniffed sarcastically. "You're thinkin' about whatever valuables could be sold for yer own profit. Don't pretend the selfless patriot with me. I know you too well for that. Yer main concern is Clifton Perkins. It always has been. Loyal and steadfast you ain't and you never have been!"

When his temper was sorely tested and his integrity was questioned, Clifton cast diplomacy to the wind. He could taste the waiting riches and he was not about to turn his back on the booty that waited in the hull of the frigate. Thomas was too devoted to the captain for his own good, Clifton mused. The first mate would bypass riches to remain in Diamond's good graces.

"We intend to take the ship," Clifton growled. "If you want no part of it go below. But you can't fight the will of the entire crew."

"Now wait just a damned minute. I'm still in com—"

Before Thomas could complete his protests he was grabbed from behind and shuffled toward his cabin. Once Thomas was out of the way Perkins took command of the *Sea Lady*. The scheme would be a simple one, he assured himself. The unsuspecting frigate would never know they were being accosted by an enemy sloop until the grappling irons were hurled onto the deck. The patriots would run up the British flag to deceive them and then ease alongside. The enemy captain would find himself a prisoner and not a shot would need to be fired. Thomas was a fool for turning his back on opportunity, Clifton told himself as he raised the spyglass to survey the peaceful ship.

While Thomas was being locked in his cabin and Clifton was snickering at his own cleverness, Derrick Redmund was lying in wait. He had loaded the less than seaworthy tub with rocks and towed it into the harbor to bait the privateers. From the secluded cover he watched and waited for the *Ranger* and the *Sea Lady* to take the bait. Although Derrick was disappointed that Diamond's ship had come alone, he licked his lips in anticipation of a confrontation with this particular American captain.

Brant had difficulty recalling where he had met Derrick Redmund, but Derrick had no trouble placing Diamond's name and face. Before the war, Derrick had entered into shady dealings with the black market in an effort to establish a fortune. After making arrangements with a less than respectable merchant in the West Indies, Derrick had approached Brant Diamond to ship the cargo from the islands to a secluded warehouse in Bristol, England. Somehow, Brant had guessed that he was about to be used as the means to

315

infiltrate contraband into the Isles. Not only did Diamond reject the offer, but he informed the authorities of Derrick's plan to sneak illegal goods to England. It had taken some fast talking and pocket padding to escape imprisonment. The funds needed to buy his freedom caused Derrick another setback on the road to fortune.

Brant Diamond owed him a double debt, one Derrick fully intended to collect. He had already speculated on his popularity in the British Isles when he returned with the notorious privateer in tow. There would be a sizable reward for the capture of the elusive pirate, not to mention a distinguished promotion in the ranks of the Royal Navy.

A satanic grin stretched across Derrick's lips when he spied the privateer easing closer. Once the privateers boarded the frigate and filed into the hull to confiscate their prizes, Derrick and his sister ship would swarm the patriot schooner. When the blundering Captain Diamond was taken prisoner, the *Sea Lady* would be blown to bits. Britain would rid the sea of the pesky pirate who preyed upon her sloops-of-war and Derrick Redmund would be hailed a conquering hero.

When the schooner raised a British flag and veered toward the brigantine that was manned by a scant crew, Derrick chuckled in smug satisfaction. Diamond was about to be made to look the fool. How true it was that a man was easily deceived when he set about to deceive others, Derrick thought to himself. Diamond was not half as clever as he deemed himself to be. The arrogant pirate was cruising into a trap.

"Come closer, Diamond," Derrick jeered. "'Tis the last time you privateers will sit upon these waters."

Anxiously, he waited for the schooner to draw within firing range. His men stood by their cannons, prepared to blow away the privateer's sails, just as they had shredded his canvas in Belfast Lough. The swivel guns had been mounted on the bulwarks and the arsenal of muskets and blunderbusses lay ready for close-range fighting and boarding.

"Very soon, we will meet face to face once again, Captain

Diamond," Derrick mused with a sinister smile. "But this time the victory shall be mine!"

With his hands tied behind his back, Thomas paced the confines of his cabin and then paused to peer out the porthole. From his quarters below deck he could see the heavily weighted frigate anchored in the bay. To the east lay the abandoned harbor that was usually lined with British warships.

A wary frown knitted Thomas's brow. Something was amiss. He could feel it in his bones. Odd, he thought to himself. He had never experienced such a simple attack against the enemy. The British may have been fools, but they certainly weren't idiots. There was little movement on board the brigantine and all sails were tied to the masts. A schooner stripped of its sails was a setting target for the enemy. She could never open sail and weigh anchor before catastrophe struck. Even the most foolish of captains would never bare his vessel in wartime.

In silent reverie, Thomas stared at the coastline. When he spotted the top of the masts that were camouflaged by the gnarled vines that were draped on the trees, a groan of disgust burst from his lips. Sickening dread overcame him when his gaze swung to the far side of the inlet to spy the masts of yet another frigate lying in wait.

That damned moron, Perkins, was steering the *Lady* into a trap! The man was so greedy for riches that he had not bothered to scout the shore. He was heading straight for the bobbing brigantine. Damn, even if Perkins realized his mistake in time it would be dangerous to bring the ship about in the stout breeze that blew out to sea. The waiting enemy would ride the wind and swoop down on the privateers before Perkins could complete the maneuver of reversing direction.

Thomas spun on his heels and charged at the locked door like a bat out of hell. With a thud, he bounced back, his movement halted by solid oak. Determined to warn the crew, Thomas lowered his shoulder, using his entire body as a battering ram. This time the hinges sagged and the door dropped. Raising a booted foot, Thomas kicked away the lock and bounded up the steps.

"'Tis a trap!" he shouted for all he was worth. "Look starboard, you fool. The enemy is crawlin' from the underbrush to blow you off the sea!"

Perkins's head swiveled around in time to see the masts of two men-of-war ease into the bay. Cursing under his breath, he clambered down the ladder to cut Thomas loose. "I hope you're as adept at turning about as the captain is," he mumbled humbly.

"If not for yer idiotic blunder I would not find my abilities tested," Thomas snapped furiously. "And *that* is why Diamond is in control of this ship, not you. He would have questioned the ease of capturin' the prize while you ran blindly ahead without surveyin' the situation." He inhaled an angry breath and then shoved Perkins toward the ladder. "Man the sails! If we escape it will only be by the skin of our necks."

Thomas leaped onto the quarterdeck to assume command while the apprehensive sailors scattered to their posts. "Trim the head sails!" Thomas shouted, and then muttered sourly when he recognized the frigate they had confronted at Belfast.

Tensely, Thomas grasped the wheel and turned from starboard to port tack. Although Brant could perform this maneuver in his sleep, Thomas was apprehensive about his ability to make such a swift turnabout in this breeze. The head sails and foresails shivered as the vessel swerved around the floating decoy. The *Sea Lady* came through the eye of the wind and dipped into the trough of the sea, causing her to tilt to a dangerous angle. Lord, how Thomas wished it was Brant who manned the helm at this moment! In the face of danger, Brant was calm and controlled, but Thomas was shaking like a damned leaf!

The whistle of cannons echoed about the privateers as they scampered to the opposite side of the ship to await the crest of the wave that would take them from harm's way. As the wind caught the sails the schooner lurched backward. Gritting his teeth, Thomas spun the wheel to avoid colliding with the decoy. When the *Sea Lady* scraped past the frigate, Thomas cut back to make headway before the billowing sails collapsed.

While the two British frigates closed the distance and bombarded them with cannon fire, Thomas aimed the schooner northeast, hoping to evade the sea wolves that hungered to gobble them up. The American returned the fire, attempting to cut the sails and slow their enemies' progress, but the British kept coming, refusing to allow the patriots to sail away unscathed.

Thomas thanked his lucky stars when an oncoming cannon ball narrowly missed the hull, saving the *Sea Lady* from a disastrous blow. A round of cheers resounded across the deck when the ship surged into open waters to outdistance the cumbersome warships.

To Thomas's relief, one of the frigates gave up the chase, but Derrick Redmund had waited too long to snare Captain Diamond. He was not about to have his plans foiled. The Admiralty would force him to resign his commission if he did not keep his part of the bargain. His reputation depended on the success of this mission and he could not turn back without being humiliated.

Scowling over the unfortunate turn of events, Derrick paced the deck. Damnation, he had come so close! But at least Diamond realized he had been played for a fool, Derrick consoled himself.

Brant Diamond would sit up and take note of his enemy from this day forward. Derrick would hound Pirate Diamond until he was taken captive and tossed into a musty prison. No matter where Diamond went he would not be far behind, Derrick vowed to himself. He could not return to Britain without the infamous pirate. The Admiralty would laugh him out of the Isles.

Blast it, it seemed Derrick's lot in life was to follow in Diamond's wake. Damn the man to hell, Derrick snarled viciously. He did not relish the idea of putting so much distance between himself and Catrina Hamilton at this critical time. But he was left with no choice. He could not show his face in Britain without Diamond in chains.

Ah well, Derrick sighed defeatedly. Where could Catrina go? She would have returned to her estate by now. Once Derrick had completed his mission, he would go to her. And this time he would not allow her to escape him. There were many things Derrick wanted from Catrina; not the least of them was her fortune. And in time Derrick would make that gorgeous creature his wife. She would succumb to him and he would spend his life pleasuring himself in her shapely body and her vast fortune.

Chapter Twenty

A low rumble of laughter bubbled in Brant's chest when he awoke from a most fantastic dream. He lay sprawled in the sand, just as he had been that morning—before the seductive siren appeared on the shore to lure him into her secluded cavern. She had filled his head with Scottish folklore, not to mention how she had effectively demonstrated the powers the mystical creatures held over mortals.

Brant had been intrigued by the creature the Scots referred to as the kelpie. Cat claimed that on dry land the kelpie appeared as a magnificent steed, harnessed and ready to mount. The high-spirited horse would come prancing from the waves, its head held high, its red coat glistening in the sunlight. A man who caught sight of this stunning creature would be tempted to climb upon its back and gallop across the beach. But once a mortal straddled this mystical steed, he became glued to the saddle. The beautiful beast would rear upon its hind legs and then lunge into its swiftest gait. The creature would plunge headlong into the sea, taking its captive with it. And once the mortal was taken down under the sea, he could never return to live on dry land. He would never again be the same after he thundered into the waves on the back of this beautiful red sea horse.

Brant drew up his legs and clasped his hands behind his

head. Breathing a serene sigh, he let his eyes drift shut to relive the wild escapade that had given him most of his strength. Ah, if he lived to be one hundred he would never forget this sojourn in paradise. Catrina had introduced him to a world he never imagined existed. It was a universe of pleasure, one that swirled with both love and laughter.

Even in the middle of a war, Brant had found a glimpse of happiness. The past few days had been a fantastic dream that Brant hated to see come to an end. He did not relish gathering their belongings and rowing back into the real world.

Although he and Catrina had surrendered to their compelling attraction to each other, they had not broached the subject of their future. Brant was hesitant to break the magical spell, certain it would lead to an argument.

The sound of distant laughter filtered into his contemplations and Brant's eyes fluttered open to see the Scottish nymph emerging from her playground in the sea. Her long hair was draped about her and her skimpy garments clung to her skin. Brant set aside his wandering thoughts to study Cat's alluring form and the wild red mane that caught the spray of sunbeams. He focused on a face that was alive with pleasure, a face that could hold a man spellbound.

Brant was again reminded of the prancing red sea horse that came ashore to take an unsuspecting rider to his new home in the dark depths, never to return. Aye, Cat was like a mystical kelpie and an enchanting mermaid—an irresistible creature that took a man's soul and led him into a world that was unlike anything he had ever known.

God, she was lovely, he breathed appreciatively. Her zest for life was contagious. Brant felt a renewed inner force swelling deep within him . . . until Cat suddenly pounced on his belly, knocking the wind out of him. A pained grunt erupted from his chest as she plopped her derriere on his midsection. Playfully, Cat shook her dripping hair in his face and then sprawled on top of him to shower him with loud, smacking kisses.

"Shameless hussy," he chortled, rolling Cat to her back,

giving him the advantageous position. "Have you no self-control?"

"Have I need of any?" Cat giggled, sporting an impish smile. Her eyes caressed the tanned expanse of his chest and her hands slid over the muscled slope of his shoulder. "We have but one day left in heaven. It seems a pity to waste it."

A roguish smile skipped across his bearded face, making his golden eyes sparkle like the sun. "You do have a point, madame." Brant turned his attention to her heart-shaped lips, knowing they would be as soft as rose petals beneath his kiss. His head moved deliberately toward hers. "It would be foolish to waste even a moment . . ."

The feel of his full lips whispering over hers sent waves of pleasure rolling down her spine. Catrina molded her body against his, her eager caresses tracking along the muscled planes of his back. Her hand crept along his ribs and then traced the sinewed column of his thigh, teasing and arousing him to breathless anticipation.

"Vixen," he growled huskily. "You delight in making me a slave to your touch."

"Prude," she kidded him between kisses and then tugged at the band of his short breeches. "Again I find you terribly overdressed."

"And what would you have me wear?" he laughed softly. "You have already clipped my breeches until they barely cover me at all."

Brant returned the tantalizing caresses she was weaving over his flesh. His wandering hand dived beneath the hem of the buttonless shirt she had tied beneath her breasts. His fingertips encircled each pink bud, teasing them to tautness.

Catrina looked up into his craggy features. Her green eyes darkened with desire as his hands navigated across the curve of her waist to settle familiarly on her thigh. "I would prefer that neither of us were wearing anything at all . . ." she murmured. Cat clenched her fingers in his hair, bringing his sensuous lips back to hers.

323

Wild sensations rippled along her flesh as his mouth claimed hers in an ardent kiss. She felt the sand shifting beneath her as Brant turned her world sideways with his intimate caresses and heart-stopping kisses. Cat moved closer to the flame, aching to be consumed by the passionate blaze.

Brant's body, already aroused by her provocative movements, caught fire and burned. Breathlessly, he crouched above her, yearning to appease the need that touching her evoked. It was not enough to kiss and caress this shapely goddess. He wanted to become a living, breathing part of her, to lose himself in the world of soul-shattering emotions. When he was in the never-ending circle of Catrina's arms he could spread his wings and soar like an eagle in flight across the boundless sky.

"Make this sojourn in heaven last forever . . ." he breathed raggedly as his body settled over hers. "I need you, Cat. I want to forget there is another world beyond this abandoned beach."

When Brant bent his head to capture her inviting lips, something in the distance caught his attention. Reluctantly, Brant looked past Catrina to see the canvas sails of the *Sea Lady* growing taller on the horizon. Growling at the untimely interruption, Brant sank back on his haunches. A sour frown plowed his brow. What the hell was Thomas doing back at Graciosa a day early?

Disappointment tumbled down around Catrina like an avalanche when she twisted around to follow Brant's gaze. The *Sea Lady* had come to retrieve her captain, stripping him from Catrina's eager arms. Damnation, she didn't want this romantic interlude to come to end. It had been so peaceful, so perfect. She and Brant had enjoyed a serenity, unlike their experiences in the past. Cat didn't want to go back to the throng of sailors and the *Lady* that demanded all of Brant's attention.

Begrudgingly, Brant grabbed his discarded breeches and stood up. When he did, he sorely wished his eyes deceived him.

There, tailing the *Sea Lady*, was the same warship he had battled off the shores of Belfast with John Paul.

"Damn," he cursed under his breath. His disgruntled gaze flew to Cat, wondering if she had any idea who captained the British frigate. Confound it, Thomas had disobeyed orders, Brant thought angrily. The first mate had taken it upon himself to seize the vessel, but apparently the scheme had backfired in his face.

Grasping Cat's hand, Brant jogged back to the lean-to to gather their belongings. While he was frantically throwing their supplies together, Catrina tapped his shoulder to gain his attention.

"Leave me here," she pleaded, fighting like the devil to keep the tears from sliding down her cheeks. "Manuel will see to it that I am safe. And perhaps a British ship will one day cruise into the lagoon and I can . . ."

"Nay," Brant snapped, and then continued with his chore. "You are coming with me."

Her misty eyes drifted to the two ships that sailed steadily toward the bay. "Let it end here and now, Brant. At least we can part without ill feelings for each other." With trembling hands, Cat removed the gold wedding ring that was inlaid with emeralds and diamonds and offered it back to him. "What we shared on this island cannot be surpassed . . . Please don't make me go back."

Scowling, Brant grabbed the outstretched hand with the ring in it and pulled Catrina along with him. "Dammit, don't you understand? I feel responsible for you. You are my wife, whether you wish to be or not. I can't leave you here, not knowing what would become of you."

Despite Catrina's protest, Brant herded her toward the skiff and forced her onto the bench beside their belongings. Keeping a watchful eye on the trailing frigate, Brant rowed toward the *Sea Lady*.

Catrina did not utter another word. She could tell she was no longer in Brant's thoughts. His mind was on the enemy ship and their stay on the paradise island was no more than a dim memory.

It baffled her that Brant seemed so distressed by the appearance of the British frigate. In the past he had been eager for battle. But now he seemed leery of the approaching warship. He kept growling and glaring at the ship as if he were staring at impending doom.

To the trained eye, the British man-of-war might have been familiar, but not to Catrina. All the brigantines in the Royal Navy looked similar to her. She didn't give it a thought that Derrick Redmund could be a league behind her. If she had considered it, she would have been more apprehensive about the British ship that followed in the privateer's wake.

As the *Sea Lady* approached, Thomas tossed a rope ladder over the side, along with the hope of towing the skiff. There was no time to drop anchor. The British were breathing down their necks and Thomas did not relish the idea of sustaining more cannon fire. Brant would demand to know what had happened off the coast of Pico and it would be difficult to explain to the irate captain while bombs were bursting about them.

After securing the skiff, Brant lifted Catrina onto the ladder and scurried up behind her. The moment his feet hit the deck his furious glare pinned Thomas to the mast. "You disobeyed my orders, didn't you?" he exploded. "Dammit, Thomas, I told you . . ."

"It wasn't Thomas's fault," Clifton murmured, afraid to meet Brant's fuming glower. "I took command when Thomas refused to seize an enemy frigate that was sitting in the harbor. 'Twas a trap. If not for Thomas we would have been taken prisoner."

Brant's golden eyes riveted over the sailor with disdainful disgust. Roughly, he grabbed the front of Clifton's shirt, twisting it about the man's neck and lifting him up until his feet dangled in midair. "You disobedient son of a bitch!" Brant hissed into Clifton's whitewashed face. "I should have you hanged for mutiny." He gave Clifton a hard shake, leaving the sailor's teeth rattling in his head. "But your end would come all too quickly to satisfy my fury. Torture is what you deserve for your greedy blunder!"

Catrina had never seen this malicious, ruthless side of Brant Diamond. She winced when his booming voice echoed across the deck, bringing the activities on board the schooner to a halt. A vicious snarl curled Brant's lips and his eyes flared like torches. In him, Catrina saw something that triggered painful memories of Derrick Redmund. The menacing twist of Brant's lips was all too familiar. She could feel the fury exuding from the irate captain. His harsh words rang in her ears and she turned away before she caught herself making more comparisons between the man she thought she loved and the man she detested.

Brant shoved Clifton away as if their close physical contact repulsed him. The forcefulness of Brant's actions sent Clifton sprawling backward. With his chest heaving with furious breaths, Brant stalked over to loom above the grimacing sailor.

"You will spend the rest of the voyage in the brig," he spumed. "You thought to dine on wine and fresh meat, but you will survive on rations of bread and water. You can breathe the musty stench in the bowels of this ship and consider your foolhardy greed, Perkins. You deserve no better, you selfish bastard!"

Catrina fought to recompose herself. The incident had thoroughly shattered the spell that Brant had weaved about her on the island. Although she had never provoked Brant's wrath to such violent extents, she could not overcome the lingering apprehension that he might turn on her as Derrick had. Brant had roughly manhandled her on two occasions and now he had exposed another, more terrifying facet of his volatile temper.

Only a fool would allow herself to believe that Brant was different from any other man she had known. Except her father, she amended. He had never been prone to violence, Cat recalled. Randolph Hamilton had never raised his voice to his daughter in anger. He had allowed his exuberant daughter to live life to the fullest without crushing her spirit. When Cat misbehaved, Randolph set her down to speak to her, not rant and rave at her like a madman. But now her father was gone and Cat found herself thrust into a man's world of ruffians, pirates, and war.

Her gaze drifted over her shoulder to see the dark, imposing frown that was chiseled in Brant's features. He was cold and unapproachable and Catrina could not face him just now. Not that he had time for her, she reminded herself.

For a few days she and Brant had set aside their differences to succumb to the passions they aroused in each other. But the fantasy was over and done. She had to control her obsession for this raven-haired pirate with the flaming golden eyes, she lectured herself.

It was becoming increasingly apparently to Catrina that she was a poor judge of men. How could she possibly have imagined she could live with Derrick Redmund, even when she knew she had only leaned on him in her time of need? And how could she survive a marriage to Brant Diamond when they made their homes on opposing sides of the war?

Would she ever learn, Catrina asked herself dismally. She knew all men were conniving philanderers who would resort to violence to get what they wanted. She knew that the male of the species used women to satisfy their lusts. Men were notorious for seeming pleasant and agreeable until they had taken what they wanted from a woman. And so it was with Brant, Catrina reasoned. When he needed her to appease his passions he could be kind and gentle. But when his needs were satisfied, he put her out of his life and his mind. And like a witless wonder she had allowed herself to fall in love with a rebel pirate who saw her as a convenience, not really a wife.

Catrina stared down at the wedding ring in her hand, debating whether to fling it into the sea or slip it back on her finger. Golden chains could not tie Brant to her, not when his wild, reckless heart would eventually yearn for freedom.

Grappling with conflicting emotions, Catrina tucked the ring in her pocket and descended the steps to shut herself in the cabin. She was unsure how she would react when Brant approached her. Could she forget the sweet memories of the past few days? And worse, could she overcome her nagging apprehension that Brant would someday become as brutal and ruthless as Derrick Redmund?

A black scowl clouded Derrick Redmund's features. He was smoldering with barely contained fury. When he peered through his spyglass to watch the two occupants of the rowboat glide toward the *Sea Lady*, he gasped in disbelief. It infuriated him to learn that the arrogant Captain Diamond was not even on board his ship when the trap was sprung. But what outraged him most was the sight of the woman who accompanied the crafty pirate.

Derrick kept telling himself that the wench only resembled Catrina Hamilton. But that lustrous mane of auburn hair and that captivating figure could belong to only one woman. There was no mistaking that feisty chit, Derrick assured himself bitterly. It was his runaway fiancée who had been crouched in the skiff with Captain Diamond.

How the devil had Catrina wound up on board a pirate ship? And how long had she been Diamond's prisoner? The scanty attire Catrina was wearing triggered thoughts that totally frustrated Derrick. The implication gnawed at him like poison.

The memories of his months with Catrina came rushing back like a tidal wave. It was not difficult to recall the craving he had been forced to hold in check. Aye, he had hungered for that gorgeous wench and it was all he could do to keep from ravishing her. Portraying the gentleman in her presence had been no easy task and Derrick had come away with a craving that no other women would appease. And although Catrina had been restrained and unreceptive to his amorous assaults, she was traipsing around with a ship of pirates, garbed in the most indecent attire.

Damn, she would pay dearly for this last bit of humiliation, Derrick vowed vindictively. His blue eyes narrowed on the *Sea*

Lady. The sight of Catrina cavorting with Brant Diamond on a secluded island was like pouring salt on an open wound. Damn that Pirate Diamond to hell and back! Derrick swore he would follow that pirate ship to the edge of the earth if need be. But he would not rest until his vengeance had been appeased and he had Catrina in his custody.

Somehow he would close the gap between his frigate and the swift-sailing privateer. When he did, he would unload ammunition in the schooner's hull and take Catrina as his wife. Derrick swore he would face no more humiliation at Brant Diamond's hand. And if Catrina refused to wed him he could blackmail her, swearing she had turned traitor to the Crown. This time she would not escape him, Derrick promised himself. He would have that tempting chit *and* her fortune.

A thoughtful frown creased his brow. If Diamond had made Catrina his whore she would probably thank Derrick for rescuing her, he thought confidently. In that case he would have no need to bribe her into a wedding. The thought of taking that elusive pirate's leavings annoyed Derrick. But his pride recovered from its nasty gash when he reminded himself of the vast Hamilton fortune that would lie at his feet after he took Catrina for his wife.

Mulling over his contemplations, Derrick paced the quarterdeck, leaving his competent first mate to man the ship. Derrick was not as experienced at the wheel as the salty British officer who had been placed under his command. If not for Argus Blake, Derrick knew he would have found himself in more hot water than he already was with the Admiralty. Argus was capable of steering the brigantine, leaving Derrick to stew and fume over the upsetting turn of events.

Aye, one day Derrick would have Diamond's head and retrieve Catrina from the despicable pirate's clutches, he vowed to himself. Chewing on that positive thought, Derrick leaned against the rail to keep a watchful eye on the schooner that cut through the sea ahead of them.

Chapter Twenty-One

After Thomas finished relating the incident that left the British frigate trailing in their wake, he frowned at the distraught expression that cut deep lines in Brant's features. He knew Brant would be annoyed, but Thomas had not anticipated this reaction. Brant had faced adversity scores of times. Indeed, the captain thrived on challenging situations that tested his talents and his competency at sea. So why was Brant so distressed by the appearance of the same frigate they had attacked in Belfast? Now was Brant's chance to capture the cowardly captain who had slipped into the channel to avoid defeat.

"Would you mind tellin' me what's botherin' you, Cap'n?" Thomas pried. "I knew you wouldn't be pleased about this bungled mess, but yer takin' it a mite harder than I expected."

Brant peered at the man-of-war that followed like a foreboding shadow. Heaving an exasperated sigh, he bent his gaze to the curious first mate. "Jean-Martin informed me that the captain we faced in Belfast was Derrick Redmund. I have the feeling the two of us have met somewhere before, but I cannot recall the place nor the incident that might have put us in conflict. It must have been before the war . . . either in the Isles or possibly the West Indies."

"Redmund . . ." Thomas thoughtfully stroked his stubbled

chin and mentally sorted through the myriad of associates with whom they had dealt the past few years. A long silent moment passed while Thomas wrestled with the name. "It does ring a bell," he agreed. Suddenly, Thomas jerked up his head to stare at Brant. "Wasn't Redmund the swindler who wanted you to import contraband from the Indies? It was in Bristol, wasn't it? Redmund appoached me three times while you was ashore, dallyin' yer way through the brothels and taverns on the wharf. He kept insistin' that he meet with you and he would not be put off."

The incident began to unfold in Brant's mind and he nodded affirmatively. "Aye, I believe you are right. It was Redmund. He kept boasting that his cousin, some influential earl, had sent him to make the arrangements for delivery of goods to his warehouse."

"And remember, you sicced the authorities on that cocky dolt." A muddled frown plowed Thomas's brow. "Nay, this can't be the same Redmund. The Admiralty would never commission an officer who served a hitch in prison."

"Unless the same Redmund *paid* his way to freedom," Brant speculated. "If a man would stoop to trading illegal runs he would not think twice about bribing an official. If a man is desperate he can always find someone who is willing to overlook the law . . . especially if the price is right . . ."

Brant's voice trailed off as bits and pieces of the confrontation with Redmund returned to haunt him. Late one night Redmund and his unsavory associate had boarded the *Sea Lady* to propose the transportation of cargo from a merchant in the West Indies. Brant was aware of the merchant's reputation of selling anything to anyone if there was profit in it. Brant instantly suspected that he was to be used as an unknowing agent in the black market. If his ship were searched, *he* would be the one carted off to jail, not Derrick Redmund.

Explaining that he would require a few minutes to consider the proposition and determine if it would be profitable to him,

Brant had left Redmund and his companion in the captain's cabin with a bottle of brandy. After climbing to the main deck, Brant had crept into the arsenal to eavesdrop through the hatch. After hearing his guests' comments, Brant's suspicions were confirmed.

Brant had wasted no time in returning to the wharf to contact the authorities and explain the swindlers' scheme. Redmund and his friend were immediately herded off to jail. Redmund had loudly denounced the accusations and insisted that he had been set up by the conniving American captain. Brant had scoffed at the lie, further infuriating the scoundrel. When the blackguard was shuffled off to prison, Brant had set the matter aside and weighed anchor, never to return to Bristol.

Grumbling to himself, Brant's narrowed gaze circled to the frigate that hung behind them. He was certain Redmund wanted revenge on both counts—the incident in Bristol and in Belfast. But what agitated Brant was that the bastard had attempted to corral Catrina into marriage while she was grieving the loss of her parents. The man was capable of anything, Brant reasoned. Redmund was a swindler and a coward and he had threatened Catrina with violence, forcing her to flee from her own home.

Brant was sorely tempted to slow his pace and turn about to engage in open sea battle with Redmund. But he did not dare risk Catrina's life. No doubt, the British frigate was heaping with ammunition. Although the *Sea Lady* could run circles around the cumbersome brigantine, Brant was not prepared to take a chance. One lucky blow to the hull and the *Sea Lady* could find herself sinking. During their confrontation with the *Countess* Catrina had sneaked onto the British ship in attempt to escape. If she attempted the same tactic she could play right into Derrick's hands. The thought soured Brant's disposition. Nay, he would not give Derrick even the smallest hope of recovering his runaway fiancée.

"Are we goin' to veer around the man-of-war and fight?"

333

Thomas queried, instinctively grabbing the drum to call the seamen to their battle stations. "I will be glad to roll out the cannons and blow holes in that ship. I never did relish the idea of havin' a British tub hangin' on the *Lady*'s skirt tails. We'll make mincemeat of that frigate on the open sea."

Brant grasped Thomas's hand before he could drum the signal. "Nay, we are not going to fight," he said flatly.

"Why the hell not?" Thomas hooted in disbelief. Brant Diamond run from a battle? It was inconceivable.

Grimly, Brant stared at Redmund's ship. "Twice we have dealt with the less than honorable captain," he muttered. "No doubt, the man craves retaliation. And so do I. But there is a complication, my friend, one that makes me leery of taking even the slightest risk." Golden eyes probed Thomas's weather-beaten features. "Redmund is also the man who put the bruises on Cat's face when she refused to marry him."

The news knocked the props out from under Thomas. With his jaw sagging he gaped at the British frigate. Now he understood why troubled thoughts were buzzing through Brant's head. "Redmund cannot help but know Catrina was the woman in the skiff. Even at a distance a man could recognize that long mane of auburn hair." Thomas groaned miserably as he set his drum aside. "Lord, Cap'n, we may as well have shaken a stick to stir a den of vipers! Redmund won't back off, come hell or high water! You've given him one too many reasons to hate you."

Those were Brant's exact thoughts. "We have Perkins to thank for putting Redmund in our wake. I would feed the fool to that British shark if I thought the exchange would pacify him."

"Somehow I don't think Redmund would consider swappin' yer lady for that wooden-headed sailor," Thomas grumbled.

"Nay, not after Redmund has gone to great lengths to entrap us on our return voyage to the colonies." Brant sighed. "'Tis blood Redmund wants . . . mine. And I would imagine the man would become even more bloodthirsty if he were to learn that

334

his runaway fiancée is my wife. That would add unforgivable insult to injury."

Thomas gulped hard. His wide eyes focused on Brant's sullen frown. "Does Catrina know who captained the ship we battled in Belfast? Does she know this frigate is one and the same?"

"I don't think she does and I do not intend to tell her just now," Brant insisted. "She harbors enough painful memories of Redmund, ones that occasionally resurface to torment her. I will not inform her that the man she deems to be a closed chapter from her past is floating a half-league behind her."

As Brant strode away, Thomas noticed the captain's bare legs. He had been too involved in their conversation to comment on Brant's unusual style of clothes . . . until now.

"Oh, Cap'n?" When Brant wheeled around, Thomas raked the captain's exposed physique and broke into a wry smile. "I've got a few yards of fabric if you would like me to stitch some legs in yer breeches."

Brant glanced down at his buttonless shirt and short breeches and grinned sheepishly. "I suppose you are wondering why I am dressed in such unusual attire."

"I am a bit curious to know what became of yer breeches legs." A wide grin curved the corners of his mouth upward. "Were there man-eating sharks in the lagoon, Cap'n?"

"Nay, only mermaids and kelpies inhabit those waters. And as you can see the creatures are very handy with a knife," Brant chuckled.

"Kelpies?" Thomas frowned puzzledly. "I never heard of them."

A mysterious smile tugged at Brant's lips as he tied his drooping shirt in a knot around his waist. "I'll tell you about them one day. They are fascinating sea creatures and a man knows he has been taken for a ride when he meets up with one of them. I very nearly lost my breeches and shirt when I confronted one of them."

Thomas gave Brant the once-over, wondering what he was

335

babbling about. But before he could pose the question, Brant glanced instinctively over his shoulder and growled under his breath. It was obvious the captain's mood had soured once again and Thomas decided it best not to badger his captain when he was preoccupied with frustrating thoughts.

Brant strode across the deck to peer over the bow. Already he had grown tired of staring at the sails of impending doom. His only recourse was to keep his enemy's identity a secret from Cat. Brant could only hope to lose the trailing frigate during their voyage across the Atlantic.

Ironically, he found himself wishing a storm would separate the two ships. Brant often relied on celestial navigation to guide him across the sea. He had no fear of being blown off course since he had followed several routes across these familiar waters. But Redmund would be at the disadvantage. The British captain had obviously been commissioned to protect the home shores. Redmund had ventured to the Azores to set his trap, but he was not accustomed to cruising the Atlantic at such great extent.

Without the aid of the *Sea Lady* Redmund could find himself entangled in the moss that lay in the treacherous waters east of Bermuda. A sly smile skipped across Brant's lips when he anchored on that thought. Redmund would not be the first unsuspecting captain to have his rudders snagged in the floating kelp of the Sargasso Sea. What better place to lure Redmund then into the Devil's Triangle, Brant thought spitefully. The demon would be right at home in those eerie waters.

If he could entice the frigate to follow him into the hazardous sea and then veer north, he might reach Charleston without permitting Redmund to know his destination. Brant could deposit Catrina with Old Matthew and deliver the much-needed supplies. Only that order of events would grant Catrina protection from Redmund. At least there was one man in Charleston Brant could trust. No matter what happened to Brant during his dangerous mission of running the British blockades to deliver army supplies, Catrina would be in competent hands. Old Matthew, as he was known by the townspeople, would take Catrina under his wing and keep her from harm.

Now all Brant had to do was elude Redmund and reach Charleston, he told himself. And *that* might take some doing with the vengeful Derrick Redmund nipping at his heels. The scoundrel thirsted for Brant's blood and coveted his wife. Aye, Redmund held a triple vendetta against Brant. Derrick could prove to be a most imposing enemy, Brant reminded himself.

Damn, Brant scowled as he pounded his fist against the rail. Why must it be this particular man who sailed in his wake? Didn't Brant have enough trouble controlling his rambunctious wife and battling the British without involving himself in personal grudges? Redmund's timing was terrible. He had seen Catrina boarding the *Sea Lady* and he was probably, at this moment, speculating on Brant's connection with Catrina. If the situation had been reversed Brant knew what he would be thinking when he saw a man and woman, garbed in little of nothing, rowing away from a secluded lagoon.

Aye, Derrick was probably fuming in outrage and envy, Brant predicted. Redmund would kill to get his hands on Catrina and the awaiting Hamilton fortune. Blast it, what a distressing predicament, Brant muttered. And yet, he could not help but ask himself when he had confronted a convenient disaster. Catastrophe struck in droves and it always had. War was, in essence, one disaster followed by catastrophe. What the hell did he expect, Brant quizzed himself as he glared at the bobbing brigantine.

While Brant was silently praying for a storm to whisk them off course, Catrina was pacing the deck. She had never seen Brant so preoccupied or distressed by the sight of an enemy warship. The trailing frigate spoiled his disposition and kept him glued to the helm, night and day.

There had been little communication between them since they returned to the ship. In the early hours before dawn Brant would come to her, whispering words of need. Catrina was too vulnerable to deny him the pleasure he sought in her arms. For those few hours it was as if they were still marooned on the mid-Atlantic island, rapt in a splendorous dream. But when the sun sprinkled its intruding rays through the porthole Brant would withdraw into his own private world and return to the helm.

Catrina longed to express the love that was bottled up inside her. And yet she was still wary of the darkly handsome privateer. There were many things she didn't know about Brant. Try as she might, she could not help comparing Brant to Derrick. Her past association with men compelled her to doubt Brant. All men were conniving, complicated creatures. Catrina thought herself to be in love with Brant Diamond, but she wondered if she were seeing things in him that were not really there—things like sincerity, affection, honesty. All men wanted something from women, Catrina firmly reminded herself. No matter what she felt for Brant she must never forget that.

A thoughtful frown knitted Catrina's brow. Just what did Brant really want from her? Why did he insist that she stay with him when he had never mentioned love or forever? Passion? Aye, he was the first to admit that. But did he truly care for her or was he dragging her along for some ultimate purpose? Did he want to make their marriage a long-term relationship or a convenient bed of desire until he tired of her? Did he hunger for her fortune? Was he planning to use their marriage as a link with the British, turning opportunity to profit, no matter what the outcome of this war?

Heaving a troubled sigh Catrina turned to survey the sea that sprawled endlessly before her. A curious frown puckered her brow when she realized the ocean had changed color since they had veered around the British colony of Bermuda. The water was much calmer and it had begun to take on a deep blue color. It was warmer and clearer than it had been before, she realized. And it was thick with deadly inhabitants—sharks. In the distance it looked as if patches of wide-spreading meadows dotted the ocean.

" 'Tis called the Sargasso Sea" came the quiet voice from so close behind her that Catrina flinched in surprise. Brant gestured a tanned finger toward the blanket of thickly matted seaweed that floated off the port bow. "There are many myths and legends associated with this mysterious sea that lays amidst this vast ocean."

Catrina's gaze shifted to Brant's rugged face, one that denoted lack of sleep and considerable stress. His amber eyes boasted dark circles and they were not as vibrant as they had been two weeks earlier. "What sort of legends?" she questioned, casting aside her rambling thoughts.

The faintest hint of a smile grazed his lips as he propped both elbows on the rail. "The stories are not as intriguing as the Scottish folklore of mermaids and kelpies. These are eerie yarns that offer mortals no alternative life in the sea. Sailors carry tales of mysterious islands of waving seaweed. These bottomless masses are said to be inhabited by hideous, huge monsters of the deep." Brant inclined his head toward the southwest. "Yonder lies the area known as the Devil's Triangle where many ships have disappeared without logical explanation. Some say 'tis the monsters' feeding grounds. Other seamen believe the shipwrecks are caused by strange, violent storms of the devil's making."

Catrina gulped hard, her green eyes wide with apprehension. "And we are charting a course through monster-infested waters?" she chirped.

Brant chuckled at the horrified expression that was frozen on her features. "Aye, my pet, but I have no inclination to feed you to the sharks and the sea monsters of the deep. We are cruising through a sea where Spanish galleons and pirate ships have been spotted, draped with barnacles and weeds. Their

339

crews have mysteriously abandoned their decks and they drift like ghost ships searching for port." When Catrina stared at him as if he had just sprouted another head, Brant laughed out loud. "You think me mad, don't you, Cat?"

Without thinking, Catrina nodded affirmatively.

"Rest your fears. There is method in my madness. I have sailed the perimeters of the Devil's Triangle dozens of times . . . but with extreme caution." His gaze swung to the ever-haunting frigate that hung behind them. "The approaching mass of seaweed can entangle an inexperienced navigator, such as the man who captains the British warship. I intend to lead him into the devil's sea during darkness and then change our course, allowing the enemy captain to tackle the most difficult waters by himself."

"Do you know the man who pilots the ship?" Cat queried, appraising the chiseled expression that claimed Brant's features.

"Aye, we have met twice," Brant informed her, his voice carefully devoid of emotion. "Once in Bristol and again in Ireland. 'Tis the same ship we encountered when we were cruising with John Paul off the coast of Belfast."

Catrina glared at the other ship. "That is the coward who turned tail and ran from you?" Catrina sniffed disgustedly. "The captain hardly proved himself worthy of a British command. Why do you suppose he has decided to pursue you wherever you go?"

Brant's face was an unreadable mask. He could not bring himself to confess the captain's name or his ulterior purpose. "He has been disgraced twice and I imagine he is out for revenge. The enemy captain has his reasons and I have mine for leading him into a maze of seaweed. I do not wish to be trailed when I run the blockade and slip into Charleston."

His golden eyes probed the fathomless depths of emerald green. Gently, he lifted Catrina's face to press a fleeting kiss to her lips and then he held her hostage with his inquiring gaze. "Tell me, Cat. Are you such a staunch Loyalist that you would be appalled if I left one of your fellow countrymen snagged in the Devil's Triangle?"

The feel of his caressing lips sent her heart leaping into double time. It would have been easy to confess that her loyalty lay with him, but pride and lingering suspicion turned the key to lock the words in her heart.

When Catrina did not respond immediately Brant frowned. His hand dropped away from her face. He had detected the hint of suspicion that flashed through her eyes. He knew he was constantly being compared to Derrick Redmund, that she would never truly trust him. There had always been an invisible wall between them, one that even passion could not destroy. Catrina could look at him and see every fault the male species possessed. Not that he blamed her, Brant mused. She had good reason to be suspicious of men, just as he had cause to be wary of women.

"You will always think of me as a ruthless pirate, won't you, Cat? You cannot and will not perceive me as a man with an honorable cause since we have always been at cross-purposes."

"Perhaps if I knew your reason for dragging me on this cruise and refusing to allow me to sail home, I could begin to understand what motivates a man like you." Catrina met his unblinking gaze, wishing she could peer into his mind and pluck out each secretive thought.

A wry smile bordered his lips. Brant knew he was being baited, but he was not about to humiliate himself by baring his emotions. "I like having you around, Cat." He did admit to that, much to her surprise. "While you are underfoot there are no dull moments." Brant indicated the frigate that sailed behind them.

Catrina wrinkled her nose and flung him a withering glance. "Surely you do not think I am naive enough to consider myself responsible for your British escort across the Atlantic. In case you have forgotten, there is a war raging between your country and mine."

Soft laughter rumbled in his chest. "The rebellion is not

easily forgotten, minx. But 'tis the battle of wills between us that disturbs me most. I am not certain if you would be for or against me if I decided to turn about and attack the Crown's frigate."

Cat was too cautious to commit herself, but she heard herself say, "I want things to be as they were . . . when we were alone on the island . . ."

One dark brow quirked and a smidgen of sparkle returned to his eyes. The wind swept his raven hair about his bronzed face, giving him that dashingly attractive appearance that made Catrina catch her breath. When he broke into that rakish smile that affected every tanned feature, Catrina's legs turned to rubber.

"You wish things to be as they were?" he chuckled. "To what extent, I wonder." Brant traced her delicate cheekbone and then glided his fingertip over the fine line of her jaw. "Is it just my body you want, Cat? You were persistent in seeing that I wore the skimpiest attire while we were castaways on Graciosa. Sometimes I swear you are more the rogue than I ever claimed to be."

Catrina blushed seven shades of red. She had been unbelievably bold with Brant those few days in paradise. It set her to wondering if she had been a harlot in another lifetime. My, but she had behaved shamelessly. Lord, the things they had done!

Recomposing herself, Cat raked Brant up and down. She was determined not to let this ornery pirate embarrass her. There was no modesty left between them. They had been as close as two people could get. "Aye, I will admit that your virility and prowess arouse me. But your body is only part of my conquest," she informed him breezily. "I have told you before that I crave your heart and soul as well."

Cat intended to strut away, allowing him to chew on that thought. But Brant snagged her arm and spun her around to face him. His smile evaporated and his amber eyes bored into her, holding her steady gaze.

"And what would you do with them if I placed them in your possession?" he demanded to know. "Would you serve them to your king for an appetizer or would you consider exchanging them for your *own* heart and soul?"

Indecision etched her brow as she pensively gnawed on her bottom lip. Did she dare give Brant the truth? Was he only taunting her? If only she could be sure of his intentions, she mused in frustration. Sometimes Brant behaved as if he cared and other times he was so distant that it left her feeling as if he had no room for her in his life.

One by one, Catrina pried his lean fingers from her forearm. "'Tis a hypothetical question, Captain. What good would it do for me to announce my intention when the possessions are not in my custody? After all, I have yet to hear you declare that you would even consider an exchange. Why on earth should I voice such a proposition? The last proposal I made landed me in a most unusual marriage to my own enemy."

Damn that elusive little witch! Would he ever know where he stood with Cat? "A cautious man never makes an offer unless he knows the consequences he faces in doing so. I have been burned once, my dear. Only an absentminded moron takes a second stroll through fire before he remembers how painful the experience can be."

"My ex-fiancé left me nursing painful *bruises*," she countered, staring him straight in the eye. "Do you think you are the first and only person embittered by affairs of the heart? Forgive me for being the one to break the news to you, Captain, but Samson had his Delilah and the wives of King Henry the Eighth lost more than the hair on their heads when their affairs turned sour. I have already turned the other cheek, only to have it punched black and blue. And I have been forced into a marriage against my will. Tell me, Brant, do you still see yourself as the only human on God's green earth to waltz from an affair unscathed?" Catrina did not give Brant the opportunity to reply. She rushed on without inhaling a breath.

343

"If you cannot forgive and forget, why should I? As you said, to blunder blindly ahead when one's heart hangs in the balance would be very foolish indeed. If you wish to brood over the past and compare the future to it, then so shall I. We shall see which of us makes the most cynical spouse, the pirate or his wife."

Brant expelled an exasperated sigh. He and Cat were talking circles around the subject, going nowhere. "You and I have never resolved any of the problems that stand between us. We only detour around them and continue onward, crossways of each other. There is much we need to discuss . . . openly, frankly. We will make no progress if we cannot . . ."

"Cap'n?" Thomas called from the helm. "The seaweed grows thick. I think 'tis best for you to navigate yer way through the devil's playground. It gives me the jitters just to think we chose this treacherous route."

Brant stared at Catrina for a long moment before he stepped away. "The decision of our future lies with you. It will be entirely up to you to choose the direction our marriage takes. I will no longer force you to stay when you plead with me to go. You may return to Scotland at the first opportunity or you can reside with me when I have concluded my mission along the eastern seaboard."

When Brant spun on his heels and strode away, Catrina's jaw swung from its hinges. How could she make that choice when she didn't know if she were welcome in Brant's home? If Brant were attempting to do the honorable thing by offering her free run of his house, Cat wanted no part of it. She had to know that Brant wanted her with him, needed her as much as she needed him to feel whole and alive.

Catrina let her breath out in a rush and then pivoted around to peer at the entangled mass of weeds that was about to engulf the schooner. What difference did it make what course she chose? Before the week was out she might find herself gobbled up by a monster or drifting like a restless spirit on a ghost ship. Daredevil Diamond could get her killed in his attempt to elude the Crown's man-of-war.

Wrestling with that unsettling thought, Catrina grimaced as the *Sea Lady* threaded her way through the mass of choking weeds. Brant was utterly mad, Catrina decided. Only the devil himself could cruise thorugh this eerie sea and emerge in one piece!

Chapter Twenty-Two

Relief washed over Brant's wary features. For the first time in more than two weeks he could look toward the stern without seeing the British sloop-of-war trailing behind him. During the night Brant ordered all lanterns to be snuffed out. Just as Brant had carefully calculated, the moon had not appeared at all, shedding no light to guide the trailing frigate. Navigating by the stars, Brant had veered north, leaving Redmund to pick his own way through the floating weeds or perish.

After several days of sailing, the coast of Charleston appeared on the horizon. Brant still faced the pesky British who blocked the sea lanes surrounding the important colonial port. But at least he could maneuver into the channel without Redmund breathing down his neck.

A peaceful smile blossomed on Brant's lips as he studied the port that had been his first home. His parents had owned a plantation to the east and Brant had enjoyed his childhood, parading through the meadows and strolling through the bustling streets of the colonial port. Charleston . . . it was a city that held both happy and bitter memories for Brant, but it was still a magnificent city, second to none. Charleston lay between two rivers—a town built on a peninsula. To the west, the Ashley River flowed gracefully into the sea. On the far side of the narrow neck of land that joined Charleston to the mainland was the Cooper River. In the distance Brant could see the dark block of the Exchange, the customhouse, post office, and business center where he had often lingered to trade merchandise before the outbreak of war.

Impatiently, Brant waited for the night to envelop them. Once the *Sea Lady* was cloaked in darkness, Brant eased the schooner through the chain of sea islands along the coast. Although a beacon shined from the tower of St. Michael's Cathedral, Brant fixed his gaze on the beam to the northwest. From the lighthouse that towered above the clump of oaks on the far bank of the Cooper River came the soft glow of light that lured Brant closer.

At last Brant was sailing in familiar waters. During the first years of the war he had delivered cubes of indigo, rice, coffee, and molasses from the West Indies and salt from the salt springs of Bermuda. Since he had traveled from the Caribbean to the eastern seaboard he had come to know the tributaries and channels along the coast and he could navigate them in his sleep. A score of times he had weaved his way through the maze of small islands, gliding through the gray-blue waters that were lined with moss-covered tupelo trees, dodging British warships between Charleston and Philadelphia.

Brant had often made connections to exchange supplies with the militia that came up from the swamps around Charleston. There were overland trade roads weaving through the back country as well as sea lanes that were employed to deliver rebel supplies to the regiments. The trade roads connecting Charleston with New England were just as precarious as the sea lanes. The rebels never made the mistake of taking the same route twice when transporting supplies. The British attempted to attack every wagon and schooner in the area, confiscating supplies and taking prisoners.

Rebel supplies had to be discreetly shipped up and down the rivers between the schooners and the wagons. Brant had once been an important part of that scheme to sneak goods past the British. But because of the high price the Loyalists had placed

348

on his head, his superiors had urged him to take to the open sea as a privateer. The Continental Navy feared they would lose a valuable sailor and sent him across the Atlantic to seize British prizes and raid the Mother Country's shores.

Brant massaged the tension from his neck and then clamped both hands on the wheel to swerve into the channel that separated the sea islands from the coast. It was a quiet night in Charleston, he mused. But in the early years of the war the South Carolina Continentals had kept guard at Fort Moultrie to protect the rebel port. The British had attempted to seize the fort but rebel cannon fire had cut the Redcoats to pieces. Because of that victory, Charleston had become the gateway for the revolutionists. For the past two years the townspeople of Charleston had not heard the blast of British cannons. Aye, the Tories were there, but without reinforcements they could not capture the port.

Brant predicted that one day the British would plan another attack. They had to if they hoped for victory in the colonies. Supply shipments from the South were keeping New England alive and the British could not crumble resistance if the rebel armies continued to be equipped with goods shipped into the port from the West Indies.

Aye, it was peaceful now, Brant thought to himself. But this serenity could not last forever. Another battle would rage in Charleston. But until it did, he would resume his mission of slipping goods along the sea lanes. The name Diamond would again become a curse voiced by the Tories who wished to see him rotting in their prison ship that bobbed in the bay near the British post of Fort Johnson.

As the lights of Charleston grew brighter, a sea of memories flooded over Brant. He recalled the days of his youth—the carefree days when he had strolled down Lamboll Street to stare across the Cooper River. It was here that he had met Cynthia Marsh, a shapely blonde whose unequaled beauty had immediately captured his interest. Together he and Cynthia had ambled down Tradd Street, the avenue that stretched between the Cooper and Ashley rivers.

In the beginning, their affair had been like a dream come true, and Brant had decided to make Cynthia his wife. But Cynthia's aspirations had not included wedding a man who had established his fortune in trade and who had set up a plantation in the West Indies. She had no intention of leaving Charleston and the luxuries of society. Cynthia had strung Brant along, hoping for a better offer. And when it came, she had leaped at the chance to marry established wealth, the kind offered by a British nobleman who had strong ties with the king.

Brant gnashed his teeth, remembering the night Cynthia had lain in his arms and then announced she was marrying Colonel Pinkerton, a British nobleman twice her age. Brant couldn't believe his ears. For several minutes he lay there staring at her, certain she was only taunting him.

But Cynthia could not have been more serious and Brant watched in disbelief as the love of his life made arrangements for an extravagant ceremony that had rivaled a king's coronation. Not two weeks after the elaborate wedding Cynthia had sought Brant out, inviting him to come to her while her husband was out of town. The mere thought that Cynthia would cuckold her new husband repulsed Brant. Resolving to remain a bachelor to avoid the wiles of women such as Cynthia Marsh Pinkerton, Brant returned to the sea, drinking and whoring his way from port to port.

Brant sighed heavily as he focused on the beacon in the lighthouse. He had learned a great deal about love and life during his bittersweet affair with Cynthia. Because of those painful lessons Brant had hardened his heart to love. He had never forgiven Cynthia for using him and then parading over him as if he were a stepping-stone on her path to prominence and wealth. Aye, Cynthia had made her bed of roses, but Brant could not help but wonder if the wench had found her older husband to be a disappointment. Obviously, Pinkerton could not satisfy her wild passions if she had gone searching for her former lover after two weeks of wedlock. Wedlock? Brant laughed bitterly at the thought. Cynthia's wedding had not *locked* her inside her husband's bedroom. The deceitful wench probably had a stable of studs chomping at the bit each time poor old Pinkerton was called away on business.

Brant scowled to himself, wondering how he had gotten himself into this tangled mess with Catrina after he vowed never to take a wife. Damn, he should have known better after watching Cynthia's cunning maneuvers. Brant had set his rigid philosophy on the vices of women and wedlock and then along came that feisty, auburn-haired temptress to upset his life. Suddenly Brant had found himself chasing that minx until he forced her to marry him. *Him* the man who had sworn off women indefinitely! And against his better judgment he had kept Cat with him, even when she begged him to let her go.

Catrina had come to mean more to him than he had imagined possible, more than Cynthia had ever meant. And, thankfully, in some ways, Catrina was everything Cynthia was not! But Catrina, in spite of her redeeming qualities, was still a woman. Brant could not quite unchain his battered heart and dedicate himself to a woman, especially one whose loyalties strongly contrasted his.

He and Cat had pleasured themselves with each other the last months. But the time had come to put Catrina ashore. The sea routes along the coast were dangerous and he would not risk her life for a cause she did not believe in. And, being suspicious by habit, Brant could not rule out the possibility that Cat might attempt to undermine his mission if she were on board the *Sea Lady*. Brant cared too much about that little minx to give her the chance to betray him. And it was time to determine if absence made the heart grow fonder or if it severed the fragile bond between them, Brant reminded himself.

Determined to see the matter done as soon as they docked, Brant turned the wheel over to Thomas and aimed himself toward his cabin. Catrina would be left in Old Matthew's capable hands. She would be relieved to set foot on solid ground, Brant assured himself. After all, she had been pleading to leave the *Sea Lady* since the day they prepared to set sail from France. But again, in Catrina's case, Brant misjudged her reaction to his demand of packing her belongings for departure.

"I am going nowhere!" Catrina insisted, stomping her foot. "I will not be drydocked on foreign shores where I know not one soul!"

Brant stared incredulously at his irate wife. "I thought you would be relieved to leave this ship. 'Tis what you have wanted from the beginning."

"I wanted to go home, not to some unfamiliar culture that I know nothing about," Catrina snapped brusquely.

"Charleston is divided in loyalties," Brant declared. "Tory planters live on the outskirts of town. You will have no difficulty locating your own kind. They always wear a touch of Tory green on their clothes."

"My own kind?" Catrina sniffed sarcastically. "How many Loyalists hereabout are married to rebel pirates who cannot wait to discard their wives and set out on another daredevil adventure?"

Brant compressed his lips into a thin line and counted to ten twice. He was not going to be provoked into another shouting match with Cat. There wasn't time. "Blockade running is *not* an adventure. 'Tis difficult work under tense conditions. The penalty for a man who already wears a price tag on his head is death. I will not have you involved."

"And if you go traipsing up the sea lanes you will be signing your own death warrant, Brant Diamond," Catrina scolded him. "I swear I do not know whether to applaud your bravura or ridicule it."

"Thus far I have had a generous helping of the latter," Brant smirked. "I was hoping you might wish me well and send me off with a heart-warming kiss."

Catrina thrust out a stubborn chin. He was making light of a dangerous mission and it unnerved her to think she might

352

never see Brant again. "I am not sending you off. I am going with you," she told him firmly.

"Nay," he insisted sternly.

"Aye!" Her chin tilted a notch higher.

"Nay," Brant scowled, his patience deteriorating. "I don't tru—" He slammed his mouth shut and glanced away.

Catrina studied his rigid back and the grim set of his jaw for a long moment. "You started to say you don't trust me, didn't you, Brant?"

Brant did not wish to lie to her, nor did he wish to admit his lack of confidence in her devotion. So instead he quickly changed the subject.

"I think 'tis best for you to stay with an old friend of mine in Charleston."

"I will not be thrust upon one of your acquaintances for the duration of this war," Catrina adamantly protested.

"You are not going with me," Brant said through gritted teeth. "I will not have you become an innocent victim if I should meet with difficulty during one of my cruises. Old Matthew will welcome your company. He gets lonely with only Nicodemus to entertain him. Matthew has no quarrel with either the Tories or the Whigs and he will treat you kindly."

"No man is harmless, no matter what his age," Catrina argued. "And who the devil is Nicodemus?"

"A tomcat, but don't tell him that," Brant advised. "Nicodemus thinks he is human and he expects to be treated as such."

"I don't care if Nicodemus speaks seven langues! I am *not* staying with an eccentric lecher and his peculiar tomcat!" Catrina all but screamed.

Brant was finished arguing. He scooped Catrina's belongings into his arms and stuffed them in her satchel. "I should think you would delight in putting some distance between us, madam. I am not so foolish to think you have enjoyed wedded bliss since we spoke the vows. 'Tis just that you are so contrary that you object to any suggestion I make."

Their marriage could have been heaven if Brant would have offered his love as generously as he offered his name, she thought disheartenedly. Catrina shook aside her whimsical musings and began undoing Brant's packing. "I am remaining on board this ship!" This time she was screaming.

"Nay, Madam Attila, you are going ashore!" Brant bellowed as he wheeled around. "Thomas! Get down here immediately!"

The order was passed through the companionway. Within a few minutes Thomas was relieved of his duties at the helm and he came barging through the door to find Catrina slung over Brant's shoulder like a feedsack. Catrina was kicking, squealing, and pounding on Brant's back for all she was worth.

"I assume Cat didn't warm to the idea of goin' ashore," Thomas observed with a snicker.

"Aye, my stubborn wife set her feet," Brant tattled as he gave her wriggling backside a stinging swat. "Fetch her belongings while I cart her to the yawl."

"Put me down this instant!" Catrina yelped furiously.

"Request denied," Brant grumbled. "You, madam, are going ashore, even if I have to carry you every step of the way."

This was the beginning of the end, Catrina assured herself. When he deposited her on Old Matthew's doorstep she would never see Brant again. The thought left an unbearable emptiness gnawing at the pit of her stomach.

As Brant rowed the skiff to shore, Catrina could do nothing but stare helplessly at him. She had loved him from afar all these months, but not at such great distances. Not seeing him at all would be intolerable.

When Brant set her to her feet, Catrina reacted impulsively. If this was to be their last moment together, she would give Brant Diamond something to inflame his dreams. Catrina held nothing back. The fear of losing Brant overwhelmed her and pride slid down around her ankles, she not caring that he saw the raw emotions. She kissed Brant with all the pent-up feelings that had plagued her since she fell hopelessly in love with this golden-eyed devil.

Brant found himself on the receiving end of a kiss that carried enough heat to turn the Cooper River into a cloud of steam. His senses came alive like dry kindling exposed to a torch. His body roused to the feel of her curvaceous body molded to his hard contours. His lips tingled when she breathed fire into him. His arms involuntarily came around her, crushing her closer, savoring the delicious taste of her, inhaling the alluring feminine scent of her.

For that moment there were only the two of them standing on shore. The only sound to reach their ears was the accelerated beat of their hearts. His hands splayed across the front of her gown to caress the tips of her breasts and then drifted down to cup the curve of her hips. His hard body moved suggestively against hers, allowing her to feel the devastating effect she had on him.

Catrina clung to the sensations that spilled through her like bubbly champagne. A parting kiss should be no less than this, Catrina thought deliriously. It was an all-consuming embrace that left a fierce, uncontrollable craving inside her. She knew Brant had been similarly affected, but she prayed the memory of this moment would be potent enough to lure him back to her arms, no matter how far he strayed.

The sound of someone loudly clearing his throat broke them apart. Brant scowled at the untimely interruption. His glare shot across the top of Catrina's head to meet the amused grin that was plastered on Old Matthew's whiskered face.

Catrina twisted in the circle of Brant's protective arms to view the stoop-shouldered old man who was propped against the stone and timber lighthouse. He looked as old as Father Time with his long wiry hair, gray beard, and mustache. From the open doorway, a shaft of golden light silhouetted Matthew's overweight frame. His hands were wrapped in tattered gloves and his exposed fingertips were curled about a gnarled cane. The man appeared a harmless pauper in his homespun coat and breeches. And yet, there was a hint of devilishness lurking in those dark eyes that were partially shielded by spectacles.

Old though he was, Catrina detected a glint of timeless youth. She wondered if Matthew had once been a daring captain such as Brant. Perhaps Matthew had run aground to keep the beacon light burning when age finally caught up with him, she speculated.

"Don't let me interrupt you, Captain Diamond" came Matthew's hoarse voice. "These old eyes function well enough to see that you would prefer to continue what you are doing than to greet an old, forgotten friend." He chuckled lightly and then stretched his lame leg, shifting his weight as he leaned back against the outer wall of the lighthouse. "'Tis been more than a year since your last visit. 'Tis not difficult to guess how you have spent these past months. Ah, to be so young and zealous again . . ." he breathed forlornly.

"Youth does have its advantages," Brant agreed with a short laugh. "But then, we must also remember that age also has its purpose, Matthew." Possessively, he draped his arm over Catrina's shoulder, absently toying with the wild stream of fire that cascaded down her arm. "Cat, I want you to meet Old Matthew. But do not pity the burden of years he bears. Inside that decrepit body lies a young man who is sharp of wit and even sharper of tongue. I'm sure the two of you will delight in fencing words. It should prove to be an amusing pastime."

Catrina nodded a silent greeting and then tensed when Matthew hobbled forward on his cane to scrutinize her at close range. Those dark eyes pierced right through her, making her wince uncomfortably.

"Cat, is it?" Old Matthew cocked his gray head to the side to peer up at Brant. He reached out a gloved hand to stroke the silky mane of hair that spilled over her shoulder. "A fitting name, I should think," he murmured pensively. "She appears to be the type of lass who would keep a man on the prowl." His discerning gaze made another deliberate sweep of Catrina's voluptuous figure, overlooking not even one minute detail.

"Catrina is my wife," Brant blurted out, flashing Matthew a warning frown. "I expect you to mind your manners while she is about, lest she will be calling you a lecher . . ."

"Your wife?" Matthew croaked, staggering back to maintain his balance. He tapped the side of his head, as if testing his ears to ensure they were functioning properly. "My God, I must be hearing things. I could have sworn you said this woman was your wife!"

"Aye, I did," Brant mumbled as he snatched up the discarded satchel and propelled Catrina toward the door. "I beg a favor of you, Matthew. 'Tis safer for Cat to lodge with you while I am tending my duties in the colonies. Will you keep an eye on her for me?"

The old man beamed as brightly as the beacon in the tower above them. "It seems I should be the one thanking you for such a privilege, Captain. 'Tis been a century since I had the pleasure of such lovely company. I'm sure Nicodemus will also be delighted." Matthew frowned suddenly. He still wasn't sure he believed Brant. Craning his neck, he glanced up at Brant from his stooped position. "Married, you say? Truly?" It seemed inconceivable.

Brant muttered under his breath. "Aye, married. I'm sure you find that difficult to believe, but . . ."

"To be sure," Matthew grunted. He shuffled around to view the auburn-haired beauty in full light. "But 'tis not difficult to see why Cat became your stumbling block. You're a pretty one, missy . . . the most bewitching little lass I've laid eyes on in years."

"Thank you, sir," Catrina murmured self-consciously.

Matthew's brows shot straight up. "And a Tory to boot. Well don't that beat all," he mused aloud, shocked by her accent. Recomposing himself, Matthew smiled broadly. "You must call me Matthew, my dear. Since we will be living together I think it proper for us to be on a first name basis."

While Matthew reassessed the shapely beauty, finding not

one visible flaw and doubting there were any hidden beneath her form-fitting gown, Brant herded Catrina through the hall. "Matthew has a spare bedroom. I suggest you put away your belongings while I talk privately with the old man."

When Catrina closed the bedroom door, Brant strode back to park himself in a chair. After Matthew shuffled over to ease into the adjacent seat, he stared Brant squarely in the eye. "A Tory?" He shook his bushy head in disbelief. "I am on the edge of my seat, waiting to hear your explanation. Good God, man, I still find it impossible to believe you are married!"

Brant squirmed uncomfortably in his chair. "Sometimes I cannot believe it myself," he grumbled, half aloud. His eyes swung to the closed door and a hint of a smile caught one corner of his mouth. "Once you come to know Cat, I think you will understand my fascination."

"I already do." Matthew sighed heavily. "Ah, were I forty years younger . . ."

"I would still expect you to remember that Cat is my wife," Brant cut in to make his point.

"Why, Captain, don't you trust me? A harmless old man who can no longer move fast enough to chase women?" Matthew snickered.

"What you do not possess in agility, you compensate with craftiness," Brant snorted. "And you do have a habit of forgetting your age. Your life expectancy may be cut in half if you do not keep your hands to yourself."

Matthew chuckled at Brant's overprotective attitude. "I do not know what has come over you. Could it be that Cupid's arrow has struck a fatal blow after all these years?"

Brant gnashed his teeth. He was in no mood for Matthew's taunts, nor was he about to blurt out some reckless confession that might reach Cat's ears. "Do you wish to hear about my mission in Europe or are you content to harass me during the little time I have left here?"

Laying his cane aside, Matthew drooped back in his chair and nodded agreeably. "Please do explain how your voyage landed you a Tory wife. I'm sure this will be fascinating."

Smoothing his ruffled feathers Brant began to unfold the misadventure. "John Paul and I instigated several raids along the Scottish coast. Against my better judgment I allowed John Paul to persuade me into helping him take the Earl of Selkirk captive for a prisoner exchange. The plan was foiled since the earl was not in residence, but the situation demanded that I take a ragamuffin hostage before he alerted the village to our presence. I made the waif my cabin boy, but he was not a lad at all. It was Catrina Hamilton, a cousin of the Earl of Selkirk."

Matthew chuckled at the hasty explanation. "Ah, that is ripe. Cat employed a disguise. What a resourceful lass she must be."

"Only you would appreciate the humor of my finding myself roomed with a young woman," Brant grumbled. "When I think how often she played me for a fool I cringe."

"Are you suggesting that you married the chit to save face? Or possibly to redeem the young maid's virtues?" Matthew burst into snickers. "How unromantic, Captain. Because of your notorious reputation with women, I would have anticipated a more flamboyant affair."

"Believe me, Matthew, 'tis been one wild escapade since she asked me to marry her," Brant assured him.

"*She* proposed to you?" Matthew squeaked.

"Aye, and then the fickle wench changed her mind. She dived overboard into the bay of Brest and took refuge on a French merchant ship."

Matthew frowned dubiously. "Now let me think this through, Captain. You took an urchin hostage, but she transformed herself into a lovely duchess who begged for your hand in marriage. When she realized you were not the charming prince she had conjured up in her dreams, she threw herself overboard."

The incident, phrased as such, did sound a mite incredible, Brant thought to himself. Plunging on, Brant attempted to relate the rest of the misadventure. "Cat said she was in love with me and that was the reason she decided not to go through with the wedding," he ended on a bitter note.

Matthew rolled his eyes toward the ceiling. "That makes no sense at all."

"That is what *I* said," Brant grunted. "Cat then declared that she had misinterpreted her feelings for me and that she wished to return to Scotland to face her fiancé alone."

"What fiancé? I thought you were her fiancé?" Matthew chirped, wondering if Brant's skull had cracked, allowing the salty sea water to seep into his brain to rust the cogs.

"The fiancé from whom she was trying to escape when she disguised herself as a boy . . . The one we battled off the coast of Belfast and the same one who attempted to entrap me in the Azores." Brant leaned close to divulge another piece of guarded information, wondering why he had unfolded these details in the first place. "But Cat doesn't know it was her ex-fiancé who chased us across the Atlantic and I intend to keep it that way."

"I have heard more than enough," Matthew snorted, gathering his feet beneath him. "The more you explain the more confused I become. I wish I hadn't asked."

At least Matthew's initial curiosity had been appeased, Brant thought to himself. Now perhaps the old man would not attempt to pry information from Cat. The last thing she needed was Matthew's badgering.

"I will return to the tower while you say adieu to your lady," Matthew offered as he extended his arm to clasp Brant's hand. "Do not fear. While you are away I will keep a watchful eye on Catrina."

When the old man's footsteps faded on the winding stairs, Brant ambled over to tap on Catrina's door. His breath lodged in his throat when he stepped into the room. The lustrous tendrils of auburn flowed down her back like a river of fire. Cat had changed into a fresh gown, one that accented every curve and swell she possessed. Brant had serious misgivings about leaving Cat in Matthew's care. The old man's blood pressure

360

would burst when he viewed this stunning temptress in her provocative gown.

"Don't you own something less seductive?" Brant grumbled crabbily.

One delicate brow arched in response to his disapproving frown. "You assured me Matthew was harmless," she reminded him flippantly. "Surely you do not expect me to make my debut in Charleston, garbed in men's pantaloons."

Brant expelled his breath in a rush. Nay, he didn't. But dammit, why did Cat have to be so attractive? She would tempt everything in breeches. Discarding his jealous thoughts, Brant moved a step closer to feast on Cat's flawless face and wide green eyes.

"Take care of yourself, Cat," he murmured softly.

This was good-bye. Catrina was stung by the frightening premonition that she would never see Brant again. The mere thought left a void of emptiness somewhere in the region of her heart. He hadn't said the words, but good-bye was written all over his craggy features.

"Aren't you going to offer me a few words of warning before you leave me stranded in unfamiliar territory?" she queried, fighting like hell to maintain her fragile composure.

A low rumble echoed in his chest. "I think perhaps I should sound the alert to prepare Charleston for your arrival, my lovely spitfire. I'm not certain the colonies are capable of handling a woman like you. You, my dear Catrina, are much ahead of your time." His head came slowly toward hers. His eyes focused on her heart-shaped lips, memorizing their gentle curve and velvety texture. "Always keep your wits about you, Cat. I have taught you to use your pistol and dagger. Keep them with you constantly. Have a care in selecting your friends. In these troubled times one can never be certain if even a friend will feel the need to turn on you."

When his mouth took firm possession Catrina abandoned thought. She was drowning in a one-sided love, fighting to contain the words that ached to fly free. Since she did not dare to voice her confession of love, she translated the emotion in her embrace.

Brant inwardly groaned when Catrina melted against him, ardently' responding to his kiss. God, his cabin would seem empty without her. For so many months she had been no more than a glance away. But he *had* to leave her, Brant reminded himself. He had already exposed her to a lifetime of danger. There was a rebel army depending on him for supplies and he was honor-bound to deliver them, no matter what personal sacrifices had to be made.

Yet, in that breathless moment, Brant found himself questioning his patriotism. He longed to keep Catrina in his arms until these soul-shattering emotions subsided. But these sensations would never go away, Brant reminded himself. They were too fierce and deep-rooted. If they would have withered with time, they would have long before now. He would turn and walk away from Cat because duty demanded it, but part of him would linger in this lighthouse.

Reluctantly, he dragged his lips from her addicting kiss and breathed a ragged breath. A rueful smile quivered on the corner of his mouth as he brushed his knuckles over her satiny cheek. "Cat, I . . ." Brant clamped his jaw shut, refusing to give the thought to tongue.

When he spun away Catrina swore the entire town of Charleston could hear her heart breaking. "Brant, when will you come back?" she questioned, her voice trembling.

His shoulder lifted and dropped in a noncommittal shrug. "I cannot say. It depends on the course of the war and the number of British ships I can seize to confiscate merchandise."

Her lashes fluttered up to stare at his broad back, her chin tilting to a courageous angle. "And if I find the opportunity to book passage to the British Isles, shall I take it?"

His head swiveled around to hold her unblinking gaze. "The decision is yours. I have refused to allow you to do your own bidding far too long. I will not dictate to you again. I have meddled in your life far too much as it is."

"You don't care if I go or stay," she speculated, her tone deflated.

The silence was so thick it could have been cut with a knife. Brant stared at her for what seemed an eternity. And then a trace of a smile rippled across his lips. "I care, Catrina, much more than you know."

"You care that I *stay* or that I *go?*" she pressed him. "Which is it, elusive pirate?"

"Ah, I have long enjoyed your keen wit, Cat. I wondered if you would attempt to pin down that remark. I shall sorely miss fencing words with you." Setting his tricorn atop his head, Brant flashed her a charismatic grin, turned around, and swaggered out the door.

Catrina threw up her hands in exasperation. As the door swung shut behind him a silent tear trickled down her cheek. Once she thought she would be better off without the daredevil pirate. But oh, how wrong she had been. She felt empty and dead inside. The lonely ache had already begun to torment her and she feared it would never ease. She was doomed to pine away, wondering if Brant would find a willing wench to replace her, waiting to catch a glimpse of the amber-eyed devil whose dark charm had enchanted her.

Catrina heaved a heavy-hearted sigh and rerouted the tears that streamed down her cheeks. Her blurred gaze swept the small compartment and she fled its confines before the walls closed in on her. Catrina focused her attention on the spiraling stairs that led to the tower. What she needed just now was a diversion, she told herself. She would search out Matthew and quiz him about the colonies—anything but dwelling on these depressing thoughts.

After scaling the first mountain of steps Catrina paused to catch her breath. How could a crippled old man make this exhausting climb without suffering heart seizure? Matthew must have been healthier than he looked, Catrina decided. The climb had very nearly winded her. There was no telling how dearly it cost that lame old man.

Opening another door to yet another set of steps, Catrina lifted her skirts and trudged upward. Finally, she reached the main tower where a huge lantern burned into the night, directing incoming ships to port. A stained glass had been hung over the window, giving the beam a red glow. Yellow and blue stained glasses were set beneath the window, leaving Catrina to wonder at their purpose.

A bemused frown knitted her brow when she realized Matthew was nowhere to be found. Odd, where else would one expect the keeper of the tower to be, she asked herself. Her gaze strayed back to the window. When she spotted the spyglass lying on the table, she scooped it up to survey the ship that had once been her floating home. She could barely make out the silhouette of the *Sea Lady* setting silently in the bay below. The sight of her masts glowing in the moonlight made Catrina's heart lurch with bittersweet memories.

The muffled sound of Matthew humming a soft tune drew her attention. Catrina laid the spyglass aside and frowned bemusedly. The old man must have walked into the rock wall, she concluded. Her gaze landed on the wooden panel beside the wide window. Upon investigation she found it to be a hidden door. When she pried it open she confronted another row of steps leading into the peak of the lighthouse. As she rounded the corner she found Matthew amid several cages of pigeons.

Unaware that he was being observed, Matthew tied the message to the pigeon's leg and leaned out the obscure opening between the rocks. "Be on your way, Mildred. You have a long night ahead of you," he mused half aloud.

"What are you doing?" Catrina blurted out.

Matthew very nearly jumped out of his waistcoat. When he spun to face the intruder, his arm bumped against a nearby cage, sending it and its squawking inhabitants plunging to the floor. The racket set the other birds to screeching. Suddenly the crow's nest atop the lighthouse sounded like an inexperienced orchestra tuning up for a performance.

"What the hell are you doing up here, girl? You scared

364

twenty years off my li—" Matthew strangled on his breath when the candlelight filtered over Catrina's ivory skin and curvaceous figure. His eyes betrayed him and he could not help but gawk. Before him stood an enchantress so spellbindingly attractive that he was paralyzed for a long fanciful moment. "My God . . ." he sighed.

Catrina was vividly aware that she was being ravished by a pair of dark, perceptive eyes. Attempting to steer his attention elsewhere, she indicated the upturned bird cage at Matthew's feet. "What are you doing with those pigeons, Matthew?"

Matthew grasped the cage and returned it to its normal resting place. "Nothing," he lied through his smile. "These pesky birds took up residence in the loft and I decided to make them my pets. 'Tis lonely in the lighthouse. I amuse myself with the pigeons and turn them loose occasionally to let them stretch their wings. When Mildred returns, I'll send out George, her mate." A merry twinkle glistened in his eyes. "I don't dare send the two of them out together. They might decide to make a nest of their own. But if I send them separately, their attraction for each other will always bring them back to the tower."

Catrina had not one good reason to doubt the old man's explanation. But she was suspicious, just the same. Although Brant assured her that Matthew was innocent and harmless, Cat didn't quite trust the shabbily dressed watchman of the tower. She had the uneasy feeling there was more to this stoop-shouldered old man than met the eye. And Brant did warn her to carefully select her friends, she reminded herself. One couldn't be too cautious in enemy territory. Matthew would have to earn her trust and her friendship . . .

A surprised shriek flew from Catrina's lips when she felt some unidentified creature inside her petticoats. Catrina shot toward the door and then half collapsed when she spied the overweight tomcat that had become entangled in her skirts.

Matthew's hoarse laughter resounded around the loft as he hobbled over to scoop Nicodemus from the floor. "Shame on

365

you, Nic. That is no way to treat our guest."

Catrina surveyed the huge black cat and then glanced at the pigeons. "Your cat wouldn't by chance have made several feasts of your pigeons, would he?"

"Aye," Matthew affirmed. "Once or twice. Nicodemus is a clever one. If I do not secure the door he will be waiting for Mildred to perch on the ledge." He affectionately stroked the coal-black cat's head and then gestured a gloved hand toward the portal. "Come along, Tory. I will brew a pot of tea while you and Nicodemus become better acquainted. The two of you must become good friends if you are to share the same space."

Eyeing the odd pair with a wary frown, Catrina stepped aside to allow Matthew to close the door to the loft. Damn that Brant. He had deposited her in the belfry with a loon and his peculiar pets. Everyone knew cats and pigeons didn't live a peaceful coexistence.

Something very strange was going on in this musty lighthouse, Catrina mused as she followed Matthew through the sliding door in the wall.

Before Matthew continued on his way, he paused to change the stained glass that hung in front of the window. "The color gives the room a quaint glow, don't you think, Tory?"

Catrina nodded mutely, her gaze swinging around the tower that was now bathed in muted shades of blue. "I suppose the changing of colors serves no purpose, just like your caged pigeons," she remarked, the faintest hint of skepticism lacing her voice.

Matthew checked the supply of oil in the large lantern and then presented Catrina with a carefully blank stare. "Their only purpose is to amuse a lonely old man, my dear." His dark eyes glided over the full swell of Catrina's breast and then he broke into a leer. "But now that you are here to keep me company, I will not be so dependent on Nicodemus, my pigeons, and the varying shades of lights."

Catrina didn't like the way Matthew was looking at her and she intended to clear the air, then and there. Her chin jutted out and her eyes glittered threateningly. "I am not certain what thoughts are dancing in your head, Matthew, but I can guess. I feel it fair to inform you that I did not come here willingly. If you prove yourself to be less than gentlemanly in your behavior I will have no qualms about striking out on my own. I am not here to ease your loneliness in any capacity besides conversation."

Matthew threw back his head and guffawed. "Ah, Tory, you do have spunk," he managed to say between snickers. "But you need not fear a molesting at my hands. Your husband has already cautioned me to keep my distance at the risk of having my hands chopped off at the wrists." His amused gaze flickered down his broad torso and then flitted back to Cat. "At my age such strenuous activity might be the death of me. Please forgive an old man for staring, but you are an exquisite sight. You are young and lovely and you make me feel as if I have been old forever. I am looking to admire, not to ravish."

A sheepish smile spread across Catrina's lips. She felt like a fool for making such an outburst to her generous host. "Forgive me, Matthew. I fear I am not a very trusting soul. And I am a bit on edge tonight," she said in self-defense.

An affectionate grin swept across Matthew's bearded face. He extended an arm to assist the feisty beauty down the tedious steps. "Shall we sign a truce over a cup of tea?" When Catrina curled her hand around his proffered arm, he started down the stairs. "Before Mildred returns from her jaunt I will tell you about the time I was shipwrecked off the coast of China. We had sailed in midwinter, trailing on the tail of a northwester. The wind smelled strong of land, but the sky hung heavy and the gales were wicked on the sails. It was an eerie night when Saint Elmo's fire settled on the riggings." Matthew paused to suck in a ragged breath before continuing on his way. "Saint Elmo's fire is the mysterious flame that appears before a disastrous storm," he explained. "And what a storm it was . . ."

Catrina clung to Matthew's arm, captivated by the tale he

was weaving about her. Perhaps she had misjudged the old man, Catrina thought to herself. But before she could pursue her musings Matthew drew her back into his descriptive rendition of a catastrophe that had very nearly claimed his life.

It was much later that night when Catrina dropped onto her bed to face the emptiness she knew would inevitably come. Brant . . . She could almost see him poised by the door, his golden eyes glowing down upon her, his raven hair absorbing the candlelight. A choked sob bubbled in her throat, remembering the feel of his sinewy arms about her, the musky fragrance that fogged her senses. Her lips tingled, recalling the taste of his kiss. A knot of longing unfurled inside her, knowing she might never experience those sensations except when she was lost to the memories.

Impulsively, she threw her legs over the edge of the bed and moved toward the window to stare at the river. The *Sea Lady* had come out of nowhere and faded into nothing. There was no sign that the schooner or her pirate captain had been there at all. Catrina clutched her arms about her and sighed heavily. Would Brant sail into her life and now disappear? Would he ever think of her? Maybe she should go in search of a British vessel to take her back to Scotland. Then this madness would be over and she could get on with the rest of her life.

Just as Catrina started to turn away from the river of glistening silver, she caught sight of Matthew scurrying along the shore to disappear into the clump of oak trees. Where could he be going at this late hour, she wondered. Shrugging away the thought, she ambled back to bed, her mind drifting back to Brant and the remarks he had made before he left her that night.

He had insisted that he would make no attempt to stop her from leaving if that was her want. But if she left Charleston she would never have any hope of seeing Brant again. But if she stayed, he might return. Oh, what had she done to deserve such torment, she asked herself bitterly. She couldn't go and she couldn't stay. She was hanging in limbo, trapped in a world of impossible dreams.

Catrina flinched, startled by the light footsteps that padded across her shoulder. Soft laughter echoed about the room when she heard Nicodemus's quiet purr beside her ear. The tomcat had made himself at home, curling up by Catrina's arm as if he belonged there.

"Isn't that just like a man," she chided as she brushed her fingers across Nicodemus's notched ear, evidence that he had not emerged from a scrap unscathed. "You think nothing of joining a woman in bed without so much as an invitation." A faraway look passed across her face. Catrina wondered if Pirate Diamond was tomcatting his way along the American coast. The thought sent Catrina's spirits plunging like an anchor.

Exhaling a dismal sigh, Catrina closed her eyes and mind to the tormenting vision of Brant holding another woman in his arms. Since Nicodemus could well be the male in her life she made no move to rout him from his nest. And Nicodemus was in no hurry to leave since Matthew had locked him out of the loft when the pigeon returned from her late night flight with a message clasped around her leg.

Matthew picked his way through the heavy underbrush to wait at the designated site. After several minutes, he heard the crackling of twigs and crouched beneath the cover of bushes. When a familiar face appeared in the moonlight that filtered through the canopy of trees, Matthew struggled to his feet to confront the stout man who had braced himself against the tree.

"Your message was relayed to me not more than an hour ago," the man whispered. "I very nearly ran a good horse in the ground to arrive here at the appointed time. What news do you have for me?"

Matthew grinned wryly. "Captain Diamond is back in the colonies," he informed his comrade.

The man's shadowed face registered shock. "Diamond dares

369

to return. The high price for his scalp alone should have been just cause to dissuade him from venturing into these waters. Where is he now?"

Matthew shrugged. "I cannot say for certain. He would divulge no information before he set sail. You must alert your superior and inform him that Diamond has returned. No doubt he will be running the same course he pursued before the rebels insisted that he abandon the eastern seaboard before he was caught and hanged."

"I'm sure my superiors will appreciate the information, Matthew," the man murmured. "And keep up the good work. You are most valuable to the cause."

As the man disappeared in the direction he had come, Matthew pivoted around to make his way back to the lighthouse. It would not be as easy to sneak off into the night with his guest underfoot, but he was determined not to allow Catrina to restrict his coming and going. He would be cautious, Matthew told himself. Catrina would never know that he was involved in other activities besides manning the beacon in the tower.

Sporting a wry smile, Matthew hurried back to the lighthouse and tiptoed down the hall. Diamond was back and the British would not be pleased to learn that the elusive pirate would again be terrorizing the seas and slipping supplies to the rebels. The man lived dangerously, Matthew mused as he eased onto his bed. And now his precious wife was stashed in the lighthouse for safekeeping. Chuckling, Matthew closed his eyes and conjured up an enchanting vision with bright green eyes and a thick mane of fiery hair. Ah, what an interesting few months lay ahead of him!

Chapter Twenty-Three

A sour frown puckered Derrick Redmund's brow as he aimed himself toward Colonel Clinton's headquarters at Fort Johnson, the British stronghold on the bank of the Ashley River. Because of the efforts of his experienced first mate, Derrick had managed to negotiate his frigate through the Devil's Triangle. As Brant had anticipated, the vessel had bogged down in the seaweed. But a gusty gale had finally given the ship the force she needed to sail free of the entanglement.

Derrick's men had depleted their supplies while they were becalmed in the Sargasso Sea. If they had been forced to endure another week, Derrick was certain they would have become a ship of skeletons. The fact that Brant Diamond had led them on a wild-goose chase before slipping away in the night incensed Derrick. He could think of nothing but revenge.

Because of the near brush with disaster Derrick was forced to limp into the colonial port of Charleston to replenish supplies. It infuriated him that he didn't have the slightest notion where to locate Brant Diamond. But Derrick swore he would track the man down, even if it took the duration of the war. Diamond was lurking somewhere along the eastern seaboard, Derrick assured himself.

As soon as Derrick's frigate was spotted in the bay of Charleston, the commander at Fort Johnson sent a signal for

Derrick to come ashore and identify himself. Derrick did not anticipate the encounter. He had committed himself to the pursuit of the pesky privateer and he had no inclination to be handed another mission in these backward colonies.

The moment he set foot in Clinton's office, Derrick winced uncomfortably. Stern eyes focused on Derrick's battered uniform and then surveyed his weary features. Derrick knew the colonel was not impressed by his ragged appearance and he had Brant Diamond to thank for that.

"What is your name and mission, Captain?" Clinton demanded to know.

Striking a sophisticated pose, Derrick rattled off his name and explained the unsuccessful mission that had landed him in the British outpost below Charleston. When he completed his soliloquy, Clinton gestured toward the vacant chair.

"It seems your search for the elusive Captain Diamond has been as unsuccessful as ours," Clinton snorted. "Although you have randomly selected Charleston to restock supplies you may be closer to Diamond than you think. My Tory spies have reported sightings of Captain Diamond in the area. We have received reports about his activities. But, as of yet, we have been unable to capture him. My informants are certain there is an intricate scheme between the militia and the privateers. But we have had no success in determining the whereabouts of the rebel ringleaders." Clinton eased back in his seat and heaved a frustrated sigh. "We know Diamond is one of the masterminds behind this scheme but we are unsure how he delivers news of his arrival and manages to sneak his supplies to the inland trade roads."

"Diamond is in the vicinity of Charleston?" Derrick could not believe his luck. "I should like to offer my assistance to the cause," he said eagerly. "I have an axe to grind with Diamond, both personally and professionally."

Clinton assessed the sable haired, blue-eyed captain for a long, thoughtful moment. He could see the fierce determination in Derrick's eyes, the grim set of his jaw. It was obvious that the rebel pirate had made a grave enemy in Derrick Redmund. A man with a personal vendetta against Diamond would aid in the capture, Clinton decided.

"Very well, Captain, I will introduce you to Colonel Pinkerton. He can brief you on our findings."

Derrick was dismissed and directed to Pinkerton's home on the far bank of the Ashley River. Since Derrick was an unfamiliar face in Charleston, Pinkerton decided to give his fellow officer the run of the town. Dressed in civilian clothes, Derrick could follow up any bit of information he might pick up in the taverns and on the streets. Derrick was elated with the opportunity of easing his needs, ones that had long gone unappeased. It would be a relief to set up housekeeping on solid ground once again. He could pursue his pleasures and still be well paid for his efforts of breaking the underground network of rebel resistance.

When Pinkerton finished briefing Derrick on the activities of Captain Diamond and Francis Marion, or Swamp Fox as he was referred to by the British troops, he clasped Redmund's hand. "It will be a pleasure to have you working with us, Derrick. I hope our combined efforts will break the force that has kept the Continental army alive. I would like you to join me and my wife Cynthia for dinner this evening." A wry smile slid across Pinkerton's lips. "You have no objection to partaking a home-cooked meal after all these months at sea, do you?"

Derrick broke into a broad grin. "It would be a pleasure to sink my teeth into something besides sea rations, sir. I look forward to this evening."

Had Brant Diamond known Redmund had accidentally stumbled into Charleston he would have slept worse than he had the past several months. Brant had often flirted with danger and spent long, nerve-racking days playing a game of sheer wits. But even with his time-consuming activities he could not keep Cat off his mind.

373

Brant eased back from his desk and took a long draw on his cheroot. He brushed his hand over the bandage beneath his ribs, reminding him of his encounter with a British frigate near Norfolk. Brant had attempted to run the blockade in darkness, but the enemy captain had spotted the *Sea Lady* and had given chase. The deck of the schooner had been splattered with cannon fire and flying debris had left a nasty gash in his side. Although he managed to escape and successfully deliver the supplies to the rebel troops, he had been forced to waylay for repairs.

On the return cruise to the southern ports to restock supplies, Brant had stared at the beacon in the lighthouse on Cooper River. On several occasions these past months Brant had cruised the sea lanes near Charleston. Tempting though it was, Brant refused to delay long enough to see if Catrina had packed her belongings and sought out the first ship bound for the British Isles. This was no time for distraction, he had lectured himself time and time again.

There were rumors that the British were gearing up for a major offensive in the South. Brant had suspected that Charleston would become the target of another attack, but his information led him to believe the siege would come sooner than he had anticipated. The port was receiving excessive goods from other American ships that ran the route to the West Indies. The British had every intention of cutting off the incoming supplies that sustained the rebel army and navy.

Brant blew several smoke rings around his head and stared at the bare wall of his cabin. The supplies he had confiscated from British vessels had begun to dwindle. Before long he would be forced to take to the open sea for more prizes or return to the West Indies to restock. He had debated about taking Catrina with him, but he kept telling himself that she was safe with Matthew. With Catrina's British ties and Matthew's neutral position between the Tories and Whigs she was in no immediate danger. But if Brant gave way to the whim of carting her back to the *Sea Lady* there was the risk of battle . . . and even defeat.

Nay, when he was forced to set sail to the Indies, he would leave Catrina in Matthew's hands, Brant decided. After all, she had probably forgotten about her unwanted husband and booked passage for Scotland.

The rap at the door stirred Brant from his pensive contemplations. After granting Thomas entrance, the first mate strode into the cabin and dropped into a chair. Brant had put ashore the previous night to transfer supplies to the guerrilla bands who pestered and raided British troops along the seaboard. Thomas was anxious to hear about the progress of the rebellion.

"Well, what news have you received about the war?" Thomas questioned impatiently.

Brant took a small sip of brandy and glanced at his curious first mate. "John Paul has finally received a command. King Louis gave him a French ship, renamed the *Bonhomme Richard*. She has been armed with forty guns and John Paul is en route around the British Isles to pester the Royal Navy."

"I'm sure Cap'n Jones is pleased to be back at sea," Thomas remarked as he poured himself a tall drink.

"No doubt," Brant murmured absently. "But as far as the colonies themselves are concerned, it seems we are no closer to independence than the day we signed the proclamation. King Louis has signed an alliance with the colonies and part of the French fleet has arrived to reinforce Narragansett Bay. But we have yet to win a decisive victory. I have received word that Parliament offered to negotiate a truce, but the Continental Congress refused to discuss peace until Britain withdraws her armies and fleets and formally announces American independence."

"Have there been no respectable rebel victories in the North to force the Crown to recognize the strength of the rebels?"

"Nay," Brant muttered discouragingly. "The rebels were forced to evacuate Rhode Island and seventy American sloops were burned at the wharf in Dartmouth, Massachusetts. Now the British have decided to make a stronghold in the South. Savannah has just fallen into British hands. My informant heard the British plan to bring in reinforcements to sweep up the coast while northern troops march south. If the two enemy armies meet it will not be peace the Congress is forced to consider, but defeat itself."

Thomas slumped dejectedly in his seat. "The men ain't gonna like the news. Their spirits are low. They ain't been ashore for almost three months."

Brant nodded grimly. "I know." Gathering his feet beneath him, Brant wandered across the cabin to stare at Catrina's empty bed, just as he did three times a day.

Watching the direction Brant's footsteps took him, Thomas knew exactly what was troubling the captain. "Perhaps we could give the men shore leave when we slip back into Charleston to exchange supplies," he suggested. "It wouldn't hurt none of us to enjoy a little rest and relaxation."

"This is not the time for an extended vacation. There is a war going on," Brant snapped.

Thomas expelled his breath and glared at Brant. The captain had thrown himself into his missions the past months. He seemed to be driven by a restless force that granted him no peace. The emotional battle Brant had been waging had taken its toll. Thomas wondered if Brant had purposely avoided returning to the lighthouse in hopes of forgetting his feisty wife.

If that had been Brant's intention, the theory had failed, Thomas mused. A six-month absence had only intensified Brant's obsession for that high-spirited minx. He had tried to preoccupy himself, but Thomas knew Catrina's memory weighed heavily on Brant's mind. Brant would never find peace with himself until he and his wife came to terms.

"I, for one, would like to know how Cat has managed on foreign soil. Or if she packed up and sailed home," Thomas blurted out. "Do you suppose she is still in Charleston?"

Brant's head swiveled around to glower at his grinning first mate. "Don't you think Matthew can keep Cat from harm's way?"

Thomas's grin grew broader. "No doubt, he could were he in his prime," he snickered. "I would imagine it ain't easy on Matthew to have such a lovely houseguest. It should keep his blood circulatin'." His shoulder lifted in a lackadaisical shrug. "But I guess 'tis none of my concern how Catrina and Matthew spend their long months together . . . alone . . . in the lighthouse . . ." His smile vanished when he met Brant's black look. "But what disturbs me most is *you*, Cap'n. How long do you think you can pretend Cat don't matter to you? You ain't foolin' nobody, you know. It's killin' you wonderin' if she is still in Charleston and if Matthew has managed to keep his hands to himself when faced with temptation."

"I would appreciate it if you would keep your observations and predictions to yourself," Brant scowled. "I seem to recall having a similar conversation once before. I did not appreciate it then, nor do I now."

"Aye, we've had this conversation before and we're havin' it again, whether you like it or not." Thomas cocked a mocking brow. "Ain't you the least bit curious to know if Cat has revived Old Matthew's youthful spirit, even if you go on kiddin' yerself into thinkin' it don't matter to you? Hell's bells, Cap'n. You are in love with Cat and we both know it."

"Silence!" Brant bellowed, his voice booming off the walls to come at Thomas from all directions. Angrily, he puffed on his cigar until his head was surrounded by a thick cloud of smoke. "If you can talk of nothing else, do not speak at all. You are worse than a nagging old woman."

"They say confession is good for the soul, Cap'n," Thomas persisted, undaunted by the threatening sneer that was stamped on Brant's features. "Why don't you get it off yer chest? You'll feel better when you finally admit that adorable little spitfire has taken a firm hold on yer heart."

Brant lost what was left of his temper. He had found himself

377

fighting a losing battle and he detested his weakness. After six months Brant had come to the frayed end of his rope. "All right, dammit, I do love her," he exploded. "But what would you have me do about it? Disregard my duties? Abandon my mission and cart Cat off to the West Indies to wait out the war like some spineless coward?"

Thomas stared Brant straight in the eye. "Nay," he said quietly. "But yer bein' a bigger coward by holdin' back what you feel. It seems Cat is the last one to know you care about her and she should have been the first."

"How many times have you fallen in love, Thomas?" Brant questioned soberly.

"A time or two," Thomas confessed.

"And how have these affairs of the heart ended?"

Thomas suddenly realized he had been baited. "That was different," he argued, tilting a stubborn chin.

Brant arched a dark brow and flashed his first mate a taunting smile. "Pray tell me how you can distinguish one man's romantic encounters from another. I cannot wait to hear your explanation."

" 'Tis completely different because I didn't fall in love with nobody like Cat. She's as ornery and willful are you are and she gives what she gets. I never met my perfect match, but you have, you damned fool! Quit draggin' yer feet. One day you might lose her . . . if you haven't already. And you will sorely regret yer blunder the rest of yer days," Thomas prophesied.

"And what do you suggest I do, counselor?" Brant queried sarcastically. "Burst into the lighthouse, determine if Cat is still there, and blurt out my affection when I have no idea what type of reception to anticipate?"

"It ain't yer method that is important," Thomas snorted. "What's important is that you stop running circles around the truth. You'll be a hell of a lot easier to get along with when you come to terms with that woman."

Brant's eyes soared toward the ceiling. Thomas was pressing hard and Brant was tired of being pushed. "Oh, very well, we will dock in Charleston on our return cruise and I will venture to the lighthouse." Brant wagged a lean finger in Thomas's beaming face. "But if this theory of yours proves disastrous, I will never heed your advice again."

"If you would have handled Cat properly in the first place you wouldn't be stewin' in yer own juice," he shot back.

"Thank you for your vote of confidence," Brant grunted caustically. "'Tis a wonder you see fit to work under my command since you consider me to be a bungling idiot."

"I got no complaints about yer abilities in battle," Thomas snickered, coming to his feet. "But what you know about women wouldn't fill a thimble. If you weren't so unconscious you'd know that girl has been in love with you since the very beginnin'. I couldn't understand why Milton watched yer every move on board ship . . . until I learned he was a *she*. If you could have seen the way her eyes followed you when you wasn't lookin', you'd know the feelin's are mutual. But you have been too busy tryin' not to get involved, even when you was already in way over yer head."

Brant's mouth dropped open as Thomas strutted toward the door. Catrina was in love with him? Brant was afraid to let himself believe it. Maybe Thomas was only trying to encourage him, giving him the incentive to approach Cat with the truth.

A contemplative frown plowed Brant's brow. No matter what Thomas said, Brant intended to employ the cautious approach. The only time in his life he had confessed to love had ended in disaster. He was not about to blunder into another humiliating catastrophe after being thrown over for a man twice Cynthia's age. After all, if Catrina loved him as Thomas predicted, she could have said so. But she hadn't . . . except for that night he had compromised her virtues and she threw herself overboard. Obviously, Cat had been so rattled by the incident that she didn't know what she was saying or how she felt. At least that was the explanation she had given later. Or was she trying to hide her true feelings for fear of being hurt?

Brant breathed a perplexed sigh. Who could know why Cat

said and did the things she did? The woman was a baffling contradiction. She always reacted exactly opposite of the way Brant anticipated.

Grappling with conflicting emotions, Brant paced the confines of his cabin. Suddenly he was anxious to complete his mission along the coast and dock in Charleston. It had been half a year since he had stared into those fathomless green eyes. Perhaps it was time to at least test his reaction to that gorgeous minx. Aye, he would set sail for Charleston as soon as he transported the remainder of his supplies to Philadelphia and spoke with his superiors. He and Cat would settle their differences once and for all . . . if she was still there, he amended.

His pensive gaze swung to the abandoned cot in the corner. A quiet smile touched his lips as visions began to rise like a jinni from a bottle. He could see Milton's smudged face, those mischievous green eyes. He could hear that twangy voice she had employed while she charaded as Milton. And then the image changed and the smudged cheeks turned to flawless ivory. There, in the shadows of his room, Brant watched a vision of loveliness blossom and grow until it consumed him.

He could hear Catrina's merry laughter drifting across the sand as she darted across the beach to plunge into the sea, wearing nothing but that radiant smile of hers. He could see her lying beside him in the underground cavern, sharing a passion that compared to no other experience.

Brant shook his head to shatter the fantasy. He had work to do and this wasn't helping matters, he chided himself. And yet, in the back of his mind, he could not help but wonder if the impetuous whirlwind with the fiery auburn hair had decided it best to set sail for Scotland.

At least Brant was assured that Derrick Redmund would not be hounding Cat upon her return to the Isles. By now the blackhearted scoundrel should have been a member of a ghost crew, lost somewhere in the Devil's Triangle. If Derrick *had* miraculously managed to escape the tangled seaweed he would still be miles away from Cat, he reassured himself.

Satisfied with that positive thought, Brant shrugged on his coat and climbed to the helm. He was eager to make connections with the guerrilla band in Baltimore and sail up the coast to Philadelphia. It would be at least a month before he returned to Charleston, but that would give him time to plan his confrontation with Catrina . . . if she were still there. Would she be? he asked himself. Did she truly care enough to await his return, even after all these months? He had made it easy for her to go, Brant reminded himself. Knowing that, he should be prepared for disappointment when he returned to the lighthouse. Indeed, he was a fool if he were the least bit surprised to walk through the door and find Catrina gone for good.

During the passing months that led from the quiet days of fall to the cool, crisp days of winter, Catrina's cynical attitude toward Matthew faded. But then, the old man was more discreet in his secretive maneuvers after Catrina had barged in on him that first night.

Catrina found herself leaning heavily on Matthew for companionship. She had tried not to think about Brant, but his memory came uninvited to her dreams. It was difficult not to wonder what had become of the daredevil who defied the British by attacking their frigates and slipping supplies through the blockades.

When Catrina would become depressed or restless Matthew would ferry her across the river to amble along the streets of Charleston. He brushed shoulders with Tories and Whigs alike, introducing her as his niece who had come to visit him during the winter.

Catrina had strolled along the brick sidewalks to browse in the shops and ventured into the boutiques to take fittings for new gowns that would suit the climate. But nothing could fill the aching loneliness of wanting a man she knew she could never have. She had heard nothing from Brant, only quiet rumors that the black-bearded pirate was still playing havoc with British vessels and supply warehouses.

One afternoon while Catrina was waiting for a fitting at the dress shop she overheard a conversation that made her frown curiously. The mention of a woman's name made her sit up and take note.

"Now, Cynthia, I think you are making much ado about nothing," Barnaby Swanson chided gently. "You know these are troubled times and 'tis difficult to procure the finest silks. I am doing my best to locate the precise fabric you have requested."

"Your best is obviously not good enough." The woman's chin jutted out in an exaggerated pout. "I have already told you to spare no cost in finding the fabric and sewing the dress. I must have it by the end of the month. My husband is giving a ball for the most distinguished British officers in the area and I cannot entertain my dignified guests in these rags!"

Catrina bit back a grin as she assessed the woman whose lustrous golden hair was immaculately pinned on top of her head. Rags? Catrina chuckled to herself. Cynthia whoever-she-was had donned an expensive velvet gown to match the color of her snapping blue eyes. Corset bows descended from her daring bodice to her waist. Row upon row of dainty white lace circled the floor-length skirt. If Catrina hadn't known better she would have sworn the fussy wench had just stepped from British court after an audience with the king.

Could this be the Cynthia who had turned Brant's heart to stone? Catrina reappraised the huffy wench and snickered to herself. Although Cynthia was an attractive bundle of velvet and lace and her face was comely, she had at least one flaw. There was no delicate way to put it, Catrina mused as her eyes sketched Cynthia's generous figure. The woman was plump. Cynthia had eaten her way into a larger size dress, judging by the fact that she was poured into the one she was presently wearing. The rebel troops might have been starving but the

British had seen to it that their Tory wives were well fed.

If this was Brant's Cynthia, he might not recognize her as the trim young girl who had stolen his heart, Cat thought smugly. Cynthia looked to be nearing her thirtieth year. Catrina guessed the woman to be well traveled, considering the mile lines that tracked across her face.

Whimsically, Catrina wished Brant could get a look at the broad-hipped wench he once professed to love. It was most comforting to know that her competition had blossomed with age. It was as it should be, Catrina thought delightedly. Her husband's ex-lover had begun to wrinkle and bulge. Aye, in Cynthia's case there was a lot of woman to love, but if she lost her temper and sat on Brant she could have squashed him flat.

The wicked thought caused an impulsive giggle to burst from Catrina's lips. She quickly sobered when Cynthia Pinkerton looked down her nose at the bewitching chit who was amusing herself with some secretive thought.

"What is it that you find so humorous, *child?*" Cynthia sniped.

Catrina shrugged, undaunted by the woman's snobbish attitude. "'Tis a private joke that suddenly popped to mind. I doubt you would find it amusing. But if you like, I can relate the anecdote and you can decide for yourself if 'tis worth a smile."

"That won't be necessary. I have more important matters to attend than to endure a long-winded story," Cynthia sniffed distastefully. Having dismissed Catrina with a condescending frown, Cynthia turned her attention to the dressmaker. "Since I am entertaining the most influential of guests, I expect you to locate the proper fabric for the gown I have designed. See to it that I have my first fitting by the end of next week. If not, I shall take all my business elsewhere and pass the word to my friends that you and your assistants are irresponsible."

When Cynthia stuck her nose in the air and stalked toward the door, Barnaby let his breath out in a rush. He did not appreciate being threatened, especially by one of his steady customers. Cynthia Pinkerton could make trouble for him. It was difficult enough to scratch out a living in these unsettled times without losing his clientele.

Cynthia paused by the portal and turned around to stare pensively at the lovely chit who had seemed not the least bit intimidated. The attractive wench was still smiling to herself and Cynthia swore she would have her revenge.

Pasting on a civil smile, Cynthia addressed Catrina with stoic poise. "I am having a tea Thursday afternoon in my home. Why don't you join us. It should prove enjoyable. Perhaps you can relate your amusing anecdote to my friends."

Catrina studied the full-figured wench for a long pensive moment. She had the feeling the invitation had been made in spite, but Catrina could not resist the temptation of accepting, not when the woman could have been Brant's former lover. "Why, thank you, madame. I should like that very much."

Cynthia's blue eyes twinkled with wicked delight. "Good. We shall expect you at two o'clock. It should not be difficult to locate my home. Ask anyone for directions to Colonel Pinkerton's mansion."

As Cynthia spun around to make her regal exit Catrina muffled another giggle and glanced at Barnaby. "Is Mrs. Pinkerton always so difficult to deal with?" she could not help but ask.

"Aye," Barnaby confessed. " 'Tis a pity she does not possess your disposition. You have been patient with me." The gleam in his eyes brightened as he strode over to fetch the gown he had stitched for the shapely redhead. "But because I find you so charming I have created a dress that will do justice to your beauty."

Catrina blinked bewilderedly at the exquisite gown and then broke into a wry smile. "This would not happen to be cut from the bolt of silk that Mrs. Pinkerton demanded, would it?"

Barnaby grinned guiltily. "It would. Let Mrs. Pinkerton wear her so-called rags. She has never complimented one of my gowns, but you . . . you will make my creation come alive."

384

"You are very kind," Catrina murmured as her fingertips sketched the delicate lace and rich silk.

"Try it on for me," Barnaby requested. "I should like to see it before you go. I have imagined how the gown would become you."

Catrina consented and Barnaby clasped his hands in pleasure when she emerged from the dressing room. Feeling quite satisfied with the dress and her belief that she had just met Brant's old sweetheart, Catrina walked back down the street to find Matthew.

Cynthia Pinkerton had made her day, Catrina thought with a mischievous grin. She settled herself in the carriage beside Matthew and continued to smile like the cat who had feasted on a plump canary.

"What has you looking so smug this morning?" Matthew inquired, eyeing his companion curiously.

"I have just had the pleasure of meeting Mrs. Cynthia Pinkerton," Catrina announced. "Would you happen to know if she is the same Cynthia who at one time walked these streets on my husband's arm?"

A wary frown knitted Matthew's brow. "And if she were?"

Her green eyes sparkled with deviltry when she glanced up at Matthew. "Then I will be quite satisfied. To my delight I found Mrs. Pinkerton to be frightfully spoiled and as broad as an axe handle."

Matthew threw back his head and laughed out loud. "Then you should be gloating, Tory . . . though I would not dare repeat such a description of Mrs. Pinkerton to those who travel in her vast circle of friends. She might come after you with a hatchet, intent on lifting your lovely scalp. She prides herself in her beauty and her expensive wardrobe, not to mention her effect on men, young and old alike."

Catrina frowned at the insinuation. "I hope I have not insulted you, Matthew. Are you one of Cynthia's admirers?"

Matthew chuckled as he popped the reins over the steed's rump and started down the street. "Whatever put that idea in

385

your head, Tory?"

"Well, you do disappear at night," she defended. "I thought perhaps you were gallivanting about with Cynthia."

"Nay," Matthew assured her. "I am not among her stable of waiting studs."

"That comes as a relief," Catrina breathed and then giggled softly. "I cannot imagine how any other man could afford that wench. It must cost Mr. Pinkerton a handsome shilling to keep his wife in food and clothes," she snickered. "It looks as if she can eat enough for three women and it would require an entire bolt of cloth to cover her blossoming figure."

"Shame on you for saying so," Matthew chortled as he aimed the carriage toward the river. "Although I do not see her as being as plump as you suggest, I have often wondered if Captain Diamond would still feel the same affection for the wench if he laid eyes on her the last few years."

The possibility stifled Catrina's amusement. Perhaps there was something about Cynthia that would still attract Brant. What, Catrina could not imagine. But a man in love could not always see a woman's faults. Ah, why was she speculating, Catrina chided herself. Brant would probably never show his face in Charleston when there was such a high price on his head. And if he were interested in her or Cynthia he would have returned long before now.

Brant was too absorbed in his purpose to give any woman a second thought, Catrina reminded herself. Although she had satisfied her curiosity about the woman from Brant's past it would do her little good in earning the cynical pirate's love.

Catrina brushed her hand over the exquisite gown Barnaby had designed for her. If only Brant would find her as appealing as Barnaby did, she mused whimsically. If only . . . Catrina halted in midthought. There was no use dreaming impossible dreams. She would set sail in the spring. It was obvious that she was fighting for a lost cause. Brant didn't care enough to send a message or come to see her all these months. She could not wait forever.

Praying that Brant would return, Catrina had sent a notice of her whereabouts to her lawyer in the fall, requesting that he continue to handle her affairs. But if Brant had not sailed into the harbor in the next two months, Catrina fully intended to return to Scotland to see to her own estate. She was going to have to put Pirate Diamond out of her mind once and for all!

Chapter Twenty-Four

Feeling a mite apprehensive about her social debut in Charleston, Catrina shifted from one foot to the other, waiting to be granted entrance to the grand mansion. The Pinkertons' sprawling home was constructed of brick and decorated with white wood trim. Balustrated promenades jutted out from each side of the house, overlooking well-manicured gardens. Although the manor was elegant it was built on a smaller scale in comparison to the spacious, Regency-style mansion that sat on the Hamilton estate near Dumfries.

Catrina decided not to make mention of that fact to her hostess. Besides, Cynthia wouldn't believe it. Let the wench think her home was a palace, Catrina mused as she impatiently tapped her foot.

When the door swung open, the butler surveyed the petite beauty and then broke into a smile. The young woman's face was exquisite and her greeting grin carried a hint of mischievousness. The servant felt a stirring of delight just gazing at the auburn-haired enchantress. She was like a fresh breath of spring.

Bowing elegantly before her, the servant gestured for Catrina to enter. "Give me your name, miss. I will formally announce your arrival to the other ladies."

Catrina rattled off her name, but not her married one.

Matthew had already warned her not to boast about her husband when she was brushing shoulders with distinguished Tories. And as notorious as Brant Diamond was, Matthew insisted that Cat would find herself strung up from the tallest tree in Charleston. Diamond was a household word, Matthew had said—the four letter kind.

Lifting a dignified chin, Catrina followed the servant through the foyer and up the wide stairway. The reception room was located on the second floor and was equipped with large windows that boasted a view of the Ashley River.

The moment Catrina swept gracefully into the room, Cynthia's face fell like a rock slide. She had not anticipated that the woman she had met in the boutique could afford such finery. But the gown Catrina had selected for this affair was a masterpiece of royal blue velvet and lace. The tailor-made dress enhanced Catrina's curvaceous figure and Cynthia's blue eyes turned mutinous green. The white lace ruffle that framed the deep square neckline exposed Catrina's alabaster skin, creating an altogether enchanting vision that had Cynthia gnashing her teeth in irritation.

This was not at all the scene Cynthia had pictured when she invited the chit to her party. It annoyed Cynthia that the butler had made such a big to-do about announcing their late guest. Catrina's grand entrance and stunning looks were like Oriental acupuncture treatments—tiny needles positioned just beneath the skin to prick her pride. It further irked her when the group of women raved over Catrina's gown and fluttered about the chit as if she were one of their closest friends.

Catrina was assaulted by several curious questions about her life in Scotland, but she was careful in supplying answers. She was determined not to expose herself as the infamous pirate's wife and twice she was forced to give bald-faced lies to protect herself and Brant.

When Brant Diamond's name cropped into the conversation, Catrina quietly sipped her tea and hung on every word. She acted as if she were intrigued by the bits and pieces of information that were being flung about. And she was! Cat was curious about these Tory ladies' opinions of the swashbuckling pirate. But most of all, Cat wanted to hear what Cynthia had to say about her ex-lover.

"Well, it will only be a matter of time before my husband and his new associates put a stop to Pirate Diamond's activities," Cynthia scoffed unpleasantly. "They are constantly sniffing at his heels. The sooner Diamond is apprehended, the sooner this frightful war will come to an end. That rebel rouser has kept the patriots in food, clothing, and ammunition far too long."

Cat bit back a wry smile and innocently inquired, "Have you ever met this Pirate Diamond?"

Cynthia was startled by the question and it took a moment to recompose herself when all eyes fell upon her. Fumbling with the spoon, she dumped several heaps of sugar in her tea and snatched up a fruit tart. "I . . . er . . . well, as a matter of fact, I did make his acquaintance before the war," she begrudgingly admitted, wishing she would have lied through her teeth. Her reply only invited more questions.

"You never mentioned it before, Cynthia," Mrs. Collier remarked. "Do tell us about him. We are all quite curious about the legendary pirate." A meek smile pursed Mrs. Collier's lips. "I have heard he is a dashing rogue, handsome as well as cunning."

Cynthia strongly resented Catrina's uncanny technique of dredging up little known facts, but she had already blundered into the conversation and there was no way out. "Aye, I knew him," she admitted before gobbling down her tart. Cynthia stared at Marshall Collier's wife, wondering if the woman knew her husband's late-night duties entailed an occasional tête-à-tête with the party hostess. The naive little fool, Cynthia thought arrogantly. Bernice Collier probably didn't have a clue that Marshall was slipping around behind her back. "Brant Diamond is very attractive, but he always seemed a mite rebellious and belligerent, even in those days."

"Rebellious? How do you mean?" Catrina prodded, delighting in watching Cynthia squirm in her tuft chair.

Cynthia shot Catrina a discreet glance. Sparing though it was, the look was meant to slice Catrina in two equal pieces. Damn that chit, she was pursuing a touchy subject. "Diamond was always a free spirit who refused to be dominated. He is very much his own man and he has never had the slightest interest in catering to the king's wishes. He would make a miserable husband as well as a poor subject of the Crown. I would think a woman would never have her way with a man like that."

"Ah, but he sounds intriguing," Bernice Collier interjected, breaking into a coy smile. "I am fascinated by bold men. And I have heard it rumored that Brant Diamond is that and more." Her eyes twinkled impishly. "They say there is a glitter of devil's gold in Diamond's eyes and a rakish smile upon his bearded face—one that can make a woman swoon."

Cynthia stuck her nose in the air. "I still prefer a man like my Virgil. He caters to my every whim. Brant Diamond would do no such thing. He prides himself in his independence. A woman who found herself wed to Diamond would be constantly battling for her rights and her freedom. Diamond is *too* much man for an ordinary woman to handle."

At least Cynthia had landed on one accurate point, Catrina mused. Brant Diamond was as wild and free as the wind. No woman could successfully tie her apron strings to a cyclone. But it was not the freedom to seek other lovers that posed the problem as Diamond's wife. It was the acquisition of Diamond's love.

"What do you suppose will become of the pirate if the Loyaltists catch up with him?" Cat inquired.

"Virgil vows to have him carved into bite-sized pieces and served to the king," Cynthia insisted and then smiled a gloating smile. "I think Virgil is jealous that I once knew the dark daredevil. For that reason alone Virgil would take drastic measures against the elusive pirate."

"Did you know him well or did you only know *of* him?"

Catrina interrogated with seeming innocence. If the angelic look on her face was any indication of her guileless nature, Catrina should have, at that moment, sprouted a halo and wings.

Cynthia grabbed another tart and vigorously chewed upon it, giving herself time to think. Blast it, that girl had Cynthia on the firing line! "A . . . well . . . he did call upon me once or twice while he was in Charleston, selling his cargo," she admitted.

"How fascinating," Catrina enthused. "Did you ever in your wildest dreams imagine that a man of your acquaintance—indeed a man who actively courted you—could be terrorizing the coastline? To think you once knew and perhaps found yourself in the arms of the notorious pirate!"

Cynthia gnashed her teeth in her tart. What that chit had implied with her careless remark had the guests silently speculating. Lord, the next thing Cynthia knew she would be hauled in for questioning and soiling her reputation with the socially elite of Charleston! The thought made Cynthia suck on her breath, lodging the tart in her throat.

When Cynthia sputtered and choked, Catrina leaned over to whack her hostess between the shoulder blades. "My goodness, Mrs. Pinkerton, you nearly strangled," Catrina observed and silently wished the wench had done so.

Cynthia dragged in a ragged breath and then caught sight of the wedding band on Catrina's finger. It suddenly occurred to her that the young chit had not mentioned her husband. Cynthia gestured toward the gold band that was inlaid with emeralds and diamonds, thankful she had found the opportunity to steer the subject away from her affair with the infamous pirate.

"Tell us about your husband, Catrina. Is he leading one of the regiments near Charleston?"

Catrina blossomed into a proud smile. "Nay, he captains a ship in these waters," she declared. "And it could well be that he will one day come face to face with the notorious pirate.

They are much alike, I think . . . from what I have learned about Captain Diamond."

"Oh, in what ways?" Cynthia inquired, becoming more interested in the chit's husband by the second.

"My husband is a man among men, fighting for the cause he believes in. He also possesses bold daring on the high seas and he thrives on challenges," she boasted, her eyes sparkling with mischievousness. "And he is undeniably handsome as well."

"Hamilton . . ." Cynthia thoughtfully chewed on her bottom lip and sorted through her mental repertoire of who-was-who in Charleston. "I don't believe I have heard that name before."

"One day I predict you will hear it frequently," Catrina insisted, fighting to keep from bursting into snickers. "Perhaps I can formally introduce the two of you when my husband is granted shore leave from his time-consuming duties. At the moment he is in the thick of things. But when you do chance to meet, I'm certain you will agree that he is everything I said he was."

Cynthia returned the smile with spiteful glee. Aye, how she would delight in luring this lovely chit's own husband from home and landing him in the guest house bed. It would provide wicked satisfaction to dally with this woman's husband, Cynthia thought to herself. That would prove to Catrina Hamilton that she was not in the same class with Cynthia Pinkerton.

She could have any man who met her whim, Cynthia reminded herself arrogantly. Indeed, she had spent a lifetime perfecting seduction. And she had learned a great deal from the infamous Captain Diamond, though she wasn't about to reveal her tutor's name to the upper echelon of Charleston.

"I'm sure I will," Cynthia agreed, a wicked twinkle in her blue eyes. "You must bring your husband by my home when he returns to shore."

From there, the conversation veered down several avenues. The women exchanged information about the progress of the war—from the Tory point of view. Catrina listened intently, wishing she could convey the information to Brant, to prove to him that her allegiance was to him. But she was still in an uncomfortable situation, she reminded herself. She was neither rebel nor Tory, but rather an outsider who had been transplanted on foreign soil.

When the party broke up two hours later, Catrina walked from the house and disappeared into her rented carriage. Cynthia lingered by the door, wondering why she felt this strange animosity toward the attractive chit. The girl upset her and, for the life of her, Cynthia was not certain why. Perhaps it was because she had the feeling Catrina was silently laughing at her. Or mayhap it was because Catrina had dared to probe into Cynthia's past, revealing her association with Brant Diamond. Or perhaps what distressed Cynthia most was the fact that the young beauty possessed such natural poise and grace when she mingled with the upper crust of society. More likely, it was the combination of all three, Cynthia reckoned.

Cynthia drew in a deep breath and let it out slowly. Aye, Pirate Diamond was a most intriguing man, she recalled. But Cynthia had her heart set on established wealth and she was not about to sail off to some secluded island in the West Indies to live out her life in a social vacuum. She thrived on gay affairs and a variety of lovers, ones Virgil had no idea she had taken to her bed. Brant Diamond had been a most satisfying lover but Cynthia had greater aspirations in life than to raise his brats on some humid island. The night she had offered Brant an open invitation to rekindle their affair had been a humiliating disaster. Brant had scorned her, mocked her, and walked away. And for that reason alone Cynthia longed to see the rebel dangling by his arrogant neck. No man declined an invitation from Cynthia Pinkerton without paying dearly for it. And Brant Diamond was the only man who had been made an offer he refused. Cynthia could not wait to see the look on Diamond's face when he was brought before Virgil Pinkerton for sentencing. Aye, he would rue the day he had spurned

Cynthia. Virgil would show him no mercy!

Setting those spiteful thoughts aside, Cynthia weaved her way through the mansion to sneak out the back door. The covered archway led her past the servants' quarters to the quaint guest cottage beneath the canopy of tupelo trees. A provocative smile hovered on Cynthia's lips when the handsome gentleman emerged from the bedroom to greet her.

"I had almost given up on you this afternoon," Derrick Redmund murmured as he strode over to unfasten the stays on the back of Cynthia's gown.

"I had to bid my houseful of guests adieu," Cynthia cooed. Her palms splayed across Derrick's chest, quickly aroused by the thought of lying in his capable arms. "One woman in particular was more upsetting and I longed to put the wench in her proper place. I hope your kisses will make me forget my irritation with the chit." Cynthia was not about to divulge the woman's name for fear Derrick would be curious about the wench. Once he laid eyes on Catrina Hamilton he might turn his attention from Cynthia and her vanity could not tolerate that!

Derrick broke into a rakish grin. He hungered for the pleasures this full-figured blonde could offer. "I promise to take your mind off the pesky wench," he assured her huskily. "But our time is short. I have to meet with your husband later this afternoon . . ."

Cynthia chortled seductively, her hands mapping the expanse of Derrick's shoulders. "It would never do to keep Virgil waiting . . . nor his wife . . . We both can be very demanding and impatient."

Derrick roughly took her parted lips, longing to drown himself in the taste and feel of this passionate woman. The mere thought that he was toying with his superior officer's wife stimulated him. Cynthia was generous with her lust and her money and Derrick had coasted quite comfortably these past months. Although he was determined to catch Brant Diamond and retrieve his long lost fiancée from the pirate's clutches, Cynthia proved to be a distracting pastime and he had no complaints about accommodating her.

They both knew they were not playing for keeps. They were only taking passion from each other. Derrick knew he was not the only man sampling Cynthia's charms, but he was not jealous of her. Cynthia had managed to marry position and wealth and that was still Derrick's aspiration. He and Cynthia had a great deal in common, not to mention their mutual lust . . .

Giving way to that thought Derrick steered his eager consort toward the bedroom and temporarily set aside his intention of catching up with Catrina. One day he would locate that evasive chit and make her his wife. Until then he would satisfy his male needs with the anxious blonde whose appetite for passion was insatiable . . . at least while she was sleeping somewhere other than her elderly husband's bed.

Chapter Twenty-Five

While Matthew was in the tower keeping watch on approaching ships with his flock of pigeons, Catrina settled into her bath. A contented sigh escaped her lips. The hot water eased the chill of the damp, drafty lighthouse and Catrina contemplated spending the remainder of the evening where she was.

A faint smile pursed her lips as she eased against the back of the tub to languidly sponge the water across her arms. She could not quit thinking about the prissy Cynthia Pinkerton. Since the party the previous week, Catrina had seen the woman three times. And each incident confirmed Catrina's opinion that the woman was as spoiled as a three-day-old fish.

It seemed Cynthia had worked herself into a snit, preparing for her grand ball. Catrina had heard Cynthia threaten every shopkeeper in Charleston to procure the supplies she needed for her extravagant party. No doubt, Cynthia intended to impress her guests and attempt to rule the ball like the resident queen. And all the while, the plump wench would probably be flittering about, propositioning everything in breeches, Catrina thought with a snicker. It was a pity one of her male guests didn't tattle to poor, naive Virgil. How could the man ever hope to locate Brant Diamond when he couldn't even uncover the fact that his promiscuous wife was tumbling in the quilts with a score of other men?

When Matthew's tomcat bounded onto the chair beside the tub Catrina tossed aside her musings and smiled fondly. "Are you still awaiting your supper, Nicodemus?" she questioned. "I suppose Matthew was too preoccupied with those squawking pigeons to remember to feed you."

Nicodemus mewed in response and Catrina hurriedly finished her bath to accommodate the spoiled cat. "We will find you something to eat," she promised.

When she rose from the tub Nicodemus leaped from his seat and trotted around the edge of the door, mewing his way to the kitchen. Since Matthew was still upstairs, locked in the tower, Catrina did not bother to dress. She wrapped a towel about her and followed the tomcat, intending to return to her tub for a thorough soaking.

"Get down from there," Catrina scolded when she spied Nicodemus perched on the table. "You may think you are human but you will still eat on the floor."

When she set the bowl of scraps and milk on the floor, Nicodemus hopped down to devour his meal. Catrina squatted down to stroke the oversized tomcat. "It would never do to let you or Cynthia go hungry," she chortled. "I only hope Colonel Pinkerton is catering as obediently to his wife as I am to you. Let the wench grow round and plump. It serves her right after the way she treated Brant."

Matthew rounded the corner and froze in his tracks when he noticed Catrina wearing nothing but a towel. Her glorious mane of auburn hair was haphazardly pinned on top of her head and several renegade strands curled about her exquisite face, one that was alive with spiteful amusement. The towel parted to reveal a generous proportion of her thighs and Matthew did the natural thing—he gawked before his spectacles completely steamed over. Although the fabric covered most of her shapely anatomy, there was enough bare skin exposed to send Matthew's blood pressure soaring. Clutching the collar of his shirt to relieve the sudden pressure,

Matthew swallowed over the lump that had collected in his throat. His chest rose and fell in a shuddering sigh as he ogled the tempting nymph and succumbed to fantasy.

A muffled groan drew Catrina's attention and she gasped in surprise when she glanced up to see Matthew gaping at her like an unblinking owl. Embarrassed red flushed her cheeks as she rose to her feet to rearrange the drooping towel that exposed more bosom than was decently permissible.

"I . . . thought you were in the tower," she stammered.

With great difficulty, Matthew plugged his eyes back in their sockets and composed himself as best he could. He and Cat had managed to share the same space for more than six months without mishap, respecting each other's privacy. But tonight was an entirely different matter. His hawkish gaze flooded over Catrina's barely clad figure, visualizing what lay beneath the skimpy towel. His imagination was running rampant, making him more uncomfortable by the minute. If Catrina could have known what he was thinking she would have run through the nearest wall to avoid him!

"I came down to fetch a drink," he chirped, his eyes making another thorough sweep of her appetizing figure.

Feeling devoured, Catrina inched toward the door, trying not to break into a run. "I had better return to my bath before I catch my death of cold."

"It doesn't seem cold in here at all, Tory," Matthew grinned. "I suddenly feel as if I have been warmed from inside out."

"Lecherous old man," she teased, attempting to make light of an uncomfortable situation. "The way you have been sneaking in and out of the lighthouse I would imagine you have been warming yourself in . . ." The words died on her lips when Brant Diamond's powerful physique filled the doorway. If looks could kill Catrina would have fried alive.

"Madam, do you always make a habit of flouncing under Matthew's nose in such an indecent manner?" Brant snorted disdainfully.

A sick smile twitched Matthew's lips as he shuffled around

to face the fuming pirate who had yet to shave the dark beard. Brant looked like black thunder with his eyes flashing and his stony features cemented in a threatening scowl.

"Why, Captain, how good it is to see you again," he squeaked. "I had not expected you before the spring thaw."

"Obviously not," Brant muttered. The expression on his face would have sent a mountain lion cowering in his cave. Blazing amber eyes lanced off Matthew's face to drill into Catrina's whitewashed features. "Get dressed, woman. I would expect even Matthew has difficulty controlling himself with you prancing about in your skimpy towel." A thin smile stretched across his lips until they very nearly snapped under the intense pressure. "Or was that what you had counted upon?"

Catrina's volatile temper flared in response to Brant's insinuation. She drew herself up proudly after being slapped with the insult. "You have no right to presume that I . . ."

"No *right?*" Brant howled. "Blast it, I am your husband! Perhaps other men can stand quietly by to watch their wives purposely seduce . . ."

"Seduce?" Catrina sputtered in outrage. Her green eyes fastened on Brant's breeches, mentally selecting the most vulnerable place to kick him. "How dare you suggest I threw myself at Matthew!"

"By God, if a woman sashayed across my kitchen in no more than a towel, I would conclude that she was craving more than a morsel of food to curb her appetite!" Brant bellowed, his voice rising until it cracked like thunder.

"You don't have one!" Cat flung sarcastically, putting a dent in his theory.

"I don't have one what? A kitchen or a woman?" he growled, eyes blazing. "Are you trying to tell me that you and Matthew have . . ." Brant could not bring himself to voice the speculation. The thought of Catrina spreading herself beneath old Matthew was like a knife twisting in his back. Brant didn't know who to strangle first, his infidel wife or her lover!

When Brant decided to go for his wife first Matthew hooked the crook of his cane around the pirate's arm to detain him. "Your imagination is running away without your brain attached to it. For God's sake, man, she only stepped from the tub to feed Nicodemus," Matthew defended as he gestured an arm toward the preoccupied tomcat.

Brant didn't believe it for a minute. "Of course, she did," he scoffed. "One would never think to wait until one was dressed before obliging a damned cat! I am not as naive as you would like to think and I do not appreciate the two of you making me look the ignorant fool!"

"You are managing the feat quite well without our help," Catrina sniped.

When Brant coiled to lunge at Catrina, Matthew stepped between them. "Both of you calm down," he ordered. If Cat and her jealous bulldog didn't clamp a tight rein on their tempers fur would be flying. "'Tis all perfectly innocent. Catrina didn't know I had returned from the tower and I had no idea she had come to feed Nicodemus. If I had not forgotten to see to the tomcat none of this would have happened. 'Tis the first time we have found ourselves in this uncomfortable situation. There has been nothing going on here during your absence, Captain. And why would this lovely lass want a decrepit old man like me? Answer that one and I think you will realize that you have leaped to a most inaccurate conclusion."

Brant slumped, the tension draining from his body as he allowed the words to soak in. While he was contemplating the matter, Catrina tilted a proud chin, flung Brant a go-to-hell glare, and stormed from the room with all the dignity one could muster when one was garbed in nothing but a towel.

When she sailed out the door, Brant released the frustrated breath he had been holding. He had sneaked to the lighthouse in high spirits, anxious to see Catrina after their long separation. What he had not anticipated was Matthew ogling Cat's barely concealed figure. When Brant had barged into the kitchen, his good intentions blew away with the brisk

December wind.

"I suggest a brandy," Matthew snickered, hobbling toward the cupboard. "You look as if you could use a drink to cool your blazing temper."

Brant accepted the drink and downed it in one swallow. Matthew watched the anger drain from Brant's rigid body and then he chuckled softly.

"She's mad as hell, Captain," Matthew declared.

"Well, so was I," Brant muttered in self-defense.

Matthew stared at Catrina's closed door. "Are you going in there unarmed?"

Brant chugged another drink. "It would be rather foolish to approach a wildcat without a shield," he agreed.

"What are you going to do?" Matthew questioned, eyeing Brant over the rim of his spectacles.

His shoulder lifted in a shrug. "Plead insanity?"

Matthew nodded thoughtfully. "A wise decision, Captain." He set his empty glass aside and pushed into an upright position. "But in case your method fails, I think I will venture out for the night. I do not wish to be around if war breaks out. I might get caught in the cross fire." Amusement danced in his dark eyes. "Tend the lantern for me, will you, Captain?"

As Matthew limped down the hall and out the door, Brant poured himself another drink of courage. It was now or never, he told himself. He had to confront Cat and he was not going to crawl to her. His legs would not bend into such a humiliating position. By damn, she should not have been traipsing about the lighthouse in her towel, no matter what the circumstances!

While Brant was polishing off his drink Cat was stomping about her room, muttering epithets to Brant's name with every step she took. The nerve of that man! He had spoiled his own homecoming, she thought furiously.

Catrina would have flown into his arms to shower him with welcoming kisses if he had hadn't verbally crucified her. How could he have jumped to such a ridiculous conclusion? Brant Diamond obviously possessed the intelligence of a potted plant!

She had lived and breathed for this day and Brant had shattered her dreams. She had ached to feel his arms about her once again, but at the moment she was sorely tempted to scratch out the varmint's eyes.

Grumbling at the disastrous chain of events, Catrina threw on her chemise and went to fetch her gown—the most provocative one she owned—the one Barnaby had styled for her. Let Brant think she delighted in tempting Old Matthew, she thought spitefully. What did she care? There could never be anything strong and enduring between her and Brant if he couldn't trust her.

He had listened to Matthew's explanation, but he would not accept *her* rendition of the incident. What was she to him, a common whore? Did he think he could strut into the lighthouse after a lengthy absence and take her to bed whenever he could spare the time? That would be the day, she thought bitterly. The Sahara desert would sooner be stricken by a flood! She was not about to bow to that wooden-headed pirate who had sap flowing through his veins! Damn him. He made her so furious she was seeing red—red walls, red tubs, red everything!

When the door slammed against the wall, Catrina glowered at the intruder. "You could have knocked," she snapped hatefully.

"If I had I might have missed something," Brant taunted. "Why should Matthew be the only one to enjoy such tantalizing scenery?"

Brant surveyed the thin chemise that clung to her curvaceous body, feeling the quick rise of desire. It was as he had feared. One look at this impetuous beauty and his body smoldered with passion. Cat had yet to slip into her gown and for that he was most grateful. It was easier to deal with Cat when she was unarmed and undressed.

Catrina reacted impulsively. Her hand folded around the book that sat on her nightstand and she hurled it at him. Brant grunted uncomfortably when the makeshift weapon collided with his belly.

"Dammit, woman, must you always throw things at me when you lose your temper?" Brant snorted, scooping up the book and setting it aside. "If I hurled rocks at you each time you annoyed me you would be buried beneath a pile of stones."

"Get out," Catrina hissed, her eyes flaring in fury. "This marriage of convenience is no longer convenient for either of us. I am setting sail as soon as weather permits. Why I waited for your return is beyond me."

Brant pushed the door shut with his boot heel. "If you truly wanted to go you would have gone long before now. Why did you wait, Cat?" he questioned. His voice was softer now and the mocking glint had vanished from his eyes.

Catrina retreated when Brant marched toward her like an invading army. "Why did you come back?" she countered.

"For this . . ." Brant lunged at her, but Catrina sprinted across the bed to take cover behind the chair.

"If 'tis passion you wanted, you could have found it anywhere," she tossed at him. "If you dare touch me I'll scream this lighthouse down around us and Matthew will come running."

"Don't count upon it. Matthew has gone out for the evening," Brant informed her. Agilely he strided across the bed, grinning roguishly. "You still have not answered my question. Why did you wait for my return? I'm not leaving here until you tell me."

Damnation, Matthew was *always* out for the evening, she thought acrimoniously. The one time she could have used his assistance he was out gallivanting about on another of his mysterious missions.

Catrina's frantic gaze darted from the wicked grin on Brant's face to the closed door. Without calculating the possibility of successful escape from the devil's clutches Cat darted from behind her chair. But Brant sprung like a crouched panther. Catrina yelped when she found herself spun around and

406

plastered against the door through which she had intended to flee.

"Answer me, damn you," Brant growled.

He crushed his hard body into hers, allowing her no means of escape. The musky fragrance of his cologne warped her senses. Catrina's mind ceased to function, just as it always did when he touched her. It had been seven agonizing months since she had experienced his soul-shattering kisses and felt his muscular contours molded familiarly to hers.

Catrina wanted to reject him, to lash out at him. But she could no longer deny the love that had blossomed in her heart. Perhaps it was foolish to sacrifice her soul to this rebel pirate, but she could not fight what she felt. The emotion had finally consumed her. She loved Brant Diamond with every part of her being. It had been an eternity since he had made love to her and she wanted him now more than ever, even if she had to sacrifice her pride.

Her thick lashes fluttered up to meet his probing gaze. The words she had held so long in captivity flew from her lips. "God help me for saying so, but I stayed because I love you."

To her utter humiliation his taut body relaxed and soft laughter bubbled from his chest. Catrina glanced away, too ashamed to face the haughty amusement in his eyes. She should have known better than to blurt out the truth, she chastised herself. She had made the blunder once before and Brant had mortified her with laughter. But this second chuckle of amusement was far more pride-shattering than the first. Catrina felt like bursting into tears. Damn him! She had been completely honest with him and he was too insensitive to consider that he might be breaking her heart into a thousand jagged pieces.

"I answered your question, now let me go," Cat choked out, fighting for hard-won composure.

Brant didn't budge. "Don't you want to know why I came back?" He curled his hand beneath her chin, forcing her to meet his beaming smile.

"Because duty demanded it," Catrina predicted. Refusing to give him the satisfaction of mortifying her again, Catrina jerked her head away to stare at the far wall.

"Cat, look at me," Brant commanded. "I am not mocking your confession. Far from it. I am laughing at my own foolishness. You see, I am very much a coward."

A muddled frown gathered on her brow. "A coward?" she echoed incredulously. "You? The daredevil who risks life and limb to deliver supplies to your fellow countrymen?" Catrina scoffed at the absurd admission. "I never thought I would hear myself say this, but you are much too modest, Brant Diamond. Last week I attended a gathering of Tory women who were intrigued by your daring and elusiveness. I think each of them were silently wishing the dashing pirate would sneak ashore to whisk them away on some fast-paced adventure. A coward?" Cat flung him a withering glance. "Nay, not by any stretch of the imagination."

Brant's captive embrace became a meandering caress. His hands flowed over her supple curves like a blind man cherishing what he could not see. "I was afraid of you," he humbly confessed. "I found something in you that I could not lightly dismiss. The emotions you stirred frightened me. I fought the vulnerability and for months I detested my weakness for you. But I cared too much to let you go and yet I was afraid of being hurt again."

Brant breathed a heavy sigh as his fingertips glided across her bewitching face. "I didn't marry you for your convenience or mine, Cat. Despite what you might have thought, I was not using our marriage as an opportunity of regaining my trade with the British if the revolution were to meet with defeat. My reasons for wedding you were far more sentimental than the mere exchange of vows for postwar amnesty. I cared for you but I tried to protect myself by shutting you out, by snapping at you when all I really wanted to do was hold you close and pray you would not one day betray me. My strategy proved to be torment in itself.

"When you came down with the fever I feared I would lose you and I could not imagine what my world would be like without you in it. I swore if you survived I would no longer stand in the way of what you wanted. If you longed to return to Scotland, I would let you go. At least I would have had the memories . . ."

Catrina probed the depths of his eyes to decipher the emotion Brant was talking circles around. He *did* love her, she realized. Although he was cautious of love after his painful experience with Cynthia, Catrina did mean something to him.

The poor man, she thought to herself. He couldn't spit out the words without choking on them. He had kept them locked away for so long that they had become like a foreign tongue.

A seductive smile pursed her lips as she laid her arms about his shoulders. Her hands tunneled through the crisp raven hair that curled around the nape of his neck. Then her fingertips trailed across his cheeks to trace the curve of his lips. Provocatively, she arched against him, her breasts pressing wantonly against his chest.

Her lips melted against his like summer rain replenishing a desert. Brant felt his heart collapse against his ribs. He inhaled a ragged breath that was scented with jasmine and he drowned in the aroma that was so much a part of him, so much a part of a never-ending memory.

He kissed her with devouring impatience, starving for the taste of her. "Lord, I've missed you. I've been miserable without you," he whispered when he finally came up for air. "Thomas says I've been hell to live with these past few months."

"And you have been hell to live without," Catrina chortled, her moist breath caressing his lips. "Despite what you were thinking, Matthew has never appealed to me in the ways you do."

Her quiet laughter died when she pushed back as far as Brant's encircling arms would allow to meet his golden gaze. Their eyes locked and the need flickering there overwhelmed both of them. Catrina ached for him. It had been months since she yielded to the sensations he instilled in her. She yearned to lose touch with reality, to rediscover the ecstasy of his lovemaking.

Brant scooped her up in his arm and carried her to bed. When he set her to her feet, she slid her hand inside his shirt to make arousing contact with his muscled flesh. Catrina drew the garment away and allowed her eyes to drink in the glorious sight of him.

She stared at him as if he were a treasured portrait that had been stashed from her sight for years on end. It felt so good to look at him, to touch him and know this was not another tormenting dream. He had come back to her, no matter what complications life held for them.

Her worshiping gaze flooded over the dark expanse of his chest but Catrina gasped in alarm when she noticed the healing wound that lay above the band of his breeches. He had returned, but not with all the flesh he possessed when he left her, Cat realized. His dangerous missions had cost him a few pounds of hide!

Brant's soft chuckle filled the apprehensive silence. His hand folded around hers, removing it from the scar that traced his waist. "'Tis nothing serious," he assured her. "Tories tried to ambush us while we were sneaking supplies ashore. 'Tis only a flesh wound."

Catrina didn't care if it were only a scratch. The thought of Brant thrusting himself in and out of life-threatening situations terrified her. Losing him would be more than she could bear. "Let someone else ferry the goods ashore," she pleaded with him. "If I am left to wonder where you are and who is lying in wait to fire the bullet with your name on it, I will never sleep another night."

A grin of eager anticipation caught the corner of his mouth, slanting it upward. "'Tis certain, madam, that you will not sleep tonight . . ."

His arm curled about her, taking her with him to the bed.

Caresses, as hot as the leaping flames of a campfire, seared her flesh, making her tremble uncontrollably. The feel of his hair-matted flesh moving suggestively against hers was a foretaste of heaven and Catrina hungered for more.

"Cast your spell over me, sweet witch. Protect me from harm. If I have your love, no musket ball can penetrate my heart." His mouth opened on hers, his questing tongue searching the dark recesses of her mouth. Willfully, he withdrew to meet the glowing reflection of emotion in her eyes. "But please . . . do not ask me to turn my back on the rebel cause. I cannot do that any more than I can stop loving you. I will do what I have to do. But know this, my love, wherever my missions lead me, you will constantly be in my thoughts."

He had finally spoken the words. Catrina's heart swelled with so much happiness she felt as if she were soaring. When his fingertips feathered across the curve of her hip and slid beneath the short chemise, Catrina forgot the dangers Brant invited by running blockades. He was here with her, loving her as deeply as she loved him.

When his skillful hands roamed unhindered across her skin, a thousand fires began to burn and spread like wildfire. A surrendering moan tumbled free as his lips followed the arousing course of his hands. Catrina was sailing on wings of fire, gliding toward some distant horizon.

Brant drew back, suddenly aware that the bright glow which usually streamed through the lighthouse had faded into darkness. "Damn," he scowled, cursing his forgetfulness. "I promised Matthew I would refill the lantern while he was away. As always, you have distracted me."

Catrina pulled him closer, reluctant to let him go. "The lantern can wait, but I cannot. 'Tis been too long . . ." she murmured. Her voice was so soft and inviting that Brant wondered if it would require an army to drag him from this temptress's arms.

When better judgment tapped him on the shoulder a second time, Brant muttered in exasperation. "And I fear it must be a

411

few minutes longer, love. If I do not tend the beacon the darkness might draw suspicion. I cannot risk having some inquisitive Tory pounding on the door." Brant groped to locate his discarded breeches and hurriedly stepped into them.

As he felt his way toward the bedroom door, Catrina punched her pillow, grumbling over the fact that a blasted lantern had torn Brant from her arms. For a moment she lay there, resenting the world and everyone in it.

And then a smile the size of Charleston spread across her lips. The wait wouldn't be as long as either of them had first anticipated. Catrina bounded from the bed to rummage through the trunk Matthew had made for her to store her belongings. She shook out the sheer nightgown she had purchased at Barnaby's boutique. After fastening the one stay that held the seductive creation together, Catrina sailed out the bedroom door . . . wearing little more than an impish grin.

Brant muttered at his fumbling attempt to refuel the gigantic lantern. In his haste to tend the beacon and return to Cat's waiting arms, his fingers turned to useless thumbs. The lingering taste of Cat's kisses was a tormenting reminder of where he would have preferred to be and with whom! He was wasting precious minutes and he was very nearly hopping up and down with impatience. When he finally restored the beacon he heaved a relieved sigh. But he stopped breathing when a movement beside the door caught his attention.

There, beside the portal, bathed in the bright flame of the lantern, stood Catrina. Her tousled auburn hair sprayed about her like a silky cape. There was a naughty look in her green eyes, one that delighted Brant. It assured him that she was thinking what he was thinking. Excitement sizzled through his bloodstream like rivers of fire spreading in all directions.

Catrina was dressed in a transparent muslin gown, held together by the silver brooch on her left shoulder. The gossamer fabric stretched diagonally across her breasts and hugged the curvaceous contours of her body as Brant ached to do. The white gown swirled about her like a long flowing caress, rippling provocatively with every breath she took. Brant could see the thrusting pink peaks through the sheer gown and he inwardly groaned at the alluring sight. She was all woman, every well-proportioned inch of her.

"If you have been strutting about in such seductive garments these past few months, 'tis a wonder Old Matthew is still alive . . ." Brant managed to say without choking on his breath. Lord, she looked so tempting that he was like a man suffering from oxygen deprivation and the condition had nothing to do with racing up the long flight of steps that led to the tower.

Catrina eased the door closed behind her and turned the lock to ensure their privacy. That living fire Brant remembered so well flared in her eyes as she floated gracefully toward him. Her sylphlike movement drew his undivided attention and Brant stared through the provocative gown that made such an intriguing wrapper for this exquisite package.

"Matthew has yet to see this creation. I have been saving this negligee for a special occasion," Catrina assured him, her voice like soft velvet.

The way she smiled, the way she moved, stirred Brant as no other woman ever had. He was awestruck by her beauty, hypnotized by her seductive tone. There was no need to refill the lantern, Brant thought as he dragged in a shuddering breath. Catrina had him blazing as brightly as the beacon.

"The beam may have burned itself out, but the fire you ignited in me is like an eternal flame," Brant confessed, giving the thought to tongue.

When he raked her with blatant hunger, Catrina came to stand directly in front of him. "Then you do approve of my gown?" she questioned. Suggestively, she ran her hands across the sheer bodice and then followed the generous curve of her hips, taking his eyes on a most arousing journey, sending his heart leaping into triple time.

"I would like it better if it were draped over yonder chair," Brant growled seductively.

With one quick flick of his fingers he sprung the silver clasp, allowing the gossamer fabric to tumble over the full swells of her breasts. Brant slid his arm around her waist to send the waterfall of muslin cascading into a pool at her feet. The taut peaks of her breasts brushed against his laboring chest, sending a fleet of tingles sailing down his spine.

"I prefer that you wear nothing at all . . . I always have . . ." Brant murmured against the curve of her neck.

As his practiced hands flooded over her flesh, Catrina sighed contentedly. His caresses trailed over the tips of her breasts and then glided lower, investigating the silky softness of her thighs. His touch was like an arousing massage, one so tender and yet so devastating that Catrina trembled in his arms.

Her body quivered in anticipation as Brant drew her to the rug beside the lantern. She felt the sinewed columns of his legs moving intimately between hers, heard his strained breath as he nibbled at her lips. The aching need for him rose like a cresting river inside her and she drowned in the pleasures he had created within her.

"God, I love touching you," Brant whispered hoarsely. "Your skin is like silk and satin . . ."

His kisses trailed along her collarbone to hover over each dusky bud while his bold caresses stroked her hips. His hand receded, following a sweet tormenting path to her breasts, and then flowed downward, leaving her to shiver in anticipation. Not once, but again and again, his caresses flooded and receded.

She was aching and breathless to satisfy this maddening craving he had created with his black magic. The feel of his hair-roughened flesh pressing into her drove her wild with unfulfilled desire. He had aroused her to reckless abandon and Catrina arched toward his seeking hand, trembling with a passion that knew no logic.

With all the gentleness he possessed Brant took her higher

and higher still. He wanted to erase any lingering doubts that he was as rough and ruthless as Derrick Redmund. Tonight he would assault Catrina with a tenderness that she would never forget. His touch would be embroidered with love and there would be no mistaking the emotions he felt for her.

Catrina could not think. She could only respond to the wondrous sensations that channeled through every part of her being. Her body was like clay in the hands of a master craftsman. He was molding her into his own unique creation. As his moist kisses glided between the valley of her breasts and descended to map the curve of her hips, Catrina caught her breath.

Indescribable feelings shot through her like the leaping flames of an inferno. Catrina clutched at him, longing to become a part of him and he a part of her. She yearned to fulfill these wild, tormented cravings his fondling had evoked. As Brant twisted above her Catrina's tangled lashes swept up to see the beacon of love shining in his eyes. Lord, how she adored this ruggedly handsome pirate. How she longed to sacrifice her separate identity to become of one heart and soul.

When her hand folded about him, guiding him to her, Brant trembled with a need he was barely able to hold in check. He came to her, slowly at first, arousing her until she could endure not another second of the sweet torment. Her body was eager for his and he was quivering with undeniable hunger for hers.

Brant moved within her, offering his love in physical pleasures that the flesh understood, whispering his devotion in words that came from his heart. He was giving of himself, sharing his heart and soul, relaying a message that sent Catrina soaring in ecstasy. For Brant it was the ultimate gift he could give—a gentleness that cost him dearly. He wanted to crush her to him, to surrender to passions that blazed like a crown fire.

Words that had once been so difficult to pronounce bubbled from his lips and he spread them across her skin, repeating them until they were like a cloak of flowing emotion. He thrust against her, striving for ultimate depths of intimacy, wanting her more than life, loving her with the very essence of his being. The sensations crept through him, sensitizing every fiber of his body.

There was no past or future, not even the present. Brant was tumbling through time and space, buffeted by such soul-shaking feelings that he could no longer think one coherent thought. His body was driven by a will of its own, one so fierce and potent that he could do nothing but respond.

Heated emotions exploded like smoldering lava bursting from the cone of an erupting volcano. Brant shuddered in satisfying release when passion spilled forth like a river of fire. Shock waves rippled through him as he clung to Catrina and it was a long, breathless moment before his sanity returned.

When his scattered thoughts finally converged, Brant propped himself on his elbows to stare into Catrina's flushed face. An adoring smile melted his rugged features as he sketched her kiss-swollen lips with his fingertips.

"I love you, Cat," he murmured. "Lord, I long to take you with me, but I dare not. But one day . . . when the world is again at peace, you and I will have our own tropical island paradise."

Catrina brushed trembling hands across his bearded face, memorizing the way his golden eyes crinkled when he smiled. "Please let me go with you. I don't care what dangers we face, as long as we endure them together."

Brant gave his raven head a negative shake. "Nay, love, not now. The war is escalating and the coast becomes more treacherous with each passing day. You are safe here with Matthew . . ." A wry smile dangled on the one corner of his mouth. "At least you will be if you stash yonder gown from his sight and garb yourself in high-collared dresses. No man can resist temptation indefinitely, not even Matthew."

"And what if I become unbearably lonely for a man's touch?" Catrina taunted.

A low rumble rattled in his chest. "I suggest a cold

bath . . . but do *not* abandon it to feed that damned tomcat. If I am forced to wait to appease my hunger, so must Nicodemus."

An impish smile lighted Catrina's flawless features. She squirmed away to sit atop Brant's belly. "I have met your Cynthia while I was in Charleston," she announced, startling Brant with the quicksilver change of subject.

One dark brow arched dubiously. "And . . . ?" he prompted, unsure where this conversation would lead.

"Have you seen her of late?" Catrina demanded to know.

"Nay, should I?" Brant questioned bemusedly.

Catrina stretched above him, her shapely body blending into the muscular planes of his. "If you dare I will scratch out your wandering eyes," she threatened.

Brant chuckled as his caresses absently glided down her back. "Are you jealous Cat? If you are, you have no need to be. My feelings for Cynthia died long ago. You once asked me how you compared to the bittersweet memory of my youth. I was afraid to admit it then, but not now. In you, I have discovered a contentment that surpasses all others."

His words pleased her. She had intended to tease Brant about the shape and disposition of his former lover, but her mind was on much more arousing matters. "Then show me some proof that I alone stir you . . ." she murmured against his sensuous lips.

Brant needed no invitation. His body roused to the feel of her soft flesh moving languidly against his. Again he strived for tenderness, arousing her passions to a fervent pitch . . . until she reciprocated by mapping the hard planes of his flesh with her special brand of kisses and caresses. And then the beacon in the lighthouse became a dim flame in comparison to the raging fire that crackled between them. It was their special time, a moment that transcended eternity, an instant rapt in the sublime expression of love.

They clung together as if there were no tomorrow, compensating for the long months they had been apart and the uncertain separation that lay ahead of them. Although war played havoc with the colonies, there was sweet, companionable peace between Catrina and Brant. The bond between them strengthened through the night, blossoming and growing until it overshadowed all other emotion.

When Brant was forced to leave the loving circle of her arms, Catrina succumbed to tears. She offered him the information she had obtained at Cynthia's party, but it was given through a succession of choked sobs. When Brant walked out into the night a stabbing pain sliced through her soul. She wondered how she would endure the months that lay ahead of her, stewing over his safety, wondering when he would return.

"This damned war," Catrina sobbed as she squirmed beneath the quilts. If she had her way, every weapon known to man would be collected and tossed into the sea. Let the fish fight among themselves, she thought bitterly. This revolution prevented her from holding the man she loved in her arms. She knew it was a selfish whim, but she was too distraught to care. God willing, they would survive this conflict between the colonies and the Mother Country. And one day . . . Catrina sighed whimsically as she closed her eyes and drifted into a rapturous dream. One day she and the handsome pirate would sail away to their own secluded paradise. If wishing could make it so, Catrina would have already been nestled in white sands, just like the enchanted lagoon on the Everlasting Mountains of the Sea.

When Brant climbed from the skiff and shinnied up the ladder, Thomas was waiting on the deck of the *Sea Lady*. The tension lines around Brant's eyes and mouth had vanished after his rendezvous in the lighthouse. Thomas chuckled at the dreamy-eyed expression that claimed Brant's features. If looks were any indication, Thomas predicted Brant had not spent the entire evening engaged in battle with his feisty wife.

"So, how is yer lady?" Thomas questioned the moment

Brant hopped to the deck.

"As lovely as ever," Brant murmured, lost to the vision that rose from the bay to preoccupy him.

Thomas flashed Brant a withering glance. "I didn't doubt that. Beauty like hers don't vanish overnight. Did you tell her how you felt or didn't you?" he demanded impatiently.

A devilish twinkle flickered in Brant's eyes as he propped his forearms against the rail to peer at the beckoning light that splashed silver across the bay. For a moment Brant was captivated by the memory of Catrina standing by the tower door. As long as he lived he would never forget that gorgeous sight. Never again would he stare at the beacon without thinking about this splendorous night.

When Brant did not respond immediately, Thomas grumbled under his breath. He would never know what had happened. Brant was in another world, one so far from reality that he would need a compass to chart his way back.

"Well, if you ain't gonna tell me about what went on between you and Cat, will you at least tell me how Matthew has fared with that lovely distraction underfoot?" Thomas snorted and then gouged Brant in the ribs to bring him to his senses.

"Matthew?" Brant's absent gaze swung to his first mate for no more than a split second before focusing on the distant tower.

"Aye, Matthew. You do remember the man, don't you? For God's sake, Cap'n, you've known him almost all yer life," Thomas sniffed sarcastically. "How the hell is he?"

"Ah, Matthew," Brant sighed when his circling thoughts finally returned to Thomas's line of questioning. "He seems to be managing quite well . . . although I didn't tarry long to speak with him."

This conversation was going nowhere, Thomas realized. Frustrated, he relinquished his attempt to pry information from Brant since it would have required a crowbar and Thomas was without one. "I just returned a few minutes ago from deliverin' supplies to Swamp Fox," he announced. "We narrowly missed bein' intercepted by a British patrol. It seems to me the communication lines between the rebel army and navy are in danger of bein' severed. Each time we row ashore there is more resistance awaitin' us."

Brant dragged himself from his whimsical musings and focused on Thomas's concerned frown. "Tory spies are thick in these parts," he reminded his first mate. "And the price on my head offers great temptation. It has come to the point that one cannot distinguish friend from foe. And conditions will not improve since the British are moving into Charleston in hopes of sealing off the rebel port."

"And that don't make our job any easier, does it, Cap'n?" Thomas heaved a weary sigh as he retrieved the envelope from his pocket and handed it to Brant. "Swamp Fox wants this message delivered to the regiments at Wilmington. He is sorely in need of reinforcements."

Brant unfolded the letter from Francis Marion and hurriedly scanned its contents. Grumbling over the state of affairs, Brant ordered his men to open sail. There was no time to dally in the harbor. As much as he would have liked to shrug off his duties and return to Cat, he couldn't, not if he intended to live with his conscience. Brant had dedicated his time and his schooner to the rebel war efforts. But leaving Catrina with Matthew was the most difficult chore he had ever undertaken.

"Until we meet again . . ." Brant breathed, his eyes focused on the facing beacon.

"Are you sure yer feelin' up to snuff?" Thomas questioned, biting back a sly smile. That was the second time in the past hour that Brant had mumbled to himself. It was obvious Brant was hallucinating and Thomas didn't have to guess whose vision was dancing in Diamond's head.

Brant straightened his slumped stature, concentrating on maneuvering through the sea lanes along the coast. "I'm fine," he assured his snickering first mate.

"I'm glad you think so," Thomas chuckled as he swaggered across the quarterdeck. "It seems to me that this love affair you've been carryin' on with Cat boasts of aftereffects that are worse than a bout with the fever. I swear you are suffering from *cat*alepsy, Cap'n."

If Brant would have heard Thomas's remark he would have agreed. His night of passion had a most devastating effect on him. Not one thought breezed through his mind without Cat's name and lingering image attached to it. If Brant didn't get a grip on himself he would be colliding with every island that protected the coast.

But at least he would sink in peaceful thoughts, Brant mused with a dreamy sigh. A strange contentment flooded over him when Catrina's memory skipped across his mind for the hundredth time that night. It was as if she were there beside him, sharing her warmth against the chilly breeze, lighting his way with her radiant smile.

He hadn't really left Catrina behind, Brant realized. He would always carry a little of her delightful spirit with him, no matter how far he wandered. And part of him would linger in the lighthouse on Cooper River. Satisfied with that revelation, Brant fixed his gaze on the flickering light that signaled the whereabouts of another rebel regiment that awaited the delivery of much-needed supplies. He prayed for a stiff wind to take him along the coast to Wilmington. The sooner he completed his mission, the sooner he could return to check on Catrina. And what a pleasurable duty that would be, he thought with a rakish smile.

The grin faded from his lips when he realized something was amiss. The breeze carried the sound of voices to his ear and Brant quickly wheeled the schooner out to sea. This was not the usual procedure for exchanging goods. He had yet to send a signal to the rebel troops, announcing his arrival. Catrina had warned him that several British regiments had been ordered to guard the shore—their purpose to apprehend Brant Diamond and the *Sea Lady*. When the underbrush along the beach came alive with the flares from exploding muskets, Brant knew Catrina's information had been correct. He had very nearly walked into a trap. It was Tories who were waiting to ambush him!

Damnation, it was becoming increasingly difficult to sneak in and out of the channels without the British monitoring his every move. How did they know when he planned to put ashore? Someone in Charleston had the British army sniffing at his heels like a bloodhound. No matter how careful he was, there was always danger lurking in the shadows. He would dearly love to know who was responsible for attempting to sabotage his missions.

Before the *Lady* was swarmed by approaching rowboats, Brant shouted the command to unfurl the head sails. He was bound for Wilmington and there would be no more detours. The rebel militia needed supplies, but he could not risk rowing ashore when the British had been alerted to his presence.

Chapter Twenty-Six

Drearily, Catrina stared across the bay from her lookout post in the lighthouse. It had been two weeks since Brant slipped off into the night. Although he had promised to return the moment time permitted, Catrina missed him terribly and he could not sail into the harbor soon enough to satisfy her.

"He will come back," Matthew chuckled, reading the sullen expression that clouded Catrina's brow. "I think you have become Diamond's beacon light. No matter how far he roams he never loses sight of you."

Catrina's gaze swung to the shaggy-haired watchman and she frowned thoughtfully. Although she and Matthew lived a compatible coexistence, the old man remained a puzzle to her. There was no close confidence between them, only a teasing camaraderie that broached upon thought-provoking subjects. Catrina would have preferred a deep relationship, if only to ease her loneliness. But Matthew seemed wary of it. Catrina wasn't certain why, but there was an underlying obstacle between them, caused by Matthew's standoffish manner. It was as if he were reluctant to commit himself to a strong friendship. For what reason, Catrina could not say.

"Ah, Tory, don't look so glum," Matthew encouraged as he shuffled over to fill the evening's supply of fuel in the lantern. "Shall we wander through Charleston a bit before dark?

Perhaps a carriage ride will lift your sinking spirits."

One perfectly arched brow lifted in surprise. "You are inviting me out, Matthew? What will your lady friend think when you do not keep your customary rendezvous with her?"

An amused grin touched Matthew's lips. "What makes you think any woman would have a shriveled-up old man like me?"

Catrina touched her fingertip to the ragged glove that covered Matthew's hand. "You are not a bad sort, Matthew. You have kindly consented to put up with me these past months. I only wish you would take me into your confidence. Sometimes I don't feel as if I know you at all."

Before Matthew drowned in the sparkling depths of her eyes he turned away to stare across the harbor. "'Tis not an easy time for any of us, Tory. And 'tis not wise to become overly fond of friends and acquaintances. There may come a time when the world about us crumbles. Each of us must be prepared to make our own way, the best way we know how. Strong ties and loyalties in these frustrating times can bring about a man's demise." Matthew paused by the door and glanced back over his shoulder, his emotions masked by a carefully blank stare. "Come along, Tory. Like my pet pigeons, you have been cooped up much too long. You need to spread your wings and catch a breath of fresh air."

As Matthew hobbled away, Catrina followed in his footsteps. A contemplative frown knitted her brow. Was Matthew warning her not to become too fond of him? Or was he subtly suggesting that she refrain from leaning so heavily on Brant? Catrina wasn't certain. But then, she was never sure of anything that concerned Matthew.

The old man perplexed her. At times he seemed eager for her conversation and at other times he appeared frustrated by her mere presence. They would share a few moments of closeness and then suddenly Matthew would withdraw, almost as if he resented any affection he might have felt for his guest. It seemed Matthew was a loner and he was afraid of living any other way. He liked her, Catrina reassured herself. But for some reason there were very strict limitations on their friendship, ones Matthew had established and seemed determined to obey.

Catrina set aside her attempt to analyze Matthew's moody behavior when they climbed into the rented carriage. Matthew aimed the white nag toward Tradd Street and made his way toward the Exchange. There was always a throng of people milling about the business center and Matthew could call all of them by name.

After Matthew had greeted the passersby and purchased a few supplies, he veered toward Broad Street. A familiar face caught Catrina's attention and her body involuntarily tensed with fury.

Derrick Redmund! What was he doing in Charleston? She thought she had put an ocean between them, but it was apparent that slimy snakes could swim great distances. The painful memories came flooding over her and Catrina reacted impulsively.

"What the hell are you doing, Tory?" Matthew squawked when Catrina bodily attacked him to snatch the pistol he carried beneath his waistcoat.

Catrina was too intent on her belated retaliation against Derrick to reply to Matthew's question. Squinting down the barrel, she aimed the flintlock at Derrick's tricorn, planning to blow it off the top of his head, along with a few strands of his hair.

The color waned from Matthew's cheeks when he realized what Catrina was about. Her target was a tall, attractive man who wore the trappings of a gentleman. His back was to them and he was totally unaware that he was about to become the victim of an ambush.

"Gimme that!" Matthew growled, yanking the pistol from Catrina's hand.

Furiously, Catrina lunged to retrieve the weapon Matthew held just out of her reach. When she met with no success, she jerked up the hem of her skirt and grasped the dagger she carried in her garter. If she could not lift Derrick's hat and a portion of his scalp, she would at least pin his ear to the supporting post of the building, she instantly decided.

"Blast it, Tory! Have you gone mad?" Matthew hooted in disbelief.

Moving faster than he had in years, Matthew sprung on Catrina as she cocked her arm to release the stiletto. They fell to the floor of the carriage and Catrina's breath came out in a rush when Matthew's heavy body sprawled on top of hers. The commotion in the buggy alarmed the nag. Releasing a frightened whinny the steed bolted sideways and then lunged into a gallop.

Cursing a blue streak, Matthew crawled onto all fours and glared at the flushed-faced chit who was muttering several disrespectful epithets to his name. Brant had warned him that Catrina had a mind of her own and that she possessed a temper to match her fiery auburn hair. But until now, Matthew had only seen occasional evidence of her feisty temperament. It was apparent that Cat was everything Brant proclaimed her to be and more! This daring witch was a handful. She was not easily subdued when she had her heart set on blowing an unsuspecting man to smithereens for only God knew what reason!

"What has gotten into you, girl?" Matthew snapped, groping to retrieve the reins and bring the runaway steed under control. "You don't just pull a pistol on a man and gun him down in the streets! My God, you'll start a private rebellion right here in the middle of Charleston. Tension already runs high. It would be like igniting a keg of gunpowder!"

Catrina was still smoldering when she clutched the side of the carriage and flounced onto the seat beside Matthew. She was in no mood to apologize. She wanted revenge for the painful beating she had received at Derrick's hand and Matthew had refused her the satisfaction.

"That man is a British officer and the devil in disguise," she ground out between clenched teeth. "I would have done the

426

world a favor if I would have been allowed to separate his head from his shoulders."

A wary frown clung to Matthew's bearded features. "How do you know the man is a British officer when he wears no uniform?" he prodded. "Are you suggesting he is a spy?"

"I know for certain that he is . . . or was a captain in the Royal Navy. Why he has run aground in Charleston I cannot fathom. But he was once my fiancé, a conniving scoundrel who would do most anything for money. I swear he would sell his own mother if he thought there were profit in it."

The dawn of understanding registered in Matthew's eyes. He remembered what Brant had told him about the fiancé Catrina had tried to avoid in Scotland. Matthew peered around the back of the carriage to study the man who had paused to stare curiously after the careening buggy.

After a long moment he twisted in his seat to stare straight ahead. "I think 'tis best to take you back to the lighthouse and keep you under lock and key," Matthew commented. "Another outburst like this and the whole town will be up in arms. I swear, woman, you alone could incite a riot!"

Catrina inhaled a deep breath and slowly expelled it. "I'm sorry, Matthew. 'Tis just that I was startled by the man's appearance in Charleston. I have spent the better part of this year wondering how I would react if I ever laid eyes on that viper again. I suppose I lost my head."

"Aye, the British would have seen to it that you *lost* your head if you would have followed through with your spiteful deed," Matthew lectured. "Tories don't take kindly to being ambushed, even by a woman, not even one of their own kind."

Catrina opened her mouth to protest being lumped in the same category with Derrick Redmund's "kind." And yet she wasn't a rebel either, she reminded herself. She loved Brant Diamond, but she did not share all his opinions. But neither did she hold to the philosophy that the colonists should be financially responsible for the staggering debts incurred by the Mother Country. Catrina could see little reason why

427

Americans should be forced to pay for the Crown's exorbitant taxes when they received nothing in return. Obviously, the rebels could not follow that reasoning or they would not have put up such a fuss.

The fact was that Catrina was a misfit. She had become a misplaced subject of the Crown and her own independent nature left her favoring the policies of the rebels . . . but from a liberal British point of view. She was wedged between a rock and a hard spot, Catrina realized dismally. She was a woman without a country. Her love for a rebel pirate complicated her loyalty. If she dared to voice her opinions she would make enemies of both Tory and Whig sympathizers.

Perhaps she should follow Matthew's philosophy of straddling the fence. The old watchman went about his business and kept his nose out of affairs over which he had no control. He was a crippled old man who could be of little use to either side. And so he remained neutral . . . or was he truly apathetic? Catrina frowned dubiously. Who was paying Matthew's expenses? Was Matthew slipping about in the cloak of darkness to see a lover or was he up to something that he wanted Catrina to know nothing about? And why did Matthew spend so many hours in the loft of the lighthouse, playing with his pigeons and staring out over Charleston with a spyglass?

Come to think of it Matthew was an odd bird, Catrina reminded herself. He never confided his opinions to Catrina and he confined most of his activities to the dark hours between twilight and dawn . . . when he presumed Catrina to be asleep. Perhaps she should pay closer attention to Matthew's habits, she lectured herself. After all, she knew nothing about Old Matthew. He was as tight-lipped as a clam. Never had he divulged his surname or spoken of his past, except to recite some wild tale of his experience at sea. Never had he willingly offered information about himself. He patronized Catrina with that quiet smile of his and tactfully steered her away from serious conversation.

Aye, she would keep tabs on Matthew's activities, Cat

428

promised herself. Matthew had always been a puzzle to her. The more she thought about it, the more she realized the pieces didn't fall into place. Catrina was prepared to bet her right arm that Matthew was not everything he seemed to be. But she had been too busy fretting over Brant to devote much thought to Matthew. Catrina intended to rectify that problem. She was going to keep a watchful eye on Old Matthew. And the next time she crossed paths with Derrick Redmund she was going to give him what *she* had gotten—a black eye, a bruised cheek, and an ultimatum that he had damned well better honor or she would do more than attempt to put a new part in his hair!

After the episode in the streets of Charleston, Matthew locked himself in the tower for two full days. Catrina had seen very little of the old watchman except when he limped down the steps to partake of a meal or to steal off into the night.

While Catrina was ambling about the shore near the lighthouse she noticed a flock of pigeons coming and going from the tower. Catrina swore there was something *foul* in the lighthouse besides Matthew's pigeons. She was certain the birds served some other purpose besides occupying Matthew's idle hours.

When she interrogated Matthew about his solitary confinement and his busy birds Matthew smiled tritely and shrugged off her questions. Matthew simply wasn't talking and Catrina's curiosity was burning her alive.

In dismay, Catrina watched Matthew hobble out the door after he thought she had retired to her room for the night. Unable to endure the suspense, Catrina slipped into her boyish garb and followed after Matthew. When he had crossed town in a rented carriage, Matthew confronted a British sentinel. He was promptly assisted into a rowboat and ferried across the Ashley River to Fort Johnson.

For a moment Catrina merely stood at the street's end, gasping for breath. Her wide, disbelieving eyes followed the

British coach that rolled toward the encampment on the far side of the river. Matthew was spying for the British, her mind screamed at her.

The thought made her half collapse in astonishment. So that was why Matthew had subdued her when she attempted to take shots at Derrick's departing back. And the pigeons . . . An accusing glare settled on Catrina's features as she stared at the distant coach. Was Matthew sending messages to the British about rebel activities along the Cooper River? He knew when the rebel ships slipped into the bay and sneaked supplies upriver to the trade roads. She had heard the British had an uncanny knack of attacking rebel supply wagons and Matthew was the *eye* of the Tories, spying from his lofty perch in the lighthouse!

Another unsettling thought avalanched upon her when she recalled the nights she had milled about the riverbank under the red glow of the huge lantern in the tower. Occasionally the beacon would shine with a blue cast and at other times the light appeared gold against the evening sky. Matthew had not been amusing himself by altering the colors of the beam, she surmised. He had lied to her! Matthew was sending signals to the British frigates that guarded the neck of the harbor!

My God, it was a wonder Brant had managed to sneak into the chain of sea islands before the brigantines seized the *Sea Lady* and set her afire! Matthew was probably responsible for the wounds Brant had sustained during his missions, she predicted. The miserable traitor had sicced the British on Brant each time he had the chance.

Matthew *appeared* to be uninvolved in either Tory or Whig activities, but he was truly in the thick of things! He was not manning the lighthouse to protect both rebel and redcoat ships. He was looking out for himself. Matthew was a mercenary without a conscience.

The realization disgusted Catrina and her mind was in a quandary. Should she return to the lighthouse to await

430

Matthew's return from his traitorous mission? Or should she pack her belongings and find lodging elsewhere? How could she get in touch with Brant to warn him if she didn't know where to find him? If Brant returned while she was away, would he think she had left for the Isles? Would Matthew attest to that theory to deceive Brant?

Grappling with a myriad of depressing thoughts, Catrina pulled the brim of her cap down over her forehead and pointed herself toward the opposite side of town. Instead of taking aim at Derrick Redmund she should have turned the pistol on Matthew. That deceitful old goat was a greater threat to Brant and the rebel cause than the entire British infantry that was camped on the Ashley River!

Shifting from one foot to the other, Matthew waited for Colonel Clinton to fetch Captain Derrick Redmund. When Clinton introduced the two men and excused himself, Matthew dropped down into a chair and leaned his hands on his cane.

"What is it you wish to see me about, old man?" Redmund demanded impatiently. He was just on his way to the elaborate party given by Cynthia Pinkerton when Clinton caught up with him. The last thing he wanted was to be detained by this crippled beggar.

Matthew sized up the long, lean captain. Derrick Redmund was a striking officer, but there was a sardonic glint in his eyes. Matthew sensed a certain ruthlessness in Redmund. Although he could not pinpoint his reason for not warming to the man, there was something there, hovering just beneath Derrick's immaculate, refined exterior. For a moment Matthew had second thoughts about coming to British headquarters this night. But it was too late to withdraw. Matthew had decided on his plan of action and he was going to see it through.

Derrick frowned in annoyance when the crippled old buzzard gave him the once-over twice, still refusing to state his business. "Well, what is it you want? I haven't all night."

Matthew set aside his wandering thoughts and stared at Redmund. "I have some information that will please you, Captain . . . if we can agree on the compensation due me."

The old goat was looking for a handout, Derrick mused cynically. "I haven't the time for your nonsense," he scoffed arrogantly. "I doubt anything you have to tell me would be worth a shilling to me or the Crown."

In all his dealings with the Tories, Matthew had never been treated so rudely. Gritting his teeth to contain his temper, Matthew watched Derrick spin on his heels and strut toward the door. Matthew's mocking tone halted the cocky rooster in his tracks.

"You are much too arrogant for your own good, Captain. And you might sorely regret not hearing me out. Does the name Catrina Hamilton mean anything to you? I know where your runaway fiancée is. And I can also lead you to the elusive Brant Diamond. I should think such interesting information would be worth a king's ransom."

Derrick's head swiveled on his shoulders. His jaw gaped wide enough for a brood of hens to nest. The old buzzard was obviously brimming with knowledge, Derrick decided. The man probably knew more about Derrick's affairs than he knew himself. Why, the old goat probably even knew where Derrick intended to spend the evening and which colonel's wife had been slipping around to meet him for a tumble in the sheets.

"How did you learn that I am after Diamond and that I have misplaced my fiancée?" he demanded to know.

A wry smile blossomed on Matthew's bearded features. "You may perceive me to be a useless old man, Captain, but these eyes are sharp and these ears are keen. I miss nothing. Of course, I tend to forget what I've seen and heard until I feel the weight of British coins in my hand."

"You knew there was a price on Diamond's head. Why haven't you come to me before?" Derrick queried. "I have been in Charleston for five months and you have never shown yourself to me."

Matthew's dark eyes danced with amusement. "There is a time and a season for all things, Captain. Before, the time was not right. But now it is. I considered that it would take a great deal of money to raise me from my level of poverty. I have been waiting until the price on Diamond's head had escalated to the point that it would make me a wealthy man. You see, if I betray a would-be friend, I must pack and leave Charleston for good. The rebels will then be after my hide." Matthew eased back into his seat to toy with the butt of his cane. "When you and Colonel Clinton decide how much extra you are willing to pay for this valuable information I will probably regain my memory. I will also expect a goodly sum for handing your fiancée over to you."

Derrick peered at the shabbily dressed pauper for a long, pensive moment. Nodding agreeably, he exited to confer with his senior officer. Within ten minutes the captain returned with a heaping purse of British coins.

"Will this cure your amnesia, old man?" Derrick chuckled as he watched Matthew lick his lips in anticipation. "Colonel Clinton promised to reward you with the other half of the price on Diamond's head as soon as the sum can be collected."

Matthew wasn't spilling his knowledge until he had the full amount in his hands. "If the good colonel cannot gather the coins in the next quarter of an hour I will have nothing to say."

Derrick gnashed his teeth. Although Clinton had handed over the complete amount, Derrick had intended to keep it for himself. But it seemed impossible to put anything past this spry old codger.

"I know the customary procedure for exchanging information," Matthew smirked. "Do not think to keep a share for yourself. Colonel Clinton would be disappointed to learn that one of his fellow officers was trying to make a profit at his informant's expense."

Begrudgingly, Derrick fished into his jacket to drop the other purse in Matthew's gloved hand. "Now tell me what you know, old man," he demanded gruffly.

Matthew tucked the money beneath his tattered coat and grinned in satisfaction. "I have received word that Brant Diamond will be returning to Charleston tomorrow night."

"How do you know that? No one has been able to predict the elusive captain's activities," Derrick snorted suspiciously.

A slow smile worked its way across Matthew's lips. "I have my ways, Captain. But if I divulge my sources I will be of little service to the Crown."

Derrick was struck by the odd feeling that Old Matthew knew each time anything or anyone moved in Charleston. "Where can we find Diamond?"

"He will be transporting supplies to Monck's Corner. If you and your men are lying in wait at midnight, you can surround Diamond and confiscate the rebel supplies before they reach Swamp Fox on the trade roads."

A devilish gleam flickered in Derrick's eyes. If he could entrap Swamp Fox as well, he could collect his own reward. Casting aside his greedy thought, Derrick focused intently on Matthew. "And what about Catrina? How will you deliver her to me?"

"When you have captured Diamond, come to the lighthouse on Cooper River. I will find a way to lure her there and she will be in safekeeping until you arrive," Matthew promised.

A skeptical frown etched Derrick's brow. "How can I be certain you speak the truth? Perhaps 'tis a ploy to make off with British currency."

"What good would it do me to lie to you?" Matthew countered. "I am an old man. How could I possibly outrun an entire British cavalry when I am not as swift and elusive as Diamond? I am only trying to ensure my future. I have lived my life in poverty, scratching and clawing to have the *luxuries* a man of your station in life considers *trifles*." He patted the purses tucked beneath his coat and then struggled to his feet. When he shuffled to the door he paused to lean heavily on his cane. "At the hour before midnight a red glowing light will shade the harbor. 'Tis the signal for the rebels to cruise into the

434

river channel without the risk of being confronted by the British. Diamond will suspect nothing out of the ordinary. He will drop anchor and row the supplies up the Cooper River to Monck's Corner. At long last you and your fellow officers will capture the man who has continued to elude you these past few years, Captain Redmund. No doubt there will be a promotion awaiting you." A faint smile skipped across Matthew's lips and dived into the heavy growth of hair that covered his features. "Aye, Diamond will be there. On that you can depend."

When the door drifted shut behind Matthew, Derrick plopped into his chair. The past five months he had been told the red glow from the lighthouse was a warning for British ships to remain offshore because of dangers, such as fog and ill winds that might make the bay treacherous. All the while the beacon had been a signal to the rebels to coast behind the blockade. What other signals were the rebels using to dupe the British? How Derrick would love to catch the ringleader who had devised this intricate scheme. Derrick knew Brant Diamond was partially responsible for the surge of supplies that were reaching rebel troops. Colonel Clinton had complained that the infiltration of rebel goods had doubled since Diamond reappeared to terrorize the British warehouses and the frigates that sailed along the coast from Charleston to Philadelphia. But there had to be other men involved in this secretive network.

A wicked grin caught the corner of Derrick's mouth. Soon Diamond would be a prisoner of the Crown. Colonel Pinkerton would have him drawn and quartered to satisfy his own personal vendetta against Diamond. And Derrick would also have his revenge. This time Diamond would not slither from the trap and Derrick would be hailed a hero. When he had repossessed his runaway fiancée he would then round up Old Matthew and drag him in for questioning. Derrick was willing to bet the old goat knew who else was involved in the intricate ring of rebels that infiltrated the coast.

Soon Derrick would have everything he wanted—a promo-

Chapter Twenty-Seven

Matthew rapped lightly on Catrina's door and waited a long moment. It was unlike her to remain in bed so long in the morning. He had begun to wonder if she had taken ill. Since he was guarding such precious merchandise it behooved him to ensure Catrina was healthy enough to endure the upcoming events of this evening.

"Catrina? Are you all right?" Matthew questioned.

Still there was no answer. Matthew eased open the door to find an empty room. A curious frown gathered on his features. Perhaps Catrina had gone out to amble along the shore or to walk into town. When Cat was restless she ventured out on her own. Ah well, he thought to himself. By the time she returned he would have conjured up some excuse as to why she should remain close to the lighthouse this evening.

Dismissing Cat's absence as nothing out of the ordinary for the independent beauty, Matthew called to Nicodemus to join him while he went about his chores. There was much to be done, he reminded himself as he marched up the winding steps that led to the tower. He had laid a trap and all must be right if it were to be sprung without mishap.

By twilight Matthew's nonchalant attitude had transformed into panic. He had seen nothing of the auburn-haired sprite who had been underfoot all these months. Where the devil was

Cat the moment he needed her, Matthew wondered sourly. If Catrina didn't appear, and soon, his meticulous planning would be for naught.

"Damn," Matthew muttered as he turned away from the empty parlor and trudged upstairs.

Once he reached the tower, he banded a message to one of his pigeons and set it to flight. Still grumbling over Cat's unexplained disappearance, Matthew hobbled into the glass tower to check the harbor. Raising the spyglass, Matthew peered across the bay, his eyes fixed on the northern horizon. Brant Diamond should be entering the sea lanes within the hour and still there was no sign of Catrina.

When the huge lantern was filled with its evening supply of fuel Matthew lifted the red stained glass and placed it in front of the window. Brant Diamond would cruise into the bay, note the signal for safe passage, and ease his supply skiffs up the Cooper River. The plan had been set in motion, but one important link was missing—Catrina. Scowling, Matthew paced the confines of the tower. He should have known the scheme would not unfold without a hitch . . .

His head jerked up when he heard the creak of the door. His dark eyes swung to the lady who was dressed in men's garb and he flinched when he spied the flintlock that was pointed at his chest.

"Catrina? What the devil do you think you're doing? I swear you have taken leave of your senses," Matthew scolded.

"Nay, I have just recently come to my senses," Catrina hissed, her green eyes snapping.

"Put that pistol down before it accidentally goes off and you blow me to bits!" Matthew ordered. "And where the hell have you been all day? Why are you dressed like that?"

Catrina did not bat an eye at the old man's rapid-fire questions, nor did she bother to answer them. "Take the stained glass from the window and replace it with the blue one," she demanded abruptly.

Matthew gulped hard and then forced a smile. "Do you have

some aversion to red? 'Twas the blue glass that I used last night. You know how I delight in variety."

Catrina scoffed at his flimsy excuse. "You have been sending signals to the British and the rebels as well," she harshly accused. "You have been lying to me, Matthew. Those pigeons are messengers, not pets. And the stained glasses are used as color codes." Her gaze narrowed threateningly. "I should blow you to smithereens for betraying Brant Diamond. He considers you a friend. But you don't know the meaning of friendship. You use people to accomplish your own selfish purposes." Her voice was growing higher and wilder by the moment. She had spent the day comparing Matthew to Derrick Redmund, finding them so much alike that the old man's image repulsed her.

"Now, Tory, calm down," Matthew coaxed, taking a bold step toward her. "You have jumped to the wrong conclusion. If you will let me explain . . ."

"Calm down?" Cat sneered. "I most certainly will not! You plan to ply me with another of your lies, just like the ones that have tripped from your lips since the first night Brant brought me here." Her flashing eyes raked Matthew's overweight frame with disgust. "I followed you last night. I watched you cross the Ashley River to parley with the British. *That* is why you have been sneaking about late at night, isn't it? You didn't want anyone to know what you were about because you were up to no good."

"I can explain," Matthew insisted nervously.

"No more lies," Catrina gritted out. "From this day forward I will never believe anything you tell me. Now remove the red glass before I lose what's left of my temper."

Matthew refused to budge from the spot. He glanced out of the corner of his eye to see the mast of a schooner in the distance. It was the *Sea Lady*, he guessed. If he could only stall Catrina for a few more minutes, Brant would receive the signal and veer upriver.

"It's not what you think, Tory," Matthew blurted out. "You

are wrong about me. I am not aiding the British. I have no loyalty toward them. I went to see your ex-fiancé last night."

Catrina's face flushed furious red. "So it was *I* you intended to betray," she snapped acrimoniously. "Did you tell that woman beater I was in Charleston? How could you, Matthew? Do I mean nothing to you?"

"Of course you do," Matthew assured her, and then glanced sideways to check the progress of Diamond's ship.

An ironic smile touched Catrina's lips. "What are you planning, old man? Have you sold me out to Derrick Redmund?"

"Nay," he loudly protested. "How could you think such a terrible thing about me? I only wanted to see the man for myself, to learn his purpose for being in Charleston. I was only trying to help you, not *hurt* you."

Catrina scoffed, not believing him for a minute. "'Tis too late, Matthew. Once I was blind to your scheming, but no more. I have finally realized that no words of truth pass across your lying lips. Now, remove . . . the . . . red . . . glass!" she demanded as she cocked the trigger.

Matthew's gaze flew over his shoulder to see the *Sea Lady* pass the beam of light and cruise into the mouth of the river. Silently, he breathed a sigh of relief. "Very well, if you insist. I will change the colors to prove to you that the light is no more than a beacon. The color makes no difference to anyone but me."

A wary frown knitted Catrina's brow. She had expected Matthew to adamantly refuse to obey her command. Had she leaped to the wrong conclusion after all? Why was Matthew being so agreeable if the lights were signals? Damnation, she had been so certain he had been spying for the British.

After trudging her way back across town the previous night, Catrina had decided to seek out a room in the inn. She had been so furious with Matthew for traveling to the British headquarters that she didn't trust herself to face him until she regained control of her temper. After deciding on her plan of action, she waited until dark to return to the lighthouse to confront Matthew with her suspicions. She fully intended to change the color of the beacon light and garble whatever message Matthew was sending to the British fleet that cruised the neck of the harbor.

When Matthew had replaced the stained glass, Catrina gestured for him to park himself in a chair. "You can stand watch from the tower. But you will not be sending your pigeons out tonight." Her gaze riveted over the slouched old man. "And if even one British soldier comes to inquire about the lack of communication from the lighthouse, I will know beyond a doubt that you have been deceiving me."

"Catrina, you must listen to me," Matthew muttered as Catrina held him at gunpoint and tied him to his chair.

"Nay." Catrina sniffed distastefully and then stuffed a gag in his mouth. "Time will run out, Matthew. I will know the truth and I will hear it without the confusion of your lies."

When Catrina turned away Matthew raved in inaudible epithets, ones Catrina was thankful she couldn't decipher. She had the feeling Matthew was calling her by every derogatory name she had ever heard, along with a myriad of curses that had yet to reach her ears.

"I will be downstairs, waiting to greet any visitor who might happen by," she taunted. "For your sake, Matthew, you had better pray this will be a quiet night."

When Catrina slammed the door, Matthew slumped against the back of his chair. Confound it, he should have known better than to think he could deceive that vixen. Brant had warned him that Catrina was a force to be reckoned with. Matthew had witnessed her blazing temper when she tried to part Derrick Redmund's hair with a pistol. Damn, Matthew had been so certain she suspected nothing. His overconfidence had been his downfall.

How was he to persuade her to release him when she refused to listen, when she bound and gagged him in the tower? Why couldn't he have been dealing with some simple-minded twit instead of this strong-willed beauty? Blast it, this was all Brant Diamond's fault. If he hadn't delivered Catrina to Matthew's doorstep life would have been much less complicated. Now here he was, tied in his own chair on the eve of history making events. If he managed to wiggle loose he was going to shake that woman until her teeth rattled, Matthew swore to himself.

Keen golden eyes scanned the banks of the Cooper River. Brant had received the message from Matthew while he was delivering supplies to troops north of Charleston. He had relayed an answer by way of a guerrilla band to the lighthouse. This was to be the last transportation of confiscated supplies to reach the trade road. Brant intended to set sail for the West Indies at dawn. There he could purchase more goods and then ship them back to Charleston before the inevitable invasion of the British regiments.

The rustle of underbrush along the banks caught Brant's attention and he crouched behind the stack of goods that formed a barricade on the rowboat. With his ears pricked he waited a tense moment, but no other sound alerted him to trouble.

"Do you see anythin'?" Thomas whispered softly.

"Not yet." Brant cocked the trigger on his musket and kept it aimed at the shore.

"I sure hope nothin' goes amiss," Thomas grumbled. "I don't relish havin' my head blown off by a bunch of redcoats."

While Brant and his small fleet of boats were making their way toward Monck's Corner, Derrick and his infantry were lying in wait. Derrick grinned wickedly when he spied the yawls cutting through the water. Brant Diamond was walking into another trap and this time there would be no escape. Derrick had ordered his men to crouch in the brush and wait for the rebels to come ashore before opening fire. While the rebels were unloading their goods they would be virtually defenseless. Derrick and his men would pick off the rebels as if they were pesky flies.

The crackling of twigs behind him made Derrick swivel his head around. Fury blazed in his eyes when he saw a guerrilla band swarming around him. He had anticipated a handful of backwoodsmen to meet Brant Diamond but the force that was surrounding him and his men was staggering. Dammit, Matthew had tricked him! The old man had set a trap, but Derrick was to be the bait, not Brant Diamond!

That infuriating thought exploded in Derrick's mind as the rebels swarmed up from the swamps and the pirates bounded ashore. The crack of muskets, both British and rebel, filled the silence. Derrick ducked away from a whistling musket ball and growled under his breath. He and his men were trapped!

Brant Diamond knew full well what awaited him at Monck's Corner, Derrick speculated. Diamond was the ringleader of this crew of pirates and nothing moved in the area without the elusive Captain Diamond learning about it.

Derrick glanced frantically about him, searching for a means of escape, uncaring that he was about to abandon his regiment, leaving them to fight for their lives without leadership. He had no intention of being captured or giving his life for the Loyalist cause. His only concern was for his own hide.

Like a snake slithering for cover, Derrick crawled through the heavy underbrush and dragged his body along the shore. He squinted in the darkness to plot his path. After scrambling through the brush he fled before a rebel musket ball could make a target of the yellow streak that stretched down his back.

When he was a safe distance away Derrick slowed his frantic pace and breathed a relieved sigh. At least he would have Catrina, he vowed to himself. He would snatch her away from the crippled watchman and wait out the war in some secluded niche. When the British had brought the colonists under thumb he would return to Scotland with Catrina to enjoy the wealth she could offer him.

Satisfied with that thought Derrick abandoned Monck's Corner and aimed himself toward the lighthouse. Old Matthew would rue the day he played Derrick Redmund for a fool. The old man would not live to see another sunrise. Derrick would make certain of that!

Brant groaned when a British musket ball seared across his left arm. Gritting his teeth, Brant crawled along the bank to close in on Derrick Redmund and his cavalry. He had waited almost a year to face that coward who had abused Catrina and abandoned his sister ship in Belfast, Ireland.

As Brant and his men reached the nest of British soldiers that were pinned down in underbrush, the rebel militia closed in the ranks from the rear. For several minutes the fighting continued, but the British were outnumbered and they had no choice but to surrender.

Brant shouted the order to throw down the muskets or be massacred. One by one the Loyalists discarded their weapons and filed from the bushes. A dark scowl claimed Brant's features when he realized the commanding officer was not among the prisoners. He should have known Derrick would turn tail and run at the first sign of trouble. That spineless viper, Brant thought furiously. No wonder Brant had difficulty recalling where he had met Derrick Redmund and what the varmint looked like. Who the hell could recognize a *faceless* coward?

Francis Marion threaded his way through the thicket, his rifle cradled in his arms, a triumphant grin pursing his lips. "We made fast work of these Tories," he chuckled. "Ah, Diamond, I do so enjoy battling the British when I know you have command of the other rebel ranks."

It had been several months since Brant had seen Marion, but he had no time to gloat over their victory. Derrick Redmund was still running loose and Brant wanted him nowhere near Catrina.

"The prisoners are yours," he said to Swamp Fox. "When you have unloaded the supplies my men will return to the *Sea Lady*."

As Brant wheeled away, hastily wrapping a bandage around his wounded arm, Swamp Fox frowned bemusedly. "Where are you off to in such a rush?"

"To the lighthouse," Brant called over his shoulder and then glanced at Thomas. "Send a skiff to fetch Cat's belongings."

Thomas nodded in compliance and then smiled when Brant vaulted onto a British mount and thundered off. It was obvious that Brant was not leaving Catrina in Charleston when the area was gearing up for another major battle. And especially not when Derrick Redmund was still fancy-free, Thomas mused. Brant wouldn't let that cowardly Tory near Catrina. She would be sailing on the *Sea Lady* where she belonged. And if Thomas knew Brant, which he most certainly did, Derrick Redmund wouldn't have a snowball's chance in hell of escaping this time. That weasel had slithered away to safety once too often. But tonight Brant would spare Derrick no mercy when he caught up with him.

"Cat?" Swamp Fox repeated puzzledly. "What was Diamond babbling about?"

"He's goin' to collect his wife," Thomas explained, turning his attention to the short, slight woodsman.

"I didn't know he had one," Marion choked in astonishment.

"Diamond's got one all right." Thomas's grin was as broad as the Cooper River. "Wait until you get a look at her. You'll want a dozen just like her."

Marion raised an eyebrow. "That pretty, eh? Then I shall count the minutes until I have the pleasure of meeting her."

Thomas extracted his watch from his pocket. "And that should be in precisely two hours. After you stash the supplies and tie up the prisoners, Cap'n said to meet him in the bay near Fort Johnson. 'Tis up to you to confiscate the rowboats that will ferry the freed prisoners back to shore."

Nodding in compliance, Swamp Fox turned to issue orders to his men and then walked Thomas toward one of the skiffs. "I am most anxious to confront the Tories who guard the British

445

prison ship. Many of my friends and comrades are rotting away in the hull of that musty frigate."

"Aye, and many of our friends are wasting away in the bowels of that hell hole," Thomas concurred. "But with any luck, they'll be free before dawn."

"I wonder what Diamond has in mind to catch the sailors off guard," Swamp Fox mused aloud.

Thomas shrugged. "I don't know, but you can be sure the cap'n has a plan."

"And I anticipate that it will be as successful as his last one." Swamp Fox glanced back at the string of prisoners that were being led away. "Two hours it is, my friend. We shall give the Tories a night to remember."

Huffing and puffing to catch his breath, Derrick burst through the door of the lighthouse. He had very nearly run himself into the ground in his haste to confront Matthew. The spiraling steps that awaited him appeared an unconquerable mountain and Derrick groaned miserably at the thought of climbing up them. Inhaling a deep breath, Derrick grasped the rail and hauled himself upward. Matthew had double-crossed him and Derrick was determined to pay the old man retribution . . . if he had any strength left.

Gasping for another breath, Derrick paused before the closed door in the tower. It took him a few moments to gather his strength before he burst in on Matthew. Once his heart ceased racing around his chest like a runaway stallion, Derrick retrieved his pistol from his belt and shoved open the door.

Matthew rolled his eyes in disgust when he was greeted by another loaded flintlock. My, but he had acquired vengeful enemies in a short span of time. He wasn't certain how Derrick managed to escape the trap he and Brant had set for Redmund, but the slimy snake had managed to crawl away unscathed.

"You lied to me, you conniving bastard," Derrick growled. Angrily, he stalked over to yank the gag from Matthew's mouth. "I see someone else has spared me the trouble of hunting you down and tying you up." Cold blue eyes pelleted over Matthew's scraggly beard and unruly hair. "Where is she, old man? And do not think to send me on a wild-goose chase. I have run short of patience after you thought to use me as bait for your trap."

Matthew raised a defiant chin. "I don't have the slightest idea what has become of Catrina, but it will do you no good, even if you locate her."

A dubious frown furrowed Derrick's brow. "What the hell is that supposed to mean?" Derrick snorted in question.

"Did I forget to mention to you that Catrina is married to Brant Diamond?" Matthew inquired, a mock innocent expression claiming his features. "How thoughtless of me."

The color seeped from beneath the smudges on Derrick's cheeks. "You're lying," he snarled, cocking the trigger of his flintlock. "Where is she? I did not plot and scheme to make that wealthy chit my wife, only to have you deter me from my purpose with your preposterous tales. Catrina would never marry that rebel pirate."

Matthew caught the slight movement in the hall, but he was careful not to draw attention to the fact that they were not alone in the tower. If Catrina was eavesdropping, Matthew intended to sway her loyalty back to him . . . if at all possible.

"Now what are *you* babbling about, Captain?" Matthew tossed the question in Derrick's enraged face.

"I suppose no harm will come in telling you," Derrick smirked. "After all, you will endure the same fate as the duke and duchess."

"What duke and duchess?" Matthew demanded to know.

"I called upon Catrina's parents to seek audience with their only child. Unfortunately, my reputation preceded me to their manor in Dumfries. It seems they were acquainted with the family of another wealthy heiress I tried to wed in Edinburgh." Derrick laughed bitterly as the memory returned to irritate him all over again. "The haughty duke, Randolph Hamilton, threw me out of his home, swearing I was not fit to *serve* his daughter, much less court her." A demented flicker glistened in Derrick's eyes as he focused on the gigantic lantern that set before the glass window.

"Shortly after my confrontation with the duke and duchess, their mansion caught fire and burned during the night. 'Twas then that I made my way to the Hamiltons' country estate, waiting to console their bereaved daughter."

"You burned them alive?" Matthew croaked.

Derrick's sinister gaze swung back to Matthew who looked a mite peaked in the lantern light. "There is something fascinating about fire, don't you agree, old man? A victim of flames soon becomes a part of the blaze." Derrick's menacing grin grew broader, his eyes dancing with deviltry. "And dead men can tell no tales. This lighthouse is of no benefit to the British. 'Tis a den of deceiving spies." He moved closer to stare down his nose at Matthew's whitewashed face. "If you do not tell me where to find Catrina you will be sentenced to death without so much as a trial, old man."

The threat hung heavily in the air. Matthew had the uneasy feeling he was to suffer the same fate as Catrina's parents. Dammit, had she overheard Derrick's confession? Or was she waiting for Derrick to set it aflame before she dealt with the man who had maliciously murdered her parents? Obviously, Catrina had no use for him or Derrick, Matthew reckoned. Or perhaps Catrina was not there in the shadows at all, he contemplated. Perhaps it was one of Derrick's henchmen, waiting to assist him with his dastardly deed.

"I paid you a small fortune to hand Catrina over to me," Derrick sneered. "Spill the truth, old man!" Grasping the handle of the lantern, Derrick tilted it sideways. "Tell me where Catrina is or I will toss the lantern at your feet and you will become a human torch!"

A surprised yelp erupted from Derrick's lips when Catrina's dagger sailed through the air to pin the sleeve of his jacket to the wall. He wheeled around to point his flintlock at the intruder and then gasped in dismay when Catrina's outraged face materialized from the shadows.

Catrina had been plastered against the wall, listening to Derrick's grizzly confession. For several moments she had been paralyzed by the information Matthew had pried from Derrick. All the pain and grief she had suffered at the time of her parents' death came back to haunt her.

How she detested Derrick Redmund's ruthlessness, his pretentiousness, his abuse. And Matthew was no better, she added bitterly. He had sold her out to the very man who had murdered her parents. Catrina was anxious to be rid of both of them.

With her hand clenched around the flintlock, she glared at the despicable man who had wrought terror and violence on her family. "At least Matthew has told the truth once in his wretched life," she spat at Derrick. "Aye, Brant Diamond is my husband. But even if he weren't, I would never wed you, not then and especially not now. The British may curse Diamond for aiding the rebel army and preying on the Crown's frigates. They may call him a marauding pirate, but he looks the saint compared to you." Catrina's features were rigid with fury. "I loathe the sight of you, Derrick. My father was right. You are not even worthy of being a servant, not to me or the king. You are so greedy and selfish that you give no thought to anyone else."

Matthew sat tensely wondering which one of them, if either of them, would survive a duel at such close range. Not only was Catrina aiming at Derrick, but Derrick had his pistol pointed at Catrina's heaving chest. Catrina had no intention of allowing Derrick out of the tower alive. Derrick was vicious enough to set the lighthouse ablaze if he thought he could escape the fire with only minor burns.

The silence was so thick it could have been slashed with a sword. Catrina and Derrick were glowering at each other, their fingers laying heavily on the triggers of the flintlocks they clutched in their hands.

"Put the pistol down. You won't walk out of here alive," Derrick jeered at Catrina.

"At least I will die knowing I will take you with me," Catrina countered in a deadly tone.

Derrick's unblinking gaze swung to the abrupt movement behind Catrina. The tenseness of the situation caused his finger to jerk and set off the trigger. The pistol misfired, grazing the side of Catrina's head. He scowled furiously when he heard the screech of the tomcat that had come to complain that he had yet to be fed.

As Nicodemus sailed across the room to seek comfort in Matthew's lap, Derrick threw his useless pistol aside. Before Catrina could recover Derrick lunged at her, snatching the weapon from her hands. Matthew strained against the confining ropes, cursing his inability to come to Catrina's rescue. As Derrick dragged his hostage toward the door, Matthew stared at the dagger that had fallen to the floor. But it might as well have been a mile away for all the good it would do him, Matthew thought disgustedly.

When Catrina's fogged mind began to clear and she realized what had happened, she struggled in earnest. But Derrick's arm tightened about her waist, threatening to squeeze her in two if she put up a fight.

"Don't force me to do something drastic," Derrick hissed as he jabbed the pistol beneath her ribs.

Catrina stiffened in response, but she was too furious to be afraid. Derrick had murdered her parents and used her in hopes of gaining her fortune. How she detested him and his touch. Catrina swore there was no lower form of life slithering upon the earth than Derrick Redmund. He was the most selfish, ruthless man she had ever met, and even his good looks could not disguise his maliciousness. People were only stepping-stones to be walked on in his pursuit to wealth and power.

"You despicable vermin," Cat spat venomously.

Derrick's harsh laughter rang in her ears. "'Tis no matter

what you think of me," he snorted. "You will become my wife or I will expose you to the Crown. You wouldn't like what the authorities do to traitors."

"'Tis impossible," Catrina reminded him through gritted teeth. "Matthew told you I am already wed."

"Aye, but to a rebel pirate," Derrick parried. "The marriage will be annulled when I explain that Pirate Diamond took my fiancée captive and forced her to speak the vows for his own selfish purposes."

"I will deny it," Catrina protested as Derrick herded her down the steps.

"Then you will be signing your own death warrant, my dear. A willing marriage to that notorious pirate will be the same as a confession of guilt." Derrick paused on the landing and grinned wickedly. "You have no choice, my dear Catrina. You must marry me or hang on the gallows. 'Tis no choice at all."

Catrina intended to declare she would prefer to die than to wed him, but Derrick's mouth swooped down on hers, strangling her protest. Repulsion sizzled through her body and she writhed for freedom until Derrick jabbed the pistol painfully between her ribs.

"Before the week is out you will be my wife and I will enjoy the pleasures of your luscious body," Derrick growled, his voice heavy with disturbed desire. "I will make you forget that pirate's touch. You will belong to me in every way."

Derrick reached out to open the door that led to another set of stairs. He tensed when he heard the echo of approaching footsteps on the stairs below.

Derrick had the uneasy feeling he knew to whom the footsteps belonged. It had to be Captain Diamond, coming to fetch his precious wife. But Derrick had his hostage and he was not about to give her up to that rebel pirate. Brant Diamond had spoiled every money-making proposition and promotion Derrick coveted. He held the upper hand and he vowed to show Brant no mercy.

Catrina also heard the sound on the steps below and she

grimaced, praying it wasn't Brant. Derrick would kill him, she thought frantically. Her wide, apprehensive eyes focused on the stairs, hoping Brant's face would not appear from the shadows. She had lost her family to Derrick Redmund. She would not lose Brant as well.

"God, don't let it be Brant," she murmured half aloud, her body rigid with grim anticipation.

Chapter Twenty-Eight

Brant swore under his breath when he rounded the corner to see Catrina held captive in Derrick's arms. Another curse sprung from his lips when he noticed the blood trickling down the side of Cat's face. How Brant itched to get his hands on that blackhearted scoundrel and tear him to pieces, bit by bit.

Again Derrick found himself facing a flintlock, but he was confident Diamond would not risk Cat's life. "Drop the pistol," he ordered, maneuvering Cat in front of him to serve as his shield.

Brant stared down the barrel of Derrick's weapon, indecision etching his brow. If he took aim at the cowardly bastard, Catrina could be killed. If he cast his weapon aside, Derrick would not bat an eye at putting a bullet through his heart.

While Brant and Derrick were staring each other down, hating each other on sight, Catrina's eyes were glued to the stained sleeve of Brant's jacket. No doubt Matthew's treachery had earned Brant another wound, she thought bitterly. Finally, Catrina raised her gaze to survey Brant's face. She could see the dilemma in his chiseled features, the barely controlled fury that tightened the lines around his mouth.

When Brant started to lower his pistol and fling it aside, Cat screamed at the top of her lungs, begging Brant not to become a defenseless target for a murderer. With no concern for her own safety, she came uncoiled like a wildcat, scratching and clawing for freedom. When her elbow connected with Derrick's midsection, his grip eased. Catrina threw herself from his arms, but to her dismay it was Derrick who fired the first shot.

Brant had recovered before he lost his grasp on his pistol, but he refused to fire until Catrina was a safe distance away. That split second cost him dearly. Although he dodged the bullet, it lodged in his left thigh. Before Brant could recoil to fire his pistol, Derrick leaped on him, growling like an enraged panther.

As they tumbled down the flight of stairs, Brant's own fury numbed him to the two wounds he had sustained. When they landed in a tangled heap, Brant snarled at the face so close to his. His body was taut with the craving for revenge and he reacted purely upon instinct. His doubled fist connected with Derrick's cheek and the force of the blow sent Derrick's head snapping backward.

With a demented snarl, Derrick shoved Brant away and scrambled to his feet. Diamond's bloodthirsty attack brought out Derrick's cowardly instinct and he took flight down the steps. By the time he reached the landing just above the ground floor, Brant was upon him, pelleting him with one painful blow after another.

Brant was like a wounded lion consumed with rage. He ached to repay Derrick for his rough abuse of Catrina and he would not be satisfied until he had beat the scoundrel to a pulp.

While Derrick whimpered and groaned beneath the punishing blows, Catrina snatched up Brant's pistol and bounded down the steps. It sickened her to see Brant's left arm and leg drenched with blood. She knew if it had not been for her, Brant could have dropped Derrick in his tracks.

When Brant sent Derrick's senses reeling with another well-aimed blow to the jaw, Derrick toppled from the landing. His unconscious body rolled down the last flight of stairs and collapsed in a crumpled pile. Heaving an exhausted sigh Brant staggered to his feet and hobbled around on his wounded leg to face Catrina.

A relieved smile drifted across his swollen lips and Catrina melted into sentimental mush. Brant had never looked worse. His raven hair was in disarray. The buttons of his shirt were strewn on the steps, leaving his heaving chest bare to her admiring gaze. His face was battered and the left side of his body was stained with blood. Although this daredevil pirate was a mass of wounds and bruises Catrina had never loved him more. This swashbuckling rebel was her champion. Even in that nerve-racking moment when Brant was peering into the barrel of Derrick's pistol, there had been no fear in his eyes. The reckless outlaw had stared death in the face without batting an eye. He had been prepared to sacrifice himself to ensure Catrina's safety.

Impulsively, Cat flew into his arms, showering him with kisses. For a long moment she clung to him, oblivious to his wounds, grateful he had survived what could well have been disaster.

Brant chuckled at Catrina's overzealous greeting. He pried her away before she squeezed the stuffing out of him. He had lost enough blood without Catrina forcing it to pour from his wounds.

"Later, love," he murmured softly. "There will be time enough for both of us to properly show how grateful we are to be together again. We have to fetch Matthew and abandon the lighthouse. The British will be swarming the place when they receive word of the confrontation at Monck's Corner."

Catrina didn't know exactly what Brant was referring to, but she frowned at the thought of sparing Matthew his just reward for betraying Brant. The old man was Brant's enemy, not his comrade, she thought resentfully.

"I tied Matthew in the tower and there he deserves to stay. He intended to sacrifice you to the British, just as he tried to sell me to Derrick."

Brant flicked the end of her upturned nose. "Nay, Matthew loves me like a brother," he insisted, setting her away from him to trudge back to the tower. "He would never betray me."

"A brother!" Catrina scoffed at Brant's blind loyalty to the treacherous old man. "Would a brother become a British spy? Would he sell you out for a handful of British coins? Let Matthew rot in the tower with his carrier pigeons."

Brant ignored her attempt to discourage him from rescuing Matthew. "Fetch your belongings, Cat. We still have a long night ahead of us."

Muttering at Brant's fierce loyalty to a man who would stab him in the back, given the chance, Cat stalked down the stairs. She stepped over the crumpled pile at her feet and continued on her way, grumbling all the while. How could she convince Brant to leave Matthew behind? How could she expose that traitorous mercenary for what he really was? Catrina had overheard enough in the tower to know that Matthew had received payment from Derrick and she would never again be swayed by the old buzzard's lies.

The shattering of glass in the parlor jerked Catrina from her contemplative deliberations. Setting aside her clothes, she stepped around the corner to investigate the cause of the disturbance. A horrified gasp burst from her lips when she found the room ablaze. The flames were spreading like wildfire, consuming all in their path.

"May they both roast in hell!" Derrick sneered behind her.

Catrina wheeled around to stare into Derrick's disfigured face. Before she could dart away, Derrick's hand snaked out to ensnare her. His fingertips bit into the tender flesh of her arm, making her grimace in pain. Catrina cursed her preoccupation with Matthew. She should have paid more attention to the man who lay at the foot of the steps, she chided herself.

When Derrick propelled her toward the door, Catrina pivoted around to plant her doubled fist in his face. "Nay, I will go nowhere with you," she all but screamed at him.

The thought of Brant perishing in the fire, as her parents

had, was too much to bear. Catrina had suffered through hell once before and she refused to do so again. She fought Derrick with the only weapons at her disposal—her hands, feet, and teeth. Her fingers curled into his dark hair and she yanked for all she was worth. Derrick squealed in pain when Catrina attempted to pull his hair out by the roots. When she sank her teeth into the arm Derrick had raised to restrain her, he yelped and backed away.

Derrick had never seen this side of Catrina and he was unprepared for her ferocious attack. He had known her only in her depressed state of grief. But all too quickly he realized he had misjudged this she-cat. Gritting his teeth, Derrick lunged at Cat, but she kicked him in the groin before he could capture her. While he was doubled over, protecting himself from another painful blow, Catrina snatched up the stone figurine that sat on the stand beside the door. With every ounce of strength she could muster, she pounded Derrick on the head as if she were driving a stake into the ground. His eyes rolled as he wilted onto the floor like a delicate flower left too long in the blazing sun.

With her mission accomplished Catrina glanced up to see the smoke choking the staircase that led to the tower. And then Brant appeared like a dark angel emerging from a black cloud. As he darted through the sea of flames, Matthew scampered along in his wake. Catrina frowned at the old man's agility. She had never seen Matthew move so fast. He was matching Brant, step for step, clutching his cane rather than leaning upon it.

When the choking twosome reached Catrina, she found herself whisked toward the door. Although Matthew had delayed to snatch up her discarded satchel of clothes, he was one step behind them in less than a minute, much to Catrina's surprise. As they raced toward the awaiting skiff, Catrina stared bewilderedly at Matthew. He suddenly seemed as spry as a man half his age. Perhaps it was the fear for his life that gave the old man winged feet to match the speed of Mercury, the swift messenger of the gods.

While the lighthouse blazed up in flames, an infantry of British converged upon the beach. When the soldiers spied the skiff they opened fire. Catrina found herself shoved facedown in the boat as a barrage of musketballs sailed past them. The mew of a frightened tomcat reached her ears and Catrina reared her head to see Nicodemus bound into Matthew's lap.

Brant's pained groan intermingled with the musket fire and Catrina eased up beside him to inspect his wounds. Carefully, she drew away the tattered cloth to survey the injury on Brant's left thigh.

"Someone up there doesn't like me," Brant moaned as he strained to row toward the *Sea Lady*.

"But someone down here loves you," Catrina said tenderly. Her eyes locked with Brant's, exposing the emotion mirrored in the depths of misty emerald.

"Here, gimme them oars," Thomas ordered gruffly. "You ain't in no condition to row."

His stern gaze swung to Matthew who was trying to console the panicked tomcat that had been singed in the fire. Nicodemus was certain he had sacrificed eight lives during his escape and he was not at all happy to find himself surrounded by water.

"Hell's bells, Matthew, that cat can wait. Start rowin'. We got troubles!"

Matthew glanced up to see an infantry of British swarming down the beach to pick off the occupants of the skiff. Dumping Nicodemus in Catrina's arms, he took up the oars and the boat suddenly lurched forward. Catrina's astonished gaze swung to Matthew who had another burst of energy. The man was a bundle of surprises, Cat thought to herself. Her pensive musings dispersed when Brant's fingers curled beneath her chin, forcing her to meet his curious smile.

"Would you remind repeating what you said," Brant requested, his golden eyes glowing down at her. "I will never tire of hearing it."

"She said she loved you." Thomas snickered and then

ducked away from a howling musketball. "I tried to tell you that six months ago, but would you listen? Nay, yer as stubborn as she is." Thomas straightened in his seat when the danger had passed and then regrasped the oars. "And the cap'n has been in love with you since the beginnin'. Brant Diamond would never take a wife unless she meant so much to him that he couldn't let her go." Thomas looked to the bearded old man for confirmation. "Ain't that right, Matthew?"

Matthew's broad grin glowed in the distant flames of what had once been the lighthouse. "Aye, that is true."

"How would you know?" Catrina snapped sarcastically. Her irritation with Matthew had suddenly been refueled. "You have been too busy negotiating with Derrick to notice anything else."

"I was only trying to help," Matthew defended, chuckling at Cat's outburst of temper.

"With a friend like you, we don't need enemies," Cat hissed spitefully, and then wheeled to face Brant. "Your friendship is blind to Matthew's faults. He is only pretending to favor your cause because he fears for his own neck."

"Humor me, Cat," Brant breathed wearily. "I am not a well man. You can try and hang Matthew when we're safely aboard the schooner, sailing to the Indies."

Reluctantly, Catrina clamped her mouth shut and silently glared daggers at Matthew. She didn't trust Matthew for a minute, but she complied with Brant's request to hold her grievances until his wounds were tended. To her further astonishment Matthew wrapped a supporting arm around Brant to assist him up the rope ladder. Catrina stared bug-eyed as Matthew hoisted the injured captain to the deck and called to the crew to fetch makeshift bandages.

Catrina set aside her annoyance with Matthew the moment Brant staggered across the deck. She feared he would collapse from loss of blood before she could steer him toward his cabin.

"Damned fool," Thomas admonished grouchily. "I knew you was invitin' trouble when you stormed the shore like an immortal warrior!" His gaze fell to the jagged gash in Brant's thigh. "How'd you get this one?"

"He was saving my life," Catrina answered for Brant, her loving gaze focused on his bruised features. "And now I plan to tend to your wounds . . . with great care."

Brant smiled at the underlying meaning of her words, but he gave his head a negative shake. "A tourniquet will have to suffice for the time being." He gestured his good arm toward the British fort near the Ashley River. "Swamp Fox awaits us. Before we leave Charleston we are going to free the prisoners who are rotting in the hull of the ship that is anchored offshore."

Catrina's eyes narrowed. "And what, pray tell, do you plan to use for a leg when you go charging across the gangplank, my dear captain?" She indicated the wound that had Brant limping noticeably. "This one is hardly sturdy enough to stand on, much less run on!"

Brant shrugged noncommittally and hobbled toward the helm. "It has held me these past thirty years. Surely it will not fail me in my hour of need."

Catrina rolled her eyes and muttered at the mulish man. "Brant, for God's sake, you must . . ."

When he flashed her that charismatic smile of his, Catrina's words evaporated. "I have no doubt that you will make a very efficient wife and nursemaid, but I do not need a mother hen."

His tone was so sincere that Catrina could not take offense, even though she was sorely tempted to. "I may never have the chance to test my nursing abilities or tend to my wifely duties if you do not have those wounds treated," she grumbled. "You are always too busy trying to get yourself killed to remember you have a wife."

Brant propped himself against the wheel and tossed his pouting wife another grin. "That, my dear, is one thing I have never forgotten, no matter where I was or what I was doing."

"You ain't gonna change his mind," Thomas commented, leaning close to relay the message in confidence. "The cap'n won't rest until he's freed his fellow countrymen from the hell hole on that prison ship."

Sighing defeatedly, Catrina ambled over to the rail to watch their progress across the bay. As Brant had anticipated, the stir at Monck's Corner had drawn the available manpower of the British to the banks of the Cooper River. The towering flames of the lighthouse had attracted further attention, leaving Fort Johnson short-handed. Thankfully, Brant would not face a full militia when he attempted to seize the British frigate that set in the bay.

As the *Sea Lady* cut through the water toward the Crown's prison ship, Catrina spied a small fleet of rowboats venturing from the beach. A muddled frown knitted her brow and she glanced over at Thomas who had propped himself on the rail beside her.

"Are those Tories, coming to defend the prison ship?"

Thomas shook his head and gestured toward the rough-edged woodsman who crouched in the lead skiff. "Nay, 'tis the Swamp Fox. He was to confiscate the boats to ferry the rebel prisoners back to safety. It seems he has accomplished his mission and now 'tis our turn to tackle ours."

Before Catrina could question the method, Brant limped up beside her. "I want you to remain below deck until we have seized the frigate," he ordered. But he might as well have asked Cat to fly to the moon. She was going nowhere if Brant was not going with her.

Her chin tilted to a rebellious angle, her green eyes glittering with determination. "I am boarding the ship beside you . . . to protect your blind side." Her gaze flickered over his wounds. "And also the side that carries British ammunition."

"You will not!" Brant bellowed.

As quick as a cat pouncing on a mouse, Catrina lunged at Brant to rob him of the pistol he had just retrieved. Grinning into his startled face, Catrina stepped back to tuck the weapon in her belt. "Are you coming, or do you intend to stand there gaping?"

Before Brant could respond Catrina lost herself in the swarm of sailors who had surged toward the bow of the ship. Although the guard shouted a cry of alarm, warning his fellow Tories that trouble was approaching off the starboard bow, they were no match for the invading privateers. Brant's men leaped from the gangplank while the Swamp Fox's men poured over the rail. Only two shots were fired before the prison ship was in the rebels' hands.

While the rebels dashed down the steps to free the prisoners and assist them to the main deck, Brant limped toward the captain's cabin. The commander of the prison ship was tardy in answering the cry of alarm and was stuffing his arms in his shirt when he confronted Captain Diamond and his daring wife.

Marshall Collier froze in his tracks, his eyes wide in disbelief. "What . . ."

Brant grinned devilishly at the startled captain. "You have your choice, sir. You can go down with the ship or surrender your weapon and be ferried back to shore."

"Marshall, what on earth is going . . ."

Catrina's mouth fell open when the plump blonde she had seen in the dress shop appeared in the doorway, garbed in Marshall's robe. The disheveled sight of the prissy Cynthia Pinkerton caused Catrina to burst out laughing. Willfully, she stifled her giggles to watch Brant's reaction to meeting his ex-lover who seemed to have a difficult time remembering where to locate her own bed. From the look of things Cynthia suffered from the well-known disease—roving eye. Her affliction had landed her in Captain Collier's cot.

Brant cocked a bushy brow and appraised the woman he had once fancied himself in love with. Time had not been kind to Cynthia. She wore her years as poorly as she managed her marriage to a man twice her age. Obviously her bed of roses had become a nest of thorns and the one-time beauty went in search of men who could satisfy her cravings. Brant regretted that he had once been attracted to the fickle wench. If there

462

was any love left in the memories of the past, it died the moment he glanced back and forth between the vivacious sprite at his side and the full-figured blonde who couldn't find her tongue to save her life.

"How good it is to see you again, Cynthia," Brant said in a tone that implied otherwise. "I trust you will be able to sufficiently explain this incident to Colonel Pinkerton when you arrive home." His golden eyes danced with deviltry as he raked Cynthia one last time. "Ah, I would love to be a mouse, hiding in the corner, when you unfold your rendition of this incident to your husband."

Cynthia stuck up her nose and breezed past the threesome as if she were a regal queen in her flowing robe. "I am eternally thankful I had the foresight not to marry you, Brant Diamond," she sniffed, flinging him a glacial glare. "I would be even more humiliated, wed to a renegade pirate."

Brant grasped Cynthia's arms as she sailed by, his eyes flickering with amusement. "You cannot be more grateful than I, Mrs. Pinkerton. I have found a woman who will remain by my side through thick and thin. Cat is twice the woman you could ever hope to be."

Cynthia gasped indignantly and raised her hand to slap the insolent smirk off Brant's face. Her arm halted in midair when she felt the barrel of Catrina's pistol ramming into her side.

"I wouldn't if I were you, Cynthia," Catrina told her calmly. "I cannot say which would disturb Colonel Pinkerton more, the loss of your fidelity, if indeed there ever was any, or the loss of your life."

"How dare you threaten me, you little . . ."

"Tsk, tsk," Brant taunted. "It would never do for the pot to call the kettle black, Cynthia. And if I were you, I would not provoke Cat. She will come at you with claws bared."

Cynthia glared at the shapely beauty who wore an ornery expression to match the one that was plastered on Brant's face. Furiously, she wheeled around and stormed down the companionway, forcing the embarrassed Captain Collier to scurry along in her wake.

When the twosome were out of earshot, Brant steered Catrina around and ushered her toward the deck. "She was once a lovely young woman," Brant murmured, half in his own defense. "But I doubt that you would believe it."

An impish grin pursed Cat's lips as she replaced her pistol in her sash. "It does leave me to wonder at your taste in women. I do hope you don't see similarities between us."

Brant paused at the foot of the steps and turned Cat to face his somber countenance. "You, my love, are in a class all of your own," he murmured affectionately. "What I felt for Cynthia, no matter how misdirected it might have been, is nothing like the emotions that touch me when I lose myself in those fathomless emerald eyes." His fingertip traced her delicate cheekbone, marveling at the satiny texture of her skin. "Cat, I . . ."

"Brant?" Matthew called from the top of the steps. "We are ready to return to the *Sea Lady*."

Reluctantly, Brant withdrew from what would have been an ardent embrace and sighed wearily. "Coming, Matthew."

Exhaustion had begun to settle into Brant's features and Catrina curled her arm about him to assist him up the steps. Brant had drained every ounce of his strength completing his task. The harried events of the night were rapidly catching up with him. When Swamp Fox had saluted his fellow officer and climbed into his skiff, Catrina followed behind Brant who had accepted Matthew's supporting arm to propel him across the gangplank.

Although Catrina strongly resented Matthew's sudden burst of patriotism for the rebels she bit her tongue. When Brant's wounds had been tended and he had time to rest, she would broach the subject. To her way of thinking, Matthew should have been shuffled ashore with the other Tories.

The moment Brant eased onto the deck of the *Sea Lady* Thomas flew to his side. "'Tis time to tend yer wounds, Cap'n," he insisted. "You've waited too long as it is."

Brant drew Catrina to his side to give her an affectionate squeeze. "Give us a moment, Thomas," he requested, never taking his eyes off Catrina's exquisite face.

"In another moment you will collapse in a lifeless heap," Thomas lectured.

It seemed he and Catrina would not be granted a minute of privacy until Thomas had his way. Brant had warned Catrina away from mothering him, but Thomas was by far the worst offender. "Then fetch your medical bag, Dr. Haynes. But be quick about it," Brant grumbled irritably. "Catrina and I need to have a private conversation."

"If you don't lie down before you fall down you won't live long enough to tell her you love her all over again," Thomas snorted.

Brant pouted like a spoiled child all the way to his cabin. "If you are so damned happy that Cat and I have come to terms, why do you insist upon ruining what might have been a quiet night alone with my wife?"

"It will be a quiet one," Thomas snickered, flashing Brant a teasing glance. "You seem to have a hard time rememberin' you've been shot to pieces. You won't be no use to anyone until yer patched up, especially to yer wife." As Thomas steered Brant toward the bed he shot Catrina a quick look. "Fetch some boilin' water, lass, plenty of it. These wounds need attention. I think the cap'n is too numb to know how serious his wounds really are."

Catrina reversed direction to obey the command. Hurriedly, she darted through the companionway to reach the galley. When she returned to the cabin, Thomas was pouring liquor down Brant's throat to prepare him for primitive surgery. Gently, she eased down on the edge of the bed to cleanse the ragged flesh surrounding the wound.

Loving hands moved across his skin, making Brant relax beneath her tender touch. A smile mellowed his craggy features as he studied Catrina's flawless face. They had been through hell together, he thought drowsily. And one day soon

465

they would find a touch of heaven . . .

When Brant drifted off to sleep, Thomas sank down on the bed to care for his patient. "Why don't you use my room to bathe and dress," he suggested. "Matthew will be here shortly to assist me."

Catrina frowned distastefully. "I'm not at all sure I want Matthew near Brant. 'Tis his fault that Brant was wounded in the first place."

Thomas laid the sterilized knife aside to smooth the frown from Catrina's features. "I think yer bein' a mite too hard on Old Matthew. Life has been difficult for him these past few years. Besides, he wouldn't do nothin' to hurt the cap'n."

"Life has been no picnic for any of us," Catrina countered, rising from the bed to fetch her satchel. "And I don't think any of you know Matthew as well as you think! The man is a walking contradiction. I, for one, don't trust his motives."

With that Catrina sailed toward the door. It seemed Thomas was as stubborn as Brant when it came to the subject of Matthew. How could they defend a man who sold her out to Derrick Redmund? Exasperated, Catrina paced the small cabin, waiting for the sailors to fetch water for her bath. When Brant was back on his feet Catrina intended to hold a trial of sorts. She would force Matthew to explain his actions in Brant's and Thomas's presence. Let that old rascal talk his way out of this one, Catrina thought spitefully.

Matthew might have gone aboard the prison ship, but his life had not been in jeopardy. The rebels had overrun the unsuspecting frigate, but they had met with little resistance and there were no reinforcements to come to the Tories' aid. Brant had made certain of that.

A wary frown captured Catrina's features as she eased into her bath. Matthew was a sly old man, she decided. He had probably received money for Brant's capture, as well as attempting to hand her over to Derrick Redmund. If the opportunity presented itself, Matthew would probably head straight to the authorities, insisting that he be compensated for betraying a friend. Why, the man could become rich giving information as to Brant Diamond's whereabouts. And if the Crown was unable to ensnare Brant it was all the better for Matthew. Brant would become Matthew's meal ticket and Brant was too fond of the pretentious old goat to realize it.

And just why did Brant feel such fierce loyalty to Matthew, she wondered. What link did Matthew have to Brant's past? Matthew seemed to know a great deal about Brant, although he had refused to explain how and why to Catrina. Aye, there were several questions Catrina wanted answered. As soon as Brant was up to it Catrina intended to put Matthew on the firing line.

Chewing on that thought, Catrina mentally listed her suspicions about Matthew's conduct. When the moment was upon her, she intended to be prepared. Matthew had a hell of a lot of explaining to do before she accepted him as a trustworthy friend!

Chapter Twenty-Nine

"Catrina?" Thomas's quiet voice came to her from across a sea of dreams. "The cap'n is awake and he wants to see you."

Drowsily, Cat pushed herself into an upright position on Thomas's bed. After her bath she had lain down, intending to rest for only a few minutes. But she had gone almost an entire night without sleep and exhaustion had caught up with her.

Her tangled lashes swept up to peer out the porthole and she frowned when she was met with darkness. "What time is it?"

Thomas chuckled at the bewildered expression on her face. Catrina seemed disoriented, as if she had been caught up in Rip Van Winkle's one-hundred-year nap. "You slept the entire day away," he informed her. "'Tis eight o'clock."

Catrina bounded from the bed to run a quick comb through her hair. "Is Brant all right? I only intended to catch a short nap, but . . ."

"He's fine. Well, not exactly fine," Thomas amended as he watched Catrina dash about the room in search of her shoes. "He's lost a lot of blood and he's weak, but he'll live."

Breathing a relieved sigh, Catrina aimed herself toward the door. "Is there any sign of infection?"

"Aye, a little in his leg," Thomas admitted. "But if we can keep him in bed for a time, he should mend nicely."

The moment Catrina eased open the door to the captain's

cabin her heart lurched in her chest. Brant looked so pale and vulnerable lying there. His dark hair lay recklessly across his forehead and the beard he had worn these many months was gone, displaying his chalky complexion.

Catrina was by his side in less than a heartbeat, her small hand folding around his. The sight of Brant weak and bandaged had her cursing Matthew all over again. Damn that man. He could have gotten Brant killed, she thought furiously.

Brant's heavily lidded eyes lifted to meet the annoyed frown on Catrina's face. "Is something amiss?" he questioned hoarsely.

"Aye, plenty," Catrina blurted out. "I would like to have Matthew thrown overboard for his treachery. Even though you seem to hold that old goat in high esteem, I consider him personally responsible for your plight. I'm certain he was using signals from the lighthouse to lure you into an ambush. He swore the varied colored lights meant nothing, but they did, didn't they? You thought he was giving a sign to sail into the harbor unhindered, didn't you?"

A wry smile twitched Brant's lips. "Aye, they were signals," he admitted. "And without them, we would never have been able to slip past the blockade."

Catrina sniffed distastefully. "'Tis a wonder to me that Matthew hasn't had you served up to the British on a silver platter long before now. I swear he has been sending signals to alert the British to your presence each time you cruised the coast . . ."

A movement behind her caught her attention and Catrina twisted around to see a tall, lean young man leaning leisurely against the wall. Although he clung to the shadows, there was something oddly familiar about him. But Catrina could not place the face. She knew for certain the man was not a member of the crew. Where had she seen him?

Noting Catrina's blatant appraisal of the stranger Brant broke into another smile. "Since you seem to be in such a snit over Matthew's motives I think 'tis time the two of you aired

470

your grievances." He indicated the young man who was grinning wickedly at Catrina. "Come forward, Matthew."

Cat's narrowed eyes swung from Brant to the dark stranger in the corner, wondering if the pain and the liquor Thomas had forced down his throat had pickled his brain. "That isn't Matthew."

"But it is." Brant chuckled and then sucked in his breath when Thomas applied the burning poultice to his leg wound.

While Thomas went about his chore of tending Brant's injury, Catrina stared at the man who ambled into the light. Her eyes flew to Thomas for confirmation. The first mate nodded affirmatively.

"Aye, 'tis Matthew," he concurred as he packed the wound and replaced the bandage. "The cap'n ain't teasin' you and he ain't out of his mind with fever . . . at least not yet."

"But . . ." Catrina's words died on her lips as the light reflected the devilish gleam in the man's dark eyes.

"Don't you recognize me, Tory?" Matthew said in the low, graveled voice Catrina had heard for half a year. "You, of all people, should know that disguises often serve a useful purpose."

Cat's face whitewashed. "You *are* Matthew," she squeaked. No one else had ever called her Tory, she reminded herself.

"At your service, madam," he murmured, bowing exaggeratedly before her.

Nicodemus, who had been lounging at the foot of the bed, bounded to the floor to brush against his master's leg. Catrina stared at the tomcat and the powerfully built man who had removed his gray beard, shaggy wig, and floppy hat. Somehow Matthew had managed to shave off several pounds when he stepped from his disguise.

As if Matthew read the myriad of questions in her eyes, he pivoted to fetch the familiar coat and breeches that were piled on the chair. "Padded linings," he explained, shrugging on the garments that added fifty pounds to his muscular physique. "They make for warmth in the winter, but I very nearly cooked alive in the summers."

Catrina's wide eyes swung back to Brant for a lengthy explanation and he snickered—but more cautiously this time—at the stricken expression on her features. "Cat, I would like to formally introduce you to my little brother, Matt Diamond."

"Your brother?" Catrina's astonished gaze lifted to the young man's handsome face. When she had recomposed herself, she glared at Brant. "Why didn't you tell me he was your brother? Didn't you trust me?"

His hand cupped her chin, bringing it down a notch. "You are a Tory, remember?"

Catrina removed his lingering hand. "I am also your wife. That was a rotten trick, Brant," she sniffed in irritation.

"It was also a rotten trick to pretend to be my cabin boy and feed me fire for supper," Brant countered.

"I am anxious to hear the rendition of that incident," Matt interjected enthusiastically and then sobered when Brant shot him a silencing frown.

"But there is no need for you to be insulted that you were kept in the dark, love. No one in Charleston knew of Matthew's identity. All young men in the colonies are required to join the ranks of the British unless they are physically unable to serve. If Matthew had not used the disguise he would have drawn suspicion and the Tories would have insisted that he take arms against the rebels. The revolutionists needed a neutral party to relay messages between the shipping lanes and the trade roads. We planted Matt in the lighthouse to send lantern signals and dispatches by carrier pigeon. With Matt keeping watch over the British troops and fleets, we were able to slip past the frigates off coast to transfer goods to the trade roads.

"When you recognized Redmund, Matt sent me a message through the militia commanded by Swamp Fox. We devised a plan to trick the British into paying a bounty for my head and ransom for your return to Derrick Redmund." Brant paused to grit his teeth when Thomas checked the stitches on his arm.

472

"Damn, you have all the gentleness of a grizzly bear." When Thomas had been properly chastised for his lack of tenderness, Brant continued. "It was Derrick who walked into a trap at Monck's Corner. Swamp Fox was waiting to hem Derrick in from the rear while my men converged on the bank. But the coward showed his true colors and abandoned his command. He headed straight for the lighthouse and Matthew."

"Unfortunately, a certain young firebrand, believing me to be a British spy and traitor to the notorious Captain Diamond, tied me to my chair," Matt mocked dryly. "Believe me, Tory, had I known you were going to become a force too difficult to reckon with, I would have confessed the truth before you blew a hole in my padded coat. And you scared ten years off my life when you tried to gun Redmund down in the street."

"What?" Brant squawked, his eyes swinging to his younger brother.

"We had a terrible tussle in the carriage the day she saw Redmund in Charleston," Matt chuckled, tossing Cat a taunting smile. "Instead of cowering like a timid lamb when she recognized the beast who once abused her, Cat came apart at the seams. I feared she was going to incite a riot in the street if I did not subdue her . . . and quickly."

A crimson red tide flowed into her cheeks when Brant cast her a condescending frown. "I had an axe to grind with Derrick," Catrina defended.

"Had she been armed with a hatchet, I have no doubt she would have buried it in Redmund's back, then and there," Matt snickered. "Your lady is aptly named, big brother. She is indeed a she-Cat. With malice and forethought, I'm certain she would have bounded from the carriage, marched up to Redmund, and shot him. Not that I can blame her. After meeting the scoundrel, I contemplated violence myself."

For a long moment Brant and Matt exchanged stares. Brant was well aware of the affection and respect Matt had kept so carefully disguised these long months. He could not help but wonder if he would be competing with his own brother for

Catrina's affection. If Catrina were not Matt's sister-in-law, Brant wondered if he might find himself vying for the daring beauty's attention. Matt had that awestruck look about him and his eyes were constantly meandering over Catrina's shapely contours.

Thomas sank back and heaved a tired sigh. "That should do it, Cap'n. Yer stitches are holdin' and the wounds are healin' as well as can be expected after you lost half yer supply of blood. But yer gonna have to go lightly for several weeks." His eyes drifted to Catrina and he smiled apologetically. "It will be up to you to give the cap'n tender lovin' care. He don't think much of my rough handlin'."

"I will be happy to offer my services while you are on the mend, Brant," Matt offered, a wry smile catching the corner of his mouth. "I will assume your duties at the helm while Cat nurses you back to health." The grin broadened to encompass each of Matt's dashing features. "Or if you prefer, I will keep Cat company while you recuperate. 'Tis no time for you to overexert yourself. You might split a stitch. And since that is all that is holding you together, it would never do for you to exert any energy in any amorous activities. If your wife needs kissing I would be willing to stand in your stead . . ."

"Out!" Brant's good arm shot toward the door. "And take Dr. Haynes with you."

Matt detoured by the bed to uproot Catrina from her spot. "The good doctor needs to give Cat medical attention as well," he insisted, indicating the wound she had sustained at Derrick's hand. "Although 'tis only a flesh wound, it has long been left unattended."

Weariness was catching up with Brant again. He raised heavy eyes to his brother. He might have protested leaving Cat in Matthew's care if the left side of his body didn't feel as if it had been run through a grinder. There was so much he wanted to say to Cat, but it would have to wait until he regained his strength.

"I trust you, Matt," Brant whispered raggedly.

"I know," Matt grumbled, his admiring gaze falling to Catrina's spellbinding green eyes.

He knew what Brant was implying. And if the invalid had been someone other than his older brother, Matt would not approach Catrina with gentlemanly reserve. He had spent half a year drooling over this auburn-haired enchantress, hiding behind a disguise that protected his identity as well as his affection. It had taken a great deal of effort to remain distant and remote with Catrina. And it had been so long since he had a woman that made him melt as he did each time his eyes lingered overly long on Cat's delicious contours.

"Someday, all will be right for you, Matt," Brant prophesied sluggishly. "I have found my treasure. In time you will find yours . . ."

Catrina glanced up at Matt for a translation as Brant sank into an exhausted sleep. "Do you have any idea what he is babbling about?"

"He was assuring me that one day I would find someone as special as you. And he was also warning me to keep my distance from you," Matt murmured. "He seems to think he is not the only Diamond who has fallen in love with you." When Catrina's mouth dropped open, Matt reached over to push her jaw shut. "Why do you think I was so standoffish, little minx? It wasn't only my identity I was protecting . . ."

Catrina paused by the door. Her longing gaze circled back to the bed where Brant lay in a pained sleep. When she looked up to Matt a fond smile blossomed on her lips and he melted into sentimental stew.

"I am truly flattered, Matt. But a dashing pirate stole my heart long before he even knew I existed. I even turned traitor to the Crown to fight by his side. I have very nearly lost him twice. What I feel for him is too strong to wither from the strains of time and distance."

The genuine emotion in Catrina's voice touched Matt's soul. Masking his own emotions, he tossed Catrina a grin. "Really, Cat, I should think a sophisticated heiress like you would know better than to get mixed up with a pirate. I wonder at your taste in men."

Her green eyes flared with mischief as Matt led her to Thomas's room to tend her wound. "Haven't you heard that reformed outlaws make the best husbands?"

"Nay, is that an ancient Scottish proverb?" Matt teased, basking in the warmth of Catrina's radiant smile.

"Aye, sir, I canna name its true origin, but me mother passed it along to me when I was but a wee child," she replied, reverting back to her twangy Scottish accent.

"Come along, lass," Matt mimicked. "I canna wait to hear the legends and folklore of Scotland. And then you can tell me about the night you brewed your potion and fed my poor brother a meal of fire."

Their merry laughter echoed down the companionway. Brant roused to consciousness long enough to hear Catrina and Matt's voices intermingling in lighthearted conversation. Groaning, Brant eased onto his right side, but there was no comfort there either. His entire body felt as if it had been used as a punching bag and pistol target.

Damnation, this was not at all how he had envisioned the cruise to the West Indies. He ached to take Catrina in his arms and compensate for all the nights he had slept alone. But more than that he *ached* from the physical abuse he had put his body through the past two days. He had been shot, beaten, thrown down the stairs, and had walked through fire to get to Catrina.

And how was he repaid for his bravery in the face of disaster? He had been tossed in bed, stitched back together, and abandoned, he thought crabbily. And there was Matt, the picture of health and virility, doting over Cat as if she were a fairy princess. If his little brother made one amorous pass Brant would have Matt strapped to the mizzen mast to ensure that his hands never again strayed. Aye, he would have to keep an eye on his little brother, Brant assured himself . . . just as soon as he found the strength to crawl from his bed. Even a man's brother could not resist a temptation like Catrina.

When Nicodemus hopped up on the foot of the bed and plopped down at Brant's feet he glared at Catrina's substitute. "'Tis no justice in the world when I get you and Matt waltzes away with Cat," he grumbled at Nicodemus.

The tomcat pricked his ears to study the sour expression that was stamped on Brant's ashen features. Unalarmed about Brant's gruff tone, Nicodemus curled up and went to sleep, despite the invalid's reluctance to have him there.

Thomas had predicted Brant's irascible disposition would improve dramatically after he was able to climb from bed. But being back on his feet didn't help a smidgen. With the use of Matt's discarded cane, Brant limped about the schooner looking like black thunder. He chewed on his crew for between-meal appetizers and snapped at Matt each time he spared a glance in Catrina's direction.

Finally Thomas worked up enough nerve to approach the brooding captain and broach the subject of his permanent bad mood. Brant had his men hopping about the ship like migrating frogs each time he barked an order. Thomas walked toward Brant as cautiously as he would have edged toward a wounded lion.

"Cap'n, I got somethin' to say," Thomas blurted out with more bravado than he felt.

Fiery golden eyes sizzled across Thomas's weather-beaten features. "Then spit it out," Brant growled.

Thomas inhaled a courageous breath. "You've been as mean as Lucifer since you were wounded in Charleston. What's eatin' on you?"

"'Tis none of your business," Brant snapped grouchily, his eyes fixed on the sea.

"I'm makin' it my business. You've been limpin' about like a bear with a thorn in his paw."

Brant grunted at the comparison and then gestured toward the heavy bandage that was wrapped around his left leg and

477

forearm. "'Tis exactly how I feel and for good reason."

"But that ain't what's botherin' you," Thomas speculated. "You've been shot up before. But it didn't make a growlin' monster out of you."

Brant's gaze magnetically swung to the shapely nymph who stood at the helm beside Matt. Catrina's face was uplifted to the sun. The sea breeze caught the glorious wisps of auburn hair like an unseen hand tunneling through the long tendrils. She looked like a goddess standing there, her curvaceous body silhouetted by the spectacular rainbow of colors that adorned the afternoon sky.

"How the hell would you feel if your wife and your own brother were gallivanting about the ship while you were incapable of walking without a limp, much less exercising your husbandly rights?"

So that was what tormented the captain, Thomas thought with a wide grin. Brant Diamond had spent too long in celibacy and he was jealous of his brother's prowess. No wonder Brant's disposition was sour as a lemon.

"I see yer point, Cap'n," he murmured pensively. Thomas's gaze shifted to the tiny speck of land that graced the wide horizon—the mystical island in the West Indies known as Diamond's Den. His arm lifted to draw Brant's attention to the secluded headquarters, the home Brant had built with his inheritance and his fortunes of privateering. "But I got the feelin' yer mood will improve when you and Cat settle down on Diamond's Den."

Brant peered at the island with a melancholy smile. "I'm sure the three of us will have a charming time at home—Cat, Matt, and me. 'Tis hardly what I anticipated."

"Diamonds are all alike," Thomas snickered. "They have a penchant for beautiful women. And some of them even spy on lovely ladies . . ." When Brant jerked around to glare at Thomas he burst out laughing. "I was checkin' the arsenal supply the other day, Cap'n. When I noticed the strange wooden box nailed to the floor of the storeroom I investigated.

478

It finally dawned on me why you had spent so much time down on yer hands and knees in the arsenal." His amused gaze darted back to Matt and he cocked a mocking brow. "At least yer brother ain't sneakin' around like a Peepin' Tom. You should be ashamed of yerself, Cap'n. Unless I miss my guess, Cat don't have the slighest notion that you were watchin' her long before you told her you knew she was a woman, not a scrawny cabin boy."

It was the first time Thomas could remember seeing Brant Diamond embarrassed. "If you breathe a word of that knowledge to anyone I swear I'll . . ."

"I won't tell nobody if you promise to ease off on the men. They're beginnin' to think yer Blackbeard's double," Thomas snorted.

Brant brushed his fingertips over the dark beard that lined his jaw and then ran a restless hand through his unkempt hair. "Very well, Thomas. I'll mend my ways if you will guard your tongue. I am not at all proud of my underhanded tactics. Had I to do over again . . ."

"If you had to do it again, you'd still be crouchin' in the supply room," Thomas finished for him, sporting a broad grin. "Yer a devil, Cap'n."

Reluctantly, Brant returned the teasing smile. "Aye, I suppose I am at that." His thoughtful gaze sought out Catrina. "I only hope the devil's bride has not begun to regret her marriage to the wrong Diamond . . ."

"You know Cat loves you. Where's yer confidence, man?" Thomas snorted.

"Directly under my handsome younger brother's boot heels," Brant grumbled before hobbling toward the steps to shave his beard and whack off some length from his shaggy head of hair.

While Brant was stewing over his fall from Catrina's loving graces, Matthew was describing the elegant plantation his brother had built in the West Indies. Catrina was captivated by the vivid blue sky and fluffy sun-tinted clouds that marched across the horizon in a boundless parade. A warm breeze kissed her cheek as she stared across the crystal waters of the Caribbean. Radiant walls of mountains, volcanic peaks, and colorful reefs stretched out before her. Behind the precipices of green loomed shades of hypnotic blue. And beyond them a haze of gray—all towering against the sky. Oyster-white beaches sprawled into the sea and faded into the foliage that rose to entangle the lower rim of the mountains.

She could almost see the clear waterfalls trickling from the mountain plateaus that Matthew had painted with words. The image brought back memories of another island in the Everlasting Mountains of the Sea. Would her life in the West Indies be an endless honeymoon, a dream from which she would never want to wake?

Her eyes fluttered down to watch Brant limp across the deck. To her relief he paused to glance up at her. The scowling frown that had been carved in his features had finally vanished. His dark brow arched as he shot a quick glance toward the island. A tingle of anticipation raced down her spine when she saw the tightness around his mouth fade after two agonizing weeks at sea.

The cruise had been a bitter disappointment to Catrina. She had longed to spend each night in Brant's sinewy arms. But she had clung to her corner of the cabin for fear of injuring Brant while he was recuperating from his wounds.

The first week had been torturous for Brant. The infection inflamed his thigh and a high fever had kept him flat on his back. But with Thomas's meticulous care, Brant began to recover his strength. He hobbled about the decks, growling and snorting. Catrina presumed his constant pain was the source of his cantankerous disposition. She silently suffered, watching his mood turn black as pitch. Although Matthew entertained her, she yearned for the raven-haired pirate who had left her soul to burn.

Catrina's heart flip-flopped in her chest when Brant finally broke into a smile, the first she had witnessed in a fortnight. But her thundering heart broke loose and tumbled around her ankles when Brant turned and walked away without calling to her to join him in the cabin.

For an hour Catrina remained where she was, listening to Matt praise the tropical paradise that grew larger on the horizon. But she wondered if she were to enjoy the spectacular scenery without the man of her dreams. Would Brant sail back to Charleston without her? Was he putting a wall between them, thinking to make their parting easier for both of them? Dammit, she still didn't understand the many facets of Brant Diamond and she wondered if she would ever figure that man out.

Her eyes dropped to the main deck when Brant reappeared, clean-shaven and his hair neatly clipped. A rakish grin skimmed his lips. When he tossed Cat a come-hither glance, she left Matt in midsentence. Her footsteps took her from the quarterdeck to Brant's outstretched arms, despite the fact they had an audience.

"I've missed you, kitten," Brant murmured as he affectionately brushed his lips over her forehead. "I was beginning to wonder if you were partial to all Diamonds or to one in particular."

Catrina laid her head against his good shoulder. "When you have properly healed I will show you where my loyalty lies, Pirate Captain." Her misty green eyes settled on the lofty peaks and tropical forests that capped Diamond's Den. "'Tis a beautiful place, Brant. I am most thankful I will have you to share it with . . . at least for a time."

"There is a special place amid the forests, a secluded haven I want you to see. 'Tis like nowhere else in the world," he whispered, his eyes full of promise.

Her gaze lifted to meet his gentle smile. "Will you show it to me . . . as soon as you are well enough to make the journey?" she stipulated, cursing herself for wishing they could spirit

481

away this very moment. Lord, if she were forced to keep her distance one more night she swore she would go stark raving mad! She wanted Brant in the worst way, but she would not go to him until he considered himself healthy enough to withstand her overzealous embraces. And they would be most ardent ones, Catrina reminded herself. There could be no other kind when she and Brant touched. The fires of passion blazed up like a thousand bonfires.

"This evening," he replied with a grin of roguish anticipation. "As soon as we dock."

The suggestive smile that brimmed his lips was very nearly her undoing. "Are you certain you are up to the exertion?" she questioned breathlessly.

He combed his hand through the lustrous auburn tendrils that caressed her face. "Madam, if not this night, I swear I will wither away from neglect. My little brother has proved to be a proficient substitute . . . all too proficient to suit me."

"Were you jealous?" One delicate brow arched in question as she surveyed Brant, wondering if that had been another source of his irascible mood.

"Insanely," Brant growled, his narrowed eyes darting to his grinning brother.

Catrina's countenace sobered. Adoringly, she reached up to smooth away the harsh lines that clung to his features. "There is no need to be, my handsome pirate," she softly assured him. Her voice was so hauntingly seductive that every nerve in his taut body was twitching. "Matthew is indeed amusing company, but he is not you and he never could take your place. I have loved no other man. I have never felt these stirrings that affect my entire being when I'm near you. Can you say the same, Brant? And if I cannot be the first and only love you've known, let me be the last . . ."

His lean fingers traced the delicate lines of her face. Nothing compared to the emotions that gripped him when he stared into Cat's emerald green eyes. He could not deny that he once felt affection for Cynthia, but that was long before he truly knew what love was, how endless its boundaries could be.

"I may have taught you the meaning of passion, Cat, but you taught me the definition of love," Brant whispered, holding her steady gaze. "You have given new meaning to the word and to my life."

"Do I now, Captain?" she taunted saucily. "I canna wait until we run aground so you will have ample time to explain what love truly is, now that you hail yourself as an authority on the subject."

Brant grinned outrageously. "I pray you have nothing planned for the rest of your life, my dear. I have prepared a long-winded explanation and several detailed demonstrations. And I expect you to attend every lecture."

Catrina's arm curled about his neck, uncaring that the entire crew was watching the goings-on on the main deck. "I shall hang on your every word, sir. When the sessions begin, you can count upon me to be all ears . . ."

His wandering caress glided down her spine to settle familiarly on her derriere. "Odd, you don't feel like all ears to me," he teased playfully.

The feel of his practiced hands mapping her supple curves ignited the fire Catrina had never been able to extinguish. The flames had been banked by circumstances beyond her control, but the coals still smoldered beneath the surface.

When he bent his dark head to hers, Catrina raised parted lips to accept a kiss that carried enough heat to leave the Caribbean Sea a sea of steam. Her mind was fogged with the heady pleasure she had been denied for more days than she cared to count. It felt so right to be in his arms. There was no other place she would rather be. She loved this reckless daredevil with all her heart. And these feelings would never go away. If they could have, they would have died long ago— during those agonizing months they had spent apart.

"Well, it seems the cap'n and Cat are purrin' in

contentment," Thomas observed with a snicker. "I don't think either of 'em know they're on display."

"I doubt it would matter," Matt said absently. His envious gaze was glued to the striking couple who were wrapped in each other's arms. "It seems the vagabond pirate Diamond has found his precious gem. I only wish Cat had a twin sister."

"Hell," Thomas grunted. "I wish she was triplets."

Chapter Thirty

Catrina's eyes grew wide with astonishment when she rode through the tangled underbrush to see the secluded clearing among the thick canopy of trees. The warbling of exotic birds intermingled with the sound of the wind rustling through the palm fronds. And there before her was a paradise exploding with oranges, yellows, and violets. In the distance, sparkling in the light that filtered through the trees was a river of bubbling springs and waterfalls that cascaded from the rocks high above her. The fine mist glistened with the brilliance of diamonds, casting a mystical rainbow over the rapids and the rippling pools below. For a moment Cat sat atop her horse, spellbound by her colorful surroundings. It was as if she had walked into a dream.

A soft smile pursed Brant's lips as he reached up to assist Cat from her steed. "I must assume that you approve of my secret hideaway," he chuckled.

Catrina allowed herself to be drawn from the saddle, but her eyes were still glued to the clear blue pool that offered an overwhelming temptation. It had been so long since she had splashed about in something besides the confines of a tub.

Casting Brant a flirtatious smile, Cat peeled off the pale yellow gown and recklessly tossed it aside. The sight of her exquisite body glowed like honey in the waning light and

Brant's good leg buckled. He staggered to maintain his balance when Catrina pulled the pins from her hair and scampered up the steps of rock to reach the waterfall.

A sigh of sheer pleasure escaped Brant's lips as he dropped down on a nearby rock to watch Catrina's ascent. This truly was heaven and Cat was the resident angel, Brant thought to himself. The picture she presented when she drew herself up to full stature on the ledge caused Brant's heart to skip several vital beats. Her hair appeared a wave of fire tumbling over her shoulders to contrast her alabaster skin. The pastel rainbow arched above her in the spraying mist, giving Cat a mystical appearance that kept Brant hypnotized for a long moment.

And then, like a graceful dove taking flight, Catrina spread her arms. Her body arched into the air as if she had unfolded her wings to dangle in space. When she dived into the pool and disappeared into its clear depths Brant came to his feet to watch the glorious bird transform herself into a fish. He could see her beneath the surface, as if he were staring through a tinted glass window, and the sight sent his overworked heart lurching again.

The cool water was invigorating and Catrina felt whole and alive. As she burst to the surface she wound her long hair over one bare shoulder and wiped the water from her eyes. When her vision cleared she saw Brant poised on the bank. His gaping shirt parted to reveal the thick matting of hair that shaded his chest. His black breeches strained against his muscled legs and gave evidence that her subtle seduction had aroused him.

Her eyes floated over his powerful physique and desire began to unfurl within her. She longed to draw away the hindering garments, to run her hands over his hair-roughened flesh. She ached to hear the words of love Brant had whispered to her that night at the lighthouse. The memories of the past swirled about her like an alluring whirlpool. It seemed a lifetime since they had kissed and caressed, but Cat could remember the taste of his kisses, the way his hands expertly moved over her yielding flesh.

A provocative smile traced her lips as she glided through the water toward the dashingly handsome rogue. "Again I find you are overdressed," Cat chided playfully. "A pirate needs but wear a roguish grin."

One heavy brow shot up when Cat emerged from the water to dig her fingers into his gaping shirt. His eyebrow arched even higher when she gave the garment a forceful tug, popping the buttons. "Wildcat," he teased. "I had no idea there were uncivilized creatures hereabout."

"Aye, the forest is thick with them," Cat assured him huskily. Her adoring gaze was focused on his broad chest as she pulled away his shirt and flung it aside. Her eyes sketched the swarthy expanse of flesh that stretched across his shoulders and down his lean belly. Carefully, she traced her fingertips around the tender wound on his arm. "And occasionally these creatures demand a human sacrifice. You, my handsome pirate, have been selected for the ritual."

Mock terror flickered in his eyes. "What is it you intend for me, some horrible form of torture?"

Her poignant gaze raked his hard, masculine flesh. Brazenly, she grasped the band of his breeches, freeing the buttons. "*Sweet* torture," Cat purred seductively. Her hands splayed across his hips, pushing the garment downward until it lay in a pool around his feet.

Brant groaned in unholy torment when her velvety lips flitted across his flesh. An infantry of goose bumps marched across his skin as her hands and lips taunted and caressed. "Lord, how can any form of torture be worse than this maddening ache that has hounded me these past few months," Brant said hoarsely.

"From whence comes this mysterious pain?" Catrina questioned. Her caresses swirled around the mending wound on his thigh, causing his quick intake of breath. "Does it come from here?" Her inquiring hand ascended across his belly to flow over his tender arm. "Or here, Pirate Captain?"

A rakish grin dangled from the corner of his mouth. "I

think you know the cause and cure of my affliction," Brant growled, his voice heavy with disturbed passion. "Pains of the flesh cannot hold a torch to the agony of being with you without touching you."

"Do you want me, Brant?" Catrina queried, her caresses continuing to work sweet magic on his flesh.

"Aye, like a starving wolf craves a feast," he breathed raggedly.

"Do you need me?" she prodded. Her lips whispered across his cheek. Like a bee courting the nectar of a rare blossom, her mouth hovered against his. "Do you need me only in the way a man wants *any* woman?"

"Nay," he confessed without hesitation. "I *have* to have you with me, like the day cherishes the sunbeams and the night counts upon the stars." His arms wound around her waist, lifting her to him, molding their naked flesh together. His mouth descended upon hers, savoring and devouring the sweet taste of her. Brant could feel no pain, could barely remember his name. He was wrapped in the taste and scent of a woman who had come to mean more to him than life. "I love you, Cat . . . madly, passionately, without rhyme or reason. I cherish you with every beat of my heart. I know I have not said it often enough, but for such a long time I was afraid of the words, of the vulnerability it represented."

Cat leaned back in the circle of his arms to gaze into those fathomless gold pools that rippled with unmistakable emotion. "There is strength in a love that flows from two hearts to join in one soul. I witnessed it in the affection my parents shared. But I thought it too rare to happen in my lifetime. Yet, it has, Brant. There are those, like Cynthia, who are too vain to be satisfied. And there are others, like Derrick, who cherish gold far more than the contentment of the soul." A tender smile grazed her lips. "My love for you had me diving overboard and soaring from tumbling waterfalls. I once was afraid of heights, afraid of the inevitable fall. But falling in love with you was the easiest thing I have ever done."

Her index finger traced the sensuous curve of his mouth and the smile lines that sprayed across his cheek. "Do you know, I think I first fell in love with you the night I fed you that fiery concoction for supper?" Her mischievous giggle caught in the breeze to mingle with the chirping of the birds that fluttered in the trees. "You were trying so very hard to spare my feelings, even when I had purposely set about to fry you to a crisp, from inside out."

"Ornery witch," Brant grumbled as he nipped at her neck. "Had I known then who was hiding beneath those baggy garments and that ridiculous hat I would not have been so lenient with you."

Cat jerked back, eyeing him curiously. "And what would you have done if you had been aware your clumsy cabin boy was a female?"

"This . . ." His lips skimmed the swanlike column of her throat and then skied down the slope of her shoulder. "I would have made sweet love to you each night while we sailed the open seas."

When his tongue flicked at the taut pink peak, Cat moaned softly. A knot of longing uncoiled deep within her, sensitizing every inch of her flesh. "But would you have loved me even if I would have surrendered to the passion you aroused in me? Would you have cast me aside for another if I had allowed myself to become an easy conquest?"

The smile that trickled across his lips was like warm sunshine caressing the murmuring waterfall, bringing it to life. "Perhaps . . . if it had been anyone but the playful she-cat," Brant honestly admitted. "You stirred too many emotions within me and I could not let you go. You were in my blood, flowing like a boiling river."

Gently, he drew Catrina down upon their discarded clothes, marveling at her breathtaking beauty, the mystical way the light danced like fire in her auburn hair. "I came to realize that Cat has nine lives," he chortled against her satiny flesh. "A mischievous one, an adventurous one, a seductive one . . ."

"And the others?" Catrina quizzed him as her hands worshiped the raw, muscular flesh that was pressed intimately to hers.

Soft laughter vibrated in his chest. "I will be content to spend the next century discovering your other mysterious lives, my delightful wildcat." Brant sobered when he peered into those emerald eyes that were fringed with long, dark lashes. "I want to know everything about you, for you are the vital flame that gives my life purpose. You have become my reason for being. You were the beacon in the tower that glowed against the night sky. No matter where I was I could see the light shining each time I closed my eyes. I could feel its warmth burning in my heart."

His big hand molded itself to her face, lifting her eyes to his. "You are Diamond's fire," he told her, his voice wavering with barely controlled emotion. "You are this rebel pirate's cherished treasure. I have become a jealous, greedy man. I don't want to share you. I want to revel in the pleasures I never thought I could enjoy. I want you to give me children, mischievous ones who are brimming with your undaunted spirit and my craving for adventure. I want us to frolic in this tropical paradise all our days, growing more and more alive, falling even deeper in love."

Catrina looked into his eyes and saw her world. The sensation that shot through her rocked her soul. "Oh, Brant, I love you . . . wildly, completely . . ." she whispered breathlessly.

"Keep reminding me of that each time I grow jealous of my own brother and merchants who happen along to feast upon my treasure."

Catrina laid her head back on the plush carpet of wild flowers that hugged the bank. Her eyes sparkled when she reached up to sketch his rugged features. "Must I *tell* you how I feel about you? I much prefer to *show* you how much I love you. And when you leave my arms to return to the colonies, I will be with you . . . if only in sweet memories."

"Matthew has offered to make the return cruise," Brant informed her with a smile. His roving hands mapped each enticing curve and swell, making him lose all interest in conversation. "It will take time for my wounds to heal properly. They require dedicated care, around-the-clock attention . . ."

Catrina looped her arms over his shoulder, careful not to brush against his forearm. "I am eager to offer my services, Captain."

"I was counting upon that . . ."

And there, beside the whispering waterfall, in a tropical paradise, Catrina set aside all identities from her past. She was a woman, giving, taking, and sharing a love to last eternity.

They set sail on the most intimate voyage across the far horizon as the twilight blended into night. Brant whispered his love, over and over again, until Catrina had no doubt that she had captured this reckless pirate's love and held the key to his heart.

In the aftermath of love Brant gazed down at Catrina's flushed cheeks and kiss-swollen lips. All the love he had kept bottled inside him for almost a year bubbled like wine overflowing a stemmed glass. He had but to stare into her eyes to remember the passion that burst like wildfire between them. Cat had become all things to him and he could not recall an existence without her. His life had only begun. In time the war would end and he prayed peace would come quickly. The thought of leaving Cat when Matt returned to the Indies tore at his soul.

"If ever you long for Scotland, do not hesitate to tell me," Brant murmured as he absently stroked his hand across the curve of her hip. "I want you to be happy here. But if you . . ."

Catrina pressed her index finger to his lips to shush him. "The memories of Scotland are painful ones. Maybe in time I will want to go back to the country estate, but not without you. My home is wherever you are, Brant. I would follow you to the edge of the earth and back again."

"You already have," Brant assured her huskily. "Take me there again, sweet nymph. I can touch the distant horizon when I hold you in my arms . . ."

Love blazed anew when her lips melted against his. Together they charted a course across the sea of stars. And suddenly the black velvet sky was aflame with sparkling lights that reflected the sun. It was Diamond's Fire, an aurora of flickering beams and ever-changing hues cast by a love that outshined the brightest stars. And while the strange glow sprinkled the sky, Brant and Catrina reveled in the wondrous pleasures their love for each other had created, a love born and blossoming of its own unique design.

Thomas glanced around the plantation house on Diamond's Den, admiring the French-styled raised cottage built of stuccoed brick and vertical timbers. The three-story structure was built to suit the hot, humid environment of the tropics. The second level, which contained the main living area, was able to catch the stirring breeze. The wide terraces and galleries provided ventilation to each room through the double French doors.

The elegant furniture, shipped to the Indies from all corners of the world, enhanced the beauty of the majestic manor that sat amid a grove of palms. This had been the only home Thomas had ever known, but in recent years his visits had been few and far between.

Sighing contentedly, Thomas eased back in his chair on the upper balcony and then took a sip of brandy. His gaze drifted from his silent companion to the tropical night sky. "There's an odd glow in the heavens tonight," he observed.

Matt downed another glass of brandy and nodded in agreement. His dark eyes followed Thomas's to the hazy hue of light that reached across the sky. "Aye, I noticed it. 'Tis a strange phenomenon." A pensive frown furrowed his brow. "What do you suppose causes it?"

"Don't know exactly," Thomas mumbled. "Some say it has somethin' to do with approachin' storms and others think the curtains of green and gold lights are related to the heat of the sun. I've heard all sorts of speculations from this side of the world to the other." Thomas was quiet for a long moment. "What do you s'pose Cat and the cap'n are doin' so long in the forest?"

"Brant probably took her to the falls," Matt predicted. "He has always been fond of that particular place." He twirled his brandy around the rim of his glass and then took a long slow sip. "The two of them probably had a relaxing swim in the moonlight and stood in the mist of the falls . . ."

"The cap'n ain't particularly a sentimental soul, but he probably picked some orchids for a bouquet and presented them to Cat," Thomas added dreamily.

"And a few poinsettias," Matthew chimed in, a faraway look in his eyes. "And most likely they gathered bananas and other ripe fruit to curb their appetites since they skipped supper."

"Somehow I don't think citrus fruits will curb the hunger that's been gnawin' at yer big brother of late," Thomas snickered devilishly. "You saw the way he and Cat was clingin' to each other before we docked."

Matt sighed forlornly and stared into his empty glass. "The thick grass in the forest would make a cozy nest, especially with the sparkling waterfall in the background," he mused aloud.

Thomas tugged at the collar of his shirt to relieve the sudden pressure that had constricted his breathing. "Aye, and it will be a wonder if the two of them don't set the forest afire. 'Tis always been lightning cracklin' between them and this tropical settin' always turns a man's fancy to . . ." Thomas paused to wipe the perspiration from his brow. "Damned humid tonight, ain't it, Matt?"

"Extremely," Matt choked out, his body overheated by the suggestive drift of their conversation.

Another moment of silence passed, each man lost to his silent speculations about what could have kept Cat and Brant so long in the forest. When Matthew suddenly sprang to his feet and aimed himself toward the terrace doors, Thomas arched a curious brow.

"Where are you off to in such a rush?"

"I find myself in need of a cold bath," Matt grumbled. "It must be the aurora of lights that makes this such a hot night."

Thomas vaulted from his chair to follow in Matt's wake. "Have the servants fill a tub for me, too," he requested. "I'm feelin' a mite steamy myself."

While Matt and Thomas were soaking in cold baths, visualizing the romantic interlude that had detained Brant and his fiery-haired wife, the twosome were cuddled in the nest of soft grass. Catrina peered up into the face of the man who had once frightened her and yet constantly lured her closer. Brant had weaved a sweet dream about her, a web of delicious pleasure.

"Do you suppose it will always be like this between us?" she mused half aloud.

Brant dropped a kiss to her heart-shaped lips. "Nay," he insisted.

Cat drew back to cast him a wary glance and then mellowed when the moonlight caught Brant's mischievous smile.

"What is between us will grow sweeter, more potent with time . . . like a finely aged wine." He could not resist another taste of her soft lips. His head came deliberately toward hers, his warm breath whispering across her cheek.

Catrina dodged his intended kiss and held him at bay. "And you will not lose your taste for this love of ours after years of its steady diet?" she questioned, half teasing, half serious.

Brant leaned back on his good arm and then shot her a sidelong glance. "Are you asking if I might be tempted when a young, well-proportioned lass sashays past me, her long hair flowing about her supple curves? Would I yearn for a variety that some claim makes life sweet? Would I forsake the vows between us to grasp for the youthful spirit that has escaped me?"

Blast it, he didn't have to go into such great detail, Cat thought in annoyance. But aye, that was exactly what she wanted to know. Not trusting herself to speak without tossing a mocking rejoinder, Cat nodded affirmatively.

Brant's eyes fell to the hauntingly lovely body that glowed in the moonlight. Reverently, he brushed his hand over her silky flesh. "Nay, my love," he assured her, his voice soft with sincerity. "You and I will grow old together, reveling in the years that strengthen this bond between us. Variety in passion is for the restless vagabond whose soul has nowhere to call home. But like Matt's pigeons, I spread my wings to soar and my lofty flight always brings me back to you. In the magic circle of your arms, I have found all the spark and spice I need and desire in life."

Misty green eyes lifted to lock with the shimmering pools of gold. A satisfied smile touched Catrina's lips as she looped her arms around Brant's neck. "Brant Diamond, do you know how very much I love you?"

Brant chuckled when she gave him a heartfelt squeeze that might have snapped a lesser man's neck. If the fierceness of her embrace were any indication of her affection, she loved him with every part of her being. "I'm beginning to get the idea," he rasped as he bent his hard contours into the softness of hers. "But just in case I might have underestimated the potency of your love, tell me in a kiss."

Catrina giggled giddishly at the roguish twinkle in his eyes. How she adored the many facets of this complicated man. "One kiss, my love, cannot begin to express what I feel. It will take at least a score and ten."

"But talking of it will never satisfy me," he growled, his playfulness transforming into ardent passion. "At least let it begin with one . . . I ache with the want of it."

And she did. Catrina kissed him with all the pent-up emotion that churned within her. And she kept on kissing him until they were both caught in a blaze that burned with the magnificent radiance of Diamond's Fire . . .